I0611305

ZAHIR

Anthology
2011

ZAHIR

Anthology
2011

Edited by
Sheryl Tempchin

Zahir Publishing
Encinitas, California

ZAHIR
Anthology 2011

Zahir Publishing
315 South Coast Highway 101
Suite U8
Encinitas, CA 92024

www.zahirtales.com

ISBN: 978-0-9831090-1-3

Cover art (from top):
Light Intervals 02 by Michael Filimowicz
Reindeer by John Pappas
Ragged Soul by Jeff Foster
Hit the Pink by Teresa Frazee

Contents

Issue 25

January 2011

And Then This

Karen Lenar

And then this:

Wind whipping my face. Stings. Chest, enclosed in my biker jacket, warm. Fingers cold—I can no longer feel them, numbed from the vibration and the chill.

Wind whipping my face. Tastes like a Maine summer, but not July, more like end of August, when the mornings are cooler, longer. I am reminded of the camp Jacob and I went to—boys on one side of the inlet, girls housed across the way. When Mom came to visit she'd always come to see me first. "Don't tell your brother," she'd say, but visitors to the camp were no secret so we both knew she said that just to make me feel special.

At night we warmed ourselves by the fire, and even when we weren't hungry we'd still munch on roasted marshmallows. It was in the mornings that we smelled the ocean the most, and the aroma seemed to grow stronger as the summer neared its end. "A salty tinge," Jacob would remark and smack his lips. He said it the first time and it annoyed me, so he kept saying it.

I was twenty-one years old when I had the first premonition, although it is possible that it was just the first one I remembered. I suppose I dreamt it, but I was not sleeping—I was very much awake, walking. I knew things I shouldn't have known—a sense of who was important to me, an awareness of my feelings.

I saw myself—I became myself—sitting in a restaurant with an older blond-haired man, perhaps in his mid thirties. We were more than friends; I knew this before we touched under the table.

KAREN LENAR

We sat with a group of people at a long wooden table and feasted, bowls of salted brown rice and sweet pineapple chunks, thick Thai noodles with tofu squares, hot cheap sake in small porcelain cups. The restaurant was packed, a base of chatter, with a few voices rising above the rest, the lights dim, and the aroma of spicy, rich foods swirling around us.

His hands were familiar on my skin, on my wrist, my arm, the top of my thigh. I reached for my soda, trying to follow what the girl across from us was saying, something about some actor in some movie that I didn't know, or maybe just hadn't heard of yet, and then the seat next to her filled with the man returning from the bathroom, and we locked eyes. Jacob.

That was it, just that brief minute or two, or maybe three, and then I was back in the present, walking down the street in New York.

Wind whipping. Stings. Tastes like a Maine summer.

"A salty tinge," my brother used to say as he loudly smacked his lips.

"What'd you get?" my mom would ask me from across the table. It didn't matter what restaurant, what town. Boston, New York. Portland, Maine.

"Margarita. Rocks, salt."

"I'll have the same," she'd tell the waiter, and minutes later we'd toast, the drinks cold in our hands, white salt granules rimming the glasses. We'd smile. We'd feel good. Good from the drinks and the routine.

The sun on my face. The smudge in my sunglasses. Annoying, but no time to stop.

The wind whipping. Stings. The bike's engine hums, vibrates between my legs. This, too, reminds me of something: the look on Hayden's face when he came the first time.

"Are you still smoking pot?" Jacob had asked when I told him about my premonition. I called him the morning after it happened, certain he'd know exactly what I was talking about. Why I thought that I have no idea.

"Look, I know it sounds crazy, but I swear it really happened. I mean — will happen, whatever. You gotta believe me." As I spoke I realized how illogical I sounded. And desperate, yes, there was a hint of desperation. I really wanted my brother to understand.

Jacob chuckled. "Sorry, I don't mean to laugh, but you have to admit, it's kinda funny." When I didn't respond, he added — in a more serious tone, "Well, maybe you should get a scan to make sure everything is okay with that noggin of yours. You know, rule out a tumor or seizure, okay?"

I couldn't blame my brother for his response; he was in medical school, after all. But I knew what had happened was real, that *he* was real. I don't know why my faith was so strong at that point when I had nothing to go on but belief itself; despite all my searching, the only place I could find him was in my dreams. I think it was because I needed to know that there was more to life, that there was a reason for things, that there was somebody special for me. That I was special.

I rejected my brother's advice and quietly dropped the subject. I had come to the conclusion that the moment couldn't be explained, at least not yet.

Then one day I saw him. It was a few years later, when I'd moved to Boston to attend law school. At first this struck me — that I now lived in a different city than the one where I'd first had the premonition. Was I not supposed to meet him yet? Had I already missed my opportunity in New York? Or perhaps I'd changed my fate?

He came into our café, the one where I had started working in the evenings to pay for school. I saw the back of his head as he came in, and I knew before I even saw his face that it was him. I knew it from the blond hair — that blond hair I'd held in my mind for so long — almost sandy, but not quite, more of a bronzed-brown that had lightened in the sun, and from his shoulders — broad, the line across them straight, strong — and even from the thickness of his neck.

He was with a pretty woman and a child, and they sat down at a table near the window. As he held up a menu with his left hand, I could see his silver wedding band from where I stood across the restaurant. He was dressed casual, wearing slim fitting jeans and a faded light blue tee-shirt with writing that I couldn't decipher from across the restaurant, and I had the absurd thought that the shirt he was wearing was one I didn't recognize. Why would I?

I stared at him, willing him to look my way, to connect his blue eyes with mine. But he didn't, instead occupied with reading over the menu and chatting with the pretty dark-haired woman. Perhaps they are just friends, I thought, but then I saw her ring, the big diamond on her finger that rested on his arm in a familiar way, and I knew that her body knew his hands like mine did. The little girl said something, and they all laughed, the girl who looked five or six, dark-skinned, dark like the woman, and I wondered if it was their kid or just hers. Or mine? Why would it be? How could it be? I was not thinking straight.

It was not my turn to waitress, so I watched as Heather took their order. He smiled as he handed her the menu, and I saw the dimple that I knew he had but hadn't recalled until now.

The dimple was what really threw me, what made me feel sick and dizzy. How could this be? Why wasn't he looking at me? Who was that woman?

I had just one thought, one overriding emotion: He needs to see me. If he sees me, then he'll know. Then he'll remember, and it will all make sense.

Heather said she was stepping outside out for a cigarette, and I thought that this was it—this was my opportunity, and when their drinks were ready, I approached their table, my sweaty, trembling hands grasping the tray.

"Thanks," he said, barely glancing up as I placed the three glasses on the table, one at a time, slowly, trying to watch both the drinks and him at the same time. I didn't have a plan; I just wanted him to look at me. *Look at me*, I willed. *Look*. His eyes finally met mine, and then he looked down at his glass, just like that, like I was just some girl, some waitress.

I heard him shaking the cubes (I suppose I saw it as well, but nothing was quite hitting my brain as it should), and it all seemed so familiar—not this meeting but the shaking of the cubes and his voice, and his face up close, the wrinkles in his forehead and the light freckles on his nose.

14

I stood there, waiting, for what I wasn't sure. "That other girl already took our order," he finally said, meeting my eyes again, and the little girl started giggling. I felt my face flush as I turned away.

The rest of the night was so ordinary, and I kept waiting for something to happen—anything—but it never did. They ate, paid the bill, and left. I stared at the name on the credit card receipt: Hayden Roads. It had meant nothing to me.

I went home, brushed my teeth, and washed my face for the sake of routine. I changed into my pajamas, turned out the lights, and climbed into bed. I was finally able to fall asleep once I'd convinced myself that I had been mistaken, that I had wanted to meet the man of my premonition so much that I had created him—conveniently picked that random person I'd seen at the café.

But the next morning I knew that I hadn't made him up. I knew that I had known him previously, or maybe in the future, or perhaps in a different life. But he hadn't known me, and that was the thing. I'd waited for nothing the past few years. I'd turned down dates and ignored dark-skinned men—for nothing.

I finally saw him again a couple of years later. He was still married to that pretty woman, that pretty woman who turned out to be a very close friend of my brother's—a fellow resident at the hospital. I never told Hayden what I knew, and our affair lasted a good length of time, the height of it the night of the Thai restaurant, when we celebrated Jacob's graduation from residency. The night Hayden's wife was too sick to attend.

I sat there that night, at the long, wooden table, surrounded by bowls of brown rice and cups of hot sake, the girl across from me gossiping about some actor I still didn't know. Hayden's hands sought mine beneath the table, and the wholeness of it all hit me—the familiarity, the knowledge of the exact sequence of events. I had the strange feeling that I was not at the table but instead observing it, that I was watching my twenty-one-year-old self hover over my twenty-eight-year-old self. Part of me was present, part of me was watching, and then my younger self became me, so that we were one, and I was back at the table, feeling Hayden's hands on my wrist, my leg. The moment was both wonderful and sad — certainly the affirmation that I had been seeking for years — but it was not kind.

My brother returned from the bathroom, and as we locked eyes, I knew that he didn't remember my vision. I thought to tell him later but realized it didn't matter.

When my affair was done, I felt foolish. Why had life brought me a relationship like the cheap sake we'd drunk, one without shape or weight?

The sun on my face. The smudge in my sunglasses. Annoying, but no time to stop.

The sun on my face. Now on my face and my neck. I know it's getting closer.

I look for the familiar restaurant that I have seen so many times in my head, and soon I am there, passing it by — the door propped open, the waiter setting the outside tables for the dinner crowd, white tablecloths and crisp triangular-folded napkins, red roses in tall glass bottles. The girl in the floral dress flits from table to table lighting votive candles.

It is too perfect, and I'd wondered many times in the past six years if I had somehow embellished it in my mind. But there it is, like a damn postcard. I don't know why it angers me, but it does. Maybe because I still can't make out what the waiter says. I never did catch it in my premonition. He turns to say something to the other waiter who is coming through the door carrying a tray of condiments. The girl in the floral dress (the hostess?) laughs at whatever they say. There it is, then it is closer, suddenly here it is — and the smell of olive oil and baked bread — with the girl in the floral dress waving (to me?), and then I am gone. They are gone.

As I speed away, I try to decipher the words. It was in Italian, of course, but it could have been in English and I still wouldn't have gotten it. The waiter spoke too fast, and now the words that are coming to mind are others — more familiar Italian words. Words we'd heard the past few weeks.

"Dov'è il bagno?" Where is the bathroom? George teased me as we flipped through our reference translation books. We were not looking for the restroom; we were just practicing the language.

"I don't know," I answered in Italian. Then, a moment later, I exclaimed "Oh! There is the bathroom. And there is the cat."

I pass a few more shops and then the storefronts turn into apartments and then into houses. The spaces between the houses become larger, and soon there is more land than buildings. I round the bend, the bend with the house with the empty hammock, and I recall feeling that the house is sad. The hammock blows, flips up, tangles, as a gust of wind races through the porch.

Now the hammock is behind me, its oscillating motion growing farther and farther away with each breath, the town it belongs to in the distance, my past, and now it is just open sky and coastline. Beautiful. More beautiful than I had remembered. I grasp the metal lever tighter, and the hum grows louder between my legs.

A salty tinge. Now the salty tinge is all around me. The ocean will be coming up on the right—and the couple waiting at the side of the road with their daughter, the little blond girl whose face I never see. When I pass she is bending down to pick up a seashell or maybe a toy. I never know if they are arriving to or leaving from the beach. Her parents stand stiffly as my loud engine approaches. I don't meet their eyes, but I feel them on me, and the moment happens so fast that I can't assure them with a smile that their daughter is safe, that an accident is not meant to be.

Now they are already behind me, and I won't ever know their direction, just like I won't know what the waiter said.

"Rocks, salt"—I imagine the waiter say as he sets the table. His friend obliges and brings him the tray of condiments.

I see the girl in the floral dress reply, "There is the cat," and they all laugh. She waves to me, and I wave back because it finally makes sense.

It's getting a little colder now, and the sun is falling down farther into the horizon. My bike churns through sand grains scattered on the road, and occasionally one flies up to my mouth, imparting a fine crunchiness between my teeth.

When it ends today, I wonder how old my soul will be. Will it be forty-six years old, my current age? Or twenty-one, the age when I'd had my first vision? I think of Jacob, of how I couldn't prevent his death, how I couldn't alter my second premonition. Will we soon meet, and, if we do, will I recognize him? Will he still be forty? That's how old he was when he passed—forty. Just a few years after my second sight. The horrific second sight.

It was a Saturday night in late April. My affair with Hayden had ended several years earlier, and I was finally starting to feel comfortable again in my life, like I owned it. Working as a lawyer had helped; I felt grounded in logic, guided and comforted by rules and policies. My life was very organized and routine; the condo that I had purchased was small but tidy, and the gym conveniently located just a block away. I dated but not seriously; I did not have much free time, and I chose to spend much of that with my good friends and Jacob. Our mother had passed away from a heart attack the previous year, and even that had felt orderly: quick, not messy, final. Flowers and funeral arrangements and the block-lettered inscription on the tombstone.

As I left my friend's party to walk home, I took a shortcut, passing through an alley, and it was when I strode past a parked silver car that I saw the accident—I became it.

The wreck... the silver car's metal ripped and crudely disjointed... his brown hair matted with blood. I felt like I was the metal, like I was twisted and contorted, but not in an uncomfortable way, and like I was cold from the night air without actually feeling the cold. Then suddenly I became warm—human again, as red blood—*his* red blood—dripped over me. And then I was him, his oozing blood, his skull—the throbbing skull—, the taste of metal, and pain. Pain everywhere, in my head, in my leg, in my ribs—it hurt so much to breathe! Then abruptly I turned into the night—the hot air above the still warm engine, the smell of burnt rubber, and then cold, icy wind as I drifted farther away.

When I returned to the present, I collapsed, hitting my knees against the pavement. Jacob—it had been Jacob that I had seen, Jacob whom I had become. I fumbled through my purse to grab my phone, to call him, and as I attempted to dial his numbers (my fingers kept pressing the wrong buttons), I remembered that Jacob was on-call that evening, and thus at the hospital all night long. Jacob was alive.

It was another premonition, I realized, and spent the rest of the night trying to figure out what to do. I wanted to warn him, but what could I say? It was an awful thing to say to someone, to anyone, let alone the person who meant the most to me. And he hadn't believed me the first time. But this was a vision that I could not ignore.

"Don't be ridiculous," he said, taking a bite of his sandwich. We met in the hospital cafeteria the next day, and I rushed to spill out my story, knowing he had just a few minutes to eat before beginning afternoon medical rounds.

"But what are you going to do?"

"Nothing."

"How could you do nothing? You don't believe me." I stared past Jacob. My knees still hurt from the fall, and my stomach was un-settled from all the coffee I'd anxiously consumed the night before.

"It doesn't mean anything," he said, and checked his watch. "It's not real. Just your imagination. Or just a bad dream. Don't worry about it." He took another huge bite, nearing the end of his sandwich.

"Don't you remember?" I started. "The Thai restaurant? Your friend Lisa? Her husband Hayden? Don't you remember the premo-nition I had? About the older man? About—"

His beeper went off, interrupting me, and he checked the mes-sage. "Got to run," he said, stuffing the rest of his food in his mouth. "Love you. Don't worry. It'll be fine."

And then he was gone. I pushed his crumbs around on the table and watched the people around me—the visiting families, the table of nurses, the Hispanic cashier with rainbow-colored braces. They all seemed so ordinary, so *simple*. I knew I was thinking of them in a condescending manner; I'm sure they had their own troubles as well. In actuality I envied them. I wished I could be like one of them, con-sumed with a problem or health issue whose resolution was uncertain. More than anything I wanted to trust Jacob, but I knew differently.

"Jacob," I pleaded on his answering machine later that day. "Look, please, just be careful of cars. Silver cars. Please."

I attempted to bring up the issue several times in the next few weeks, but each time he dismissed me. I still tried — it was all I could do, but soon realized it was useless.

"Hey sis," he called out over the noise of the bar. I had agreed to meet him one night after work as he was trying to set me up with one of his colleagues. "We're discussing this medical case, this woman whose back pain we can't figure out. Maybe you could enlighten us." Jacob grinned and gestured to his friends. "My sister, gentlemen, has a sixth sense. She can see the future." He paused, and then added, in a Yoda-voice, "See the future, she can." They laughed, and I quickly finished my drink and slipped out the door.

How could he embarrass me like that? What now? I struggled for a logical way to react to the situation. And then I wondered: Would things be different if I had spoken to Hayden at the café?

Jacob's accident didn't happen for another two years and ten months. For nearly three years he was safe. For nearly three years I prevented it from happening. Or did I? Did I stop it from occurring earlier, with all my annoying warnings, or was it always meant to happen when it did?

The night he died I was at a holiday cocktail party. I knew when it occurred. As I took a sip of my red wine, I felt it. I had a quick rush of the metal feeling (such an odd feeling, really, becoming an inanimate object — a cold, emotionless sort of feeling, shaped by position), then I tasted blood, felt the intense pain, the pain so strong I almost fell over, but it was so fast, and then the chilling cold of the night paralyzed me, froze me so that my body locked in one stiff line, as if I were chemically paralyzed. All this in the time that it took for me to raise my glass up to my lips, and there it stayed, until I finished it completely, gulping it down, slurping to the last drop. It was only when I put the empty glass on the counter that I became aware that the people around me had hushed.

The next thing that I remember is that my phone rang. It seemed like the next minute — although in reality it was probably more like twenty or thirty minutes. My phone rang, and I gave it to the person standing next to me to answer.

Now the open stretch is shortening, and I see the second village I am to pass through coming up on my left, the cream and pale yellow and terra cotta buildings stacked into the mountainside, like rows of chairs in a stadium. This one is not as poor as the last. More shops, more stores. Again, no traffic lights, but I recall from my vision that there are a lot of people milling about, and one careless man in particular who I need to avoid by the market with the red clay roof — the one with the liquor store.

First the sea grass grows longer and longer, almost magically, and the sight of it makes me feel surreal, as if I'm dreaming. Then the gray stones scattered on the path, and then the walls, the clay walls of buildings, and the town emerges, but it is too big for me to see the tops of the buildings, or even the building above the first or second floor, but there is much to see anyway on eye level — stores and people and restaurants and bakeries.

I hear music, maybe a violin, and a few voices, one shrilly and female, climbing higher and higher than the rest, and then she hits the top note and holds it, a slight tremor in her throat. The smell of sweet baked goods comes next, like buttery croissants and glazed sugar, and with it espresso, or maybe I just imagine that, because it comes and goes so quickly.

I realize that I am hungry, or maybe not, but just that I could eat right now, and I wonder for a moment what would happen if I pull over and sit down for a cappuccino and a pastry.

But I know that I won't.

It was ironically my third premonition, the one six years ago, that brought me back the pleasure of life. It was the utter beauty that I saw on my ride: The sun's long arm extending towards me across the ribbed ocean, the little blonde girl at the side of the road whose face I never got to see but imagined nonetheless, the enormous mountains engulfing small, quaint towns where the people live simply.

All this before the silence, before the vision got abruptly cut off, and the sudden cessation only amplified the beauty that preceded it, like the exact second after a song ends in perfect pitch.

And that silence. The total quietness, not even a lack of noise but just… nothing. That, too, was beautiful.

I am coming closer to it. The woman's song has faded, and I wonder if her voice is the last one I'll hear. The market is here now on my left, and there's the careless man who stumbles into the street, but I am anticipating him, and sweep the outline of his shadow. He's barely here before he's gone, now far behind, encased in a swirl of sand dust, growing farther and farther away.

Another house on the outskirts — this one, too, sad. Underfed, with a skeletal frame and wearing splotches of paint like a leper's rash. A little too far from town to be included, but not far enough nor strong enough to be independent. It reminds me of how I felt after Jacob passed away — like I was there but not quite, doing all the things I was supposed to but not enough to feel like it was really me doing them. I continued practicing law because it was what I knew. Days passed, and somehow I continued as part of a life which I supposed was mine.

It was only when I received an early 40th birthday card that I realized it had been nearly four years already since my brother's death, and that I was approaching the age Jacob had been when he died. The night of my birthday I went to bed early, and at some point before waking up the next morning, I'd had my final vision.

Unlike my previous premonition, I didn't do anything to try and alter its course. It won't change anything; I've learned that life is dutiful, that it's more obedient than I am. I never told anyone what I saw in my vision, not even George when we began dating.

I was not surprised last week when we arrived to the village whose landscape I recognized immediately — the gentle bends in the sand-dusted roads, the clay-walled buildings stacked into the mountainside, the outlier house.

Our presence here in Italy seems almost like an accident ("incidente," as George would say), but I know better. We missed our connection and then canceled an expensive rebooking, opting to instead take a few weeks to explore the coast. We started off in a rental car but abandoned that for a couple of Vespas when our car broke down. *Incidente*. I know better.

The air is now turning cooler, the sun nearly absent. The waves fade into the blackening horizon, their frothy wings the only visible part. The wind seems to tease me, at first gently pulling me to the side, then emitting a roar so loud that its sound rather than its force makes me jump. Just as I am settling, a large gust suddenly blasts through my pathway, pulling my bike towards the left. After a momentary drag, I manage to steer straight, and I shiver, because the moist sweat in my armpits from the afternoon sun is now cold and damp.

It feels wonderful, so wonderful, all these sensations—the sting of the cooling temperature, the echo of air whipping in my ears, the vibration between my legs, rubber and metal beneath fingers, the sky darkening to mud.

The bike skids, and it happens so fast—my body flings   I'm in the air   my stomach woozy   like too much coffee when I tried to warn Jacob   head back   then forward   black rocks   smell of gas (the bike?)   black rocks getting biggercloserbigger   metallic taste   I know this taste   George—Jacob—mom—Hayden   Hayden—and then this:

Robards + Redbarn

Christopher Lowe

My daddy was a middle linebacker. In my earliest memories, he is a force, flinging himself sideline to sideline. He never got to have a name on his jersey, Coach Derby didn't allow it, and after watching him play every week for years, I associated his number, 49, with his name, our name, Redbarn. I'd sit in the stands, watching him feint up, faking a blitz, and I'd know that number 49 was my daddy, that it was my daddy bringing down all the great Bunker League players.

After the games, he would take me with him to the Generators' cafeteria. We'd eat our Protein and our Carbohydrates and talk about the game. My mother hated that I went to the games and to places where the other players were, but she was hardly ever on our Level, and even when she was, she knew better than to suggest that I stop going.

"Jackie," my father would say, his spoon hovering, full of gray Fiber, "did you see when I got that safety?"

"On a blitz."

"Right. And what kind of coverage were we running?"

"Zone," I'd say, digging my spoon into the soft pools of food, thinking that if I kept eating maybe I'd get stronger, be strong enough to play ball, even if I was a girl.

Now, I'm sitting in class, and I know better. At the front of the room, Ms. Grantham is talking about Shakespeare. This month, we're working our way through the tragedies.

"A rose by any other name would smell as sweet," Ms. Grantham says. I type the phrase into my computer. "Do a search for 'rose'," she says, and there is a clatter of typing. In a year, when I'm sixteen,

I'll join the Administration pool. It's a job that my father lined up for me when he was still playing. Here in the Bunker, women can mine or work the steam vents beside the men. Most of my classmates will work the generators, but I'll move to Level 6, where I'll have a desk. Digital paperwork will need to be processed. Digital paperwork will need to be filed.

On my screen, a picture of a flower appears, but I know that it isn't a rose. Someone in the Data Corps has messed up, put a picture of this flower in the file under "rose." I have seen roses before, in person, though I'm probably the only one in my class who has. I was five when the Generators won the twenty-fifth America Bowl, and my father brought me with him to the celebration on the lower levels. I met the President and wandered around, my father walking with me, and we looked at flowers in their sun-pots, little halos of light formed around them. I remember a man in dark blue coveralls reaching out and stopping me before I could touch the flower's petals.

"This isn't a rose," I say.

"Ask permission to speak." Ms. Grantham glares, and I look back at my monitor. "Roses smelled wonderful, clean and sweet, like Complex Sugars."

I want to tell her that she's wrong. I want to tell her that maybe the flower itself smelled good, but the soil it was in stank so bad I could smell it from several feet away, but before I can open my mouth, I feel a nudge at my back, and I slide my hand behind my desk, take the note that Kevin passes me. His fingers tickle across my palm as he slips the square of paper into it. I hold it under the surface of my desk, blocked from Ms. Grantham's view. He's written YOU HEAR ABOUT ROBARDS? in block letters on the page. Trenton Robards took my father's place on the Generators when my father quit playing and started coaching two years ago. He's not as good as my father was, but he's a sideline-to-sideline defender, and he's got some natural skill. Kevin knows that he's my favorite player. He knows that at games, I shout "Robards" almost as much as I shout "Generators." He doesn't know that at night, I close my eyes, pretend that Robards is there with me. He doesn't know that sometimes, I imagine him on the little mattress in my room, he in his full pads, his helmet still attached.

26

I reach my hand behind my seat again and, using our system, tap Kevin's knee twice to tell him that I haven't heard anything. Almost immediately, I can hear the scratching of his pencil. We are just friends, Kevin and I. Up until a year or two ago, we hadn't ever even talked. Then, he figured out that of the kids in our class, I knew the most about football. He figured out who my father was and that I can teach him things he needs to know if he's ever going to really play.

Ms. Grantham says, "Romeo is saying that names, labels, don't matter," and Kevin's pencil stops scratching long enough for him to join us all in typing *Names don't matter.*

I lower my hand again. After a moment, I feel another note nestled into my palm.

HEARD THEY TOOK HIM. THE BIG E.

I close my eyes. I know that Kevin wants me to write something back, that to him this is just conversation, another rumor to spread, but I don't know how to react.

"He's telling Juliet that her name isn't as important as her function," Ms. Grantham says, and I type the words along with everyone else, though my eyes are still closed.

My father is awake when I get back to our rooms after class. He's sitting at the desk in the corner, huddled over his dry-erase board. I sit down beside him and turn our computer on.

"Daddy," I say, "what happened to Robards?"

"He's a mike-linebacker," he says, his hand still moving the marker across the board.

My command screen is up now, and I type *Robards.* It registers zero results, and I know they've Evacuated him. "I heard he's gone."

"I was a mike too."

I reach over to him, touch his shoulder. Sometimes, contact helps bring him back, and I hope that now, for this conversation, he'll come back at least a little bit. "Is Robards gone?"

My father turns away from the play he's scribbling. His eyes are leaking fluid, and for a moment I think he's crying for Robards, but I know that this is just excess moisture, that his eyes do this now. I hand him a cloth.

"Is that a new play, daddy?"

"It's a man/zone mix," he says, smiling. This is his life now, scribbling out plays that he takes over to the field once a week. He doesn't go to practice or games. He sits at his desk, hunched over bits of paper, trying to piece together a game plan. "I'm dropping a defensive end into coverage in case of a slant."

"Sounds like a good one," I say, standing. On our computers, we can access all of the greats of literature. We read all of the works that they say are important in our classes, but on my own time, I look for information about football everywhere I can. As a girl, I scanned the lists of titles relentlessly, settling on ones that seemed the most likely to contain some bit of knowledge about the game. My father lets me do this, lets me sit in front of the monitor for hours. Some days, before he stopped playing, he'd sit with me, read from the football strategy books loaded onto our computers. Nights in our room, I'd trace formations on the screen as he showed me how to adjust them on his white board. We'd read through the explanations of the Spread-Option or the Tampa 2, and he'd show me why one formation is better than another.

My part of the room is separated by a metal and cloth partition. This has been my corner of the Bunker for as long as I can remember. When I was younger, I'd visit my mother sometimes, up on her Level, in the Nursery, but those were days and nights to be tolerated. There, in her more expansive rooms, I'd never felt at home the way I do here, with my father. Even after the last concussion, after he was forced to stop playing, forced to become a coach, I refused to move up there.

I push the partition out of the way and move into my area. There isn't much room here, just a couple of feet of floor space and my bed, attached to the concrete wall. I lie down, facing the wall. In the thick, gray concrete, I've etched *Robards + Redbarn*. At night, staring at those words, I think of the possible meanings. I think of my father and Robards on the field at the same time. They could have anchored a legendary defense. My father could have gotten the best out of Robards, could have gotten plays out of him that he can't get out of himself. One thing my father has taught me is that sometimes success depends on what the other players on the field are doing. Sometimes, it's less about where you are on the field than it is about where your teammates are. On the field together, my father could have created mismatches with the offense that would have helped Robards live up to his potential.

Looking at the words I've carved in the wall, I also think of myself and Robards, on the field together. In my mind, my muscles pulse and throb, and I imagine the two of us tackling some running back together, the force of our motion colliding. At night, when I think these things, I imagine us falling to the turf, the running back disappearing, Robards huddled against me on the fake grass.

I close my eyes and try to picture us there, together, but I can't form a coherent image. Robards shifts and disappears in my mind, and when I look at myself I don't see the woman I thought I'd be, I see the girl I am, too small, drowning in the pads and jersey.

I think of Security coming for Robards. I have seen this before, seen them haul men off the field or out of the Commons, but there was always a reason, a broken bone, a mental deficiency, some excuse for Evacuating them. Nothing happened to Robards last week.

Kevin and I watched the game together. From the first snap, I called out the plays, explaining formations and alignments to Kevin, trying to prepare him for the try-out he'll have in a little more than a year. By the end of the game, Robards had a few tackles but that was all. Coach Derby had blitzed him all game. I recognized my father's schemes, the complicated blitz packages that he is still able to put together.

My father's schemes hadn't worked, though. The Generators lost 14-0. After the game, I kept my eyes on Robards. He walked around the field, shaking hands, slapping backs. He was fine, not even a trace of a limp from the low ankle-sprain he'd had earlier in the season.

I try again to imagine a reason why they would Evacuate a perfectly healthy man. I get up off the bed, walk back past the partition to my father. He is still at work on the play, fussing over the zones his linebackers will cover. "I'm going down to the Commons," I say. "Kevin needs to practice."

He doesn't look up, doesn't say anything as I leave the room. Out in the hall, without even thinking about it, I start to move toward the field, toward where the Generators must be gearing up for their afternoon practice. Kevin is expecting me. He needs me to correct errors in his body movements, to fix all the things he's doing wrong, but I head away from the Commons, toward the field.

In the rafters, the America Bowl Championship banners sway and flutter in the breeze coming from the air vents. Players are scattered across the field, stretching. They're about to start position drills, and I think of watching my father run full-tilt into a tackling dummy.

I'm standing in the doorway, thinking about how none of this has changed since my father played when I feel a tap on my shoulder. As I turn, I'm taken in by a hug, thick and weighty.

"Let me go, Freeman." He backs up a step, but I still have to look up to see his face.

"I haven't seen you in forever, girl."

"I know. I've been busy with class."

He pats me on the head, his hand covering my hair like a hat, and I remember the way we played when I was younger. My father would be busy talking with Coach Derby, figuring up schemes, and Freeman would keep an eye on me. Most times, he'd teach me things about being a defensive tackle. He'd get down on his knees, have me drop to a three point stance, and he'd let me try to swim past his blocks. I remember trying to run around him only to find his huge form shuffling into my path, his arms roping out to stop me.

"You played good last week," I say, and he thanks me, though we both know that he's having a harder time getting through the line these days. The techniques he taught me don't work as well anymore, not with his knees gone out.

"Want to help tape my ankles?" he says.

"Sure." I follow him to a bench on the sideline, and he hands me a roll of yellowed tape. I wonder how they make this stuff, what the adhesive on the tape comes from. The rolls appear, as does most of the equipment, from the President's Area.

Freeman sits, his legs propped on the bench, and I begin to wrap.

"Make it thick, girl," he says.

"Why'd Robards get Evacuated?"

Freeman is looking at his ankles, at my hands wrapping the tape on, making thick layers of protection for his joints. I loop the tape around the ankle twice, then around his foot, then back to the ankle again, repeating the process.

"I don't know."

"Was he hurt?"

"He was just gone. Supposed to be here for practice yesterday, but he never showed up." I know what this means. The men in blue coveralls took him during the night. They came into his room and woke him up and took him. "We don't talk about this kind of thing, Jackie."

I look away from him. "I was just curious."

"It's ok."

The roll of tape ends, and I say, "Is this enough, or should I get another roll?"

"That's good, girl." He stands, and I notice that sitting, I barely reach his waist.

"Good luck this week."

"Luck ain't got nothing to do with it..."

I smile. "Skill and planning's all you need," I say, finishing my father's quote.

"Come by more often." He walks away from me, toward the other players.

I know why they don't want to talk about these things. I understand why they can't focus on Robards being Evacuated, but in the back of my mind the question is still pounding away.

I'm sitting on a bench in the Commons, Kevin in front of me. He's managed to block off a little stretch of space, and I'm running him through drills. The room, bigger than the practice field, is full of people, everyone milling around, and I think it's a miracle that he's managed to get this space.

Kevin's jogging in place until I clap my hands. I wish that I had a whistle, like Coach Derby wears, but I don't know where I could get one.

Each time I clap, Kevin drops to the ground, pushes himself back up, and resumes jogging. It's a tiring exercise, but it works his core.

"The players won't talk," I say. Kevin is facing forward, his head bobbing as he jogs. I clap, and he drops, pushes off the ground.

"Maybe they can't say anything," Kevin says, his breath coming in quick bursts. I clap my hands again.

"What do you mean?" I say.

He's back on his feet, slower this time. I think this is good for him, this is what training is for. "Maybe it isn't that easy." The words come slow, just one at a time between chugs of air. I clap twice, telling him that he can stop. He drops to the ground.

I look out at the crowd of people. In the back of my mind, I think that maybe Robards will pop up, that he'll just appear across the room. Through the crowd, I catch a glimpse of dark blue fabric, and I know it's one of them. Before Kevin can stop me, I'm up from the bench, away from our little area, pushing through the clusters of people.

The Commons is the only non-football gathering room on this Level, and there are people from all over the generator pool here. As I move through these people, I briefly imagine myself a running back, juking and weaving my way through holes my offensive line is opening. It takes me a minute to get across the room, to the place where I saw the dark blue cloth, but when I get there, I look in all directions, trying to get another glimpse of the man. My eyes move across bodies, looking for the tell-tale coveralls, and I'm about to give up, when I see a utility door closing, a bit of blue still visible through the crack.

It takes me a minute to get to the door, and by the time I'm yanking on the handle, Kevin is beside me. He's breathing hard, and for a minute, I let myself feel pride that he was able to catch up to me even after the workout I've just put him through. "What's going on?"

I open the door the rest of the way. "You'll be happier if you don't come." I don't wait for a response, and I'm through the door, not thinking about what I'm about to do, not thinking about the man in blue's job or what he can do to me, I'm just thinking hard on Robards, imagining him in a world I can't imagine, trying to place him with all those details I've pieced together from books and pictures on my computer, and I still can't do it, still can't imagine what it's like for him out there, but I want to know, and I want to know why, and I want to be there and for my father to be there too, done with the worrying and the waiting, no matter what it's like.

I'm moving down a long hallway. Utility doors are off limits to everyone except Security. From childhood, we're told not to open these doors, but right now, I don't really care about consequences.

At the far end of the hallway is the man in dark blue coveralls. I'm still moving forward, and I'm about to shout for him to wait a minute, but the door behind me clicks shut, slowed this whole time by a little hydraulic pump. The click is loud enough that he turns, sees me.

He's tall and angular, like a wide-out, and he comes toward me in long strides, covering the distance quickly.

"This area's off limits," he says.

"I know." I try to keep the sudden fear out of my voice. "I just have a question."

"It's off limits." He closes the distance between us. "Go back into the Commons."

"Just one question," I say, but he's got me by the arm, and he's moving me backward. For a minute, I let myself wish that I'd grown into a football player, that I had the size of Freeman or of my father. I picture this man trying to push Freeman back. I imagine bowling him over, standing over him, asking him all the questions I want to ask.

He leans in close as he backpedals me toward the door. His fingers dig into my arm just enough to hurt. I know I should pull away, run back into the Commons, but instead, I do the dumb thing, and just keep trying to make eye contact with him. The pressure from his fingers hardens a little, then he lets me go, swings the door open, and pushes me out. I hear a lock click into place. Kevin's standing next to the door. Some of the red has left his face, but it's still slick with sweat. "You can't do that," he says.

"I wanted to ask about Robards."

Kevin shakes his head. He walks a few feet away, to an open bench.

"I just wanted to know," I say, but the words sound weak now. I want to rub my arm where the man's fingers had been, but I think of my father, his nose broken and bloodied at halftime of a meaningless late season game against the Processors, pulling his helmet back on, getting ready to go back on the field. I'd come down to the field, held his helmet and a towel for him while he pulled his nose down until the bone that had bulged to the top formed something closer to a straight line. Blood had come out in bubbling splurts, and I'd looked away, afraid that he would lose too much of it. Now, I keep my hand away from the bruises already forming under my skin.

Kevin motions again, and I sit. "They aren't going to talk about it. 'We cannot discuss or comment on any past or potential Evacuations.'"

I shake my head. "Someone knows what happened to him. He's famous. People care."

He looks at me, but he doesn't say anything, and I can see how much he wants me to stop talking about this. Asking questions, with him around, could jeopardize his chance at getting on the team. I stand up, walk a few feet into the crowd and grab a man, by the shoulder. I say, "Do you know what happened to Trenton Robards?" The man shakes my hand off and walks away. I turn to a woman who is standing nearby, and I say, "Do you know why he got Evacuated?" She turns away too, and all around me, the crowd recedes. I look back at Kevin. I don't know what I'm doing, don't know what I expect to come from this, but I want to grab everyone in the room, ask them the same questions until someone tells me why Robards is gone.

Kevin stands up. "Jackie, no one wants to know what happened to him."

And I know he's right. They all know Robards is gone, they whisper it to each other in hallways or pass notes in class or at work, but no one will talk about these things in public. Besides, no one cares why he got evacuated. In a week, they'll forget Robards entirely.

I want to believe that I will go back to normal, that I will be like everyone else. I want to tell Kevin that it's ok, that we'll be able to joke around, pass notes in class, train even harder, but I don't believe these things. I'm looking at my feet, at the plain gray shoes with the gray velcro straps, and I want to explain to Kevin why I need to know about Robards, but when I look back up he's gone, and I'm alone, the crowd on one side of me and a locked door on the other.

It's late when I get back to the room, and my father's already sleeping. He's still in his chair, but his head has dropped to the surface of the desk. I shake him awake and guide him to his bed. He's only half-aware, and as I close the partition around him, he thanks me, the way I used to hear him thank refs on a good call. I wonder briefly if he made it down to the cafeteria today, if he got anything to eat.

I sit at the desk, type another search for Robards into the computer, and again, nothing comes up. My fingers start to type in other search terms, but they won't form coherent words. I can't think of anything to search for, so my fingers just move across the keys, beginning words that they never finish, looking for some combination that makes sense.

After a moment, I stand up and walk to my father's area. I grab his keys, and head out of our room, out into the hallways.

On my way to the field, I only pass a handful of people. Most everyone has gone to their rooms for the night. The lights in the hall have dimmed to half-power, and I notice that in the lower light, I can see more of the cracks and creases in the concrete walls. Something about the brightness of the daytime washes it out, makes those walls look smooth, sculpted, but now, with pools of shadow and yellow half-light, I can see the decay of the place.

It takes me a few minutes of winding through the hallways before I find myself in front of the big double doors. Coach Derby got my father the key for the field years ago, so that he could come and work out whenever he wanted to. I turn the key in the lock and slip inside. It's dark here, and as I walk toward the middle of the field, I imagine the world outside the bunker.

When I was eight, I failed my first placement exam. My mother came up from the Nursery, and she yelled at me and my father for a while. She said I focused too much on football. At one point, she asked what I thought I'd do with myself if I kept failing exams. I remember my father turning white, and now I know that he was imagining me being Evacuated, but at the time, I didn't understand his reaction.

I looked my mother in the eye and said, "I'm going to play football."

She laughed for a long time, then yelled more, and finally left, going back to her Level. When it was just me and my father, both of us sitting on the edge of my bed, he reached over and put a hand on my back to stop me from crying.

"Let's go down to the field," he said.

It was the first time I'd been there when the room was empty. The lights high up on the ceiling were off, so when my father let the door swing closed behind us, the room was in perfect darkness. Now, I remember the feel of the turf under my feet that night. I remember the way my shoes sank down in it a little. It seemed so much softer than the concrete flooring everywhere else in the Bunker. My father, one hand on my back, guided me out into the room. When we were near what must have been mid-field, he asked me if my eyes were open. I told him they weren't. "Why not?" he said.

I opened my eyes. "I can't see anything."

"So why should your eyes be closed?"

"I don't know," I said.

"Keep them open."

"Ok."

He took his hand off my back. "I want you to look at the walls."

"I can't see them."

"Ok," he said. "I want you to look at the ceiling."

"Nothing."

"Look at the ground."

"I can't see it."

"So you can't see. What do you hear?"

"You. Talking."

He laughed. "When I'm not talking, what do you hear?"

I let the echo of his words fade, and I listened, but there was nothing. There was no hum of generators, no buzz of light fixtures, no bustle of other people. "I can't hear anything."

"Good. Standing there, what do you feel?"

"The ground, I guess."

"Ok, you feel the ground. What's it feel like?"

I concentrated on the way my feet sank down into the turf. "Soft, like it shouldn't be holding me up, but it is."

"That's what grass felt like."

"Really?"

"Yeah. Just like that. Only sometimes, it grew out longer, and you could feel it tickling at your ankles."

"On football fields?"

"No. They kept the grass on fields short."

My father was young when everyone came here, not much past five or six. I imagined him in a field of grass. I wished I was barefoot, that the turf was longer, that I could sink my feet down in it, feel what my father had felt. I realized that I couldn't imagine my mother in that world, couldn't imagine her anywhere but here, in the bunker.

"What now?" I said.

"Now, I want you to stand there. Keep your eyes open."

At the time, I didn't understand what he wanted me to do, why I needed to stand in that dark room or why he wanted me to keep my eyes open. My mind kept shifting back to my mother, focusing on the way she laughed at me.

Now, I try to recreate those few minutes in my mind. In the dark, there are no walls, there is no ceiling. Everything is silent. There is only the feel of soft grass under my feet.

A shaft of quick light slants into the room as the door opens and closes behind me. By the time I've turned around, the door is closed again, and I can't see anything.

After a moment, a bank of lights along one wall switch on, and I see Coach Derby, standing off to one side, facing the master switches for all the room's lights.

He turns, and he doesn't seem surprised to see me. "Jackie."

"Coach."

He walks over, slowly. "How's your father doing?"

"Working on plays."

He nods, and I know that he's wondering the same thing as me. When will my father stop being able to draw up plays? When will Derby stop being able to justify his presence?

"I have a question, Coach."

He reaches out, pats me on the shoulder. "You're not supposed to be here."

"I know. What happened with Robards?"

His face is turned away from me, half lost in the shadows, but when he talks, I can hear the strain in his voice. "We aren't discussing Robards."

"Why not?"

"Let it go," he says. I've heard this tone of voice before, when he tells players to stop asking for playing time or to run another ten laps or to hit the sleds once more. There isn't an inch left between the words for discussion.

"I was just curious," I say, and though I don't want to admit it, I'm hurt that he's used this voice on me, that he's treating me the way he treats everyone else. I think of my father getting that last concussion, of the men in blue coveralls standing around him in the locker room. Coach Derby lied, told them that my father had already been coaching the defense, drawing up schemes and formations. We didn't know then how bad it was with my father.

Coach Derby looks at me, and in this dim half-light, I notice for the first time how the skin under his eyes has softened, begun to sag. He's been coaching for as long as I've been alive. In my mind, I see him in the President's Area, standing next to my father, both of them smiling, watching me as I explored. I know that I shouldn't, but I say, "Robards was hurt wasn't he?"

Coach Derby's eyes narrow, and his hand drops on my shoulder. He gives me the briefest of nods, just a quick tilt of the head. "Tell your father I said hi. Tell him that I'm looking forward to seeing those new plays."

He begins walking, his hand still on my shoulder, and I move with him, toward the door, my suspicion confirmed.

Back at our room, I sit down at the desk, listen to my father snoring softly from behind his partition, just a little wheeze of breath.

I look down at his dry erase board. Part of his arm fell on it when he went to sleep, and the play he was working on is blurred. I can tell that this one is an offensive play, but I can't tell where the play will go because the receivers' routes have been smudged. I think about waking my father, asking him if this will be a slant, an out-route, a post. Instead, I switch off our lights, and stumble through the dark, to my bed.

I remember being five, my father trying to explain why my mother didn't stay with us in our room, how her function here demanded that she be on another Level. At six, he tried to explain why I needed to focus during Engineering Class, and at eight, he told me to close my eyes and feel the grass underneath my feet. I remember him telling me one day that it was okay to concentrate on football. I'd asked him about the sky. I didn't understand how it worked, how something could just go on and on, without any edge. "There's too much to know about the world before the Bunker," he said. "Too many questions."

"I want to know."

He nodded. "And that's good, but don't try to understand everything. Find something you can know, and study that."

"Is that what you do?"

"I focus on football." Then, I didn't understand how he could stop wanting to know about everything else. "When you read something else, filter it through football. Don't try to imagine the world. Try to imagine football. When you read something about plants, think about the hedges at Sanford Stadium or about the Rose Bowl. Don't let yourself paint a picture of the rest of it."

Now, lying on my bed in the dark, I think of Robards and of Coach Derby and of my father, and I tell myself that I can't ask more questions. Everything about this place urges me to forget. Still, for a moment I remember the way Robards played, how he could swim past a tight end on his way to blitz the quarterback. How, when he dropped back into coverage, his backpedal was so smooth it looked like he wasn't going backwards at all. I reach up to the wall, feel the carved names. Tomorrow, I will scratch them out. Tomorrow, I'll pay attention to Ms. Grantham, apologize to Kevin by teaching him how to juke a defender, make sure my father eats. I'll bury myself in those actions, my focus narrowed to this world around me, though lying here now, my fingers grazing the carved names, I imagine a knife in my hand, the blade scratching the walls, bit by bit, beginning with the divoted

CHRISTOPHER LOWE

letters and moving deeper, the blade chipping and breaking through
the hard concrete. I imagine pushing free of the Bunker, out into the
dirt that surrounds us, soft after the hard resistance of the concrete,
but the blade doesn't stop moving, it shovels out dirt. I can smell the
stench of earth, can feel the grit of it, but my hand keeps moving, the
blade angling higher, working at the ground until it pushes free into
the open air, my wrist tickled by the grass. I concentrate on the rough
letters, imagine the knife. In my mind, I climb out into a grassy field,
a night wind bristling at my arms. The sky above me is so, so simple.

I'll Be Leaving

Margaret Karmazin

I knew all along that I would be leaving; it was part of the original plan. So why now, did it seem so difficult? Though I have been other places and make a professional effort to remain detached, when actually in the field I seem to lose my resolve.

Possibly it is because she hums while emptying the dishwasher. Why anyone would hum while performing this tedious chore, I cannot fathom, but she does and it's delightful. Low and hypnotizing, she hums away, sending me into a relaxed mood, almost sleepy, as if I were lying in a porch swing listening to bees buzzing in the bushes. Or dragging my hand in a stream as I lay beside it, mesmerized by sun dappled water, the aroma of woodsy air. Humming is like that and no one hums better than Camille.

Naturally, we never had children. Such a thing would create serious problems, though it all worked out without, as they say, a hitch since to my pleasant surprise Camille did not desire any. I should have warned her before we married, but I was so enthusiastic about performing my field work and, I can freely admit it now, enthralled with this woman with the round neck covered in the back by fine gold hairs that lit up in sunlight when she wore her blond mane piled high on her head. I washed this hair for her, brushed it, twirled it around my fingers. Some people pet dogs and cats, but I petted my wife.

Her skin attracted me also. The pliability of it, the way it was flexible, yet so soft. As she aged, the texture changed of course, but I still enjoyed stroking it on occasion.

I often wondered if she thought my ways odd; I wondered if other husbands did the same things, but suspected that for the most part they did not. Observing them at social events, I would usually come to this conclusion. Some hardly seemed to notice their wives, turning away from them when speaking, looking off into the distance, paying more attention to anyone who happened by than to the human being supposedly closest to them. At sporting or other events, I would listen to the males speaking of their spouses in jovial, occasionally insulting terms. Ball and Chain, my bitch, my fatter half, the list went on. I could never quite grasp it all. True, there were occasions when I found Camille irritating and even a few when I almost regretted taking on the assignment, but these would soon dissipate. I never had a desire to share my negative emotions concerning her with outside individuals.

But then I am not like the others, which goes without saying.

There did come a scare, ten or so years into the marriage, when Camille feared she was pregnant. When she told me this, my mouth grew so dry I almost couldn't speak. I didn't see how it was possible. Trying to remain calm while she called the doctor for the pregnancy test took much of my courage and energy. When I was able, I asked her what we needed to do next. She said she would go see if the rabbit died. In those times, either they tortured some poor rodent to find out or still referred to doing so. I almost lost consciousness when the news was good. She never seemed to notice that my own relief far surpassed her own, and together we drank martinis, our favorite indulgence at the time. She would never learn that should the "rabbit have died," I would have had to take measures of my own.

The assignment, in case you're wondering, was for fifty years. We married when Camille was twenty. She assumed I was twenty-two. I imagine that I looked about that age. And now, I appear approximately how someone in their early seventies should. No one has ever remarked on my appearance except to say that I seem anemic and should request a blood test for iron deficiency. I always claimed that my blood tested fine, that I seemed to have no anemia of any sort. I was Norwegian, I would say, hence my light coloring. That would usually end the discussion. I have always avoided doctors.

Camille has prepared a delicious dinner this evening, consisting of some of my favorite foods. Salade Nicoise, a reminder of our trip to Paris some twenty years ago. She had wanted to go and naturally I would not turn down any chance to observe different sections of the world and their occupants, so I was enthusiastic to accompany her. Ever since, I have craved Salade Nicoise and will find it difficult to forget in the future.

She serves me this with dark German bread and creamy garlic butter and a plate of various cheeses. If a utopia in the universe does exist, they would serve the occupants this very meal.

There have been many things I don't understand and do not know if they apply to other females or just to Camille, to the relationships of other wedded couples or just ours, but then that's why I am here, to discover and experience.

For instance, she belongs to a reading club, she calls "The Book-ies." The group consists of six to eight women and one man who take a month to read one novel (or rarely a nonfiction book) and report to each other their opinions about it. Camille frequently returns home afterwards so worked up that she is red-faced. When this occurs, I worry that she might suffer a cerebral hemorrhage. Her anger usually relates to something another member has said during the discussion, yet when she reports the content of this exchange to me, I fail to understand how it could result in such fury on her part. There is a woman in particular who is the star player in these episodes, a particularly exasperating person by Camille's description. Yet the time that I happened to meet this individual, when the group convened at our house, she seemed innocuous and even pleasant to me, which only served to further infuriate my wife.

"What is it exactly that you find so distasteful about her?" I inquired after the guests had left.

"If you're so thick that you can't see it yourself," Camille snapped, "then I don't know that I can explain it!"

It took me the good part of an hour to soothe her to the point of trying.

"She is small-minded," said Camille.

"How so?" I asked.

"She even wears her silly, tight-assed blouses buttoned to her neck. Ridiculous."

This I did not understand at all. How can blouses be "tight-assed" and why would the way a person buttons her blouse bother anyone?

"Haven't you noticed, William, that you can tell all about a person by the way they dress or, say, decorate their house? I can pretty much tell a person's political persuasion or sense of mental or spiritual adventure by these things. Just a glimpse and I can tell."

"Really?" I said, intrigued. "So I'm assuming that by your observations this woman expresses by her dress and decorations a way of thinking that you disdain?"

Camille looked at me long and hard. "Are you making fun of me? Because, if you are..."

"No, no!" I assured her. "Absolutely not. I am merely quite curious. In a scientific way, you understand." (And indeed I was.)

"In her house, she has little roosters stenciled around the top of her kitchen. Everything is red, blue, pink and white, some sort of ridiculous patriotic statement, I assume. All items in her house look as if she purchased them from a living-in-the-country catalog. She wears her hair in an insipid haircut, the exact look of someone who sings in a church choir. Her entire persona expresses conservatism and fear. She has probably never seen any other parts of the world other than her own small region. I am certain that she never permits herself an original thought, never deviates from the party line, be it religion or politics - all churchy-while-we-bomb-them, you know the type. Twists whatever Jesus might have said. I hate her."

I didn't contradict Camille, knowing better after all these years. Not if I wanted a pleasant dinner and peaceful evening. Besides, who was to say that she was not correct in her perceptions?

"How would someone dress or decorate that would meet with your approval?" I asked instead.

She shot me a sharp look, the sort that a carnivorous bird might give to its prey.

"The presence of filled bookshelves in a person's house, and *not* with Danielle Steel, but serious books, would signal to me that the owner is intelligent and probably keeping up her learning. Original art on her walls would tell me that she is open to and understands to a certain degree the arts, that possibly she knows and socializes with artists. Objects from different countries on her tables, shelves or walls tell me that she travels and is possibly open-minded toward other cultures. If her clothes are casual, yet interesting, not restrictive or buttoned up, I would assume that she is open to moving, possibly dancing, is sexual, likes her body and is ready to enjoy life. Unafraid, that's how I would see her. I could be wrong or partly wrong, but I think for the most part, I'd be right."

I found all of this quite interesting, to know that someone can glean all this information from one glance and I wondered if most people did the same or was it just Camille? Why though would it be just Camille? Since she was composed of the same stuff as the rest of them, I could only assume that others saw what she did. What then, I naturally wondered, did she, or they, see when they observed me? The mere thought gave me a shiver of fear. Should I make sure that my top shirt button was kept open? But how then would I attach a tie?

Later, while sitting on the toilet, I remembered the Masai I had seen on a TV program and their love of red and purple clothing. What did this say about them? Would Camille know? The next morning I asked her, but she brushed me off, believing I was making a joke. I never found out about the Masai and did not ask anyone else.

All of this time I have worked as an insurance agent. In this way, I've enjoyed the opportunity to travel around the area and get inside people's homes to present them with insurance options. Both sides in this transaction benefit since I have the opportunity to observe close at hand how various people live and they in turn can create safety nets for their old age or the unpleasant event of a death. Naturally, I have insured myself quite well to help lighten the blow to Camille when I part from her.

In a week, I will take Camille out for her birthday. She will become seventy years of age the twelfth of October. We'll go to her favorite restaurant, an Indian one out on the highway not far from where they built the new airport. It will be our last dinner together, though of course she won't be aware of that at the time. There's no reason to spoil things for her.

There have been occasions when Camille cried and not just when you would expect, such as at funerals and other life and death situations. I'm thinking of the times when I could not understand why she did it. I have never shed a tear, not due to emotion. Probably I could if I concentrated, but why bother? After Camille cries, she often develops a sinus infection, so I have no desire to attempt it myself. But in spite of her unpleasant aftermath, I've heard my wife do it when she believed that no one was listening. Once in the afternoon, I arrived home unexpectedly and caught her sitting at the breakfast nook, sobbing hard. When I asked what had set her off, she refused to explain. Over the next few hours, I managed to get something out of her referring to "the meaning of life," but no further information.

I too have pondered the "meaning of life," but have moved past such conjecture. I have a job to do and I do it, that's all. I am a cog in the machine of the universe, a working part of the whole, and so I do my share as I understand it. Fortunately or unfortunately, I don't seem to possess Camille's emotional depth and that of some of my other associates here, so I possibly don't suffer as much as I would otherwise. Yet, there is much of me that dreads parting from Camille and this role I have played for the past fifty years. It manifests as almost a physical pain in the center of my chest.

I must bring up the subject of sex here. You may have been wondering about our relations in that area. We performed sex, of course. It would be unlikely that I could behave as a normal husband without taking part in such activity. I usually found the task a reasonably pleasant one, though experienced little of the intense passion apparently connected with it according to what I observe in the media. It's likely that Camille felt negatively about my lackluster performance over the decades.

She said to me once, early in our connection, after one of our sedate (compared to what I have watched in films) sessions, "Don't I turn you on, William? Is there something about me that just doesn't light your fire?" She was wearing a smirk when she said this, so I wasn't quite sure of her exact emotion at the time.

"Um," I said, "Of course you light my fire. But maybe my fire is smaller than usual?" I sincerely wanted to know since after all, knowing is my function.

"Oh?" said Camille. "You suspect that your ability to experience passion is lacking? Have you noticed this with other women?" She watched me closely.

"Other women?" I said. "There haven't been any other women. You're the only one."

She sat up with interest. "Really? You're twenty-one years old, right? You're saying I'm your first?"

First what? I was confused, but then I understood. "Yes," I said.

"No wonder," she mumbled.

"No wonder what?"

"Nothing."

I knew it was not nothing. "You shouldn't hold back the truth," I told her.

Her eyes widened. "You want the truth? Even if it's painful?"

The truth was painful? That I really didn't grasp. "Of course," I said.

"All right then. You're not very good at sex."

This was interesting. "No? Explain why not."

She gave me the sort of look I'd seen people give to mentally deranged street denizens, then sighed deeply and began. "You kiss me like it's a job, not a hot lead-in to more. You keep your hands flat on my back or hip instead of running them all over me. You don't seem to enjoy what you're doing. Once you start the actual doing (here she snorted), it's okay but it's over in a minute. What am I supposed to get out of it, William?"

I was surprised. I had assumed that what she was supposed to get out of it was sperm. I was supposed to be impregnating her, though she was unaware that I could not. But from her point of view, she would be receiving the desirable sperm.

"William? You didn't answer."

"Um," I said, "sperm?"

Again that look. "Sperm? What the hell would I want sperm for? You think I want to get knocked up? Are you nuts?"

"Well, uh..." I didn't know what to say.

"I have a diaphragm in! I'm protected, for crying out loud. We're supposed to be doing this for the *pleasure* of it!" She looked quite upset.

"Oh."

"I hate you!" she yelled and began to disentangle herself from the sheets.

"Don't go!" I pleaded, grabbing at her arm. I was in a quandary. What if I was incapable of enjoying sex to the degree that she expected? Should I fake it? Go, as they might say, through the motions? Wouldn't that be dishonest? But then I'd never told her that I would never be a parent. I suppose *that* was being dishonest.

"I-I'm just a beginner. I probably need practice. A lot of practice."

I said that in a neutral tone of voice, but apparently Camille thought, I now realize, that I was being wittily sexy. Which worked. She settled back down and, with a throaty growl, began to work on my participating organs.

Eventually, I learned to relax and get a relative amount of enjoyment from the frequently expected activity. Oddly, sometimes I find myself dreaming of this.

I won't be taking anything with me from our life together. Nothing is necessary, considering that I store all the information in my mind. Camille will believe that I have gone in the usual way; there will be a body destroyed in an accident. She will undoubtedly mourn for several months, possibly a couple of years, but she'll go on, meet with her friends, travel, possibly enjoy a class of some sort. She might have twenty or more years left; her ancestors are long lived. She will never know who I really am.

The Desk Clerk and the Tattooed Maiden

Michelle Nichols

It was impossible for the desk clerk to recognize the maiden. She had
waited so long for this girl, working at the DPS, taking pictures of
women who removed thick glasses, stretched the skin at their eyes,
and tried to smile so that they looked eighteen again—at least on their
driver's licenses. When there was still a little sparkle to her, the desk
clerk advised her subjects when there was lipstick on teeth or when
collars needed straightening. She allowed retakes for blinking, taking
the extra time to delete flawed images from the computer and start
again.

But lines of angry drivers have descended on her and the word
"bitch" has been thrown at her so many times that her glamour crum-
bled. She has spent too many smoke breaks with co-workers who
complained about their husbands and kids and the DPS Patrol officers
they have kissed at Christmas parties. She has huddled in the cold,
puffing on bummed cigarettes, and checking out sixteen-year-old
boys taking their driving tests. She has learned how to shape her face
into complete passivity when her supervisor yells at her about being
gone from her post too long.

Now the desk clerk's lips have grown thin from biting them so
she won't cuss or talk about a time when she consorted with maidens
and princes and magic gourds. Now, she snaps the camera when
least expected, in the moment when a woman is folding her glasses
against a hip, one eye cast downward and the other inexplicably wandering up and to the right.

So when the maiden appears, the desk clerk is wiping her nose
with a wadded up tissue that she keeps in the pocket of her sweater.

She glances at the girl long enough to take in the purple-dyed hair, the skin of her bare arms covered in vining tattoos, the metal of her piercings shimmering under the fluorescent lights. She drops her tissue back into her pocket with a sigh. Everyone in the office is staring at the girl and by association the desk clerk. This makes the clerk angry. She directs the girl through her eye test and paper work, and when she pulls out too few wadded bills from the pocket of her jeans, the clerk announces in a loud voice that the license renewal amount is posted on the front door.

"We say it up front so that this won't happen," she says. "You're holding up the line." The people behind the girl grumble and make pointed comments to one another about freaks.

The girl lifts one leg and balances against the desk as she unties her boot. Her fingernails are painted to match her hair, and they work slowly, pulling the laces through holes and uncrossing them. She retrieves another five dollar bill from beneath her foot and lays it onto the desk. The clerk's nostrils quiver. She stares at the money, wet with a piece of lint stuck to it.

"It's still not enough," she says.

The maiden brushes away a strand of hair that has coiled around her eyebrow hoop. Her fingers lightly touch the diamond nose stud. "Please," she says and smiles widely so that her straight perfect teeth glow. "Please," she says again more softly. "I have to drive my father to radiation."

But the desk clerk can't see that beneath the sleeveless shirt, the girl's arm tattoos swirl into an image that covers her entire back — a firebird at the point of ascension. The feathers are rendered in such detail that they can rise from the girl's soft skin and tremble aloft before she steps into a shower. The wings drip when they are wet, and a flea huddles deep in the silky down to escape the shampoo. The red eyes wink and move and weep, and the crown is a pure flame that smolders at the base of the girl's neck. It steams in the shower, but it always burns, especially when she is happy, like when her father's doctor has good news. No boy has seen the firebird, though a couple have snaked thick arms up and under her shirt to undo her bra. They have been bitten. Males allow the maiden wide berth, especially be-

cause once they draw back bloodied fingers from beneath her clothing, she punches them hard enough to bruise.

On the girl's hip is a lone feather that curls and undulates as she
moves. It can be plucked by a beloved or a fairy godmother who has
forgotten how to shine. To hold the feather is to rise off the ground
and hover, unburdened.

But the desk clerk doesn't recognize the maiden. She doesn't see
the edge of the feather in the gap between the girl's shirt and the low
waist of her jeans. The desk clerk crosses her arms over her chest.
"This isn't charity," she says. She smiles as the girl retrieves the bills
and crams them back into her pocket. She then watches her exit the
building and unlock a 70s model sedan, lowering herself into the driver's seat beside an old man. The man leans forward, checks his wallet,
and the girl shakes her head. When she starts the car, the desk clerk,
motions for one of the DPS Traffic Officers. She points at the girl and
tells him that she is driving without a valid license. The officer shrugs,
starts out the door to stop the maiden with his ticket pad. The desk
clerk gestures for the next person in line.

Firestorm

Claudine Griggs

<u>Journal Entry #1:</u>

Most bad accidents happen in routine moments that suddenly skew into disaster. To stub a toe and fall in the backyard is no big deal. Embarrassment, a few curses, and on with the day. Stub that same toe at the edge of the Grand Canyon and they pack your body out on a burro.

My stumble happened as I was fueling my Subaru Outback. The pump's automatic shutoff failed, the tank overflowed, and a splash of gasoline trickled on the ground. Bland, really. This would normally produce a foul smell, fuel evaporation, and some extra air pollution. Probably happens a hundred times a day, maybe thousands. In this instance, however, that minor bit of nothing was accompanied by a static spark, and Wham! I was up to my Wonder Bra in flames. But even that should have been relatively inconsequential—a vaporous mist, a small fire, and a madwoman dash out of harm's way. Then the fire department could clean up the after-burn, slap a few bandages, and cite the station owner for faulty equipment, environmental degradation, or unclean restrooms.

But accidents don't follow scripts. I was standing at the Canyon and didn't know it.

In an irreconcilable moment, I reflexively jerked the nozzle out of the filler duct, which not only fed the fire but provided air and access to the tank. It spilled its guts. I was engulfed by the Big Bang, lost my footing, and rolled to the asphalt with thirteen gallons of unleaded regular, where I apparently kicked and screamed until somebody pulled me out.

I remember trying to stand and run, but my feet skated on Brimstone Pond. The second time I went down, I choked on gasoline and blackness. As an ironic joke, the puddle seemed cool. When I came to, the only viable skin on my body was a small stretch of forearm that I had pressed against my eyes along with the corresponding face protected by the forearm. The rest smoldered like a roofer's mop. Somebody was crying hysterically, but it wasn't me.

I was transported to Rhode Island Hospital. The emergency room doctor said that they were airlifting me to the burn center in San Antonio, but I probably would not live long enough to get there. All they could do at the moment was ease the pain.

"I'm not in pain," I said.

"You will be," he said, and shot me with enough morphine to stop an asteroid. The doc told me again that I was critically burned, which was annoying because I heard him the first time. I figured he was exaggerating for reverse psychology, but he was a good old American realist who believed in fully informed patients. Bless him. He asked if I wanted a priest. I said, "No. Just tell my boyfriend I won't be able to make dinner tonight."

To tell you the truth, that would have been a good time to die. The double-dose morphine temporarily ended all my little problems, and life was pretty good in the haze. I quite suddenly had fond memories of San Antonio and the river walk when I visited an Air Force friend at Lackland AFB. I knew their hospital treated severe burns, which happens around jet fuel, although I thought treatment was reserved for military personnel and their families. Maybe they would bill my insurance company.

It was impossible, but I survived to Texas and beyond. That's not really the story, though. Not what's bothering me, and not why I'm keeping a diary, which is surprising. My response in sophomore English when Mrs. Dettwelling extolled the benefits of journaling was several big yawns followed by a giggle. Personal writing was for humanities geeks who were too far gone to work their way up to losers. I was more interested in how to get out of fifth-period P.E. or who would ask me to the prom. But here I am. The new journal queen.

I won't bother with details about pigskin grafts, the years of cultivation and transplantation of dermal patches from my face and forearm, the repulsive goop immersions to deescalate the war against dehydration, or the blinding, screaming pain of multiple surgeries, infections, and recoveries followed by more surgery — month after month after month. The doctors and nurses said I was a living miracle, but they weren't the one in a rotating bed or eating through a tube. It's too bad the first doctor had not been right. That kind of faulty prognosis could make one lose confidence in the medical profession.

That's how I felt for many years. Quick death good; long recovery bad. But something happened to make me wonder.

I have told only one person. Junior Ryan Smythe, my best friend since fourth grade and my current boyfriend. Until recently, Junior was the egghead of our relationship; and for some strange reason, he continues to stand by me while we're trying to figure out how to manage my altered life. This is surprising because I won't be winning any modeling contracts. I have been cut and spliced more than Mary Shelley's monster. But the really weird part is the brainwaves.

JR, that's what I've called Junior since the second day we met, is a pretty fair biologist at the University of Rhode Island. He thinks my emerging intellect has something to do with five years of severe sensory deprivation. I told him from where I was sitting pain was pretty sensory. But according to JR, the pain functioned as corporeal white noise, isolating my brain from everything around me. As I'm sure you know, loss of sensory data can promote psychosis; people start to see and hear things that aren't there; lab rats might chew off body parts. So in sensory deprivation experiments, human subjects are limited to the "short-run" by ethical constraints. Mine was not. I couldn't feel through my skin. My eyes and what used to be my ears were bandaged for weeks at a time. My nose was ablated, and I couldn't eat or taste much for years (there's no such thing as a gourmet feeding tube). So the loss of sensory data combined with systemic pain suppressants set my brain adrift with nothing but three pounds of neurons as my whole reality.

JR says that people use 15-20 percent of their brain power. To survive, mine apparently went to 100 percent, which then generated extra capacity besides. JR called it a neuro-multiplier. I called it hell, but by unwillingly breaking experimentation limits, I developed a flaming IQ with kinetic abilities. Perhaps everyone has this potential.

JR wants to run controlled measurements when I am better. Me? I don't care. I'm smart enough to know I'd rather be beautiful. I miss slinking into a cocktail dress and showing off my young body on the dance floor. I liked to watch national beauty pageants and wonder how I might stack up against the competition. But my life went up in smoke, and I should have died with disco.

JR says I'll appreciate what's happened in a few more years, that I'm still growing and there's no telling where it will lead. I say to hell with JR, even if he is my boyfriend. Give me my former body and let's call it square.

Journal Entry #2 (Six Months Later):

I'm returning to Rhode Island permanently. No more extended visits to Texas, and hopefully no more reconstructive surgery or skin grafts. The surgeons say that I'm well enough for locals to take care of me. The risk of infection is about average. I've regained as much use of my hands as I'll probably ever have, which is almost nothing, though I can pinch a pencil between my right thumb stump and partial index finger. My left hand is basically a webbed lump. I can hobble with a cane for short distances, but I'm not strong enough for more than a few minutes. My arm gives out. JR promised to design a wrist-strap that will clamp onto a specially fitted walking stick to extend my distance. I had figured to rely on a wheelchair, but it's hard to sit for long periods. The skin on my thighs and back hurts, and there are circulatory issues. My legs tingle much of the time, and the pain gets worse if I'm in a chair more than a couple hours. This body is a mess, and walking for short distances is part of my physical therapy.

My eyes, protected by my arm in the fire, are in pretty good shape. If I wore a Hijab, I might be inconspicuous. Seriously, though, I couldn't handle blindness. That would be too much. I read a lot now, including the highbrow texts that JR brings. I used to laugh at his spending so much time with books, and before the accident, I couldn't make it past the titles of *Critique of Pure Reason* or *Popular Delusions and the Madness of Crowds* or *Human Action*. Book-learning just didn't click. Today I want everything. Physics, calculus, history, philosophy, rhetoric, psychology, paleontology, economics. And I'm skimming side-line languages like Chinese, Russian, Greek, German, Arabic. I gloriously failed Spanish in high school, but I now seem to remember everything that I didn't learn in Mrs. Espanola's class, or whatever her name was. I prefer reading texts in their original language when possible because translators often lie (so do authors for that matter), but reading helps pass the time. JR is sweet and goes out of his way to find what I request: Einstein, Balzac, Hugo, Tolstoy, Balzac, Camus, Stendhal, Kant and Nietzsche. Quite suddenly, I'm into Edgar Rice Burroughs and Stephen King. A real kick.

Journal Entry #3:

JR is setting up a home computer with high-speed access so I can tie into academic databases. URI, Brown, Harvard, and several other universities and nonprofits are allowing me to use (for free) their electronic journals and library resources because of my "tragedy and heroic struggle to overcome adversity," etc., etc, etc. Pity is annoying because it won't return my life to me, but I am grateful for the on-line periodicals and books. There are some smart people out there.

Brown University is providing most of my medical care, though we all agree that less is best at this point. I'm pretty sick of doctors and manage to get my pain pills refilled on-line. JR picks up a bottle of Yukon Jack when I need an extra boost. And because I'm so smart these days, I tucked away enough Seconal to provide an all-purpose escape clause if life gets too rough. Why didn't I think of this sooner?

Journal Entry #4:

Feeling pretty good today. Not much pain. And I'm having fun with the computer. I often read late into the night, sometimes to three or four in the morning. Sleep a few hours; get up and start again. I don't need a lot of rest, in fact, it's almost a distraction. Took the computer apart yesterday and put it back together. Surprising how simple these things are when you get into them. If I had a system clean room, I might try to build a better mousetrap, but there are limits to what a lone scientist can do in the modern era. We might produce a revolutionary idea, but only the corporate lab system can translate the idea into reality.

Oh, JR is coming for dinner tonight. Bringing his homemade burritos and a bottle of tequila. We had a fight two days ago. He told me I was beautiful and I spit in his face. I felt bad afterward, but I don't take well to pity-lies. JR said that he's too much of a nerd to lie and I am beautiful. I think he was almost serious, yet it took me two days to forgive him. I see a freak show in the mirror, so it's easy to believe JR is making fun of me.

Kinetic sideline: I can levitate a wet sponge for up to fifteen minutes. (Look Ma, no hands!) For some reason, it's easier when the sponge is damp.

Journal Entry #5:

I read Thoreau's *Walden* four times today, which helped me understand that JR might be telling the truth. He *thinks* I am beautiful. A week ago, I asked JR to take the short drive to Massachusetts to look at the Walden, which is now a state reservation. This was disappointing. The vehicle line getting in was longer than an amusement park ride. Then I realized how stupid I was. As if Thoreau would be found in the pond or cabin. I re-read *Walden* to confirm what I was thinking. JR does not see me as a deformed monster. He sees Thoreau's worn-out gloves that become more meaningful, more beautiful, with use and repair. A kind of existential utilitarian naturalism. In a similar way, I have become dearer to JR. We go back a long way. He cares.

That's when I started to consider time travel. Not the H. G. Wells' variety because Einstein convinced me that's impossible. Well, not precisely impossible, but requiring infinite energy, which is impossible. But I wondered about intellectual breaches along the continuum. If ideas have no mass, it might be possible to send them through time. Just a thought.

My lips still hurt when JR tries to kiss me, which I don't like anyway. The image is revolting. I sure as hell wouldn't kiss me.

Journal Entry #6:

I didn't mean to kill the man, but he deserved to die and I was mercifully quick.

JR took me out to dinner. I am getting better at solid food, and he decided we should go out for my birthday. When in public, I wear a polypropylene ski mask and gloves so as not to frighten small children. People in East Greenwich are used to me, so the facial covering is rarely a problem, but JR took me to the Federal Hill dining district in Providence. Some wise guy walked by and said something about only terrorists wear masks in July. JR was polite, but suggested that the guy should go about his business, so the jerk pushes JR aside and yanks off my mask.

Lon Chaney's phantom looks better than I do, and I swear what little nose I had left came off with the polypropylene. Felt like it anyway. I yelped and grabbed my face. JR, who cringes at harsh language, lit into Mister Bad Ass Wannabe without hesitation. The battle was over in two seconds. JR hit the ground. Mister Wannabe glanced my way and said, "With a face like yours, Babe, this dude's probably the best you can get, but Jeez-zus!"

JR staggered up to try again, but there was no need. Wannabe keeled over, and I asked JR to please take me home.

The next day we heard on the news that a man had dropped dead in Federal Hill. Medical examiners suspected a cerebral hemorrhage. When JR asked if the incident had anything to do with our birthday dinner, I told him the truth. Wannabe's brain felt like a wet sponge when I reached inside and squeezed his grey matter into scrambled eggs. JR is the only one who knows.

Journal Entry #7:

JR and I stopped at the same gas station where my accident occurred. The owner visited the hospital when I was recovering. Now he allows me to fill up for free and still cries when he sees me. JR doesn't like to accept the gifts, which makes him feel like a thief, but I told him that this makes the owner feel better. It does, too. I can sense emotions pretty good these days. The station agent is built with kindness from the ground up, and he carries a crippling remorse about my accident. So every month or two, we help him by accepting the free tank of gas. It's the right thing to do.

Journal Entry #8:

I tested my time-travel theory. Didn't work. Yet if I can levitate small objects in space, I might levitate my thoughts across time. Maybe I'm dreaming, but the difficulty seems to be with sensory perception. Without the body, how can I *know* when and where I've been? Or whether I've been at all? When I intellectually visit the past, I must somehow learn to "see" without the body's five senses. I'll study on it, of course, but nobody is researching in this area, nor does anyone else have my theoretical capacity.

I read mostly for pleasure these days, which is a bad habit. I went through the *Encyclopedia Britannica*, *World Book*, *Oxford English Dictionary*, and *The Story of Civilization* last week. I love old encyclopedias—learn a lot by examining standardized cultural viewpoints.

JR wanted to test my photographic recall and asked if I could remember phone numbers, like that savant movie, but I told him it would bore me to death. I suggested that he use the *American Heritage Dictionary*, which was on the kitchen counter and which I had already read. He gave me a page number, so I listed the headwords, described the "flipper" photo of a scuba diver, and mentioned a smudge at the entry for "flirtatious." JR doesn't bother with phonebook questions anymore.

Journal Entry #9 (One Year after Return to Rhode Island):

Out of the blue, JR pressed me about Mister Bad Ass Wannabe. I tried to avoid the topic. I mean, it's not like I'm proud, but after a brief protest, I reiterated what I told him before. I thought the guy dead.

JR did not challenge me, which was surprising, but said we should try to measure more precisely my kinetic abilities. JR also admitted that he used the university connections to talk with the coroner about Mister Wannabe. The man's brain had been mashed against the inner skull with no outside physical injury. The official cause of death is listed as "trauma of unknown origin," but the coroner said it was easier to believe in spontaneous combustion.

I don't like New England winters. I wonder how Thoreau could stand them.

Journal Entry #10:

JR made love to me for the first time since the accident. Not that he hasn't tried, but I could never allow it. The thought of his touching what's left of my body was too vile. Everything still works internally, but I don't feel like a woman anymore. How could I? I'm the fastest ugly on two legs. The creature from the blackened lagoon. The charwoman of Dresden Street

It's torture that I can't love JR the way he wants. No, that's not exactly the truth. It's torture that I can't *be loved* the way I want. Women never understand the extraordinary wonder of a female body. All the glories of a universe compressed into 120 pounds of sensual capacity that can be ripped apart in an instant or chipped away over sixty years.

After we made love, JR asked me to marry him. I cried, said no, and took the Seconal after he went home. I barely had enough finger to get myself to throw it back up.

Journal Entry #11:

I'm home from the hospital. Not the burn unit. The mental ward at Butler.

I flipped out. Started to hear voices and answer them. Started to fling pots and pans around my apartment — only I wasn't using my hands to do it.

JR got me calmed down enough that I wouldn't hurt anybody, or let on that I could throw things without touching them. We agreed that the government, if they found out, would probably lock me up as somebody's never-ending research project, but we also figured that a few days of observation with anti-psychotic medication might be good. Like chicken soup, it couldn't hurt.

What set me off? Somebody sent me a handsomely bound book entitled *The Uncanny*. When I opened the cover, there was a mirror inside. That broke me. I started screaming and making potholes in my kitchen.

The psychiatrist at Butler was pretty good. After a two-day observation, she said that I didn't warrant medication. I needed exercise and a strong dose of quit-feeling-sorry-for-yourself. "Face reality," she said. "Get out of the house, out of the books, and out of your head for awhile. And quit wearing that damned ski mask! Let the world adjust to you. If they don't like it, *they* can check in here."

At first, I wanted to scramble her brains better than Mister Wannabe. Then, pretty soon, I wanted to give her a hundred years of extra life. (I wonder if that's possible.)

When JR brought me home from the hospital, I told him we could get married if he still had interest. Believe it or not, he pulled the engagement ring out of his pocket and slipped it over what's left of my right index finger, which is just long enough to sport a ring. Looks nice, too. If it weren't for uncanny books with mirrors in them, I might have felt beautiful.

Journal Entry #12 (For Your Eyes Only):

I scrutinized every physics, chemistry, and engineering manual that I could find via my on-line data access and HELIN multi-library consortium privileges. No help with brainwave time displacement. It's pretty clear that I'll have to write my own theory and tests à la the Wright Brothers. But I'll do it inside my head because I don't want the CIA to download whatever I come up with. Could be dangerous in the hands of fools.

JR dropped by my apartment two days ago (that hyperbolically wonderful nerd doesn't want to live together until after the wedding)—very excited because he devised an easy measure of my kinetic abilities with an old barbell set bought at the local flea market for three bucks. JR claims that practical teacher training should include a course called, "Lab Equipment on the Cheap," but anyway, my test would be to levitate the iron plates in increasing increments.

I smiled. JR was so proud hauling in that barbell set. I had been keeping secrets lately, but since we were to be married in four weeks, it was time let him in.

JR arranged a series of 2½-, 5-, 10-, and 25-pound discs. He also took a can of refried beans from the cupboard in case the 2½-pound plate was too heavy, but he was pretty sure after my flying-pots-and-pans that I could handle a couple pounds. I laughed and asked if he wanted me to lift the plates one at a time, all at once, or perhaps meld them into a single unit. He was puzzled, so I levitated the four discs off the floor, stacked them nicely in air, whistled the theme from *Lost in Space*, and melt-molded them into a single 42½-pound tetrahedron. Simple, really, but you would have thought I had walked on water.

"That's impossible," said JR.

"Oh, I'm sorry," said I. "You should have told me sooner."

I reassured him that it wasn't as fancy as anybody might guess. I simply destabilize the atoms so they can slide together with a little push. Pretty easy with metals—almost like liquefaction without heat. Crystals don't work so well. I tried the diamond in my engagement ring, but the damned thing wouldn't meld at all. I reframed my theoretical underpinnings regarding quantum crystalline structures to no avail. Shape shifting won't work on a girl's best friend, but iron can be as malleable as Silly Putty.

Kinetic sidebar: I don't need a cane any more. My legs aren't any stronger, but I can make myself weigh less for short periods of time.

Journal Entry #13:

JR and I will be married tomorrow at the University of Rhode Island. Just a few friends with a minister. The bride and groom are both atheists, but so is the minister, so I suppose that's OK.

My dress is beautiful white-lace. It makes me sick to think what will be wearing it. I try to put those ideas out of my head, but they have a life of their own. Intermittent self-loathing is a beast.

JR really loves me. I know that. I try not to read his mind, which isn't fair, but sometimes there's no helping myself. His love is bottomless and warm and golden. He deserves better than he's getting. If I really loved him, I wouldn't allow this marriage. But I am a moral coward who wants to be a wife.

Three days ago, at the rehearsal, I went to the ladies room. While I was inside a cubicle, two students entered the room, washed their hands, and started talking about the woman they saw on campus.

"If I was toasted like that," said one, "I'd never go outside the house!"

The other offered, "I would have killed myself long ago. Don't see why she has to come around and gross-out the rest of us. Looks like barbequed peanut brittle."

The first woman suddenly turned generous. "Poor thing probably has no idea how bad she looks. Might be retarded."

I sat in the cubicle for fifteen minutes, crying and paralyzed with disgust until JR came to look for me. The sad part? Down deep, I agree with the students. It's hard to be ugly.

<u>Journal Entry #14</u>:

I am losing control. Difficult to tolerate my fellow man, especially women. They are so stupid. Some wacko rear-ended me yesterday in the new Prius I was test driving. JR wanted me to have more independence and offered to buy and custom fit the car, but to tell you the truth, I'm tired of traveling and lecturing. Even the brightest students and faculty can't comprehend my work. I speculate about psychic space-time or science-based alchemy, and they praise me for being an inspiration to disabled people around the world. One more dumb and dumber question or comment, and I swear I'll meld the man with the woman sitting next to him. Then *S/he* can be an inspiration to the disabled.

Anyway, the accident nutcase was putting on mascara while driving. Then she yelled at me for stopping at a red light and causing her to ram into me. She told the police that, because I had no hands, I was a vehicular menace and shouldn't be allowed on the road.

Well, I got mad, and the bitch won't yell anymore. I shredded her vocal chords along with her optic nerves, but now the guilt is driving me crazy and I really know how the gas station owner feels. Don't suppose I'll get much sleep (though I'm down to only one hour per day) until I figure out how to repair the woman; however, part of me doesn't want to. Next time she may splatter some poor kid on a bike. It might be wise to let her cry silently in the dark.

After that episode, I decided against the vehicle and further lectures. My temper can be dangerous, even lethal, and I don't want to draw attention to myself. Some people are beginning to wonder how a sexy high school socialite with a C+ average speculates about psychic time travel, so I've gone silent in the hope of a big payoff. If I puzzle through the concept, I might be able to go back to the accident, warn myself, and shut down the fuel spigot before it overflows. Slide a single thought into my head on that fateful day and Wallah! Plunging necklines are back — with no sensory deprivation, no medical torture, and no Mensa magic. Just an uninspired, self-absorbed, thoroughly happy woman. I would take that.

I do sometimes wonder whether any record of my current post-accident life would then exist. If I go back and stop the fire, there will be no Super Me to write this journal, and JR would never experience his smarter fiancée, only the dimwitted but loving girl that I was. He would never know the consequences of mental melding or the tactile relationship between scrunched sponges and Mister Wannabe's brain tissue. Neither would I.

By the way, as a byproduct to some of my research, I might have a solution to viral issues such as AIDS, but I probably won't have time to publish before the temporal brain-wave insertion.

One more thing: JR and I are pregnant.

Journal Entry #15:

Morons! Morons! Morons! The world is filled with moronic morons who can't grasp the simplest equation! Everywhere I turn, morons magna cum laude. This frustrating discovery, however, has led me to understand fully Mrs. Dettwelling's infatuation with journals. When all else fails, hammering a few choice words into the computer with a tequila chaser can perk a girl right up. Murder in effigy. Vicarious vengeance. Jackass justice.

Feels great!

Journal Entry #16:

Ideas have no mass; therefore, theoretical limitations of spatial time travel do not apply. I should be able to send a thought back nine years, or any number of years, though this presents a fundamental untested glitch. Can a concept alter the past?

I had to take a break. Threw up again. Morning sickness is the pits. You'd think my towering intellect could do something about animalistic processes. It takes a lot of energy to grow a child, not to mention hormone jolts that make Red Bull compare as a sedative. And the mommy track cuts into contemplation of the fourth dimension, which is not a dimension at all. Time is time, not space, which is a key to my science project.

Had a routine ultrasound yesterday. The baby is a girl! I am excited but also worried. How could she love anything that looks like I do? Might be afraid of me.

Journal Entry #17:

DNA from a frog will not meld with the DNA of a rat. However, strands from a *tadpole* work fine. In conjunction with this discovery, I did a little experiment. Tried to go back in time two days and report to myself about the rat-frog failure to see if it could be avoided. But in avoiding the error, I didn't learn about the lethal genetic combination and repeated it. Too bad for the rodent. On the other hand, the recombined tad-rat is an interesting species. I will not try to breed it. Just an investigative trial while I considered splicing tadpole genes into stem cells to grow a new wrapper for my body. The process might actually work, but it's complex and requires lab equipment, testing and retesting, documentation, and a competent assistant to work with me and on me. Further, the skin-job would require years of effort.

JR offered to lend a hand. Sweet thing. But he's got his teaching job, and as much as I hate to say it, he might never grasp the theoretical foundations, some of which I managed to publish in respected scientific journals by ghostwriting under his name. JR was really pissed about this, but after he received an academic grant and was promoted to full professor for his work, he settled down. In JR's defense, I'm not sure anyone else can understand what I'm doing either. Some of the measurements and calibrations require extrasensory abilities like *seeing* molecular bonds, DNA sequences, or real-time cytological processes; nor do I fully understand how I do this, which is similar to watching a PBS video in my head. *And I don't want to grow a new skin.* I want to revoke the accident, reclaim the physical youth and passion, and remove a decade of pain and suffering. I want to be intellectually average and think I'm special.

Of course, the tad-rat was interesting.

Journal Entry #18:

Baby's due in two weeks. I'm scared to death but already love her. JR is all excitement. Me? I don't know. There were moments when abortion seemed best, so the child wouldn't have to meet its mother.

Journal Entry #19:

JR is a proud papa, though he no longer manages to get a full night's sleep. I still don't need more than an hour per day, which seems to be the stabilization point, so little Susie doesn't interfere with that part of my life. She is the most beautiful thing I've ever seen. Much better than a tad-rat.

I'm temporarily breaking from research. I could be on the verge of a time-slide breakthrough, but for now, regular day-by-day clock-works are fine. Being a mommy is way too much fun.

Who would have thought that I'd end up as a housewife? Susie doesn't seem to notice that I'm ugly; and it doesn't hurt too much when I hold her, though I had to practice to change her with my missing fingers. One of my breasts has enough tissue to produce a little milk. The rest of Susie's diet comes from the organic aisle at Stop & Shop.

Journal Entry #20:

Three years have passed since my last entry. I probably wouldn't be writing now, but JR died last week. He was hit by a car walking to class. A damned freshman, and one more pointless mishap in my life.

Thank heavens for Susan. Otherwise, I could not have survived. She doesn't seem to understand that her daddy is gone. Probably thinks he's at an academic conference.

Susie and I came home from the neighborhood park yesterday (one of our rituals), and she asked me, "Why do other mommies look different?"

My heart collapsed around the edges. "They just do," I said. "I had an accident long ago. They are regular mommies. I am different."

"Oh," she said. "That's why they aren't as pretty."

I cried all afternoon. Susan might say this at age three, but at thirteen she'll be ashamed and want me to drop her off a block from school. She needs a normal parent in her life.

There must be a way to bring her father back. Time to pick up the research.

Journal Entry #21:

I did it! I mentally skipped back two months and told JR not to step off the curb. He is alive and well. JR hesitated just two seconds, and the car sped by harmlessly. The asshole driver also got a speeding ticket because I thoughtfully suggested to a cop that he might patrol the area at that moment.

JR doesn't remember being killed. When I explained the situation, he wanted me to visit the psychiatrist again. I don't care. The time paradox be damned! I know what happened. JR is alive and Susie's happy!

Further, suggestive time-thought-interface works — and surprisingly, the revised history didn't erase my memory of J's fatal match with a Camaro. It should have, and I still don't understand how I can remember something that, thanks to my intervention, never happened. Like a drug-induced flashback or a near-death hallucination, I seem to be the only person with knowledge of the dual realities.

Doesn't matter. I did it!

Susan and I aren't as close as we were. After her father died, she clung to me like she always clung to JR. And in the new space-time, she never told me that I was the prettiest Mommy. It's probably for the best, but I admit that a tiny part of me wanted to leave the accident untouched. Just for a second. I love JR, and he loves me and Susie. I can live with that lost mother-daughter moment.

But now there is the possibility of a game winning score! A self-inflicted psychic time insertion. Maybe I don't have to remain bacon-crisp. Maybe I never have to be in the first place. Maybe I can reshape my universe.

Journal Entry #22:

I'm going back. If I changed history for JR, I should be able to do it for me. Time travel is difficult. First, it's hard to find my way to the right place and moment using only brainwaves. Second, I must plant an idea into a then living person. The concomitant precision and concentration are cryptic. Practice helps, but even my accelerating genius is barely up to task. The effort makes me dizzy.

During my research, I made a number of incidental discoveries, including a gene-splice inhibiter to prevent the HIV from breaching cellular walls or reproducing. It worked on me, anyway. (All those after-burn transfusions gave me AIDS, which I haven't mentioned because it seemed meaningless in light of the rest of me.) With a little more effort, I might find the on-off switch for cancer. Anyway, there's no time. I'm scrapping this work because I don't want anyone to interfere with my time sculpture. Call me weak, but I want my former life. I have a right to it.

Journal Entry #23:

This could be my last report. I retained memory after I fragmented JR's accident, but I'm not sure how things will play when I send ideas to myself ten years past. That young, healthy, unburned woman at the station. If I succeed, the station owner won't have to give me free gas.

I admit that my flash-life hasn't been all bad. I'm generally happy, and JR and Susan are very nice. The physical pain has lessened significantly in recent weeks, though I always seem to be thirsty and there's a high-pitched humming in my ears. I appreciate being smart and having the ability to crush bad people with a thought, but I am ready for the insertion. I cannot kill the desire to be normal; it's killing me instead.

It *is* possible to revisit that horrible day and to warn myself about the defective nozzle. I know because the accident made me very, very, very smart, and I've learned that being beautiful is better. I've practiced and calculated and cross-checked, but I must act soon. The complexity of time travel increases at a geometric rate the farther back I must go.

My real concern is that I will lose Susie in the process. Lovely little Susan. Even I can't recreate an entire human gene sequence, especially when I re-emerge as my C+ self. The consolation is that JR will be there. We can still be married and have children in the altered universe, and I know CVS won't discontinue my special shade of lipstick.

I should say goodbye — no, I won't wake her. Susie is the perfect fantasy daughter, and I shall look for her across space and time. It's all right, Honey. Don't be afraid. Mommy must leave, but you won't feel a thing. And someday, when the time is right, I'll tell Daddy all about the girl we left behind.

I'll just have a cool glass of water before I go. The firestorm is calling, and my thirst is unquenchable.

Foreign Bodies

R. I. Sutton

The hills retreat from her in the half-light like mothers letting go. The creatures of the night chirp their canticle, a requiem for her last reflections in this place. Below her lies the dam, the offering upon which they feed, drawing their silver voices as silver timbrels from its glow.

The hinge of everything is bending, breaking, like bearers of a door keeping some unseen something at bay. Her legs give way and she sinks to the ground.

She feels them now, swarming their way inside and she cradles her head in her hands. In her mind she sees herself as through the eye of a microscope—a bag of fluid and jacketed organs, an amoeba swimming the surface of a slide. And there are others like her here, morphing, translucent parasites. As water beads converging on a window they slide into her. But they do not follow the nature of fluid to mingle; like foreign bodies they instead lodge themselves, black ticks chewing, perforating the membranous fineries of her brain.

It was not always like this…

She sees her brother's face as it is in the photographs—his cheeks peach-plump, his nestling hair. She sees them as they were together on a day from long ago. He is ploughing through the grass behind her, treading in her footsteps. On either side of them the hills rise, shadowed with rocks and shifting grass. She plucks a stem, chews it like Huckleberry Finn. He does the same.

"Why do you always have to copy me?" she says.

"Why do you always have to copy me?" he replies.

Leaning into the slope she toils on, clambering over rocks with moss like fertile continents, her brother's breath close behind. She snatches handfuls of dry grass as she climbs, imagines offering it on the hilltop to the birds for their nests. They will dive down on her to snatch it from her hands — speckled kestrels and hovering kites; larks, twirling like flamenco dancers' skirts; moaning ravens and arrowing pies. They will swoop their fanning dance around her, and with her outspread arms, her closed eyes, with the wind lifting her hair, she will feel what it feels to fly.

Her brother is not in this picture.

She stops and follows the valley with her eyes. It turns in its sleep below them, fogging green its autumn breath, dreaming on its mattress soaked with rain. Watching over it like a mother hangs the hill from which she and her brother came. Her bosom is veiled by the shadow-play of clouds, the dam gleaming at her feet. And couched upon her shoulder is the glint of light from the window of their home, a speck of stillness like a ship on a choppy sea.

Her father built that house with his hands. Like the swallow nest she sees each day above the door, it had formed in segments of hardening mud. But while the swallows had flitted on paper-cut wings, knitting their throatfuls of earth, her father had plied the soil with shovel and ram. On the shoulder of that hill, with his binding of straw and sweat and cow dung, he had shaped for them this home.

Her brother mimics her gaze, his cheeks flushed, the breeze tufting his hair. Suddenly, she starts, and with searching eyes, turns towards the hilltop.

"What's wrong?" he asks.

"Can't you hear them?" she says, her voice little more than a whisper. "They're coming...over the hills."

"What're you talking about?" His smile pricks dimples in his cheeks. "I can't hear nothing."

Turning her eyes on him, she motions to the south. Her voice swells, solemn, on the wind. "Spirits come from that place. They ride the clouds like horses and eat up little boys. And I can hear them—they're coming!"

All at once the hillside seems a host of bowed, whispering heads.

His dimples disappear. "It's not true," he says, "I know you're just trying to scare me—I'll tell Mum."

And now the wind surges, bending the grasses to scratching and thrashing at their knees. She glances over her shoulder, her face a mime of fear.

"Run!" she yells, dashing past him, "—run home before they get you!"

She glimpses him once—his stricken face, his tear-thick eyes—before he casts down his bunch of grass to scramble past her for the distant house, his shriek unravelling on the wind.

Her treacle of satisfaction scalds her with shame. Terror is written in the grass by his fleeing feet. But she has what she wanted—she is alone. She is very alone.

The autumn clouds drift across the sun, and the rocks and the grasses seem to emanate a light from within. And now the hills have faces, faces mottled with ichor like frowning old men. And from their ears and from their mouths branch trees that have long since died. Like the dreams of deities are the clouds over their heads—dreams of winged horses, of long lost wars, of gods on thrones of mist.

She turns from them to stare at her hands, as small and pink as newly-hatched chicks. The air seems too thick for her throat. She feels like she is drowning.

There is a woman on the hill singing the birds from the sky. They swoop their fanning dance around her, plucking grass from her hands for their nests.

In the full dark the dam is a clay bowl reflecting the stars. Beneath her hands the grass is wet with night. A solitary car cuts along the road, gutting the vale with its roar.

Her memory changes now from remembrance to recollection of a dream…

She is falling through space, an abyss as black as night turned inside-out. Stars pass by her like balloons fleeing for the sky, kindergarten cut-outs stars of cardboard and foil.

She is not frightened. There is nothing here but the soft voice of a man. She thinks it might be God. As in the Bible stories, He says, "Do not be afraid."

And now she finds that she has stopped; she hangs in her Sunday dress, suspended, ridiculous, like a birthday cake strung among the stars. Before her, floating in space, are two islands.

The first of these is little more than an eroded pile of earth. Roots hang from its base like the flailing legs of a crab. On top of it stands her father in his singlet and shorts, his skin baked brown as the earth. He is shovelling, sweating, and as the dirt flies over his shoulder, it tumbles behind him to slide back down, clotting as mud round his boots.

The other island is surmounted by a kitchen sink of smeared, teetering plates. Here her mother stands in her apron, chained to the dish-rack. As she scrubs and dips and scrubs and dips, arranging the dishes in the rack, plates upon plates appear before her, toppling into the swill.

She watches them and feels her insides sinking, as though her guts have been rammed with dirt. She feels as though it is she that has marooned them here in this waste of space, beyond help or care.

"You must choose between them," the voice of God says.
She looks from her mother to her father. "I can't," she says.
She falls…

Her father is stranded in the middle of the floor, a captain on his sinking ship. He drifts to a seat, covers his face with his hands. Her mother, slumped in the chair, is animated by little more than an indrawn breath. On her lap her hands are wrinkled red like curled dead crabs.

She glances at her brother and they smile, idiots revelling in the tickling in-draw of a murderous wave. It is coming.

Like bubbles surfacing in swamp water, Mother's eyes rise to fix on their father. "Tell them," she says, her voice a wire across a brittle blade.

He runs his hands through his hair.

Her face is thick as mud congealing. "Look at your children and tell them!"

The bird-woman on the hill watches as the girl runs out into the wakening night, tears spilling silver the grass. She watches as the girl stops, sinks to the ground.

There are no birds this night; they are all sleeping in the trees. She will not wake them until morning. And so for now the creatures of the night will have to do—the moths, the bats flitting, the crickets chirping their canticle from the dam. She calls to them her high secret keening and they come to her, flying and swooping, swarming to her back. She draws them close around her shoulders in a shimmering veil, and makes her way down the hill to the girl.

Issue 26

April 2011

Wolves at the Door

Ann Claycomb

The patient in 216 is on a waitlist for hospice care. She has not stirred since she was brought in. She does not appear to be in pain. She does not groan or shudder when the nurses turn her, clean her, change her sheets. She lies on her back, breathing gently in and out, like someone playing at being asleep to surprise a lover as they slip into bed. Her call button never rings, but still the nurses remember her. The dying are rarely beautiful in hospitals, under the greenish cast of the fluorescent lights. The nurses stop by to check her vital signs, adjust her pillows, open or close her curtains, but really they just want to look at her, to be startled all over again by the sight of her face.

Her hair is black, close-cropped. It sets off her skin, which is matte white as the inside of a seashell that's been bleached by the sun, scoured by sand. Her cheeks are only faintly pink, but the flush is enough. The nurses wear pink scrubs, but the color is so tinged with gray that they dread putting them on. The pink in this woman's cheeks reminds them of what pink is supposed to look like. Her lashes are so long that the fringe shadows her cheekbones, and her mouth is red and full as if she has just applied lipstick. One of the nurses can even name the color: Cherries in the Snow. Her mother wore that color when she dressed up; she cannot think of it or see it without conjuring the sweet waxy smell that settled onto her mother's mouth along with the deep red stain. It is that scent, more than perfume or cooking aromas, which she associates with her mother.

Whenever she leans over the patient, tucks in her sheets, arranges her limp hands, the nurse expects to smell lipstick. She longs to be reminded of her mother. But what rises off this woman is the scent of winter air, and underneath the black aroma of frozen earth.

The patient's daughter visits every day. Each time, when she first walks in the room, she leans over the bed and murmurs, "I'm here."

Then she sits down. The chair is terribly uncomfortable. She looks at the long-fingered hands lying so loose and graceful on the sheet. She's never seen those hands so still before, never noticed the fine tracery of veins and tendons along their backs.

She remembers those hands covered with blood and matted black fur, remembers them under cold running water at the tap, the blood coming unclotted, turning pink, and washing away.

I told you no shortcuts. I told you to come straight home.

She was only a little girl, eight, maybe nine. She had just seen her mother hack a wolf to pieces with the saw they used to level the trunk of the Christmas tree. In the moment before it descended in a whistling arc that yearned for a keener blade, the moment she rolled away, she smelled, fleetingly, the cold tang of wet pine.

What were you doing in the woods anyway? Why didn't you stay on the path?

She cut through the woods because the old trees did not mock her like the other children did. The trees merely tapped her with their branches as she passed. They did not poke her with pencils or walk up behind her, deliberately so close that they stepped on the backs of her shoes.

Why can't you just ignore them? Ignore them and they'll get bored and leave you alone.

She found her voice then. *You mean like the wolf? If I had just gone on ignoring him would he have left me alone?*

Her mother dried her clean white hands on a dish towel and looked at her with narrowed eyes. She was a woman who had never been afraid and so she did not understand fear, of wolves or other children.

The woman in the bed hears her daughter's voice, briefly feels the slight weight of her daughter's shadow hanging over her. Such a pale, gray shadow, so unlike her own, which has always been black and sinuous. She never needed to wear her hair long to entice her lovers. The caress of her shadow when she leaned over them was always enough.

She wonders about her daughter's lovers, how many there have been, how large their hands, how hot and rough their skin. She remembers the day she realized that her daughter was beautiful, lace and cobwebs and violets hiding in the shade, a beauty she had never coveted until that moment, until the moment she saw it in the mirror, in her daughter, and knew she could not have it.

They were shopping for a prom dress. Her daughter tried on red dresses, green dresses, gold dresses and black dresses, velvet and taffeta rustling like dead leaves around her when she emerged from the dressing room.

What's wrong? It's a beautiful dress. Stand up straight, let me see you.

And the girl wilting in front of her, in the mirror, inside the bright and dark dresses. *I look terrible. Look at me.*

Then a salesgirl interceding, offering the girl a dress the mother would never have chosen, silver lace and chiffon, a dress that she'd glanced right over. In it her daughter was moonlit, elfin, enchanting. The mother looked in the mirror and saw herself eclipsed by the shy swish of skirts, the half-smile playing over the young face.

My God, she said—she didn't mean to say it out loud—*they'll gobble you up.*

She was thinking of her own lovers, if they could see this girl, how their eyes would flare and their hands clench with the longing to tug her head back and expose her white throat, tear the fragile dress off of her, leave violet bruises on her thighs. She wanted to hurt the girl in the mirror, to rend her beauty from her. She saw her own face, her skin red and taut along her cheekbones, her teeth bared. She heard herself speak.

We'll take the red one. Box it up.

She turned away from the mirror.

The nurses come in and speak softly to the daughter. She answers them just as softly, the way one speaks while walking in a snowfall, as if words can be shaped into softness, into whiteness. The patient is comfortable, they tell her. Her vital signs are weak but discernible. Her blood pressure is low, but that's from the morphine. That's to be expected.

The daughter thanks them, smiles, shakes her head when they ask if she needs anything. Her back aches from the chair. She does not look at her mother in the bed, but she can hear her voice clearly.

Stand up for yourself. Tell people what you want. If you don't tell them, they won't know and you'll have no one to blame but yourself.

Her mother sat across from her in a restaurant, linen cloth on the table and heavy silver service at each setting, the handles embossed with tongues of flame.

I don't see why I have to be rude to people, she said. She kept her eyes on the silver flames. *It doesn't hurt to be nice.*

But her mother knew better. Once a man came upon her in the dark, on a cobbled side street. He slammed her up against the wall, put his forearm under her chin and tore her dress open. The coarse hair on his arm prickled on her skin, his belt buckle opened with a sound like a knife on a whetstone. He leaned in close and told her to beg. She felt his heat, his excitement, could picture her pleas dropping like petals onto his arm. She lunged toward him instead. She told him he was cold, small, soft. A snake dropped out of her mouth and slithered down his wrist, then a scorpion, its carapace shining with her saliva and its tail raised. He screamed and ran for the lights he'd dragged her from.

The daughter heard this story. It made her shiver, as much at the thought of spitting out snakes as anything else. When she spoke, rose petals fell from her lips, small misshapen pearls, apricot-hued in candlelight.

The waiter appeared with their food. Her shrimp were over-cooked, nearly orange, and swimming in the tomato sauce she asked him to withhold.

Thank you, she murmured. An opal dropped from her mouth and into her shrimp, gleaming wetly. She pushed it aside with her fork.

Her mother sliced into her steak, one quick cut, let the cutlery clatter onto the plate. The daughter, chewing a flabby shrimp, flinched.

This is not rare. I requested rare. Look at this. It's gray, for godsakes, all the blood's been cooked right out of it.

A silver thread descended from her mouth and a line of spiders marched down it and onto her plate as the waiter bowed, apologized, promised to replace it with something better. A spider crawled onto his shirt cuff as he removed the plate.

The woman in the bed can feel her daughter like a ghost in the room. She remembers how the girl used to slip in and out of focus even in their own house, as if willing herself lost or invisible. And then she married that man . . . her mother took one look and knew he'd match her word for word, serpent for asp. He wore custom-tailored suits, threw his head back when he laughed. He had been married before.

And what happened there? She asked her daughter. *Do you know the story? Do you know* both *sides of that story?*

He was looking for moonlight, her daughter said, *but she was made of ice. She couldn't love him. I can.* She looked down at her hands, flexed her slender fingers. The ring she wore was too big for her, too heavy, though it sparkled like a chunk of star.

The mother paid for damask roses and a string quartet, wore diamonds and black velvet and danced with the groom when the candles had burned low. He held her loosely, carelessly. When he'd danced with her daughter, she'd watched his hands bite into her waist, open and shut against the silk like mouths.

I'll take good care of her, he said. *You know I will.*

If you hurt her, she said, *I'll kill you.*

He grinned, white teeth flashing in his black beard—his hair was as blue-black as her own. *No, no,* he said. *I'll leave that to you. You do such an admirable job of it.* Then he set his hand on her back and spun her, twirling her rage faster and faster until it fell around her like a cloak.

She did not let her daughter go easily, though. She called and visited when he was not home, which was more and more often. She took her daughter shopping for clothes he would hate: sleek pant-suits, gold bangle bracelets, high-heeled boots. She took her daughter to dinner, watched her tug the neck of her sweater up higher, told her to stop spilling pearls from her lips.

There were the inevitable rumors of another woman, other women, other men. After one shopping trip the mother received a package containing all the clothes she'd bought for her daughter, sliced into ribbons. When she opened the lid, roaches and centipedes swarmed to the surface. She stood at the kitchen sink and sharpened all her knives. She called her daughter and told her how to sharpen hers, how to test the blade against the side of her thumb, not to discount the uses of a serrated edge.

Finally, the girl left him. The mother never knew if the knives had made a difference, and for once she dared not ask. Her daughter came to see her afterwards, thinner than ever, but harder at the edges, steel instead of silver now.

Why? The mother asked. *Can you answer that question now? Do you even know? Why him?*

Don't you know? The girl's mouth curved up into a smile like a tensed bow. *I thought I was safe with him. He treated me like you do.*

A tiny white spider, its body round and gleaming as a drop of milk, slipped from the corner of her mouth. The mother leaned over and pinched it away.

It is called Cheyne-Stokes respiration, a sign that the body is failing. The patient breathes in terrible gasps, something behind her about to catch up. It catches her, shakes her lifeless in its jaws for a moment. She stops breathing altogether. The daughter stands rigid beside the bed. The gasping starts again. It won't be long now. The nurses have pulled the curtains all the way around the bed and left them there, the two of them alone together.

Wait, the daughter murmurs. Wait. There's something I forgot to tell you. I meant to tell you that I have gradu-ated to snakes, only garden snakes, you understand, but still – snakes. I can only bring them up occasionally but I do not hate the feel of them in my throat. I meant to tell you that I live now on the edge of a wood in-fested with wolves. They come to the door nearly every night and slaver under the edges, scrabble with their paws to be let in. But I lean against the keyhole and I whisper to them of what I would do to them if I were on the other side, of what you did to that wolf once – do you remember? I tell them I can smell their blood already, and they go away. I eat my steak rare now, I keep a black satin blind-fold in the drawer by my bed and I never wear it myself. I bought a red hooded coat this winter, I will wear it in the snow, I will lift my face to the sting of cold air, my hands fisted and warm in my pockets —

Wait, the mother thinks. Wait. There's something I need to tell you. I meant to tell you – I can't breathe. I am frightened of the dark, I, who've never been frightened of anything. I am cold and small and I have lost my voice and the strength of my hands and my rage, that black rage I wore so proudly all my life. It is coming for me, I can feel its breath, I can smell it and I cannot run fast enough. But I meant to tell you this: when you were small, you used to slip your hand into mine sometimes – do you remember? I brushed your hair at night before bed, I tucked you in, kissed your white forehead, looked in on you while you were sleeping and saw how lovely you looked when the moonlight fell across your bed. That is what I am running to now – your bed in the moonlight, you curled un-der the covers with your hand out-stretched. I am coming to take your hand, I am coming, put out your hand —

Soatsaki

Laura Valeri

And though it's hard for you to imagine it, there was a time when time was not a measure crushed to crumbs for the hunger of people whose gods have been asleep too long. Iihtsipaitapiiyo pa, the Source of Life, was not a God, nor a man, nor a woman, but just a dreamer of dreams, a little like you, creating tomorrows with the tender blossom of thought. The Siksikawa had just crawled out from the navel of the earth to people the North American continent. Blackfoot, they were called, for they walked on the ashes of the burned prairies, and their moccasins, though beaded and tanned with various colors, were as dark at the bottom as the ashes of those fires. Soatsaki was new like the dawn, light as the sun in the morning. She slept in a tipi made of deerskin and antelope bone, a beautiful *nii toy yis* which her mother had owned before her, and which she shared with three sisters. In the tradition of her people, the *nii toy yi* had been made by her great grandfather, who painted the deerskins in the colors of the ancestors, telling their tribe's history through it's design, and then the tipi was handed down to the women, who owned it, cleaned it, set it up and took it down when the hunters followed the thunderous herds of the buffalo across the plain. In this manner, the Siksikawa spread over the valleys like the rivers and the prairie fires and the women carried their history on their shoulders.

On summer nights, the air was sweet with smoked meat and joyous with the thundering drums of the dance. The reeds swayed with the breezes and the mud of the riverbanks breathed life onto the crust of the earth. In the daytime, the sun shone bright and the moisture of the river rose and permeated the air. But at night, the sweet hot breath of the earth clung to the skin of Soatsaki, making it hard for the girl to sleep.

All the lodges had their flaps opened like great mouths gasping for cool air. Soatsaki, not wanting to wake her sisters, tip-toed out of the tipi's mouth. She quietly moved away from the earth fires as the crickets sang in waves of tingly choirs, and she collapsed on the tall grass, her hair tangling with pieces of reeds and small weeds. Tiny insects crawled through the earth under Soatsaki's clothes but the girl did not mind, as back then human beings had not yet quarreled with the gods, and insects and animals and all children of earth thought of each other as one.

I know your patience is frayed from the constant noises of your time, but listen: here you are, thousands of years later, looking for clues of the beginning, for details of the life of a tribe girl who was alive before history was the trade of learned men. Imagine Soatsaki, this girl who slept in the prairie, who lived of squirrel meat, June berries and buffalo, who made soap from the fat of animals and sewed with porcupine quills. Tonight she sleeps in the soft pillow of the prairie grasses, her feet pale in the moonlight. Half the world is still asleep and dreaming, coagulating nightmares trapped in the gossamers of superstition and wonder. And on this night of so long ago, an ordinary girl steps away from the campfires, sure-footed and un-afraid, and crosses beyond the sensory impermanence of life into the cottony eternity of myth.

Not so far from her, the men are snoring in their *nii toy yis*, curled around their wives, for the dogs are alert, and the cliffs are painted with the blood of the buffalo that jumped to its death to feed the Sik-sikawa. The girl is lying supine watching the Morning Star glow as it climbs towards its azimuth on the primordial sky. How beautiful and free seems the Morning Star, so mysterious that the girl watches it all night. And here is the part you can only believe of a folk tale: the girl falls in love; she falls in love with the Morning Star.

Do you remember the sweet breath of new love? Can you feel the tingling ghost fingers of hope dancing on the tender part of your belly? This is how Soatsaki felt as she ran to her people with her hair still tangled with bugs and pine needles. Love was Soatsaki's news;

she told it to her sisters, told it to the crackling fires, to the sharpened knife she used to cut fat and to the quills she used to fit and saw the bladder that she filled with water for the hunters' journey. Love, she said to the coyotes who watched her curiously as she toiled. But her band, the elders of the tribe, they laughed at Soatsaki's love.

Even Soatsaki's sisters, two adolescent girls covered in smoke and pelts, their teeth shining in the sun, even these sisters mocked her: "How could you fall in love with a star?" As if love could be reasoned away.

Ridicule is contagious, a virus that quickly spreads from mouth to infected mouth so that the girl endures shame as she goes about her chores. "Soatsaki, what do you want with a star? Marry this clod of dirt! At least it will feed you. Soatsaki, here is a rock that fell from the sky; do you think it's pretty? Soatsaki, look up! There goes your lover chasing a star! Oh, Soatsaki, who will you love now?"

Soatsaki cooked, cleaned, skinned the hunted buffalo and washed blood from her fingers in the cold waters of the river. She collected roots for medicine. She plucked June berries from the shrubs and pasted them into sauces for the meat. She sliced thin the flesh of hunted animals and laid it to dry for the winter season. She wove feathers together into head garments; she gathered tobacco leaves and laid them out to dry. Maybe she smelled of smoke, of leaf, and dust, and blood, of new, sweet grass, of youthful sweat, of mud and pinesap. She had her moons and passed them in her sweat lodge, and celebrated with dance, and chanted for rain, all the while speaking to unsympathetic ears about her night alone in the prairie grass.

You want to be exact about it, but you can only imagine the real details. Subconscious memory is not that precise. Focus on more important questions. For example, how did Soatsaki fall in love with what you now know is a planet shrouded in toxic ammonia and volcanic ashes? When her warm adolescent form was a hot coal in the damp earth, what did she gather in her chest, what fantasy tingled the pit of her soft belly that made her save her love for a rock in orbit? When she looked up into that black blanket of ancient sky, seeing the stars like someone had poked holes into a tarp with a hot iron… what, exactly, did she love?

Like all things unusual, her crush is so easily dismissed, as if dreams were something cheap for the trade, as if the soul itself needed no food to thrive upon, no fantasy on which to drape some shred of love.

And yet, here you are, charting her course through the geography of Montana and lower Canada, looking up the course of the Saskatchewan and the Mississippi rivers to retrace what might have been her people's journey. Imagine how that love quickened her breath and sent her blood rushing down between her thighs, a knot down there untying, loosening the restraints of daily boredom. Why has legend been so unkind to that first love, when it seemed Soatsaki's body exploded with a numinous strangeness that invalidated all caution. Her people laughed. That's all the stories will tell you.

She grew tired of the glances that people threw at her before their cheerful gossip dropped to a whisper at her approaching footsteps. They believed she had met a reason to break away from respectability in the musky tall grasses of the prairie that one night, and she was lying to cover her shame. It was a man from another tribe that she had met in the prairie. The whispers thickened, infecting daily life with the ill.

But then, one day Soatsaki walked along the river. A man stood there smiling at her, his lips bright as berries and his hair as dark as the earth under her fingernails. On top of his head his hair was gathered in a lump in the ways of the hunters with an eagle feather to hold it in place. At first, she mistook him for a villager, an inverted comma in his cheek, and the dimple in his chin so mocking. He was dressed like the hunters of her band, with leggings and a robe sewn of white buffalo skin. Around his neck he had the claws of a grizzly bear, the ornament of a mighty hunter. His face was painted in red, the color of life, the color of Soatsaki's feelings. He extended a hand to her. His smile was long across his face, holding a meaning that frightened the girl, for it seemed to hold secrets she believed only she held locked tightly in her breasts.

"Go," she shouted when she found her voice. She threw a small stone at his feet as if to scare him away like a coyote. "I will not suffer mockery from a stranger."

But from his hair he pulled out that eagle feather, which he held out to her as a gift and his hair tumbled on his shoulder, glossy and dark. At her feet he placed a juniper branch draped with glittering white, silky threads, ephemeral and fine. Caught up by the beauty and strangeness of these gifts, Soatsaki let the tips of her fingers brush against the glowing web on the juniper branch and knew at once this man was no man at all.

Then Morning Star spoke. His voice resonated like the hum of the wind. He told her he knew she had spied him from the earth in the womb of the dawn, that for a hundred nights he'd watched her from a pillow in the sky, sending his breath over the contours of her body as she, vulnerable, unguarded, opened the gates of her heart. Now with eyes full of sunlight and mirth he said, "Come to live with me in the sky nation. I promise that you'll be happy like no human has yet."

It felt to her that with his gaze he touched her in a part inside that was raw, a knowledge only just born to her now bursting to respond. The river thrummed, and the spray of the fast waters weaved a misty rainbow web from the god's lovely shine.

You wonder how she could look at him, light pouring out of his mouth so that even the tiny insects on the leaves of the elms glowed like hot, colored crystals. But she was a girl who had fallen in love with a planet. There were no limits to her faith.

"Let me say goodbye to my people," she pleaded with him but he was stern, his arms crossed before his chest and already in a hurry: "We must go now or never meet again."

"My sisters will be worried. They will not know what happened."

"The stars align only with the right season," he said sternly. Unlike the gentle voice he'd used before, there was an edge to him she should have felt, a clue that would peck a tiny crack in her memories, but he set the juniper branch at her feet, told her to touch her toes to it, and so she closed her eyes and did as was told, as one might expect of an offer for ascension.

That's how Soatsaki left the campfires behind, her sisters, her people, her history, and all the things mundane and dear: the long painted feathers she used to braid in her hair, the *nii toy yi* she was born in, the necklaces and bead bracelets her mother had made for her, she left all of it without as much as a last glance.

You would hope her lover appreciated her sacrifice, but who knows what are the motivations of the gods. He told her only "Close your eyes," and she did, not understanding how much the things that she once thought unimportant would manage to dig tunnels inside her, deep and dripping with cold grief. On that day she thought only of love, and rose up to the heavens astride his knotty shoulders with her eyes shut against all that floated away beneath her.

The star nation was a color like sunset, and speckled with golden large lodges that glowed with the hearth fires, and heavenly bodies busily orbiting about. The Moon greeted the girl; she was Morning Star's mother, gracious and pale as she bowed to acknowledge her son's new bride, but a smile was cleaved like a scar on her open face as she offered Soatsaki gifts of clothes, food, and jewelry.

Sun and Moon, who were Morning Star's parents, noticed the ashes on Soatsaki's moccasins and the dead animal skins that covered her body. In private, they voiced a tender concern, but Morning Star seemed oblivious to their complaints. Between him and Soatsaki there were kisses, hands searching secret places, the mingled breaths of god and woman whispering words that have no sense and parental worries cannot compete against such sensations.

Then, one morning Soatsaki ran her fingertips from her navel down the hair line on her belly, felt something move in there and understood only just then all the absences she had lived with. All the words that she had once found easy to sing to her lover turned into things hard and edged, things that lodged into the holes inside her where once there had been the memory of campfires, and of the teasing of her adolescent sisters.

Soatsaki groped with the rigors of motherhood without help from her heavenly mother in law, who said she knew nothing of raising human children, while Morning Star himself gradually grew too busy for Soatsaki, leaving early for his ever widening orbits, glowing in the purple realm of dusk late in the night, away from Soatsaki and their baby. Sun and Moon, who had never been sure of Soatsaki's class, her smelling of river and stone even after so many years in the star dust, decided it was time to put a test to the girl. When Morning Star was away, Moon presented Soatsaki with a special gift.

"This is a root-digging stick," Moon told her, holding an object that seemed whittled out of the very glow of the moon. "Only pure women can use it," the Moon added in a whisper, as if to add some June berry juice to the smoking meat that was Soatsaki's curiosity.

All about the star nation there were great craters covered by leafy plants of many varieties and sizes. These plants were shrouded in glimmering spider webs whose threaded ends disappeared into the glowing, puffy soil of the sky nation and spiraled down towards earth. Morning Star had told her, "Those spider webs are the roads that the gods use to travel, but you must never go near them." He had never explained why.

Soatsaki eagerly accepted the gift, and strapped Star Boy, her child, onto her back.

"Go dig good medicine root for us," Moon advised. "But wherever you go, whatever you do, do not dig the great big turnip. It has been planted by grandmother spider to plug a hole in the clouds that connects us to the earth. You must never look at earth through that hole." When Soatsaki agreed, Moon seemed to emit a different light, as if an invisible worry had just cast a shadow on her cratered countenance.

Turnips as they go are usually harmless, but Soatsaki had been warned not to dig it up. Mortals know well the temptation of warning, the hot, dangling promise of forbidden things. Soatsaki saw the turnip, enormous in the valley of the star nation, luminous and purple-hued, the only thing up there that smelled of earth and home. At first she could hardly move it, so deeply it had been plugged into that great crater of the sky nation that it seemed impossible that there had ever been anything strong enough to plant it, but a pair of storks flew by, watching her as she dug, and when she was about to give up, attempting to remove bits of star dust from her short, bitten-edged fingernails, the storks flew around her in great swooping circles and down towards the crater where, with their long bills, they lifted up the turnip just enough for Soatsaki to slide her wondrous root digging stick deeper in. Little by little, the turnip came loose, enough that it could be rolled on its side from its hole. Not for a moment had Soatsaki thought about what she could see, only that something tugged at her as she dug, a feeling as of the fragments of a dream one wakes up with in the morning, remembered only through a scent or a fluttering in the chest. But when the girl stood on her knees, looking at the funneling crater that the turnip had covered, the dream came back to her at once. Below, the Siksikiwa hunters had gathered. The smoke of the campfires rose through the hole to Soatsaki's nostrils. The dogs barked and loped around the dancing warriors as the fire stretched crackling fingers of flames. Soatsaki saw her sisters, infants strapped to their bodies. They shook rattles and chanted while their warrior husbands kicked dust in the frenzy of rite. Their chants dislodged something rooted deeper than any great turnip.

Soatsaki tried to cover up the hole as best she could, an anger beating in her chest that she could barely voice. She ran home to her in-laws, but as she grew closer to the glorious *nii toy yis* in the stars she understood Moon mother's game. She quickly wiped the tears from her nose, leaving incriminating streaks of star dirt on her cheeks.

Moon waited for her in front of her lodge. "Let me see your hands," was the first words she spoke. Soatsaki hid her hands under a fold in her dress. "Where have you been," asked Moon, relentless. Soatsaki looked into Moon's face and said nothing.

Moon nodded at Morning Star, who sat, listening, in a dark corner, shadowed by his own brooding. "She's made of mud and silt," said Moon. "No sojourn in the star could ever cleanse her. There is no home in heaven for broken promises. The sky nation is no place for dirt and blood and lies."

Soatsaki humbly handed back her digging stick, head hanging low, for it isn't often that a girl can summon the courage to talk back to the Moon.

"A promise is a promise," said Morning Star later that night taking the side of his mother. "If you are not good on your word, at least accept the price for disobeying," forgetting already the promises he himself had made to Soatsaki and the price he had exacted for his love. So Soatsaki was banished, with her child bundled on her back, his little fingers pulling at her hair and crying, responding with grief to her grief. When Soatsaki descended, the sky lighted up with a purple glow, and the rain fell on the earth for days. A wind swept and beat against the pelts of the *nii toy yis*, as if to announce Soatsaki was home.

There are great gaps in history as great as the hole of the turnip that the giant spider planted to prevent man from seeing god, so it should be no surprise that this legend skips to the adulthood of her son, Star Boy, half god, half cursed, half like all children ever born to mothers, who will grow strong, but scarred by a wound that never heals. He will leave the village in search of his heavenly father. An old seer will show him the way. He will walk all the way to the shores of the Pacific and climb to heaven on a web of sunrays spun for this purpose by the giant sky spider. He will consult with his heavenly grandparents, who will heal his scar, and he will return to the Blackfoot people with the medicine secrets of the gods, a teacher of wisdom who will overcome lore and bleed into legend for his miraculous powers. He will then ascend to heaven to take his place by his father's side, and his glory will overcome the shadow of his mothers' shame.

But what happened to her, to the mother, the young, disobedient girl in love with heaven, who first kissed a god and bore him a son? Of her, there is only one more mention: of lonely nights spent in the prairie where she once fell in love, her back pressed against the cool earth, her nose turned up towards the belt of stars above, her thinned, tired voice pleading for grace from her estranged lover, who returns only silence.

There is no logic in dream, no fairness in love. Beauty has no reward, least of all in young women who grow to be unprepared mothers.

Her story barely survives, passed on from mother to daughter, and loses its details like a washed piece of cloth. Most of the world is asleep yet, anyway: Europe is far on the other end of the ocean; history is written by men in powdered wigs. Monks in long cloaks will preach against sex and folklore from high pulpits, their words raging through stone vaults hewn and chiseled by the labor of superstitious men, and you, in your high knowledge of planets, sheltered by your stone abodes and comforted by beds of air and feathers, you, people of choices, of waking consciousness, will not know the end of my story.

But if you see a mention of me in the dry passages of a textbook, or a poem that has deliberately been casual with the details of my choices, and disregarded the consequences of my ignorance and the price I paid for it, remember, I am the origin of human mistakes. My progeny, when things go dark and sorrow chases you to places where you will chafe your knees to ask for grace or mercy, find comfort, a thread of humor at the notion that all sorrows of mankind spin from the conflict of mothers and sons, and that all curses are laid on earth for the eyes of one girl so long ago who dared to look to heaven and to love.

The Door Ajar

Jeffrey Greene

Later, after Valerie came to, her boiled thoughts coalescing on the large, self-adoring face of Dr. Vance looming over her, it troubled her that she had been thinking about Michael Riordan, the desk clerk who'd signed her in to the neurology clinic that morning, just as she had felt the first strange breeze of the aura. It had troubled her so much that she had tried mightily, with even a pushing motion of her hands, to expel his face from her mind before the seizure took her, because she had smelled Marta's perfume again, its cloying, crushed flower fragrance so intense she almost gagged, and somehow, in a way she couldn't explain, she feared for him. It was so odd, she thought later, when she could think again, that she should feel that way, protective of a stranger. But from whom or what did he need protecting?

She lay on her side on the examining room table, still too dazed and scattered to speak, feeling the first twinges of strained muscles in her stomach and lower back, and soon fell into a light sleep. They let her sleep, and when she woke an hour later, Dr. Martin Vance, the head of the neurology department, a tall man with a carefully trimmed mustache and a rocking gait, rocked back into the room trailing clouds of interns, patted her on the shoulder with his big hairy hand and told her he was increasing her dosage of anti-convulsants to three hundred milligrams a day. They'd lick this thing together, they would, they would, and knowing he was playing to the gallery as much as to her, she wanly agreed. The blows to her pride she'd endured since the big blow to her head that was the cause of all this leering medical attention and canned reassurances, were so numerous and varied that she was no longer mortified by the thought of her body writhing

JEFFREY GREENE

like a half-crushed insect on a dirty hospital floor. What better place
to have a seizure than in a clinic lousy with neurologists? In what
was certainly one of life's little mercies, she never saw herself having
the full-blown, *grand mal* event; that was for others to remember and
shudder at, not her. She recalled only the aura, the ground tremors,
as it were, of the actual eruption, which obliterated all traces of itself
in her memory.

They observed her for most of the day, and finally, late in the afternoon, sent her home. She wasn't supposed to drive a car until the
phenytoin reached the prescribed blood serum level, worked its black
magic and tamed her epilepsy, giving with one claw while taking with
the other, so she had called for a cab and was waiting at the front
circle when it happened again. First there was *jamais vu,* the familiar abruptly gone strange, and the strangeness itself evoking *déjà vu,*
as people around her seemed to recede into a grey, watery distance.
She smelled burning rubber and tasted gold — it was the only way she
could describe the metallic yellowness of it — and then brute panic
seized her, and anger, too, at her own treasonous brain. She begged
a security guard standing nearby to get her in a wheel chair and back
to the clinic before all hell broke loose. Peevish about leaving his post
but plainly rattled, the young man complied, and pushing against and
through what seemed in her altered state like a raging current of af-
flicted humanity, during which she felt herself being compressed to
the size of a Raggedy Ann doll, they reached the clinic desk. With
hardly a word he left her there, in the care of the young clerk, Michael
Riordan, for whom that very morning she had conceived a desire to
meet on terms altogether different from this one. He was alone behind the desk at that moment, as if he'd been waiting for her.

"I'm having a seizure," she said, trying to quell the panic in her
voice, and feeling another stage beginning to set in, when she might
stop speaking in mid-sentence, locked in a zombie rictus while the
bomb in her head prepared to detonate. "Please call Dr. Vance right
now. It could happen any second."

Clearly alarmed for her, he spoke to the nurse, then picked up the
phone and began dialing.

"Dr. Vance has left the clinic for the day," he said, watching her warily. "But I'm calling the neurology department. We'll find him, don't worry."

"Don't worry? Don't worry?" She beat back an almost hysterical sarcasm, tried to breathe. "I don't want it to happen here."

"I don't, either," he said. And the way he stayed behind the desk, as if she were something volatile, unstable, she believed him. He got through to Dr. Vance's secretary, who said she'd page him, and to hang on. "A nurse's aide will be down in a minute," he said.

"I hate being medically interesting," she said, gripping the arms of the wheel chair.

He smiled at that, and she seemed to feel his kindness settle over her like a soft green net that passed through her skin and held her fear in a gentle grip. His handsome, angular face was calm, like a sheltered cove that drew her gaze, until she realized she was staring, and looked away. She thought he might be twenty-seven or eight: Marta's age. Her age now, she corrected herself. What had he seen this morning? Everything, his dark eyes said.

At that moment the nurse's aide arrived and wheeled her to the elevator. Just before the elevator doors closed she looked back at Michael, and felt as if a cold hand had gripped her by the throat. Standing a few feet from him and facing him, her feet planted in the middle of the wide hallway as if she were bracing herself against a stiff wind, was her sister. It wasn't by her face but her withered left arm that Valerie recognized her, that and her thick, straight black hair. Her face was darkened or shadowed by something that was neither blood nor shadow, but instead resembled, at least from this distance, a blowing veil of dust that seemed to extend somehow from the heavy bangs that covered her forehead. In the instant before the doors closed, she realized with a shock that Marta was visible only to herself. But she knew, even though she could see no eyes in that oval of dust, that Marta was seeing him. No, not just seeing him — staring at him. And he apparently saw and felt nothing. It's the aura, she told herself over and over, as the elevator climbed with terrible slowness toward Neurology, just another symptom of epilepsy, like the smell of Marta's perfume. She had learned to expect visual, auditory and olfactory hallucinations during the seconds or minutes leading up to a seizure, and sometimes indescribable combinations of all three, and her sister was never far from her thoughts. But if that were true, why was this spiking discharge in her brain staring so hard at Michael Riordan? Should she tell Dr. Vance about it? No, she thought. Don't be an idiot.

Thankfully, the expected seizure turned out to be a CPS, complex partial seizure, which was far less traumatic, sparing her Dr. Vance's grim little joke about her being "the number one tonic-clonic drama queen" in his practice, and by early evening she was eating home-delivered Chinese food in her modest cinderblock rental house on the northwest side.

Her mother had called from Boston, as she did every night at seven p.m., demanding from Valerie the news she simply couldn't give her: that she was getting better by the day, her brain rebuilding itself after the Event That Must Not Be Named. She repeated what the doctor had told her, and then her mother raised the inevitable question: when would she be leaving the poisoned ground of Taylor Creek, Florida and coming home? As always, her mother made it seem as if her refusal to acede to her wishes was simply further evidence of her, Valerie's, cruel punishment of her and her father, the only two people left in the world who truly cared about her, and who even now were "standing by," like her own private nursing staff, to render aid and comfort to a daughter far too ill to be living alone. Valerie spoke little during these tirades. How could she possibly explain, without sounding psychotic, why she couldn't leave? When her father finally took the phone, they exchanged their usual awkward pleasantries, and as always after she hung up the phone, she felt the need for an antacid. She missed alcohol terribly, and never more than after these nightly calls. Why did she feel so much lonelier after hearing their voices?

The punishing silence of the house, the always closed door of Marta's room across from hers at the end of the hall, the slight tremor in her hands that was the phenytoin's newest side effect, the swelling shame at what had happened today at the clinic: it was all settling on her chest with intolerable pressure, like those wooden pallets they used to place on top of witches, piling stones on them until their victims were crushed. The still, humid air in the house had become unbreathable, and tossing her unfinished carton of lo mein into the nearly-empty refrigerator, she fled through the kitchen door into the back yard.

The scruffy, half-acre lot was dominated by slash pines, bamboo, and untended azaleas, the grass unmowed for weeks, and a florid, almost-full moon lolled at a drunken angle on the treetops of the eastern horizon. The air was better out here, at least until the mosquitoes found her, which wouldn't be long. She lighted a cigarette to discourage them and stretched out on the patio's one threadbare recliner chair. If she were to have a seizure right now, she thought, no one would hear her if she hit her head on the concrete and bled out. But seizures only came unbidden, like nightmares, never at her beck and call, the way the hovering, hungry boys used to, and never at such an ideal moment, when she was laid out and ready in her long, black, thrift-store dress and multiple rings and bracelets that would serve very well for cerements. She didn't want to die, she wanted her old life back. It wasn't to be had, though, none of it, ever again. Valerie Penzoldt had survived the crash; the heedless, beautiful kid sister of tough, practical, put-upon Marta, whom the boys would cruelly ask out just to get closer to her: that Valerie had died in the car with her sister.

She felt a mosquito on her neck, and slapped at it, but resisted going back inside just yet. The moon was a friend, as it had been that night, and at that she angrily snapped the ash off her cigarette and drew deeply on it, rejecting the memory, or trying to. Somebody had to drive, she told herself for the millionth time. And I was only two sheets to the wind. It didn't matter, of course. If she didn't dream about the crash, it came back during the aura, like this afternoon, when the stench of burning tire rubber had filled her nose, ten times stronger than it had in the second or two before the cars collided. Her brain was as full of the accident as the sea with shells, and if the aura was capricious and surprising in its palate of tastes, sounds, smells, and visions, sometimes combining exquisite, forgotten moments from earliest childhood, or colors more saturated than any seen with her uninjured brain, it could also take her by the scruff of the neck and grind her face in unbearable distillations of windshield glass, blood, gasoline, viscera and shit, and force her to relive those moments in tasteless and bizarre combinations, as if they were all of equal value, like the keys of a piano. The accident, the brief coma that followed, and then, nine months later, the first seizure of what had proven to be a difficult case of post-traumatic epilepsy: one or all of these insults had jimmied open a window in her brain that, for her own good, nature had kept nailed shut, and now there was no escaping herself, not even in sleep. But at least the thought of Michael Riordan made her feel like getting out of bed, and there was so little that did these days. She wished she had his home phone number, but she would call him at work tomorrow, and then, if she could get up the nerve, do what she'd never needed to do before: ask a man out.

She took her medication and watched some TV, the uncompromising inanity of which seemed just the thing right now, then turned on the wall-unit air conditioner in her bedroom, climbed into bed and tried to read. Seizures in her sleep were rare, ironically precipitated by sleep deprivation or drugs like Valium or too much liquor, which she'd all but sworn off of, but she always feared them, especially the somehow terrifying idea of a seizure occurring in the middle of a dream. All she wanted was a good, dreamless night's sleep.

She tore herself out of a short, claustrophobic nightmare in which the ceiling had lowered—or the bed had risen—to within inches of her face, like a coffin lid, and for a panicky moment she had no idea where she was. She must have been asleep a long time, because the moon had almost set, making the room much darker. For several moments she lay there, listening in the dark, as helpless with fear as she had been in the dream, before switching on the bedside lamp. There was no one else in the room. She got out of bed, her legs so weak they could barely hold her weight. She washed her face and brushed her wildly disheveled hair, then turned out the light and went to the kitchen to make a cup of tea. Still shaky, she sat down at the table.

It was just past four a.m. Her mother was right: she was a fool to think she could live alone, without help. She had a feeling that something bad would happen soon, no matter what she did, and she was waiting for it, almost eager to get it over with. Either kill me or leave me the hell alone, she thought, then jeered at herself for personalizing a medical condition. This had happened to her because her head had hit the driver's side window very hard in a certain spot, causing a subdural hematoma, which in turn had led to a build-up of fluid pressure requiring surgery to relieve it. The trauma to her brain had resulted in a type of epilepsy not unusual in such cases, which, depending on how she responded to the increased dosage of Dilantin, would soon be under better control, shaky control, or no control at all, and Dr. Vance, despite his Marcus Welby routine, clearly had no idea which it would be.

But it was undeniable that odd things had been happening to her lately, not at all in the usual range of symptoms, and far too subjective and strange to mention to Dr. Vance. She felt… how could she put it to her parents, even to herself? That she was haunted? That she dreaded the aura not for its intrinsic mystery and portent, but for some indefinable sense that it was being used against her, as a kind of opening, or door? No, she couldn't say a word about this to Dr. Vance. He'd smile around his ridiculous pipe, offer a condescending pat on her shoulder, then refer her to Psychiatry.

The next day, after putting it off all morning, she called the outpatient clinic and asked for Michael Riordan. When he answered, his pleasant voice briskly professional, she nervously rushed out the words she'd rehearsed.

"Michael? Hi, it's Valerie Penzoldt. Do you remember me? I complicated your life yesterday."

There was the briefest hesitation before he replied, a note of puzzled caution in his voice: "Actually, you made it more interesting. How are you feeling today?"

"I'm fine, fine," she said, aware that she was overdoing the cheeriness, and toned it down. "It sort of didn't happen, my little crisis. What they call a complex partial seizure. Kind of like smelling the rain and hearing the thunder from a storm that never comes."

"Well, you had me worried," he said.

"Thought I was gonna go all funky on the floor, didn't you?"

"Something like that," he said.

"The reason I'm calling is to thank you, Michael. May I call you Michael?"

"Please do," he said. "And you're welcome, Ms. Penzoldt."

"Please, it's Valerie."

"All right, Valerie."

"I also wanted to apologize if I spoke sharply."

"You didn't."

"I certainly did, and I'm sorry. It isn't every day one gets such kind treatment in a hospital."

"It must be hard, the situation you're in."

"I'm dealing with it."

"Better than I would," he said. There was a silence, then he said: "I appreciate the call."

She waited for him to say something else, then took a breath and plunged ahead. "Look, Michael, I know this is sudden, and probably a little weird, coming from a patient, but I was wondering if you'd like to come over to my house tonight. If you're not doing anything. We could have a drink, continue the conversation."

"Well... yes. I think that's, uh, a good idea, Valerie."

"Your enthusiasm overwhelms me," she said, wincing at her almost involuntary sarcasm. "It's all right if you don't feel like it," she added.

"No, I'd love to. My Fridays tend to be pretty barren. Thanks for asking."

"I can't legally drive, is why I'm suggesting my house."

"I have a car. Where do you live?"

"Is eight all right?" she asked, after giving him directions.

"Great. I'll see you then."

"Bring something to drink, okay? My cupboard's bare."

"I will. Goodbye."

"Bye."

She couldn't blame him, she thought, as she hung up, for hemming and hawing a bit. She had half-bullied, half-shamed him into accepting her invitation. Would she want to go out with him if their positions were reversed? What would the old Valerie have done? Turned him down, probably, and not very gently, either, though afterward, in the version that would become the official one, she would have told herself how considerate she'd been, and how gracefully he had taken his rejection.

She took a long nap in the afternoon, hoarding her strength for the evening, then spent close to two hours getting ready. Her blue-veined paleness was a problem, but at least her dark brown hair was as thick and shiny as ever, mostly hiding the jagged scar in her scalp, and her knack for dressing to flatter her almost too-thin figure had not deserted her. She reminded herself that he would be nervous, too. One glass of alcohol was all she dared drink, and she considered it bad luck even to wish for a night free of seizures. A calm and neutral state of mind, free of hope and fear, would serve her best.

He was on time, bearing a bottle of Chianti and a charming, uncertain smile, dressed casually in a blue polo shirt and jeans. Behind him, a storm was threatening in the southwestern sky, its massive front of clouds already drawing a ragged curtain across the setting sun. She led the way into the kitchen, rummaging in a drawer for a corkscrew. They carried their glasses into the living room and sat down together on the couch. He offered a toast to her health, and she smiled ruefully and sipped her wine.

"You look nice," he said.

"Thanks," she said. "You look like you're expecting a medical emergency."

"I'll try to stop doing that," he said, smiling. "Do you live here alone?"

She nodded. "I know, it's risky. Like smoking; like this," she said, holding up her glass and taking a healthy sip. "My doctor forbids all fun."

"How often do the seizures occur?" he asked.

"Three or four times a month, usually. For a while there it was three or four a day. And though the side effects of anticonvulsants can be pretty awful, I have to keep taking them. Have I scared you off yet, Michael?"

"Not quite yet," he said, with a laugh. The thunder had been growing louder while they talked, and the last rumble, following hard on the heels of a lightning stroke, rattled the windows. The cool, rain-smelling wind billowed the curtains, and any second now the first heavy drops would begin to splat against the dusty jalousie windows.

"Do you know what an aura is?" she asked, pouring them both some more wine. She knew she was taking a risk by drinking more, but it had been so long since she'd had someone to talk to besides doctors and nurses, and having him this close made her nervous.

"I've read about it," he replied. "The feeling of—what would you call it, unreality?—that precedes the seizure?"

She nodded. "Smells, tastes, terrible, wonderful, impossible-to-describe feelings, like being lost in space, or forgetting who you are, shouting voices in my head: whatever happens forces itself on my thoughts, takes them over for a while. Yesterday at the clinic, right before the first seizure, I smelled the perfume my sister, Marta, used to use, like a whole bottle of it broken under my nose. I hated that perfume—so flowery and sweet and overwhelming, like the stuff my maiden aunt used to wear in church. She had it on that night."

"What night?" he asked, leaning forward in the fading light.

"Oh." Why had she brought it up now, of all times? "The night she died, and I didn't."

"I heard about the accident," he said. "I'm very sorry."

"Thanks, Michael, but please don't think I asked you over to give me sympathy."

"Okay, no sympathy," he said. "Good riddance to all epileptics."

"Let's toast that sentiment," she said, laughing, and they touched glasses and drank.

"You're not really in the medical profession, are you?" she asked. "No ambitions in that area? Because I'm really sick of doctors, nurses and hospital administrators. No offense."

"None taken," he replied. "I was an English major in college, but didn't want to teach, go into law, insurance, or any other sensible profession. So now, after a blur of bad, blue-collar jobs in Polk County, I'm back in Taylor Creek, clerking at the Health Center for dirt-floor wages. As for ambition, I seem to have a deficit in that area. I'd like to keep breathing; that's about all the ambition I can muster right now."

"I like a man who knows what he doesn't want," she said. "Go on. You interest me."

"Well, how about this? I'm so shy, I have to wait for women to ask me out, a rare occurrence, so I'm usually alone or hanging out with my misfit friends. I'm twenty-eight and back in a college town, but don't want to go back to school. I'm attracted to beautiful, damaged women, and have about two hundred dollars to my name."

She laughed. "So you accepted my invitation because I'm damaged?"

"Don't forget beautiful."

"Thanks," she said, blushing. "I'll take any compliment at this point, back-hand or forehand."

It was pouring rain now, the lightning and thunder simultaneous, competing with her softly spoken words, so that he had to lean closer to her, watching her fine, dark eyes as she spoke.

"You know, before all this happened," she went on. "I was pretty full of myself, pretty wild. Marta, who saw herself as the responsible older sister with the thankless job of cleaning up my messes, never missed an opportunity to remind me of it, either. Truth is, I wasn't very nice to her. The doctor who delivered her broke her arm getting her out, and it never grew right. She had to acquire a thick skin, the way the other kids treated her. It made her tough, independent, responsible—everything I wasn't. She learned not to wait to be asked out on a date. If she liked a boy, she did the asking. And everything about me was salt in the wound for Marta, because from the time I was twelve, the boys came after me, not her. I know how vain that sounds, but it's true. I even stole her boyfriend once, a guy she really loved, just because I could. I don't think she ever forgave me for that. And why should she?"

"Little sister getting all the action," he said. "I'll bet she was jealous."

"Poisonously," she replied. "Since we were kids. Anyway, when I smell her perfume during the aura, I feel—it's hard to express—a kind of living presence of my sister. That sounds insane, I know. But I still feel her, very close to me, as if she's occupying the same space as my body, and I feel her judging me, too, with the same concentrated intensity that I smell her perfume — much more than I ever felt it when she was alive. It's as if all that's left of her is her damning judgment of my life."

"Do you think you killed her?" he asked abruptly.

She looked sharply at him. "You mean do I feel responsible? Of course I do. A drunk driver crossed the center line and hit us. But we'd been drinking, too, and if I'd been sober, I might have swerved in time. Then again, maybe not. I've gone over it a million times. I'll never know."

"Do you ever feel her presence apart from the aura?"

"No, never. Which makes me dread seizures that much more. When I come out of it, the feeling of her is gone. It's probably just a symptom of epilepsy, a kind of reverberating impression of her, personified into a sort of hallucination."

"Hallucination? Do you mean you actually see her?"

She hesitated, then nodded. "I did yesterday. It was after the nurse's aide wheeled me to the elevator. I looked back and saw her standing in the hallway right in front of you, wearing her nurse's uniform. Her face was kind of hard to see. But I'm sure she was looking at you."

"At me?" he said. "That's a little unsettling."

"I'm not saying she's a ghost. Or maybe she is: a ghost from my banged-up brain."

"Maybe it doesn't matter whether it's a medical or a supernatural phenomenon," he said. "The result is the same. You've found yourself guilty, Valerie, and Marta is the sword of justice. But it's all you."

"I hear what you're saying, Michael. But you've never had a seizure. The aura is something like a dream: it happens inside the brain, and yet while it's happening, it feels as real as this conversation. When I'm in that place, I know she's dead and so does she. I also know that she hates me."

He leaned forward. "Hates you? Really?"

"Hates me for being alive, I mean, with the potential for happiness. If she has to be dead, it's only just that I should be alone and miserable."

"Forgive me, Valerie, but the dead can't hate. They can't care about the living. What you're going through is not about Marta. It's about you coming to terms with what happened."

"I wonder if that's possible," she said.

"Have some more wine," he said.

"I shouldn't," she said. "But I want to. I'm so sick of being sick."

There was a tremendous crash as lightning struck something nearby, so loud it made them both jump. They laughed, and Michael got up and looked out the window.

"Look, there's a pine tree on fire across the street," he said. She got up and stood beside him, their shoulders touching, watching the flaming branches that were quickly put out by the intense downpour. She impulsively took his hand, her heart pounding. He turned and smiled at her. "Have you had dinner yet?" he asked.

"No. Have you?"

"I was waiting to see if you had. Let's go out and get something."

"I'd like to," she said, tightening her grip on his hand. "After the storm."

He turned into her open arms and embraced her. As he kissed her, she knew that he knew they were rushing it, that she was grabbing wildly for something because she was lonely and had lost confidence in her beauty. They lurched in the direction of the couch and half-sat, half-lay on it. At first his responses seemed dutiful, even half-hearted. But then, maybe it was the storm, the way the lightning revealed in photo flashes their faces and bodies to each other, the crashes of thunder, or the clamorous downpour on the roof and the yard, bending every branch, flower and blade of grass to its will — whatever lucky timing had driven her to start something in the middle of a thunderstorm, it no longer felt awkward and forced, it felt right. They ended up in her bedroom, and by the time they thought of food again it was to late for anything but take-out pizza or an all-night breakfast house.

She said she might have an old frozen pizza, and got up to look, feeling her way down the dark hallway. She was a little dizzy, a reminder that she'd drunk more tonight than in many months. When she opened the refrigerator door, the sound was strangely muffled and distant, as if she were hearing it through a downspout, and then, as she surveyed the desolate, mysterious landscape of the empty shelves, she realized what was happening to her.

"What's the verdict?" he called from the bedroom.

She heard Michael's voice as tinny, avid, somehow insectiverous, like a tiny mammal burrowing into her ear to feed on the termites boring steadily toward her brain, and she wasn't sure if she had just thought it or actually managed to speak the word "seizure" before the nauseatingly sweet smell of Marta's perfume assailed her with such intensity that she went down on her hands and knees and vomited on the kitchen floor. Had Michael heard, was he coming? The flavor of gold ineffably clung to the taste of vomit as she tried to stand on the surging floor, the walls of the house shaking as if in titanic laughter at her delusions of romance with the first guy to walk in the door since the accident. Wasn't he coming to help her? She couldn't endure this anymore, not by herself.

Or was it Marta who was coming, impatiently waiting for Valerie to seize and disappear into the undreaming place where the convulsions hurled her, so that she could step daintily through the gaping hole left by her sister's abrupt departure? She would have the run of the place until Valerie came back, whereupon the hole, rent, door, whatever it was, closed again.

She pushed herself off the floor and wiped her mouth, and was turning unsteadily toward the hallway, when a voice that seemed to originate both from inside her and all around her shouted: "Two good arms and no sister!" They were Marta's words in Marta's drunken voice, at the height of their shouting match that night in the car coming home from the bar, as the other car's headlights sliced sharply across the lane right at them. Her last words. Then, as the refrigerator door began to close behind her, she saw in the vanishing edge of light a flitting impression of whiteness, too fast to make out, but clearly heading down the hall toward the bedroom. She tried to call out, but it was as if she were encased in thick glass that was quickly going dark.

She was in her own bed, alone. Grey morning light seeped through the blinds. Her face was throbbing, and her fingers found a bandage over her left eyebrow. She sat up, feeling stiff and sore, hobbled into the bathroom and turned on the light. She'd seen it before, but it was still a shock: her left eye black and blue, swollen almost shut, a large bump under the bandage that Michael must have applied. She turned on the bathwater and climbed in. She lay there for a long time, incapable of thought or even remorse, her tissues swelling like a corpse, only rousing herself when the chill of tepid water began creeping into her bones. She dressed, then made the last of the coffee, doing everything in an empty-headed daze. She noticed that he had mopped the kitchen floor. She went over to the phone, looked at it, then shook her head and sat down on the couch. It was up to him to call, if he was going to. She'd expected him to stay the night, felt confident that for the first time in ages, something good had happened to her, and to him, too. He'd told her so, she remembered that much. But there was a gap in her recollections of the evening, that started shortly after she'd heard Marta's voice shouting the words she'd found impossible to forget. And Michael was gone, without leaving a note.

She read distractedly as the morning air slowly grew sultry, trying to suppress the hurt and anger rising in her, and then she heard his car in the driveway. He'd gone out for groceries. She stood up, watching him as he walked to the door, then opened it and let him in. He walked past her into the kitchen and set the bag on the counter, turning as she came toward him.

"Are you hungry?" he asked, smiling a little tentatively at her.

"Starved," she said, keeping the unbruised side of her face turned towards him. "Did you get coffee?"

"Along with bacon, eggs, juice, and bagels. Can you cook?"

"You make the coffee, I'll make breakfast," she said.

"That I can do. Are you all right?" he asked.

She lightly touched the bandage on her forehead. "Better than I look. Thanks for the first aid. Are you all right?"

"I was worried last night. You were a mess."

"Seizures don't hurt, Michael. Only the cuts and bruises. You're sure you're all right?"

"Of course. Why wouldn't I be?"

"No reason," she said. "Excuse me; I'll be right back." She went into the bathroom, shook out two pills from the Dilantin bottle, then drew a glass of water and washed them down. As she turned to leave the room, vertiginous swirls of colored sound, feeding on her slightest movement, eddied around and through her. No, not again, she thought. Please. Say please, mocked the voices hissing under pressure like the coffee machine. I can't be this way in front of him again. Not this soon. The hallway was a narrowing underground cavern through which she forced her way as if against a strong current of cold water, toward the lights, sounds and smells of the kitchen. Michael's back was turned as she entered, her hands outspread before her as if to ward off the infernal presence of Marta, who stood planted between her and her lover, her white uniform now drenched with a monstrous grime of blood, motor oil and road dirt, her unveiled face in tatters, forehead studded with windshield glass and asphalt, blood oozing from her shattered mouth. Valerie could feel the words forcing themselves up from her bowels like a spasm, words she couldn't have voluntarily spoken to save her life, but only in the paroxysm of seizure:

"It wasn't my fault."

He turned at the sound of her voice, which, instead of the banshee screech she had feared, was as flat and impersonal as a dial tone. She saw his welcoming smile fade, his eyes widen with concern, his arms extending as he came forward and, impossibly, clear through the gore-drenched figure of Marta, who, still motionless, was now behind and concealed by him. He took Valerie's outstretched hands and led her into the living room, then helped her sit on the couch.

"Shall I call the hospital?" he asked.

But the impending seizure, having forced her to say the words that she'd previously spoken only in dreams, had now sealed her lips. She looked over his shoulder, and saw to her infinite relief that Marta was gone. Michael had been wrong about one thing, she thought. She had confessed her guilt, day and night since the accident, and the ghost was not appeased. Marta, she knew, would come back, always, until the anticonvulsants controlled the seizures and the door was closed. Michael looked searchingly into her eyes, then stood up and reached for the phone, but Valerie's hands were still her own, and she held his arm, and after a moment he sat back down and waited with her for the storm.

The Stars' Chill Song

Francesca Forrest

True cold has come, cold that causes frost to form along your wind-pipe and deep into your lungs as you breathe in, cold that fingers its way through any number of layers of clothing to find what's fluttering and warm and chill it, still it.

"They'll be singing tonight. Next couple of nights, most probably." The upland farmers are saying so, and the boatmen, and Mr. Parkhurst at Five Foxes Tavern.

A cold like this peels away the blankets of air between the earth and the heavens, and if you travel out at night, you can hear the stars, singing. So beautiful, but so deadly, if you stop and unknot your scarf to hear those songs more clearly. The frozen faces of the unlucky ones are always tilted upward, lips parted, eyes wide, lost in rapturous attention. The animals too—one always finds a handful, frozen standing, out in the open, both predators and prey, wild creatures and domesticated ones whose owners forgot to shut them safe in house and barn.

Those songs etch permanent patterns in the windows of the houses of Orion Falls—flourishes and feathers of frost that never fade. That's what makes the glass produced by Orion Glassworks so valuable. When the cold comes, the foreman orders extra shifts, so all the glass made in the past months can be set out beneath the stars to catch the song and take its pattern. Sophie Brule is among the girls who have been assigned; like the rest of them, she would prefer to spend tonight at Five Foxes Tavern, because there will be dancing. Ezra Brown will be fiddling, but it's not to hear his playing that Sophie wishes she could go. Ezra Brown's fiddled in Orion Falls all Sophie's young life; he's as familiar as the hills and the 100-foot cone over the Orion Glassworks furnace. Besides, he drinks. No, if she could go, it would be to spin on the arm of Elijah Spencer and to hear the trio of fiddlers that have come down from Lower Canada.

Anna Hapgood, on the other hand, longs to hear Ezra Brown play, but she will not be at the Five Foxes Tavern either. She will be with Sophie Brule's mother, who is about to have her next baby. The night being so deadly cold, Anna will no doubt spend it at the Brule shanty, up in the hills. Little Henry Brule has come down to find Anna this afternoon, and to bring a coat to his sister at the glassworks. He practically dances as he walks alongside Anna up to the brick buildings. Is he dancing to keep his feet out of the snow? When he runs ahead, Anna can see that the soles of his boots are thin at the heels and the toes. She imagines there may well be holes in his stockings, if he's even wearing stockings.

But his cheeks are rosy and his eyes are bright. Maybe it's excitement, and not the cold, that makes him dance this way.

"I'm going to be the leader of the rescuers," he announces to Anna, walking backwards in front of her, so the two of them are face to face. "Isaac Clark got to be leader last year during the first cold snap, and Matthew Bliss was leader after him, and now it's my turn. I'm going to take everyone out of the town and up into the hills."

Every time the stars' singing can be heard, the children of Orion Falls organize rescue parties for any loose dogs, cats, or even rabbits or squirrels that are unlucky enough to become smitten. Occasionally, stray lambs have been rescued. There are hot drinks waiting for the children wherever they should call on those nights.

A wind picks up, and Henry claps his mittened hands over his ears. He turns to face forward and runs ahead, to the doors of the glassworks, then dances in place until Anna catches up.

"I made a map of the route," he says, and pulls a square of paper from his pocket and unfolds it. Broken and unbroken lines curl this way and that; there are marks for houses and woods.

"That looks like your sister's pay envelope," says Anna, noticing Sophie's name on the other side.

"She let me use it. Look, here's the stream by my house, and here's the path down to town, and here's Main Street, and here's the glassworks. Here's where we'll meet up, by the school. And this is how I'll take them. Past the Abbotts' farm, and the Lamontagnes', and the Walcotts'. We're meeting as soon as it gets dark."

Which will be soon. In the west, the sky is the color of the glassworks' furnace, but in the east the fiery shades have already burned themselves out. The men who pull the glass on metal plates to make panes for windows are coming out in twos and threes; they hastily slip into coats and jam hats on their heads. And here come the girls, who wrap and store the glass, and who tonight will climb the ladder up the side of the furnace dome and circle round and round it on the catwalk, leaning the glass against the dome, forming a temporary layer of transparent scales.

"Why did they pick the dome as the place to set out the glass?" Henry asked his sister, the year she started working at the glassworks. "Are you ever afraid you might fall?"

"Oh no, it's wonderful to be up so high; you can see the whole town. I don't know why they put the glass there. Abby told me it's because it's harder for mischief makers to try breaking it, but Molly thinks it's to get the glass closer to the stars."

The other girls are going to get supper before returning, but Sophie stays just inside the door. She has a thick woolen shawl, but that's not enough against this kind of cold.

"Ma sends you this," says Henry, passing the coat to her. "She says with the baby coming, she's not going to be going outside, so you may as well use it." Sophie puts it on and looks sidelong at Anna.

"So you'll be helping with the birth? Not Mrs. Ellis?"

"Mrs. Ellis doesn't go out much now; her arthritis is bad and her sight is failing. It's mainly me. But I've got plenty of—"

"Oh, I'm sure you'll do fine. Ma could drop a baby with Henry assisting if she had to, anyway."

"Sophie!" says Henry, and it's embarrassment as much as the cold that's making his cheeks red now. But he can't spend too much time on outrage when he's got his own news to share.

FRANCESCA FORREST

"Sophie, I'm leading the rescuers tonight. I'm going to take them everywhere. We'll save more animals than anyone ever has before. This'll be a famous night for rescuing."

Sophie runs a hand through her little brother's dark curls.

"You're staying out all night with no hat? You want to end up with clipped ears, like that crazy fiddler?"

Anna feels a pang for Ezra Brown, but her face doesn't show it.

"I can do like this," says Henry, putting his hands over his ears the way he did on the walk over.

"How can you rescue animals with your hands on your head? Here, wear this." Sophie pulls her scarlet scarf off and holds it out to Henry. "I won't need it, not with the shawl and the coat." But Henry's not taking it. "Oh, go on," urges Sophie. "Don't make a face. Are you fussed about the color? Don't you know leaders have to wear something bright to distinguish themselves from their followers? This'll mark you as the leader."

That persuades him; he even looks pleased, now, with the bright scarf. Sophie reaches for something beneath her apron—coins—and gives them to Henry.

"A leader has to look after his followers," she says. "If you hurry, you can buy your friends some roasted chestnuts." Henry squeezes her in such a tight hug that she coughs, and then he dashes off down the street.

Sophie sighs, shivers as a tongue of wind licks by the entrance to the glassworks.

"Let's close the door," she says, and doesn't wait for Anna to answer; she pulls the heavy door shut.

The furnace fire has not been banked, but it will be. They say the fire is unpredictable on nights when the stars are singing. Maybe it's salamanders, as some say—or maybe it's the fire itself that rises to hear the song. Either way, the stars' singing arouses the flames far better than bellows ever do, and it's dangerous. So no nighttime glassmaking tonight.

But because the fire has not yet been banked, it's warm inside, even by the foreman's desk by the door.

"You're not having supper, Sophie?" the foreman asks.

"I'm not hungry tonight; too much excitement," she replies, lifting her chin. He gives her a quizzical look and goes back to his bookkeeping. Anna thinks on the coins Sophie gave to her brother and bites her lip.

"You remember the way to our house?" asks Sophie. She frowns slightly. "I should have made Henry walk back with you."

"Oh, no need for that—I remember the way," says Anna. "There's the path through the orchard, and then the path along the pasture above that, right?"

"That's right," says Sophie, and then, "Stay warm."

Anna nods and smiles. "You too."

And then Anna hurries off to Mrs. Ellis's house to pick up the things she'll need tonight, while Sophie lingers by the door of the glassworks, waiting for the other girls to return from supper.

Anna has put a small bottle of Mrs. Ellis's quince brandy in a cloth bag, along with packets of dried raspberry leaves and blue cohosh that she surely won't need for someone who gives birth as easily as Mrs. Brule. They're comforting to have, though; comforting for Anna, and comforting for Mrs. Brule—and the quince brandy even more so. She has wrapped her scarf around her head and ears and tied the ends at the back of her neck, and she has put on mittens. She won't need snowshoes; there's not that much on the ground.

It's dark out now, and there they are, overhead: the stars. So big, some of them, and so bright. Such colors, too, if you look—soft gold, cold white-blue, red, green. Anna can almost hear their singing, almost. What she does hear is the sound of fiddling coming from the tavern, seeping out like light from its shuttered windows, but only faintly and growing fainter. Anna is walking the opposite direction.

"Called out on a cold night, and no one to accompany you?"

Anna looks over her shoulder and sees it's Ezra Brown, his fiddle case slung over his back. The sight warms her to the tips of her fingers and toes.

"Henry Brule called me for his mother, but he's with his friends tonight, off to rescue animals. It's easy enough to get to the Brules' place without an escort," she answers, then adds, "You're not playing

119

at the tavern tonight? They said you were." Her heart speeds up as he begins to answer, because she knows what he'll say.

"A night like tonight, my first duty is to that song," he says, pointing upward. Anna smiles and releases the breath she hadn't been aware she was holding. It makes a cloud between the two of them; some of it freezes on the edges of her scarf.

Yes, that's what she thought he'd say.

When Anna was as young as Henry, and Ezra was perhaps a year or so shy of Anna's current three and twenty years, Ezra went out on a winter's night like tonight's, went out and didn't return. Mr. Porter found him halfway up the hill to Hunter Pond, almost frozen to death, and dragged him home. When Ezra revived, all he would talk about was the stars' singing. People could understand; it had happened to others before Ezra—Ezra was lucky to have been rescued. But when it happened a second time people muttered about folk who don't learn from experience. Between those two events, he lost three fingers from one hand and one from the other, as well as the tips of his ears and nose.

He hasn't needed rescuing since then, but still on nights like these he always goes out, fortified by spirits. People argue about whether it's the stars' singing that made him drink or drinking that makes him tempt death time and time again, but Anna knows drink is beside the point. It's love. All you have to do is listen to him play the tunes inspired by the singing, his stumps of fingers making the bow dance across those strings, to know it's love.

That love. It makes Anna heartsick, vicariously. It makes her blind to the young men in town. The only face she cares for is this one, with its deep creases, half-missing nose, nicked ears, and ghostly pale eyes, and it's not so much the face; it's what those eyes have seen and those ears have heard. It's how he makes the fiddle tell the tale.

"I'll walk with you as far as the Brules'," he says.

"You're going on to Hunter Pond."

"Yes. The sound is magnified there—I think the ice must reflect it back."

"I wish..." Anna begins, but trails off. She stops walking and leans back to catch a dizzying eyeful of stars. Concentrates. Maybe. Maybe she can hear something, now. She unwinds her scarf.

Yes. It comes as if on a breath of wind, though the night has grown very still, a sound she feels in her bones more as trembling than as resonating, trembling the way the stars tremble up there, though they can't be cold, can they? No, they must be trembling with the joy of their singing.

She has unwound her scarf but wishes she could peel off her ears to hear more clearly. She stands on tiptoe. Now she's four inches closer to that sound.

Something startles her and breaks her concentration. It's Ezra, wrapping her scarf back around her head. The whiff of song is gone, instead there's the sharp scent of alcohol and the damp warmth of his breath as he speaks.

" — waiting for you, isn't she? We should keep walking."

"You enjoy whole evenings beneath the stars when they sing, but I can't even steal a minute to listen?" The words tumble out before Anna can stop them.

"A minute becomes five and then twenty, and then... well, then there's a chance of losing yourself entirely. You don't want to risk that — you can't risk that. People depend on you. Me, now. No one depends on me; so I'm free to do as I like."

I depend on you, Anna would like to say, but those words are frozen in the back of her throat.

They walk on more swiftly now, in silence, through the orchard and alongside Henry's footprints across the pasture, and then, when they have nearly arrived at the Brules' ramshackle dwelling, Ezra suddenly grips Anna's arm tightly and points skyward. As piercingly as regret, a star flashes down from the top of the sky's dome and vanishes. Before Anna can say anything, another star, from another point high in the sky, follows the first.

"They're coming," he says. He picks up the pace even more, his hand still on Anna's arm so she must trot to keep up with him. They're at the door of the Brules' place now, and Ezra releases Anna. He's already walking rapidly away.

"They're coming to Hunter Pond?"

Ezra turns back.

"Yes. I hoped. I called. Each time they sang, I called... and now they're coming."

His voice is so warm that Anna can feel it on her cheeks, even at this distance. But he's turning away now, he's disappearing into the night, and Anna's cheeks grow cold again. The door in front of her is pulled open by a child with tangled hair and bare feet, and Anna hurries inside.

Sophie, Martha, and Harriet don't speak much as they lift the plates of glass from their storage crates and lean them against the side of the glassworks' brick cone. They're working extra quickly because they're spelling Charlotte and Molly, who have gone off to the tavern. The foreman won't find out; he's not going to come out into the cold to see how many girls are up on the catwalk. In the end, all that matters is that all the glass is exposed to the stars' singing.

Charlotte and Molly have promised to return in time to let Martha and Harriet get some time listening to the Canadian fiddlers. As for Sophie, she no longer cares about hearing them. She will work the whole night through, and happily, too, because Elijah Spencer has been put in charge of banking the furnace fires, and when he's done, he'll come up and lend the girls a hand. And then — well, then Sophie intends to lead him along the catwalk until the furnace cone stands between them and the other girls, and in that privacy, she will rest her hands on Elijah's shoulders, lean in close, and see if a second kiss will be as good at that first one was. That kiss! But mustn't think about it while carrying glass on these narrow walkways.

Yes, it takes extra care. One can't handle the glass without gloves or mittens on; the air's too cold. One's hands will grow numb, and numb hands are clumsy hands. But hands in mittens and gloves are almost equally clumsy. It's carefully, carefully with each pane that must be leaned against the cone.

There are lanterns along the catwalk, so the girls can see what they're doing, and in their flickering light (wildly flickering — each little flame seems determined to escape its lantern's confines), the glass is shining. As Sophie makes her way back to the crate, she sees the plates she has already set out are already showing signs of patterning. She looks up at the sky—she can't help it—but doesn't unwrap her scarf. In sixteen years, she's never heard the stars—not to remember, anyway; never anything to make her want to stop and listen harder. And she doesn't intend to try and hear them now.

Just... when she sees the glass taking on those curls, those arabesques, that snowflake tracery, she does sometimes wish... what must it be like to be so touched? A tiny, tiny part of her asks, *Is it better than a kiss?*

But then she remembers the mad fiddler and his missing fingers. No, definitely not better.

A half an hour, maybe an hour goes by; it's hard to say. The stars are turning overhead, but Sophie's not looking. She and Martha and Harriet have hauled up the next crate of glass and are unpacking it now; that leaves only two for Charlotte and Molly, when they come back. And what's keeping Elijah?

More time goes by—here are Charlotte and Molly (and there go Martha and Harriet; they barely turn back to wave goodbye), and here at last comes Elijah, looking anxious, with soot on his face.

"Fire won't settle down," he says. "Every time I think I've got it banked, it flames back up.

Something catches Sophie's eye, something up there. A flash, a falling star. And another. A vibration travels from her feet to her head. There's a sound like distant thunder coming from the heart of the cone.

"You have to try harder!" Sophie exclaims. "You have to settle it—you can't let it go wild." More vibrations; she fears she'll lose her balance, and he must feel the same—they find themselves clinging to each other and leaning against the cone, which is warm and growing warmer.

"Too late," he whispers, face pale as the snow.

Sophie hears Charlotte and Molly scream, then a tinkling of broken glass. Her stomach turns. How many panes have broken? How many weeks' wages have just shattered? The cone is becoming positively hot, but she doesn't dare pull away from it; the vibrations are too fierce, the catwalk too narrow, and the ground too far below. She coughs; suddenly the air is thick with smoke. If the stars are to blame for this, if the stars have put the fire in a frenzy, well, they're hidden from sight now.

"Look!" says Elijah. With their backs pressed against the cone, they can't see its top, but the flashing, twisting light illuminating the clouds of smoke tell them that the flames have found their way out the top of the cone.

Will her mother's coat catch fire from the heat of the cone? Sophie doesn't even care. It can burn, and her dress too, and the skin on her back can blacken, and it won't matter, because the fire is pouring its heart out to the stars, and Sophie knows this song. It's not about love; it's about longing. *I'm bright. I shine. Know me. Own me.*

"I hope the stars are listening," she shouts, so that Elijah can hear her over the rumbling and the roar of the fire. She's still clutching his left arm with both her hands, and he's still got his gloved right hand over her mittened one.

"I hope so too," he shouts back. "The fire's going to burn itself out soon; it's going to exhaust the coal."

No! For a second Sophie wishes she could throw herself into the fire, to help it burn a little higher, a little brighter, for a little longer.

But the catwalk has already stopped rattling and shaking, and there is no longer any dancing light reflected in the clouds. Voices float up from the crowd that has gathered at the base of the cone, and the sound of someone weeping.

"It sang itself to death," says Sophie, voice quavering.

"Star-mad, like Mr. Brown," murmurs Elijah.

"No, not like him!" Sophie pulls away from Elijah so abruptly that she stumbles, but quickly catches herself. "The fire's kin to the stars — isn't that so? The fire thought so. But no man was ever no star's kin. That fiddler, he's just a fool, but the fire... "

"The fire's left us with a bigger mess than the fiddler will, if he ever gives in completely to the stars' call." Sophie follows Elijah's gaze and sees that the glass leaning against the cone has grown dark, has taken on a smoky shadow. And now she hears the foreman's angry voice, calling her and Elijah.

Marguerite Brule is comfortable now, her newborn baby, a boy, asleep on her breast. Catherine Walcott condescended to be here for the birth, too; she has helped little Marie put Peter and Paul to bed while Anna was helping Marguerite with the delivery. The three women have been alternating sips of tea and quince brandy, but Marguerite is drifting toward sleep, and Anna and Catherine soon will lie down too, or so Anna is thinking, when Marguerite's eyes fly open.

"Henry's not returned yet," she says, sitting up.

"Won't he stay with one of the boys in town?" asks Anna.

"No, no. He boasts he's the man of the house when his father's away, now that Luke's working with the boatmen. Before he left, he put his hand on my shoulder, just like his father does, and said he'd see the other rescuers home, do a final circle of Hunter Pond, and return."

Hunter Pond. Anna thinks of Henry walking along its frozen margin, in the company of the stars, with Ezra fiddling in their midst.... She stands up abruptly.

"I'll bring him home," she says.

The world of human warmth disappears like a candle flame blown out when Anna steps back outside and pulls the door shut behind her. Her eye is caught by another star streaking across the frozen sky. Is it heading to the pond? *You're late,* thinks Anna. *But I won't be late. Not too late.* She walks quickly and doesn't look at the sky again.

Hunter Pond is at the top of a wooded hill. Into the woods Anna goes, up and up; the climb is steep in places, and she finds herself breathing more heavily, feeling almost warm. Then the ground levels, and white oaks give way to swamp maples, yellow birches, and high-bush blueberries, for it's boggy by the pond. All these are nothing but skeletons right now, of course.

At last Anna is pushing through the blueberry thickets and onto the snow-covered ice of Hunter Pond. The wide, flat expanse of it breaks the tangle of woods, and overhead, bright and undeniable, are the stars. Not just overhead: in front of her too, wheeling and spinning just above the ice and perhaps right on the ice—it's hard to tell—the stars are turning in a huge, spiraling dance. Anna can't bear to look at the brightness full on but can't bear not to try, and through watering eyes it seems as if each dazzling sphere might resolve into something like a person, but maybe it's only desire that makes it appear so.

And the singing. It's not deafening because it's not heard with the ears; it's heard in the blood and along the nerves and the tree of the lungs, and down each chiming vertebra of the back. Anna's body is a bell that the stars' song strikes, and to resonate is to run toward those shimmering beings, to run and feel one is flying, to fall into a current that is more wild than a snowmelt flood stream, stronger than the tides, and older than the moon.

But her ears do catch something, one line of this polyphonic song, reduced to mere music, skittering toward her across the ice like a stone skipping on the water. What part of her was frozen just now, and melts on hearing it? She looks over. It's coming from Fisherman's Island, which really is no more than a collection of granite boulders posses-sively embraced by the roots of an old white pine. There's something silhouetted against the radiance of the stars at the edge of the longest, flattest of the boulders; it's a thin smear of darkness. It's Ezra Brown, and he's fiddling. And that bundle beside him, is that Henry, leaning against Ezra's legs?

Anna lets the song current carry her across the ice and up to Fisherman's Island. Ezra's fiddling seems more full now that Anna's standing so near. She can hear the color of it—can the stars? Can they hear how he's added blueberries and pine needles to the melody?

She must collect her thoughts. Why has she come? To hear the song, of course, and to swim in its current, to dance. No, that's not why. Henry. She looks down at him, and he smiles sleepily up at her, then turns back to the scene on the pond. Anna sees him exhale, close his eyes, and adjust himself against Ezra's legs.

"Henry. Henry, don't go to sleep here. There's a bed for you at home for that. Come along with me now."

The words are little blots and interruptions in the song, and Anna hates herself for speaking and hates the task she's come to do, but she'll do it, all the same.

Henry doesn't open his eyes. "I want to hear the song. I'll come home when it's finished," he whispers.

126

Ezra doesn't speak at all, doesn't seem to notice Henry at his feet or Anna in front of him. The fiddle is racing now, speaking to the stars of autumn leaves.

Anna leans down and gathers Henry up in her arms. She staggers a bit at the weight of him and sucks her breath in at the coldness of his cheek against hers. There's hoarfrost in his eyelashes and he seems hardly to breathe.

"You should come too," Anna says, wondering if Ezra can even hear her. A small shake of the head tells her he can.

"You know how it will end, otherwise," she says.

"It ended thirteen years ago," he murmurs, eyes not leaving the pond, bow still dipping and rising on the fiddle. "Thirteen years, no promise that this night would ever come... you think I'll trade this night for an accumulation of more long and dusty years?"

"I'll come back when I've delivered Henry home," Anna says, to herself more than Ezra. Ezra doesn't answer.

"You! You're dismissed for dereliction of duty and for destruction of property. Do you have any idea — any idea? — how much this night's glass was worth? I've sent for Mr. Friedrich; he will see you imprisoned I'm sure. You had better just hope the furnace and cone are undamaged."

Sophie has never heard the foreman in such a rage. Martha and Harriet stand nearby with tearstained faces; they've been let go too for being away without leave, and Charlotte too for the plates of glass she knocked over when the cone began to shake. But most of the foreman's anger is reserved for Elijah. The force of his words has Sophie's heart drumming, though he has not turned on Sophie yet. Elijah just looks stunned.

"But sir," begins Molly, holding up one of the fragments of broken glass.

"Be quiet! I haven't asked you to speak."

Molly shrinks, but as she lowers her hand, the glass catches the light of the foreman's lantern. The smoky shadow that has laced itself into the feathers and spangles etched on its surface glints crimson and scarlet, ruby and cinnabar. As Molly sets it down, there are flashes of magenta and violet. Sophie gasps, and the foreman looks over. His eyebrows fly up and he reaches for the fragment. He turns it this way and that in the lantern light, and everyone can see the play of colors along the stars' patterns.

The foreman orders Molly and Sophie to bring down an unbroken plate, and by the time they return, Mr. Friedrich, the old Bohemian glass master who owns the Orion Glassworks, has arrived. He laughs and shakes his head when he sees the transformed glass.

"It seems," he says slowly to Elijah, in his accented English, "your mistake with the fire has a fortunate result. Our glass is already unique, and this batch is unique among our glass. You must speak with me further about what happened. We must investigate whether we can reproduce these conditions."

"Yes, sir," Elijah manages, and sends a quick, dazed look Sophie's way. She smiles back.

"This special batch of glass will more than compensate for the wasted coal and the broken plates," Mr. Friedrich continues, addressing the foreman now. "Let us forgive this night's missteps, provided everyone behaves as expected from now on."

The foreman nods curtly and directs the girls to start bringing down the rest of the glass. Something crunches under Sophie's boot; it's a fragment from one of the broken plates. Sophie picks it up, watches it sparkle wine red, royal purple, and tucks it away.

It takes longer than Anna expects to revive Henry, to warm his body and be sure his spirit is settled within, so that by the time he is tucked into bed with a sibling snuggled on each side and she once again stands beneath the dome of the sky, the world has inched closer to morning. The night is as deep and dark as ever, but Anna knows that in the east, the sun is creeping up toward the horizon from under the earth.

The stars' song has changed. There is a gentle melancholy to it now, like the recollection of an ancient sorrow. What sorrows do stars know? Anna can't imagine, but as she steps onto the lake's smooth surface, she feels that her bones know, and her blood knows. Her bones and her blood propel her closer to the stars' spiral dance, as close as she can come before tears from their brilliance make her stop, wipe a mitten across her eyes. Her tears on the mitten shine in the stars' light, salty diamonds.

Glorious and tragic as the song is, Anna feels a lack. It's a small thing, a lack of pine needles maybe, or a lack of blueberries. Her breath catches on its way to her lungs. She breaks from the dance and hurries toward Fisherman's Island, but sees no silhouette against the sky, hears no fiddle.

Ezra Brown is sitting with his back against the pine tree, facing the dance on the lake, his fiddle in his lap and the bow still in his right hand. Anna kneels down beside him. His body has become as hard and unyielding as the rock below; his face has been tattooed with the same feathers and whorls as the windows and glassware of Orion Falls.

Anna doesn't bother wiping her tears away now. *Now who will share the stars' songs with us, Mr. Brown? Not many of us dare to listen as you listened.*

She looks out at the pond, hears the stars echoing her own sorrow back to her in tones too alien to comprehend, and hates them for it.

"Did you even know? Did you even notice how much he loved you?" she shouts, but her voice is a thin thing that lands at the edge of the rocks of Fisherman's Island, useless.

And yet, remarkably, as if in answer, now she hears clear summer sunlight, leathery leaves, dusty berries, midnight blue, each stamped with a star at the bottom — Ezra's fiddle tune, transformed. Anna rushes back out onto the lake, coming as close to the stars as she is able, and spins round, arms outstretched — she can't embrace the stars, but she can embrace the air around them — and repeats, "You did know, you did know, you did know," laughing and crying both.

Then autumn leaves flutter into the song, and Anna stops her spinning, surprised, and sees that she can look at the stars directly now, can approach closer, and so she does, and she sees they're wavering, like flames viewed through thick, thick glass. And yet surely dawn is still hours away? The sky is still black. The multitude of stars up there are as bright as ever. But the stars here on the pond have shrunk to firefly size.

"Are you—are you dying?" asks Anna, horrified. *The price of knowing blueberries and autumn leaves?* Anna looks back over her shoulder at Ezra, looks up at the dome of the heavens, looks down the path she's traveled to come here. Who can help her?

One, two, three . . . five . . . seven, nine . . . the dancers fade to nothing. Up above, so distant, the stars' melody is changing, but its sadness lingers.

The resonance in Anna's bones has become shaking in her shoulders, arms, and legs, and her teeth are chattering. It's time to retreat to the human world. She can mourn among the living, and maybe, some other winter night... but she won't even think about that now. She takes just one liberty—a quick kiss bestowed on Ezra's frozen cheek—and then it's back once again the way she came, the stars' chill song still hanging in the air.

Reunion

David Evans Katz

I never related this before, because anyone hearing the story would think me a liar or insane, but I am neither. I am, however, quite old, and have long since stopped caring about what other people think of me. Besides, anyone else who knew Alan Caldwell is now surely dead.

It all happened a very long time ago of course, and it started innocuously enough. I had recently returned from Capetown after several years as overseas representative of my family's business, and I was dining with Dickie Merton and a few other Willoughby classmates at the University Club. The dinner conversation revolved around our forthcoming twentieth class reunion and, after dinner, we retired to the smoking lounge and began compiling a list of fellows with whom we had lost touch and who needed to be tracked down. Someone mentioned Geoffrey Vickers, who had been killed in action, and we briefly digressed to debate how much the class treasury could afford to spend on an appropriate memorial.

After we sorted through the names on our list, we spent the next two hours drinking, smoking and recounting youthful escapades that were surely amusing only to those of us who experienced them. Toward the end of the evening, we became rather maudlin, and we awkwardly parted company intending to meet the following month to finalize our reunion plans.

As I made my way home, it occurred to me that no one had mentioned Alan Caldwell's name. He hadn't been one of the popular boys at school; in fact, he had been bullied unmercifully. I couldn't remember him having any friends except me — he had been my roommate, after all, and I'd felt honor-bound to defend him, even if he showed scant interest in defending himself. Poor Alan; he hated Willoughby, and he resented his parents for insisting he matriculate there.

I had spent holidays with Alan's family in the old days, and I remembered those times fondly. His mother was a gracious lady, and though his father treated Alan indifferently at best, he was kind to me. Alan's younger sister, Lavinia, was as charming and beautiful a creature as I had ever met, and I confess to having been deeply infatuated with her; I suspect she shared my feelings, but I was far too shy to pursue her. Sadly, I'd lost touch with the Caldwells within a few years after graduation. Nothing in particular caused the breach; as so often happens with schoolmates, we merely drifted apart. I had gone on to university, and then the war intervened, and after that, I was off to South Africa.

Nevertheless, I felt an obligation to my old chum, despite the fact that we hadn't corresponded in nearly two decades. I resolved to contact Alan and invite him to the reunion, but I didn't have his current address, so I sent a letter to his parents' home in Barrowdale. Within three days, however, the letter came back marked "Undeliverable."

I had some business up north the following week, so I decided to extend my trip a couple of days and visit the Caldwells. Barrowdale was a remote Yorkshire village where the Caldwell family had lived for generations. The drive was pleasant, especially at that time of year, when the orange, red and yellow leaves painted the landscape in autumnal beauty. Upon reaching Cheswick, the nearest market town to Barrowdale, I found that I no longer remembered the route—so much had changed since the war, especially the new motorways the government had mandated—and I drove about aimlessly seeking a familiar landmark. After half an hour of fruitless search, I gave it up and turned off at a petrol station to ask directions.

The attendant was a mere lad, and he offered little assistance. "I know of Burrows," he said. "That's about ten miles east, off the Willingham Road, but I never heard of Barrowdale."

He produced a motor-club road map from a rack by the cash register and spread it out on the counter, where he scanned it seeking the appropriate turn-off from the main route. After checking every place-name within a thirty-mile radius of Cheswick, he concluded that there was no such place as Barrowdale.

"Nonsense," I said. "I've been there before, many times. And I know it's nearby. Have you got the spelling right? It's B-a-r-r-o-w-d-a-l-e."

He frowned and said, "I been to school, Sir. I know how to spell."

Two men—one much older than me, and the other about my own age—appeared in the doorway leading to the garage. Although I hadn't noticed them before, they must have been standing there for some time. The older man furrowed his brows as he wiped the grease off his hands with a rag. "You won't find Barrowdale on that map," he said. "Ain't been listed on any map in more than a dozen years."

"Why is that?" I asked.

"'Cause nobody lives there no more."

"I don't understand."

"What's not to understand? No one lives there."

He eyed me suspiciously, as one would an interloper, but I refused to let him intimidate me. I stared back at him and asked, "Well then, where did they all go?"

"Well, they either died or moved away, didn't they? None of my business, and I can't see how it's yours, either."

I glared at him. "One of my oldest friends lived there, and I suppose I do have a right to ask."

The old man shrugged and said, "Can't have been much of a friend if he didn't tell you he'd moved away."

His hostility was palpable, and it seemed more than the typical country-folk aversion to outsiders. I refused to be cowed by his impertinence. "What of the town itself—the buildings—are they still there?"

He grimaced. "I couldn't say. Ain't been within miles of the place in a dog's age."

"Well, then, can you at least tell me how I might get there?" I wanted to see for myself; it was more than curiosity. I remembered my impression of Barrowdale from my school days—a typical rural hamlet with stone buildings and wooden cottages, farmers' fields and sheep meadows broken up by stone walls and tall hedgerows, and the

Caldwell estate high on a hill to the east overlooking the town. Alan, Lavinia and I had ridden over miles and miles of their father's property, cantering through the countryside.

The old man just gave me a stony gaze and shuffled back into the garage, but the other fellow spoke up at last and said, "Don't mind my father. He doesn't care for strangers."

"Will you direct me, then?"

The old man's son rubbed his chin with a calloused hand, apparently pondering my request. After a moment, he said, "There was never but a carriage lane in or out of Barrowdale, and the new motorway bypassed it, so there's no turn-off. I suppose you can drive north about ten miles to Warfield and double back on the old post-road. There aren't any signs, but it's a clear enough morning so you shouldn't have any trouble finding the carriage lane. Look for a stile on the right about seven miles south of Warfield; that'll take you in. But mind your tires — no one's tended the lane for many years now, so it's sure to be rough going."

I thanked him brusquely, feeling no obligation to reward his father's rudeness with courtesy.

It took me another forty minutes to find the stile marking the carriage lane to Barrowdale, and I saw that the man from the petrol station had given me an accurate description of the place — the lane was terribly rutted and overgrown from disuse; clearly no one had driven it in years. The hedgerows on either side were overgrown and crowding in, making it difficult to see around the curves, but I had no fear of oncoming traffic. At last, after a couple of miles, I came upon something familiar — a faded wooden sign that read, simply, "Barrowdale."

Around the next bend, I spotted the village itself and slowed my car to a crawl. From a distance, it looked normal, but as I got closer, I could see that it was no longer the pretty little hamlet I remembered. The adjoining fields had gone fallow and were choked with weeds. The buildings were shuttered, and all the signs on the business establishments were faded and peeling. In fact, there was an absence of sound and color — a pallor seemed to have descended on the place that suggested emptiness more than anything the old man back in

Cheswick could have described. But for a few broken roof tiles that had fallen to the ground, nothing littered the cobblestone street. Indeed, there was nothing at all—no people, no dogs or cats, no bleating sheep in the distant meadows, no birds—to disturb Barrowdale's grave-like quietude.

I looked up behind the steeple of the old stone church at the head of the green and saw the Caldwell mansion on the hillside beyond, stark and gray against the morning sky. I found the dirt road by the churchyard that led up to the house, and I drove along it slowly, carefully negotiating the many ruts that cratered the surface. I came to a set of wrought-iron gates—they were open, at least—and I passed onto the driveway and up to the house where I stopped the car under the *porte-cochère*. I sat there for a long time, debating whether I should bother getting out to knock on the door.

Unlike the rest of the town, the house itself looked well maintained, but it, too, had an air of abandonment. I noticed that there were no power lines connected to the house, and it occurred to me that I hadn't seen any utility poles along the carriage road, either. Rural electrification had always been a problem in this part of the country.

As I stared at the front door, I determined at last to forget this foolishness and leave. Wherever Alan Caldwell was—if he were anywhere at all—it was not likely this desolate place. I depressed the clutch and shifted into first gear, but as I started forward, I braked suddenly and stalled the car. There in the driveway ahead stood my old friend, staring at me through the windshield.

He said, quietly, but loud enough for me to hear, "What do you want here?"

I reached through the driver's side window to wave and said, "Alan, is that you? It's me, Dennis Tremaine." I leaned my head out so he could get a better look at me, and I at him. He was older—as was I, of course—but he looked haggard and unhealthy, like a man only inches away from death.

Rather than smile at me in warm recognition, he merely grunted and said, "Well, Dennis, it's been long enough since I've seen you. What is it you want?"

"I've come to find you," I said.

"I didn't know I was lost."

I smiled, trying to soften his attitude. "The class is having a reunion, and, well, we all missed you."

He ambled closer to the car and, with little emotion in his voice, said, "'All,' you say? I hardly think so, Dennis. The Willoughby boys never had much use for me."

I looked down sheepishly, acknowledging the truth of his statement. Then I smiled at him again and said, "*I* missed you, at any rate. It's been so long. I mean—"

Alan seemed to relax a little. He said, "You can come in if you like. Seeing as you came all this way, it would be unkind of me to turn you away."

I got out of the car and offered my hand to him. That small gesture softened him, and he smiled at last and shook my hand.

"I wrote to you about the reunion," I said. "But the letter came back."

"There's no post office here anymore."

"I see. Is your family here still?"

"Yes, of course they are. Where else would they be?"

"It's just that, well, the town—never mind. Is Lavinia here, too, then?"

"Yes. I expect you'll see her when we go in."

My heart raced at the thought of seeing Lavinia again after all these years. Although I had remained a bachelor, it was probably too much to expect that Lavinia hadn't married.

Alan turned and led me up to the front door and into the house. It was almost as I remembered it—spacious and elegant, yet decidedly a relic of bygone times. In fact, nothing seemed to have changed since I had last visited, except, perhaps, the air. It was cold and musty, and not nearly as inviting as it used to be.

"My parents and sister are likely in the morning room," he said.

I followed Alan through the great hall and down the gallery toward the east side of the house. He slid open a set of pocket doors and ushered me inside, where I saw Mr. and Mrs. Caldwell sitting on a settee by the window drinking coffee, and Lavinia standing by a writing desk in the corner perusing a book. The hearth was unlit, and the room was chilly, but not uncomfortable. Mr. and Mrs. Caldwell looked just as I remembered them, though older of course, and Lavinia had grown from a pretty adolescent into a beautiful young woman. She was so beautiful, in fact, that I found myself averting my eyes so I would not be caught staring.

Alan said, "You remember Dennis Tremaine from my school days. He's dropped in for a visit."

All three of them smiled broadly. Mr. Caldwell arose and came over, shaking my hand and clapping me on the shoulder. "Good to see you, lad. It's been such a long time."

"Yes, Sir," I said. "It's good to see you again, too." I recovered from my surprise and walked to the settee where I leaned over and took Mrs. Caldwell's hand. She pulled me closer and leaned up to kiss me on the cheek.

"How wonderful that you came, Dennis," she said. "We so seldom have visitors."

"I'm happy to see you again, too, Mrs. Caldwell."

Lavinia didn't wait for me to come to her. She closed her book on the desk and glided over, almost in a single fluid motion, and gave me a hug that, to my utter delight, felt more than sisterly.

Her smile was radiant. She said, softly, "You cannot imagine how much I've missed you." Then, more to her parents and Alan than to me, she said, "Dennis is staying for dinner, of course, aren't you?"

"Well—"

Mr. Caldwell said, "Of course you are, dear boy. We shall have a celebration of your homecoming."

Alan looked uncomfortable, but before he could object, and before I could respond, Lavinia said, "And you'll spend the night as well. We simply can't have you driving about these terrible roads after dark."

I was overwhelmed. "Of course I'll stay," I said.

Alan didn't frown exactly, but his face registered disapproval. In deference to my friend's obvious discomfort, I was about to make an excuse for changing my mind—a suddenly remembered appointment—when Alan said, "Come on then, we'll get your things from the car and I'll show you to the guest room."

Alan left me to settle into a suite on the second floor of the west wing of the house, where I changed my clothes and went to the adjoining lavatory to freshen myself. The facilities were unchanged from what I had remembered as a schoolboy — with no electric power, the plumbing was fed by a complicated lever-driven screw-pump in an outbuilding that raised the water from an outside well through a conduit into a large cistern on the roof, which then fed the kitchen and lavatories by gravity. If one wanted hot water to bathe, the servants would heat it on the stove downstairs and carry it up in buckets. But I hadn't seen any servants, which only piqued my curiosity about why the town had been abandoned and why the Caldwells remained behind living in such isolation.

I filled the basin, but I recoiled almost at once. The water had a distinctly pungent odor to it. Nonetheless, I washed my hands and face, and brushed my teeth.

When I returned to the morning room, I discovered that only Lavinia had remained behind. She said, "Alan is tending to some chores, and Mother and Father are making arrangements for dinner. I thought you and I might take a stroll around the grounds and get reacquainted. I packed a picnic lunch for us."

"I remember that we used to ride. Do you still keep horses?"

"Oh no," she said. "Not for years and years. Come on then, a ramble will be just as good."

She led the way out though a pair of French doors and onto a stone terrace. From there, we began a leisurely pace toward the woods east of the house.

"Shall we walk into town?" I suggested.

Lavinia shook her head. "I don't think so. There really isn't anything to see there."

For the next half hour or so, we walked along an old bridle path through the woods, making small talk and getting reacquainted. She wasn't shy about asking why I had never married, and I explained, simply, that I had never met the right woman. Since it seemed fair territory, I asked her the same question, and she blushed.

"If you must know," she said, "you were always my ideal."

I, too, blushed, as much from embarrassment as from sheer delight at hearing her say it. After an awkward silence, I confessed my long ago infatuation with her; she smiled sweetly and enfolded her arm in mine and we continued walking. We came upon a meadow overlooking the town, and, from our distant vantage point, it looked almost normal. I asked Lavinia why the town had been abandoned.

"I suppose it was the economic conditions before the war," she explained. "It was a difficult time for everyone around here, especially the tenant farmers and the journeymen laborers. People just left."

There was something about her tone of voice that didn't ring true, but I chose not to question her further on the subject. We spent a magnificent day together, and I admit that I hadn't felt as happy in many years.

By the time we returned to the house, it was well past tea and almost time for cocktails. I went up to my room and changed for dinner, returning to the great hall where the hearth had been lit and a tray of drinks was set out. Lavinia was resplendent in a close-fitting midnight-blue dress that accentuated her figure; Mr. and Mrs. Caldwell were dressed formally, too, but Alan, who remained his dour self and stood alone in a corner of the room, was coatless, wearing only an open-collar shirt and what appeared to be the same casual trousers in which I had first seen him. Even in the dim candlelight, I could see that he hadn't shaved.

Everyone else already had their drinks, and Mr. Caldwell held up a siphon bottle and offered me a whiskey and soda. I was about to accept, when I recalled the bitter smell of the local water, so I said, "Neat, if you don't mind." Mr. Caldwell obliged, and we toasted to renewing old friendships.

Dinner was served family style – I noted again the absence of servants in the house. As warm as I felt toward Lavinia and her parents (Alan remained somewhat aloof throughout dinner), I found the meal itself less than pleasing. The main course was ragout of lamb, and though I was ordinarily fond of lamb, the sauce was unpleasant so I ate reluctantly and very little. Lavinia and her parents didn't seem to notice or care about my lack of appetite, but I observed that Alan didn't eat at all. Fortunately, Mr. Caldwell produced a rare Burgundy from his cellar that more than compensated for the stew.

We retired to the drawing room after dinner, where Mr. Caldwell treated me to a sixty-year-old tawny port. Lavinia sat close by me on the sofa, and once again Alan retreated to a corner of the room and abstained from conversation. After several glasses of port, my head became a little fuzzy and I felt flush — I wasn't accustomed to drinking in such quantities — so I made my excuses and retired to my room.

I did not sleep well. Either the meal or the wine hadn't agreed with me, I suppose, for I couldn't get beyond that stage of sleep in which tumultuous dreams kept me on the verge of wakefulness all night long. When morning came at last, I had a miserable headache, an upset stomach and a mild fever.

I dressed and packed, considering all the while asking Lavinia to return with me to the city. This isolated environment was no fit place for someone so vivacious. I felt confident she would agree, but I worried nonetheless that Alan and his parents would resent me for asking her. As I made my way downstairs with my suitcase, I rehearsed in my mind what to say.

Much to my surprise, Lavinia was waiting for me at the landing. She rushed up to me and wrapped her arms around my waist. "Darling," she said, "please don't go right away. I want you to stay here with me. It's so unfair of you to come back into our lives like this and leave so abruptly."

I looked deeply into her eyes and, despite feeling ill, I managed to say, "I must return to the city, but I want you to come with me. A beautiful girl like you shouldn't be cooped up in this mausoleum."

"Oh, but I couldn't. My place is here, with my parents."

"Alan is here. They won't want for company."

She shook her head and said, "You don't understand. Alan doesn't stay here. He only came because of you."

I gave her a puzzled look. "But Alan was here when I arrived. He couldn't have known I was coming. What do you mean?"

Before she could respond, Alan stepped out of the shadows behind the stairway. He inserted himself between Lavinia and me and, folding his arm around my shoulder, he guided me toward the front

140

door. He said to Lavinia, "Dennis must go, my dear. You know that." Then he turned to me and said, "I can't say I'm glad you came, but I am glad to have seen you again."

Alan's remark was decidedly strange, but I let it go. Instead, I asked him if he would attend the reunion, and, perhaps, bring Lavinia along.

Alan said, "Please give my regrets to the class, but I will be unable to attend."

Lavinia scowled at her brother and looked away.

"But your parents — I'd like to thank them for their hospitality and say goodbye."

Alan shook his head. "There's no need. They're still upstairs. I'll convey your thanks when they come down."

It was clear that I was no longer welcome, and I assumed that my advances toward Lavinia were the reason.

"I apologize, Alan. Perhaps I was being too forward with Lavinia. I should have spoken to you and your father about my intentions."

He gave me a weak smile and said, "It's all right, Dennis. There's no harm done. I'm sure you meant well."

I kissed Lavinia goodbye. She brushed a tear from her eye and turned away without saying anything. Then Alan walked me to my car and hefted my suitcase into the back seat. "Have a safe journey home," he said.

As I drove back through the emptiness of Barrowdale and along the carriage lane toward the post-road, I tried to sort through my experiences of the previous day and evening. I pondered Alan's odd behavior but I couldn't grasp its meaning. Soon, I stopped thinking about it altogether because I began feeling more and more ill. My headache was worse, my fever was higher, and my stomach was no longer merely upset — it was now violently nauseated. When I reached the post-road, I pulled over to the side, got out of the car and vomited. Then, I felt my knees buckle and I collapsed.

The following three days were lost to me. I awoke in a hospital bed in Warfield. I was told that a passing motorist had stopped to help me and had brought me there, where I was diagnosed with nonspecific food poisoning. I thought of the lamb ragout and hoped that the Caldwells hadn't been affected the same way; considering their absolute isolation, medical attention would be difficult to come by.

I lingered in the hospital for another two days, and, following my recovery, I drove back to the city, still thinking of Lavinia and planning my return to Barrowdale. Despite Alan's objections—and I could think of no valid reason why he should object—I wanted to marry Lavinia. I was certain she would agree, and that her parents would be pleased to have me as a son-in-law.

That evening, I went to the University Club for dinner and encountered Dickie Merton in the Grille Room.

He greeted me heartily. "Glad to see you back and feeling better, Dennis. I heard you were in the hospital up north."

"Yes. Thank you," I said. "It was merely a case of food poisoning. Nothing to worry about, really."

I told Dickie that I had visited Alan Caldwell, and related the fact that he wouldn't be attending our reunion.

"Now that's a good joke," he said.

His remark baffled me. "Whatever do you mean?"

Dickie grinned and said, "I just think it's funny you said Caldwell won't be attending the reunion, that's all."

"But why would you find that so amusing?"

"It's the way you said it, I suppose. I hardly think the governors of Wilmington would let him out for the weekend, even for a school reunion."

Wilmington was a hospital for the criminally insane; it was a notorious place where only the most dangerous and deranged killers were confined.

"What are you talking about? I just saw him and his family only last week at his home in Barrowdale."

Dickie laughed. "Well I doubt that," he said. "Caldwell's been locked up at Wilmington in maximum security for years. You can look it up in the archives of the *Times* if you want. The Capetown papers might not have covered it, but I should think someone back home would have written you about what happened."

I was exasperated. "Dickie—what are you talking about?"

142

"The Barrowdale killings, of course! It seems that our old school chum went round the bend. It turns out he was psychotic — what they call a 'true schizophrenic' — a real case of multiple personalities. Very rare."

"But what did he do?"

Dickie shook his head sadly. "He poisoned the well at his house and killed his entire family — servants too. And that's not all. The poison was extremely powerful; it leeched into the aquifer and affected the wells in the whole area. Almost everyone in Barrowdale, including the livestock, got sick or died."

I was almost too stunned to reply. Finally, I stammered, "When — when did you say this happened?"

"Oh more than a decade ago, I think. You can look it up at the library. They have all the back issues of the *Times*."

I did look it up, just to make sure that Dickie Merton wasn't playing a practical joke on me. It was all true, of course.

Oñate beta

William Doonan

I. Oñate

Diego de Oñate dreamed about the comet again, a blistering fire-ball that cut through the afternoon glare and landed with a crunch in the middle of the plaza, on top of the fountain dedicated to Simon Far-rier, the wealthy American who had paid for it. The impact shattered church windows but the only other adverse effect was the unexpected resurrection of the dead who began issuing forth from their graves to eat the living.

Always the same dream.

There weren't really any graves nearby anyway, Oñate reassured himself. The dead would have to face the long walk from the cemetery or hitch a ride into town.

A mature man, Oñate had grown comfortable with a lifestyle that held napping sacred. This afternoon he had settled down on the porch for just a quick rest, and were it not for the comet, he might have slept well into the evening. And that wouldn't do. Plans had been made to meet his friend Milos Constantinos for dinner and he still had his businesses to attend. All this meant that he was now in a hurry.

He cursed the hard luck that some years back left him flush with cash, and cursed his ex-wife Lucy, who urged him to buy what was probably the only late model Audi sedan in all of Central America. The car brought him nearly three months of dripping envy from all who knew him, but had since sat motionless in front of the house, lacking some vital part that no local mechanic could identify. You should have bought a Toyota, Lucy suggested one afternoon, bring-ing her closer to a violent end than Oñate was comfortable admitting.

Rushing through the narrow streets of Pocos, Oñate passed a cantina just as Rocio Vasquez stumbled out, already considerably drunk.

"Do you know how long I've been drinking here, Diego?" he asked.

"About a hundred years," Oñate said, moving along the edge of the sidewalk.

"One hundred and fifty three years." Friends began pulling him back inside. "That's a long time."

"It is," Oñate agreed, moving along. He turned a corner and nearly collided with a funeral procession. Men and women climbed solemnly onto a bus as the coffin was loaded on top.

"The Rivera boy," confided the driver, a man Oñate had known since childhood. "So young."

"Tomasito?" said Oñate, taken aback. "He was in the store just days ago renting a movie. *Pirates of the Caribbean II*, if memory serves." And he had not yet returned it.

"Felipe not Tomasito," the driver corrected. "He and Tito Remedios and the Perez girl were up in the hills poking through the Indian burials, looking for gold. Supposedly they found a little statue of a man with the head and wings of a bird."

Oñate frowned

"And in the process of digging it up, Felipe fell into the open tomb, hitting his head on a stone pillar. They had been drinking quite a lot."

"And the statue?"

"It remains unclear. Tito Remedios claims it disappeared, but that's not likely. Such a thing would be worth something."

"I should imagine so," Oñate said. "It has been a long time since the last one was found." With the coffin lashed down and the last of the passengers boarded, the driver waved his goodbye, and Oñate made a quick path to his ice cream store.

II. Oñate Flashback

A younger, trimmer, fitter Diego de Oñate reached deeply into the sink to find the last of the spoons. Year after countless year he had traveled here to Elizabeth, New Jersey to spend a few months bussing tables and washing dishes at the Prometheus Diner. There was so little work back home once the harvest was in.

The Constantinos family, first Simon, then his son Simon, several more Simons, and finally young Theo, made him welcome, regaling him with tales of their homeland while suggesting procedures for more efficient dish scrubbing. Oñate developed a love of things Greek and read four books on the history and culture.

"You have to meet my cousin Milos," said Theo Constantinos, leaning over the sink, his arms wet with suds. "He told me he's had his eye on you these past years."

"As much as I admire your culture," Oñate answered, scraping the remnants of a kebab into the garbage bin, "I remain committed to a heterosexual lifestyle."

Theo shook his head. "No, no. He wants to talk to you about something else, about the little gold pieces."

"I don't have any more."

"No? Even back at home?"

"No. And it was wrong of me to sell that one to that fellow, the Colonel. I would never do it again. I needed the money, you see. The other time was different. I gave the statue to your grandfather when he was in the hospital. He was always kind to me and he was very sick."

Theo nodded. "He wore it on a chain, never took it off. He moved back to Crete shortly after. In fact I got a postcard from him last week. He said he rode a donkey to Church."

"Not surprising. He was a vigorous man."

"Not many men make it to their hundredth birthday party."

"Not many." Oñate wiped his hands and stole a bit of baklava from the platter on top of the refrigerator.

"That was twenty-two years ago," Theo said. "Do you like cheese?"

Oñate nodded.

"That's good. My cousin also likes cheese."

―

Milos Constantinos pressed himself into the booth. "I have a home in Crete," he said. "I manufacture cheese which I sell to Turks. It's not very good cheese but they buy it."

"That must be very nice for you," Oñate said.

"Also, I teach classes at the college in Athens."

"That must also be very nice for you."

"I teach about antiquities, about archaeology. I once participated in the excavation of a Roman cemetery in Palestine. So very many skeletons."

Oñate leaned back into the booth.

"When you dig the Indian graves," Constantinos asked, "do you find skeletons?"

Oñate crossed his arms, then his legs. "It's not legal to dig up Indian graves."

Constantinos said nothing.

Oñate frowned. "But if you were to do so, you wouldn't find any skeletons."

"I thought not."

"The ground soil is such that the skeletons are not preserved. The archaeologists say as much."

"I'm sure." Constantinos chuckled.

Oñate leaned in closer. "You think they're lying?"

"No. They don't know what they've gotten into."

"And what's that?"

"I think," Constantinos began, choosing his words, "I think that it is possible not to die."

Oñate looked out the window, watching as a pigeon picked at the remains of a melon.

"Some years back you gave something to my grandfather. It shares certain properties with some relics that turn up from time to time. I'm a member of a group that studies these relics."

"I don't have any more of them," Oñate said.

"I'm told that you sold one once, long ago. That means you had at least two. You could maybe turn up a third."

"No."

"How old are you, Diego?"

Oñate fussed with his coffee. "I think about forty. I'm not sure. There are no records."

"But there are," Constantinos replied. "I've done some research. There are records from the mission at Solano where you went to school as a young man. Do you remember the Sisters of Piety? They taught you to write and read in Spanish, though it was not your native language."

"A little," he said, reaching back into his memory. "They were kind."

"The mission was closed in 1698," said Constantinos. "You're quite old. Could we maybe become friends?"

Oñate frowned. "I'll be going home soon."

"If I wrote you letters, would you respond?"

"I might," he said, "if I had a moment from time to time. I'm a busy man."

III. Oñate's Six Happy Flavors

'Now With Ten Flavors,' read the small aluminum sign below the larger plastic one. When Oñate's Six Happy Flavors first opened its doors, ice cream was a novelty in Pocos. Truth be told, only four flavors were commercially available: chocolate, vanilla, strawberry, and guava. But Oñate had improvised, mixing to create strawberry-guava and chocolate-guava, which tasted very bad.

"I'll have a small chocolate cone," he called to Mildred Caravagio as he pressed into the store. It was his usual greeting. Mildred was ancient. Tall and solid. She licked the scoop as he made his way behind the counter to the small office where he kept his cigarettes and the fax. "Use the other scoop, please."

"Hana is looking for you," said Mildred. "She says there is a problem at the video store."

Oñate winced. He was newly suspicious about Mildred, certain that she often forgot to charge for sprinkles. But these feelings were overshadowed by his love for Hana Mora, the manager of his movie rental store.

"Did you hear about Felipe Rivera?" he asked, inspecting the cone that Mildred handed him. "Apparently he hit his head on a tomb pillar and died."

"So sad," said Mildred, shaking her head. "So sad."

"I can be thankful at least that the accident didn't happen on one of my fields. If it had, the Rivera family would probably sue me, like the family in Out of Africa who sued the Kikuyus when the coffee plantation failed."

Mildred scowled. "Nobody sued the Kikuyus. The plantation failed due to climatic issues, largely altitude. Blixen was no help."

"Maybe it was Out of Africa II, the one with Van Damme. He came back with a vengeance."

"There's no such movie, Diego."

"I read that it was in the making."

Mildred shook her head. "Hana tells me you have a visitor coming," she said, helping herself to one of his cigarettes, "the man who asks too many questions."

"He is my friend," Oñate said. Against his better judgment he had corresponded regularly with Constantinos over the years. But the phone call last night announcing the visit surprised him. Other than the time and place of their planned meeting, nothing more was revealed.

"Friend or no friend," Mildred told him firmly, "be careful what you say to him. He's not from here. Now go see Hana. She was upset."

Oñate paused by the door. "When was the last time someone in Pocos died?"

Mildred pulled hard on the cigarette and exhaled slowly, the smoke forming a blue plume above her hair net. She sat heavily, plumping down on the vinyl couch. "It was awhile back, wasn't it? Most of the young people leave."

Outside, a cat chased a little duck across the lane.

"Rocio Vasquez," she said finally. "About four years ago. He walked in front of the tourist bus, drunk as all daylight. We buried him on the hilltop."

Oñate nodded. "I saw him this morning."

Mildred frowned. She took a pen from the desk and used it to scratch her behind. "I did too. He came in for a cone. Had no money but I gave him one for old times."

Oñate finished his cone and made quick time through the plaza, admiring the neon sign that beckoned him and hopefully others, a sign that was visible even through the church windows. Oñate beta, it read.

Times had been tough ever since Donato's DVDs began offering family entertainment in the newer format, and Oñate was slow to respond. His program of converting all the betamax tapes to VHS was completed just as DVDs rendered them obsolete. Now Hana ordered all the little discs she could get her hands on, and they were getting by.

Hana Mora, her back to the door, ran an optical scanner over the DVDs that arrived with the morning mail, adding their titles to the database.

"You complete me," Oñate said, standing at the counter.

Hana turned. "I'm glad you're here."

He smiled, remembered kissing a little high-ticket girl way back when, behind the palisade near the river, before the Spanish came. "You're glad I'm here?"

"Yeah, I need to pee," she said, moving quickly.

Don Efren Cuevas was pushed through the door by his little son who came for Shrek II.

"Nothing goes with a movie like popcorn." Oñate smiled

"Just the movie," said Cuevas as the boy produced the plastic case. "We have fruit at home."

"It's quite uplifting," Oñate said as he wrote out the slip. "Truly an inspiration that the people of France can still have hope after all history has inflicted upon them."

Silence. The boy looked up in horror.

"I don't think it's about that," said Cuevas.

Oñate turned the plastic case over to read the liner. He frowned. "Perhaps I was thinking of another film. My memory is not what it was."

"We have a little problem," Hana said when the customers left.

"Tell me the new lesbian movies arrived today."

She shook her head. "But we got fourteen copies of Lion King and six of the sequel. I didn't even know there was a sequel."

"I enjoyed it. He might look like a beast but he has a heart of gold."

"The problem that I mentioned is this, there was an error made, and I made it. I checked the invoice to confirm. Apparently I ordered six copies of Transformers II. They arrived today."

Oñate braced himself on the counter to keep from falling. "We'll be ruined."

"It's not that bad."

He stared at the ceiling and held up a fist. "Only Steven Segal can save us now. He must make more movies."

"I feel a need to repent."

"Perhaps if we made love," he suggested but she ignored him as was her custom.

IV. Oñate's Bag of Indian Gold

Get Oñate sugared up with ice cream and he's inevitably going to start thinking about his ex-wife Lucy who left him many years ago to live with the Toyota salesman. The first time he saw Lucy, the Statue of Liberty came to mind. Like that famous New Jersey landmark, she was cold and beautiful and had places inside you were forbidden to go.

A city girl from the capital; he met her at a dance. There were little pink cakes and a band and Lucy was the most beautiful thing he had ever seen. Oñate drank a cold cerveza and a beaker of that Black Label Scotch. He told himself that he was as beautiful and as worthy as any of God's fauna, and asked her to dance, then later to marry him.

Lucy brought him years of sheer joy before unceremoniously morphing into something different, something who spent her days drinking wine with her friends, and sleeping with him only when quite drunk, which was blessedly often.

"Tell me about this," Lucy scowled one day just before the end, just as the rains came. She held up a tiny gold statue. It was a little man with the head and wings of a bird. "I found it in a drawer."

"It was in a bag behind the washing machine," he answered, reaching for it.

"No," she said, pulling away. "I want to know where you got it."

"From the hills. From the burials in the hills. Years ago we sometimes found them there."

"It's magic," she said. "You know that."

"No."

"My grandfather had one. He bought it from a Negro woman who told fortunes. He'd been sick. The nuns told him he wouldn't live to see the trolleys that mules would pull through the streets of the capital."

Oñate closed his eyes.

"He got better. You have more of these," Lucy said.

"I have a few."

"You have more than a few. I found the bag. There were three in it."

"Three is a few."

"I'm going to be leaving you, Diego," she said.

He stared at her.

"I feel like we've been together forever."

"That's bad?" he asked, not entirely surprised, not entirely overcome.

"Yes," she said. "It's too long."

When his first wife left him long ago, she left dancing, taking two jars of corn liquor from the shed behind his pole house, promising that he and his neighbors would be spared. When the Quetzal scouts came from across the hills, Oñate shot one through the leg with a fat drippy dart and was clubbed senseless as his roof burned.

"You can't take the gold," he scowled. "You can take the car or the couch or the little TV, not the big TV. And you can't take the gold."

"I'm sorry." Lucy stared at herself in the mirror. "I need to take them, for me and for Peter and his daughter."

"Peter?"

"Peter Montoya, the man who sells the Toyota cars. We're leaving together."

Oñate dashed for the laundry room. He pushed aside the washer but the bag was gone. "You can't have them," he shouted, running back into the bedroom. "You have to give them back."

Lucy took his face in her hands. "Are you crying?"

"No."

"Do you want me to die, Diego?"

"No," he said softly, touching her hair. "No, not ever."

He watched from the porch as she left, walking quickly past the broken down Audi. His neighbor was feeding a baby parrot on the front lawn. It was a messy job involving a big spoon and goopy oatmeal for which the baby parrot was too eager.

"I'll think of it all tomorrow," Oñate said, "at Tara. I can stand it then. Tomorrow. I'll think of some way to get her back. After all, tomorrow is another day."

"What's that from?" the neighbor asked.

Oñate scratched his bottom. "English Patient, I think."

"Are you drunk?"

"No."

"Wife leaving you?"

He nodded.

"That's really too bad. She's hot."

V. Oñate's Friend Milos Constantinos

They puffed thin cigars on the veranda at the Hotel Jardin. They ate chicken with squash and nice beans, drank Schnapps, and toasted the new moon.

"Show me the tomb," Constantinos suggested for the third time.

"No," Oñate said again.

"Why not?"

"Because I'm too old to be climbing around the hills. And because there's no gold there anymore."

"You're sure?"

"Yes. Why did you come here? Why now?"

Constantinos ordered another round of Schnapps from the hostess. "I got a call from someone in my antiquities group," he said. "We had some information that someone found a new burial with a statue in it. They sent me to meet with him, but I have not yet been able to. A boy died, as you know. And as such, the statue seems not to be for sale."

Oñate shook his head. "They can't sell it to you now," he said.

"And you know why, don't you?"

Oñate nodded. "They'll need it to bring him back."

"That's right," Constantinos said. "I'm old, Diego. I'll be eighty next week. I've got some kind of tendonitis that gets in the way of my golf. I've also got a photo of you and my grandfather in Times Square the night Taft was elected."

"Do I look good in it?"

"You look OK but you didn't smile."

"Maybe I was sad."

"Maybe. I want to see the tomb, Diego. Just to see it. They'll have to take him there to bring him back. I want to see them bring him back."

Oñate downed his Schnapps, wincing in agony. "No."

"Listen," Constantinos said. "You're my friend and I love you, but you're going to bring me up that hill to meet those boys or I'll kill you."

Oñate frowned his way into a gentle smile, allowed himself a rare moment of lucidity. "I might be quite hard to kill, Milos."

Later, they took in the night air, walking a circuit around the plaza, making their way to Six Happy Flavors. Oñate unlocked the door, locked it behind them, and double dipped two chocolate cones.

"He's not from here," called Mildred Caravagio from the dark, from the little office where Oñate kept his cigarettes and the fax. "Bad enough you let Lucy walk away with what she did. You can't be giving him anything."

Constantinos sat deeply into a plastic chair and licked at his cone. "Would that be Mildred speaking?"

Oñate handed him one of the cones.

"Sister Mildred?" Constantinos continued. "Sister Mildred from the mission that Friar Pedro de Oñate founded in 1670? You bore the Friar two children, both of whom died in infancy. You were very young. How did you come by your little statue?"

In the dark, Oñate reached for the sprinkles, sprinkled them on his cone, saw the flicker of the match as Mildred lit one of his cigarettes and moved into the front room.

"The Viceroy sent a few soldiers to defend the mission," she began, walking slowly toward Constantinos. "But they ran away the night the warriors came. There were about forty of them. Most of their people were already dead from the smallpox and they were hungry, you see. They killed the Friar when he told them to go back to the hills. They left the children alone but they drank all the wine and tied the lambs together to take with them.

"They brought the nuns into the rectory," she continued, pulling deeply on the cigarette, sitting herself across from Constantinos. "There were only three of us, and they were many. Afterwards, one of them seemed sorry. He put a bit of leather around my neck, a bit of leather with a little gold statue hanging from it. He said it would keep me safe. Then they left. They even took the cask of olive oil that the Viceroy sent. I was particularly sad about that. I'm not sure why."

Constantinos sat motionless, ice cream dripping onto his hand.

"How do you like that, fat boy?" Mildred asked, damping her cigarette in his cone. "Now I'll have to kill you with the ice cream scoop."

"No," said Oñate firmly. "There'll be no scoop killing. He's done nothing wrong."

Mildred turned to face him. "Don't take him into the hills, Diego."

"He only wants to meet with the boys. That's all."

"It's meant to be a secret," she growled. "That's why it works."

"She's right," said Constantinos, his voice a shaken whisper. "It is meant to be a secret, but that's not why it works."

They turned to him, said nothing.

"I saw someone try it once in Pakistan. It was a little girl, a dead girl, maybe eleven years old. She stood up and walked around for a moment before laying back down. It didn't work. I just want to see it," he said. "Then I'll leave."

156

VI. Oñate's Coffee Field Near the Tomb

Pale butterflies tussled among the bright red heliconias and the pointy ginger flowers. Above them, olive-throated parakeets gurgled and chirped while the little tree frogs slept. Lush fields of coffee blanketed the visible world, and beyond them, the peaks of twin volcanoes held vigil. They were quiet today.

Constantinos cut into a wheel of goat cheese while Oñate cut slices from a sausage. They had been climbing most of the morning, and stopped to take a break under a low palm.   The rain was not far off and the air had grown chilly.

"There are thousands of statues in the museum in the capital," Oñate said, "thousands."

"All fakes," Constantinos answered. "A secret cooperative of artisans makes them. And there never were thousands," he said, making a little sandwich. "At most there were a few hundred real ones. The government sold them in the 1940s. Why do you think, Diego, that this is the only country in Central America with universal health care, no significant external debt, and outstanding dental hygiene?"

Oñate pulled the cork from a bottle of wine and filled two plastic cups. "The prosperity is due to an emphasis on sustainable development, ecotourism, and a stable democracy."

"No, it is not," Constantinos said. "It is not. Every now and then a farmer would bring one of the statues to some people who got in touch with our people. They were mostly fakes, but not always. The real ones were sent to a house in Cyprus where they were sold by silent auction. Or to another house in Damascus where Saudis bid wildly. All of this was controlled by one man, a man known as the Colonel. He claims to have worked as an aide to Stonewall Jackson during the American Civil War. Do you know what the greatest commodity in the world is now, Diego?"

Oñate smiled knowingly. "Information. The computer superhighway that connects us all."

"Immortality," Constantinos told him. "The last piece sold for more than 700 million dollars. You were there that night at the mission at Solano when the warriors came, weren't you?"

Oñate took a piece of cheese and wrapped it in a corn tortilla. "I think so," he said. "I mean I know so, but I can only just glimpse it from time to time. I was hiding in the barn. I was older than the other children but the sisters kept me because I was strong and could cut wood."

"And when the warriors came?"

"They didn't find me. I felt ashamed afterwards. The Friar had even given me his name."

Cresting the hilltop where Oñate planted his first banana trees long ago, they pushed on as the rain clouds gathered.

"They might not even be there?"

"They'll be there."

"Why not Mexican gold?" Oñate asked, cutting the brush with his machete. "Is that no good?"

"No," said Constantinos, puffing along behind him.

"Why not?"

"I don't know?"

"Greek gold?"

"No."

"Why?"

"I don't know. Nobody knows."

"It's just gold from here then?"

"No," said Constantinos, leaning against a coconut palm to catch his breath. "No, not just from here. Some Etruscan gold has similar properties, but there's not much of it. Did you see the National Geographic about the archaeologist who found the tombs outside Perugia?"

Oñate shook his head.

"They ran him out of the country when the workers dug up a coin with his face on it. He had come back for more. The Vatican confiscated it all."

"Tragic."

"And some Syrian pieces," Constantinos continued, pushing forward. "And one or two hat pins from Babylon. Some cups from Zambia have been reported, but it's not yet been verified. Nothing from

Egypt or Rome or China or Peru. Every few months the Colonel gets wind of a new piece, but nothing real has turned up in decades, not here, not anywhere in the world, until just now."

"We're almost there," Oñate said as the rain came.

Constantinos pulled an umbrella from his backpack, opened it, and watched as it sailed off like a kite over the coffee fields.

"The Riveras have a shed below the ridge," Oñate called. "They own the field below. We can rest there; the rains rarely last an hour."

They moved quickly through the rain and through the low door into the shed. Inside Tito Remedios lay in a hammock with the Perez girl beside him. Her eyes were red from crying. Felipe Rivera leaned against the wall, his face and Sunday suit creased with mud. The rain fell like pebbles on the tin roof.

"Can I at least see it?" Constantinos asked.

Felipe Rivera blinked but said nothing. He coughed up a little cloud of dust. Tito Remedios gave the matter a measure of consideration before holding up the little gold statue, a man with the head and wings of a bird

Oñate leaned in close to smell it.

"How did he die?" Constantinos asked, staring at the boy.

"He caught his leg on a vine," Tito said, climbing out of the hammock. "Then he fell back, cracking his head. We had been drinking, but no matter. He's going to be fine." He clapped Felipe on the back, bringing up another little dust cloud.

"No, he's not going to be fine," Constantinos said. He handed the statue to Oñate. "It's not real, is it?"

Oñate smelled it again and touched it to his tongue. "No."

Constantinos shook his head. "So you contacted the Colonel and told him you had located a new tomb with a new statue. You dug around but you didn't find anything, so you got a fake. Then this boy died."

The Perez girl began to cry.

"He'll be fine," Tito said, clapping Felipe's shoulder. "He's walking around, isn't he? He followed us here. He just needs a little time to come back."

Constantinos shook his head. "There is a membrane between death and life, and like all membranes, it's permeable under the right conditions. You don't have the right conditions."

"He's right," Oñate said. "I remember that from Spiderman II."

"But he's alive," Tito insisted as the girl cried behind him.

Felipe Rivera blinked, poked out his tongue and drew it back.

"No he's not," said Constantinos. "He's dead. You've just got him animated a bit, probably something residual in the hills. It won't last more than a few hours."

Tito shook his head. "When I made the call, I was sure we had something. We've been digging in these hills for years," he said. "I think all the real ones are gone."

Oñate placed the palm of his hand on Felipe's forehead. It was damp and smelled like the dirt he used to dig from the Indian graves as a younger man. "We'll help you put him back," he said.

VII. Oñate beta

"So sad," he said, forcing the tears. He knew Hana would hold his hand if he cried, and when he did, she did.

"It must have been awful."

They were sitting on the bench by the fountain, the one the dream comet hit. Oñate buried his face in her hair. "We led Felipe back to the coffin and he just got in without a sound. I think he smiled but an ant crawled out of his nose so I looked away. His eyes were open when Tito nailed the top back on."

"How terrible," said Hana, stroking the side of his head. "Your friend left then?"

"Yes, he took the bus. He said he was fairly sure there was no more Indian gold here. I promised I would write if any turned up."

"At least I have mine," she said, reaching into her pocket and producing a tiny statue.

Oñate's eyes opened wide. He touched it, then smelled it. "Where did you get it?"

"You gave it to me. You gave me yours also to hold onto. Remember that day you lost it and we had to tear apart the store to find it?"

"The video store?"

160

Hana chuckled. "We'll it wasn't a video store back then. I think we were selling mostly axe heads and nails and those iron mills that replaced the grinding stones."

"And I was young and pretty," he added.

"No. You were old and ugly even back then."

"Where's mine, then?"

"In the bathroom. You spend a lot of time there."

He smiled and took her slender hands in his. "You know Hana, you truly are the wind between my wings."

"You can't say anything original," she scolded, pulling away.

"I can," he said. "I just like metaphors."

Watching her scurry across the plaza back to the store, Oñate sighed. The lamps around the fountain flickered on, and a moment later, other lamps lit the street corners and the little kiosk with the public telephones. He stood up and walked slowly towards the ice cream store to have a cone before bed.

"You've got company," Mildred said as he walked in. She frowned deeply and flicked her ash into the new cherry vanilla. Oñate turned to the man at the table in the back. It was the Colonel.

"Señor Oñate," he said quietly.

"Of all the ice cream joints in the world, you had to have a double cone in mine." Oñate made his way slowly across the room and sat across from him. "I remember you."

"You sold me something once," the Colonel said, "years back in New Jersey. I remember it like it was yesterday. I was reading the daily paper. The Confederate Army had just been rousted at Vicksburg."

"I remember," said Oñate. "The Union soldiers wore blue. You wore gray. And you had a green hat. You looked like a homo."

"I'm Simon Farrier," the man said, extending his hand.

Oñate stared at him.

"I sent Constantinos. He has some expertise in this area, but in the end I had to come to see for myself. I was informed that a new statue had turned up, though it appears I was misled."

"You've been a regret of mine."

"At least I tried to give back to the community. I built the fountain, and I paid for the new Ministry of Justice building."

"Liar," Mildred shouted from behind the counter. "The Ministry of Justice was paid for with municipal bonds."

Farrier shrugged. "Well, I paid for the fountain. And I've invested a lot more in these parts, paying local boys to dig around."

"And now it's time for the killing," said Mildred, moving fast, brandishing the big scoop.

Farrier jumped out of the way as the scoop slammed down into the table, cutting a neat cuticle of green plastic. He hid behind Oñate as Mildred raised the scoop and made her second approach.

"We've discussed this," Oñate scolded.

Mildred fumed, her great bosoms rising and falling with each breath. "You have to have more respect, Diego," she said. "You can't be telling people things."

Oñate nodded. "Leave here tonight," he told Farrier. "Don't ever come back. There's no more here."

Farrier nodded, his eyes still fixed on Mildred and the scoop. "I'll take the morning bus."

"You'll take the night taxi," Oñate told him. "Back to the capital and then get on a plane. Take up fishing or play the crosswords but don't come back here. There's nothing more for you here."

Farrier nodded. "I had the idea of traveling to Peru next."

"Won't be worth your while," Oñate said. "But you know, there's no place like Zambia."

"Diego," Mildred yelled, smacking him in the head with the scoop.

"Zambia." Farrier said the word slowly, drawing it out as if it were a piece of dental floss lodged between molars. "Good bye then, Señor Oñate."

"You've been a fool," Mildred scolded, much later, scraping residual ice from the cooler.

"I'm an old man, the world must expect that of me. What do you say we close up early tonight? We haven't had any customers since you tried to kill the man."

She put down the scoop and shut the glass window over the cooler. "You do make me angry at times."

"Mildred," Oñate began, "I think this is the beginning of a beautiful..."

"Stop it, Diego," she said, turning off the lights, leaving them in darkness. "I don't think I can manage to hear it again."

"Fine," he said, taking her by the hand. "Let's go watch Lion King."

Issue 27

July 2011

A Comfortable Chair

Tom Smith

1.

Morris Small stooped to the day's mail with little expectation. However exceptional the day, the usual bills and advertising would have been pushed through the brass slot onto the entry floor. Since he himself worked at the layout of commercial catalogs, the absurdity did occasionally occur of his receiving a piece of his own design, a kind of ouroboros event, a futility of junk.

The mail in hand, Morris resumed his upright posture and made way for his life-long friend Morton to pass. Both gentlemen wore mourning, returning as they were from the cemetery were they had witnessed the burial of Marian Small, wife of Morris, victim of stroke at fifty-eight.

Friend Morton strode across the threshold. In the middle of the foyer, he turned with arms extended. "You certainly won't want to stay on alone in this huge place."

Morris shrugged and laid the mail aside. Guests were expected and he and Morton were already not alone in the house. As they stood together within the embrace of the lofty stairway, Morris could hear the commotion of caterers at work in the rooms beyond: kitchen, pantry, dining room, parlor, library. He was glad of the catering. He could largely ignore the incipient gathering of business associates, women friends of Marian's several clubs: garden, bridge, birdwatchers; Marian's kin.

Morris himself belonged to no clubs and had no kin. He had been an only child as had been both his parents, now long deceased. Morton had been Morris' one friend since kindergarten. Besides Morton, there was Martin, Morris' son, only child of the Smalls' marriage. Martin would have been named Morton, to honor the friendship, but Marian would not allow it. "It reeks of mortality. Martin I can live with. A songbird."

Martin would arrive momentarily from parking the limousine. He had been good enough to undertake the driving, saving his father from having to ride beside the unctuous director. Morris was happy, he thought, to have the young man, a film editor living in California, with him. For at least eight years now a continent had separated them. A companionship of years, camping trips, baseball games, had been reduced to telephone conversations. Now he was home to honor his mother's demise. A stranger. They had met at the airport. In the physical presence, Morris found himself thinking: children are so strange, one is never really with them; then they grow up. And adults, though one has lived with them all their lives, are strangers. Still he loved his son. As he had always loved his friend. Strangers though they were.

And here came Martin now, closing the great front door behind him and striding toward them to embrace his father and shake the hand of his father's friend. "My father's only friend. Strange and wonderful!"

Morton sighed. "Ah, I remember the two of us, boys together, and here he is an old widower, with a grown son. Thirty something, are you, Marty? So, me? Am I an old man then?"

Morris chuckled, "You were an old man in kindergarten."

"And you! Some kind of elf. Your feet never touched the ground, flowers sprang up in your wake."

Morris blushed and protested. "Still, I'm glad someone remembers that child. I can't quite myself. Even when I dream of my childhood, everyone's there but me."

Martin embraced his father again even as Morton commented, "I ask myself... I often ask myself. Whatever happened to that boy."

"He grew up."

"Did he? I wonder."

Chimes rang. One of the catering crew acted the butler. The mourners, celebrants, arrived in small groups. Morris and Martin stood side by side to receive them.

Morton dismissed himself, wandering away into the front parlor.

The first object to capture the man's attention was the stuffed wing chair, Marian's chair, with its arms, high back, sheltering wings; its rose-garden upholstery. He felt drawn to its promised comfort; yet squeamish of invading the dead woman's precinct. They had never really liked each other, had maintained cordiality only for Morris' sake. It would be impudence to sit on her now as the first clutch of guests spilled into the room.

Beyond Marion's chair, a wide arch led into the dining room where a buffet had been spread. Morton helped himself to some refreshment, then set about the business of distributing his attentions among the company. Gradually the room filled. Later, as he introduced himself to a young woman who, he gathered, was some sort of cousin to Marian, several times removed, he observed Morris enter the room and pause just inside the door. Several persons in the group closest to the bereaved addressed their sympathies, but he appeared not to listen, distracted, it seemed, by the sight of Marian's wing chair across the room.

Morris was thinking it curious that, though every other seat in the room had been taken, Marian's chair remained vacant. At the moment, he observed David Chesterfield, a young man from the firm, drop cautiously into the seat only to stand again almost immediately and hurry away. Morris felt drawn to the chair himself, at the same time sensing how strange it would be to usurp the station always left vacant for the woman of the house.

Martin entered the room and stood close behind his father. "I'm going to have some food. Can I get something for you?"

"I think not. Not just now."

The young man made his way toward the table, stopping frequently as individual mourners sought his attention. Morris, still standing just inside the room, watched his son's progress; watched him fill a plate, look about for someplace to settle, approach the yawning wing chair, stand before it, turn away to lose himself among the guests.

Then Morris perceived that friend Morton also observed Martin. Morton seemed amused. Indeed, he laughed as their eyes met. The two friends wound toward each other through the crowd. They met near the center of the room. "Dead or not," Morton observed, "Marian still exerts control of her domain."

"What do you mean?"

"Her throne of course. The most comfortable seat in the room and no one will sit in it."

"Well, why don't you sit in it?"

"Not on my life."

"Then I shall sit in it."

"Please, don't."

Morris, startled by his friend's sudden seriousness, said, "Don't be silly." He started toward the chair. But he walked on past it to the table. Morton caught up and the two men, side by side, but not continuing the conversation, filled their plates.

Their filled plates in hand, Morris and Morton stood beside the coffee urn and contemplated the empty chair. From behind, Morris thought it like an ancient castle in a wood, an old fortress all covered over with a rose thicket. Then, even as Morton cleared his throat, Morris spoke. "The chair is empty. That's the point, isn't it."

And Morton replied. "I don't mean to be spooky, but is it empty? Or does a ghostly presence keep it? Maybe I do mean to be spooky."

Morris now ventured to surprise, perhaps challenge, his friend. "I know you never liked Marian, but now is not the time to speak ill of her."

"Not liked her? What can you mean?"

"Come now. No more than she liked you. It was nice of you both to accommodate my feelings, but did you really think I was fooled?"

"But, Morris, you're quite..."

"No, I'm not quite. And it really is no matter." Morris peered intently into his friend's eyes, as if to reassure him.

Morton lowered his gaze. "It was only that I worried about you."

"That I should have been a serious artist instead of a commercial hack?"

Morton shrugged. Morris, considering the occasion, stopped himself from laughing. In a half-whisper, he observed, "We ought to have a big hug right now, but we'd have our food all over us."

Then they rocked, awkward and embarassed by affection still after fifty years of friendship. Morton hemmed. Morris said, "Meanwhile, I should circulate."

The October afternoon drifted like a water-logged raft down a weary river. For a long while the three men lost trace of one another among the crowd. Shadows lengthened. Darkness rose. Lamps were lighted. At last, Morris found himself watching his son climb the stairs toward his bedroom. He held his friend's hand, meanwhile, in both his own. Morton the last to leave. Even the caterers had finished the cleaning up and driven away in two vans.

"I hope you'll take some days off from work. Rest. Consider your future. I'm completely available if you need company."

"I've no idea. I might prefer work. Distraction. I'll decide in the morning."

A little flurry of departure ensued. Then Morris found himself alone. The foyer, all wood and stone, gaped. Cheerless and pretentious thought Morris, though he had never thought about it before. He proceeded to wander the downstairs rooms, checking locks, turning out lights.

Only one small lamp glowed dimly just inside the door to the front parlor. As his eyes swept the room, Morris imagined furtive movements, startled glances, a little animal world lurking inside the rose thicket imagery of Marian's wing chair. The illusion was momentary and worried him only briefly: tired eyes, a weary mind. Yet, when he switched off the lamp, in the darkened room, the chair filled with a gray fog.

Morris stared a moment, then withdrew, drawing the pocket doors closed between himself and the vision. "I'm seeing a ghost," he said to himself. "Hardly surprising." He sighed. "Goodnight, Marian." He turned away and started toward the stairs.

2.

Martin stayed on through the week and weekend. Father and son, however, hardly saw each other except at breakfasts.

On the Sunday morning, Morris descended the stairs and crossed the foyer to part the livingroom doors and look in on Marian's chair. It had been his first gesture each day and, though he laughed at himself, he could not resist. He then turned toward the breakfast room at the back of the house overlooking the elaborate, but not very well-kept garden. The garden had been his affair, a passion for many years, but the passion waned.

Morris entered the room to find his son already seated, eggs and toast and coffee before him.

Martin rose to greet his father. "Kept a plate warm for you in the kitchen. Help yourself to coffee. Be right back."

When Martin returned, he found his father staring vacantly out the French doors. He placed the breakfast plate before the man who still seemed unaware of his return. "Your garden makes a very lovely autumn display. Especially the tree hydrangeas."

"My garden? Yes, I suppose it is. Though, if I remember right, it was your mother's idea I should take up gardening. We were still new in the house. You were still in the womb."

"Well, anyway, it looks lovely."

"From this distance. You can't see the neglect. I seemed to lose interest this season."

"Perhaps the weather's been discouraging. Everyone's complained of the humidity."

"Ah, people do talk about the weather. And who have you been talking to?"

"Oh, a lot of old friends from high school. And college. Some showed up at the wake. Some I've bothered to look up."

Morris attended to his plate, pushing the eggs about, rearranging the toast. "So you've filled your days with old acquaintance?"

"Can't help feeling curious about how people have turned out. What they're doing with their lives." Martin studied his father's averted face.

The older man continued to worry his food. At last he said only, "Really?"

Martin laughed, partly amused to observe his father's puzzlement that anyone might be interested in other people, partly saddened imagining the old man's solitude. He ventured. "Can't help wondering what you might do with your life. Now that you're free."

"Free?" Morris looked almost alarmed.

"Not responsible for anyone but yourself."

"Responsible." The echo flattened the word, hollowed it, drained it of any meaning.

Martin persisted. "For instance, are you going to stay on here? Big house. Big garden. Big expense. You might retire to a smaller place."

"Retire?"

"I suppose your old enough. Mother was fifty-eight."

"I'm fifty-five. Your mother didn't like anyone to know I was the younger."

Martin suppressed the little irritation he felt at this revelation, continuing instead his theme. "People do take early retirement at fifty-five these days. Pursue their own real interests."

"My own real interests? My own real interests. And what do you suppose they might be?"

"Certainly not the advertising business. I mean it's paid for everything over the years. My education. Mother's... er, comforts. But it's never really meant anything to you. Maybe you'd like to devote yourself to serious painting."

"Serious painting!" This time the echo whooped and hooted, brought the father to his feet, laughing and prancing, quite startling the son. "Aha! Ah! I gather Morton's had your ear. Good old Morton."

Martin felt pressed into his chair. He breathed deeply, reached for his cup, sipped. Morris, meanwhile, fell silent, turned to gaze out at the garden, suggested, "I've always had Morton to worry about me. You needn't take that on."

Returning cup to saucer, Martin decided to risk a suspicion. "You two could move in together now, share some smaller place. Nothing to prevent you. I think you should."

Morris turned from the view to study his son. "What are you suggesting?"

"Well, Morton has never married."

"That's true. Morton, I guess, is not interested in women. We've never discussed it. I can recall only one remark he ever made about women: they never put the seat up. Morton can be very funny."

Martin caught his father's eye and stared intently, as if to say out with it.

Morris smiled, a father's indulgence. "Yes, Morton has been in love with me since we were five. No, he's been in love with his fantasy about me. It's not a sexual thing. Morton is not a sexual being. He's like a caterpillar."

At this moment, A thud startled Morris from behind. Even as he turned he heard Martin exclaim, "A bird." The son jumped to his feet. Father and son stood together, their mutual gaze fixed upon the body of a goldfinch. It had flown against the glass of the French doors and lay, yellow and staring, on the slate floor of the patio. "Oh dear," said the father. "Yes," said the son.

3.

Martin was scheduled to return to California that same Sunday evening. Morton volunteered to drive them to the airport. He wished, if it did not constitute an intrusion, to partake of the seeing off. At the last moment, before passing through security, Martin embraced both his seniors, an unprecedented hug, firm and prolonged, that affected Morton and Morris each with a profound sense of his own mortality. This sense of impending fate perhaps accounted for the unusual silence that prevailed between them as they sped down the turnpike toward home. At last, Morris, finding the atmosphere oppressive, tuned in the radio to the classical music station. Haunting cadences from a flute filled the enshadowed vehicle.

"Strange, strange!" exclaimed Morton. "Do you recognize it?"

Morris settled into his seat, feeling adrift on the enchantment of the music. "It's familiar, but... "

"Debussy. *Afternoon of a Faun*."

"Oh, yes. I remember. *Portrait of Jennie*."

As they sat listening in the darkness and the brief, intrusive lights of passing traffic, the couple shared their silent reminiscence. They had first heard this music, budding adolescents, side by side in the flickering darkness of the movies, soundtrack to the fantasy film: Jennie materializing out of some past, disappearing into the haze of amorphous time, a spirit person of moonlight flesh. Morton asserted his friend was like that, a sort of elusive mist. "Please," had said Morris, "you're embarassing me."

The youths had, nevertheless, agreed that the music was seductive. Morton had written to a fan magazine to find out the composer and title. He had exclaimed his awe and satisfaction: "Faun, faun!"

Morris had protested. "I am not a faun. Or a jennie. What is a jennie anyway? Some kind of ass."

Morton had sighed then. He sighed now.

Less evocative music ensued. Eventually they pulled into the drive at the manse. Morton suggested his friend might want company. Morris agreed to a nightcap. Inside, he built a fire and poured two Bourbons. The couple settled to the comforting warmths of flames and alcohol.

"So you did take the week off from work."

"While Martin was home. Not that I saw much of him. All taken up with old friends."

"A very loving son though. An affectionate boy."

"Yes, I guess so."

The pair retreated again into recalling that last, almost desperate embrace. Morris felt again the warmth of the young body against his own. He was disturbed to find himself, in imagination, struggling to free himself, stifled.

"Surprisingly," observed Morton, then quickly sipped his drink, censoring his further thought.

But Morris acknowledged the unspoken. "Considering his frigid parent."

"Oh, I wouldn't say frigid."

"Something more moderate perhaps."

Morton nodded. "Speaking of work. I suppose you'll be back at it on the morrow."

"I expect so. Martin thinks I should retire. Sell the house and retire. To pursue my own real interests."

"Martin and Morton are of like minds."

"I have no real interests."

"You know what I think."

"I have no interests. Real or unreal."

The two turned again to their Bourbons. They studied the dancing fire. At last Morris chuckled. "The like mind of Martin thinks we are lovers. Or we ought to be. Ought to move in to a small space together."

"Does he indeed? And what do you think?

"I told him that's not what we're about. He seemed disappointed."

"The liberated mind! So intent on understanding everything. That anyone should be simply uninterested in sex--opposite sex, same sex, livestock-- is the last taboo."

"And a good laugh is so much better for you."

"A sweet boy nevertheless. And what about it? Should we live together?"

Morris seemed at a loss; to seek his answer on the ceiling, in the farther corners of the room, in the bottom of his empty glass. At last, casting a sidelong glance at his friend, he ventured, "I think I need to be alone."

"So call me, I won't call you." Morton rose from his chair.

Morris rose beside him. "Are you mad at me? Have I hurt your feelings?"

"Nonsense! But it's late. And I respect your need."

As Morton started toward the door, something else in the room caught his attention, a little flash of brilliance in the corner of his eye. He looked toward Marian's chair, squinting into the near darkness. "Never noticed that before." He crossed the room slowly. He peered into the inside left wing.

"What! What are you seeing?"

"Such a bright yellow bird! Has it always been there?"

"What?... Well! Of course it's always been there. I haven't suddenly taken up petit point."

"It's so fresh though. How have I missed it?"

"How indeed! But, you're right, it is late. I'll walk you to the door."

Morris managed the accompaniment without dismissive haste, but as soon as the door was closed behind his friend, he scurried back to the parlor, anxious to study the intrusive embroidery in private.

Perched among the deep reds and dark greens of the rose thicket, the yellow silk was so brilliant it was impossible to believe the creature had been there always and he had never noticed. And in the inconstant light of the fire, the black of the little round eye seemed to wink, as if the bird were alive, not the dead goldfinch that had crashed that same morning into glass. The man's knees threatened to fail him. He might have sunk into the chair's embrace.

"I'm seeing a ghost again," whispered Morris to the empty room as he backed away, backed into the foyer, closing the doors against his vision, leaving the fire, leaving the dirty glasses, leaving Marian's chair that seemed to rustle full of fairy breezes.

4.

The following morning, Morris woke abruptly at first light. He found himself sitting upright in his bed. His immediate thought was of the little yellow bird: the goldfinch dead upon the patio stone, the silken aura embroidered upon the left inside wing of Marian's wing chair. Birdwatcher though she may have been, that Marian should choose to haunt him in such small songbird form seemed. . .seemed what? Inappropriate. Unapt. An owl perhaps. A crow. No bird at all; nor any other creature. Marian was Marian. Dead or alive, she would never choose to be other than herself. He was allowing his grief (was it grief he felt; oppression?) to besiege his imagination.

But it was not hallucination. Morton had seen it also. Morton had seen it first. If it were real, it would be there still. If it be there still, then it must have been there always. Scarcely possible. Check it out, check it out.

Morris was halfway down the great stairs before he knew it. There he stopped. He was not, he told himself, afraid; neither, however, would he behave all a dither. He assumed a manly posture, commenced a measured step, a pace of normalcy. At the threshold, he was careful neither to hesitate nor hasten. He parted the doors. He stepped into the room. He strode across the floor.

The chair seemed to gape a welcome.

Standing before it, Morris experienced a vertigo, as if standing at the verge of a great chasm. He saw again, behind the rose embroidery, deep forest beneath a sheltering sky. He sensed the hidden presence of timid, or predatory, animal life. He shook himself free of this delusion.

He sought the silken image of the yellow bird. He might have gasped at what he found. Instead, he sighed, succumbing to a great hollow weariness that rose from within him. The bird was there, but now it was partly obscured behind leaf and bloom. Morris assured himself this had not been the case last night. The creature had stood foremost. He assured himself further that the image had not, before last night, been any part of the picture. But he was sure of nothing. This could not after all be happening.

Morris backed from the room. Closing the doors, he sought the breakfast room, stood close against the French doors. The dead bird was gone from the patio.

Some neighbor cat would have carted it away.

I've been too much cooped up in this house.

He would shower and dress quickly, catch breakfast at a diner, leash his imagination to his work.

5.

Morris allowed some days to pass in dogged adherence to the workaday schedule. He dined out in the evenings, went to the movies or, at home, watched television in the library. On the weekend he called his friend. They played golf, explored the nearby malls, kept themselves occupied. Morris confided he was thinking his son and friend right that he should sell the old white elephant. The friends studied the papers together to see what sort of quarters were available. Morris would want two bedrooms, Morton recommended, so that his son might visit. "And a studio."

"Yeah, right." Morris rolled his eyes and laughed.

Some weeks passed. A realtor was engaged to oversee the sale of the manse, the white elephant. A wooden notice staked the front lawn, ads appeared, couples were conducted about the premises. Meanwhile, Morris and Morton occupied evenings and weekends checking out a variety of rentals, apartments, flats, small houses. Morris found all quite grim. He began to consider small properties for sale. He could afford to buy even if the big house did not sell.

They were well into the new year, through the winter months and into spring's first burgeoning, when they came upon a small house in

178

the countryside, not too remote, a large barn behind. A small property of unmown grass and the promise of hollyhocks. It was the hollyhocks more than anything that won Morris' approval. Morton admired the barn: "An excellent work-space for a major painter."

It had happened, meanwhile, that Morris had, as his son and friend had suggested, retired... quit, in fact, his employment; in consequence of a tiff with his boss. Mr. Davenport had called him in one afternoon to criticize his recent work: desultory and unimaginative. Morris had snapped: "Geoffrey, this business is trash. How can you take it seriously!" Whereupon, Davenport had invited him to resign. In retrospect, Morris admitted to himself that his work had in truth suffered from his distracted mind, fretting obsessively about the queerness of Marian's chair, or his queer perceptions of it; then all this business of escaping the house. That's what it was really, this selling out: flight.

"At last, friend, you set forth upon a life of your own!" Morton arrived, even before the movers, at the new house where Morris awaited his furniture; arrived with gifts: an easel, paints, canvases, brushes, knives, a palette.

"Is this generosity or agression?" asked Morris.

The couple waited together for the van. Morris had tagged only those pieces of furniture he really needed. The rest could go for sale with the house. He felt somewhat unburdened; and it wasn't only Marian's chair he felt free of.

They strolled through the empty rooms of the small house, rather like a doll's house in its squareness. They carried Morton's gifts out to the barn, as swept and empty as the house.

"No promises! But maybe I will try painting again."

"You must."

"Morton, it's been years. Thirty years?"

They heard the van backing up the drive. They relaxed into laughter and small talk as they went to meet the movers. Convergence happened: the couple arriving at the front door just as the great truck came to a stop. Driver and rider dropped from the cab. "Morris Small?" asked the driver. He and his companion set immediately to opening the trailer.

Morris, groaning, took a step back, staggered almost. "Oh, God! That was not one of the tagged pieces."

Morton, even as he lay a hand upon his friend's shoulder, looked away. The movers shrugged, pointing at the bit of paper pinned to the back of Marian's chair. Morris paled, unsteady on his feet, muttering, "How could I have done that? Why would I do that?"

The movers, at a loss, awaited instruction. Morton studied the barn.

6.

Finally, Morton took charge, instructing the movers to set the offending chair aside ("We'll cope with that later.") and carry on with the rest of the furniture. He rescued a wooden desk-chair from the van, conducted his friend into the house, and sat him in an out-of-the-way corner.

Morris sagged. And allowed arrangements to unravel around him without his attention.

A week passed while Morris, having taken to his bed, seemed haunted, unresponsive, distracted. Morton stayed on in the second bedroom. "Friend," he inquired, delivering breakfast each morning on a tray, "It's old Morton. Do you know me?"

On the eighth morning, Morris answered. "Of course I know you. Do you know me?"

"I know nothing," exclaimed Morton, over-joyed.

7.

Life settled into new routines, a new idleness in a new house. "New to me, but an old house really." Morris liked the old farmhouse feeling about the place. His transported furniture, newly arranged, felt nicely unfamiliar. He liked living alone: Morton had returned to his own apartment.

Morris set about creating an environment for himself. He bought many gallon cans of paints, a variety of sunny yellows, dusky roses, blues; and set about painting each room. He loved living with the scent of fresh paint.

Then, one morning at breakfast, he realized he had finished. Each room was bright and all the furniture in place. He packed the several cans, their tops securely hammered, the drop cloths, the thoroughly cleaned brushes, into a large cardboard box. This he lifted, careful about his back, and carried to the barn.

It was by now mid-summer. Along the side of the house, on the way back to the barn, bloomed a profusion of hollyhocks: bright yellow, candy pink, blood red, and a blue purple, almost black. Morris stood awestruck, even with the heavy carton in his arms. Then, on his way back to the house, he saw the lawn was in serious need of mowing. After lunch, he would drive into town and buy himself a sit-down mower.

The following afternoon he sat astride his mower, stopped in the middle of the lawn, with half the grass mown and the other half astir in the breeze, stopped there to gaze again at the hollyhocks, tall, sunny, dusty somehow. They sang to him like sirens. They were certainly a subject. They wanted to live again: pigment and canvas. They would not take no for an answer. "Maybe I am an artist," said Morris. He seemed to be talking to the oak that over-arched the barn. He tore his mind loose of the idea, set about finishing the mowing.

But he was restless over his evening meal. He endured a sleepless night. In the morning, he could scarcely suffer the toaster. He sought the barn in a rush, averting his eyes from the flowers as if they would scold. There he found out the supplies that Morton had provided: the tubes of oils, brushes, palette and palette knife, the easel. He came to a standstill over the consideration whether to work outside, face to face with inspiration, or inside from passion "recollected in tranquility." He laughed at that naivety. He tried setting up on the lawn, but was overwhelmed; regathered his tools and carried all again inside. The idea of the hollyhocks, rather than the hollyhocks themselves, was almost bearable.

He sketched. And then he painted. He worked all day. And all the next day. And the next. On that third night, when he returned late to the house, the blinking light told him he had messages. While he poured himself a glass of milk, he listened to his son, who was sorry to have missed him but glad to know he was out and about; and to

Morton, who would try again and, meanwhile, Morris could call him at any time of day or night. Morris smiled as he pressed the button to erase the messages. He carried his milk upstairs, where a welcome bed awaited him. As if he were a kaleidoscope in some Brobdingnagian's grasp, his brain was a tumble of shapes and colors.

First light woke him. He shrugged into the clothes he had shed the night before. Thinking about the shave and shower he surely needed, he started down the stairs intending to brew coffee, but turned away from the kitchen and scuttled out to the barn, nodding to the clamorous hollyhocks as he passed.

Two small paintings awaited him side by side on the barn wall.

Morris stood, still now, even his brain falling quiet, and considered the work. At first he felt quite masterful, old master, impressed by the clarity of the image, the unmistakable hollyhocks, pink and yellow and green, solid against the brown wash behind them. But, the longer he gazed, the more dissatisfied he felt. The work was all wrong. But what was wrong about it?

The paintings were too small for what the hollyhocks were about. Not only too small. Too square. They should be taller than they were wide. Hollyhocks aspire. And why had he placed them against such darkness? Contrast.

Again, contrast was not their way. They were a soft light that shed illumination. So, it was not just the size and shape. The style was wrong. The edges were too solid, too defined. The colors were too flat: bright, but they didn't glow, didn't shimmer, didn't pour out of themselves into their setting. They were static. They needed the swift. busy brush strokes of the French Impressionists.

Morris turned away from his first paintings, dismissing them. He sought new canvases. Morton had thought of everything as Morton always did. Blank canvases of several shapes and sizes leaned upon one another in profusion. Morris extracted a rectangle, about three feet by two; extracted it almost thoughtlessly, his mind already busy with new techniques, new composition.

Another two days passed. Morris chortled, hummed and whistled, while the colors thickened, quickened the canvas. The blinking telephone messages increased. Morris no longer listened or erased.

Long after midnight, he crept into the house and tumbled onto the couch into an instant, untroubled sleep. But, in the mornings, his brain blazed. He couldn't be bothered with messages or breakfast. He was out.

In the barn, he was almost shattered to discover a new canvas finished. It would, at least, hold no more paint. A pretty, shimmering thing. . .Okay, but it wanted to be bolder, bolder, bigger. Much bigger.

The store of blank canvases was by now a sloven heap. Morris tore through the disorder. The largest, when he found it, was too small by far. Now that all had been dislodged, flung aside, Morris discovered the stacks had leaned against a large object covered by an old bedsheet, white but vaguely yellowing with age. An impulse seized Morris to hang the sheet on the wall. It would be a grand size for a grand painting.

He scooped the sheet free to discover Marian's wing chair.

"Damn," he said, vaguely distressed, impatient. He couldn't be bothered about that. Life called him to its brilliant task.

He tore about the great space, ducking into stalls and corners, dragging the sheet behind him, seeking the ladder he had purchased for his decorating. This he leaned against the vast back wall and, with a corner of the sheet and a hammer in one hand and some nails in his breast pocket, he climbed.

The sheet now stretched across the wall, Morris turned from the tubes of oils to the gallon cans of semi-gloss. These he pried open with a screwdriver. Then he hauled the ladder away from the wall, opened it, set it up about three feet away from his new surface at the center of its width. He seized a large brush, a half-full can of dusky rose, and climbed. Halfway up, he dipped the brush into the paint, lifted it out dripping, and flung the color onto the hanging linen.

He leaned away. He had created a large flower. Around it, diminishing splotches, offspring buds falling away as if from some centrifugal force off the mother bloom. He dipped the brush again and, with a sweeping motion, loosed more color, an arc of sundown blossoms. Then again, and yet again, higher up the ladder, lower. Then descending for another color. Green. He craved green. Then yellow. Blue. White.

Many trips climbing and descending. Sometimes pulling the ladder farther away, sometimes close up. Almost touching, to have the paint flow down the surface in stems and tendrils.

At last, there was no more. The cans were all empty. The sheet was a garden of colors, side by side and overlapping, a suggestive perspective, a density of blooms and buds, green stalks, blue shadows.

Morris drooped exhausted. He dragged Marian's old chair into the center of the room and dropped into its sanctum. His days of work all stood before him. The little square studies to his left. The larger rectangles to his right. In the center, the hanging sheet. Toward this, he leaned closer.

Was there? Who was there?

He was very tired. His eyes, so abused with the work, played tricks. Now there, in the lower left corner; now there, just right of center, was it a creature, an elf, a child hiding amongst the tangle?

Morris closed his eyes, inviting sleep. The garden of his imagination burned the inside of his lids; or his parents' garden remembered. He stood in his parents' garden calling: "Morris! Morris!" Oh, of course, the child was Morton. Morris hid: Seek me. Seek me in Neverland. The vision darkened. A blank.

Eyes open, Morris saw only the toil, the trials of a week or more. The child was nowhere in it. Not in the tidy little squares, the impressionist shimmer, the soiled bedsheet. He was, himself, nowhere in it, all acquired, derivative, a pointless dissolution: nowhere, nothing. Whatever happened to me? Did I never come out of hiding? He felt the wing chair grow around him, heard bird song, smelled roses, the woman's perfume. The thicket rose over him, drew him in to its asylum. Thorns teased his flesh. Shadows lengthened. Darkness rose.

The empty chair idled at the center of the empty room.

All in the Air

Allen Kesten

In a country whose borders seem unable to contain it, a Soprano stares at a pair of shoes in a nest of white tissue paper. After three separate attempts to match the aquamarine color of her gown, this pair comes closest but offends her nonetheless. Some failure of will by the shoe dyer to reach perfection, she thinks. Not the same beautiful moment between blue and green that is her gown. She has brought her favorite silver shoes to the concert hall as well, resigned to wearing them if need be. She has resigned herself to a great deal of late, indignities and snubs, for she is perceived by the National Council on the Arts to be part of the old guard: too independent and grandiose. And she has yet to officially declare herself for the ruling Party.

Her vocal warm up complete, she tucks a wisp of hair back into the elaborate style. Loud sobbing outside the dressing room door disturbs her concentration. Her assistant, a quiet, shadowy woman who knows little about music but everything about whims and how to service them, follows the Soprano's eyes and goes out to investigate.

The assistant slips back into the dressing room and reports that a member of the chorus is in tears because she has broken the heel of her only pair of shoes and now fears that she won't be able to perform. Her disappointment is made all the worse by the presence of so great a soloist.

Still in her robe, the Soprano lifts the dyed shoes in their tissue paper and carries them to the poor shoeless girl as if they are a bouquet of flowers. The young singer smiles as she reaches for the shoes, possessing them perhaps a little too eagerly.

Perhaps you are there, seated in the mezzanine or even in a box. You watch the gathering of orchestra and chorus on stage, and then the entrance of the conductor and soloists to warm applause. Everyone is in black except the Soprano in her aquamarine gown. But there among the sopranos of the chorus, you're surprised to see a pair of shoes peeking out from the hem of a black dress, the same color as the Soprano's gown, and you wonder: what strange talisman is this?

The conductor stands on the podium, and bows his head. In this moment, like a great exhale, the musicians seem to cast off everything but the music at hand. A requiem in the old style. Baton up and the sacred murmurings of the chorus begin. A spinning wheel is set in motion. Golden threads are flung into the air. After two choral passages, the Soprano enters. The voice is double-bedded, as if the solemnity and grace of the music isn't enough and needs an additional layer. It's a complex voice, with notes well landed and full of color, but you find it emotionally removed despite its gloriousness. The baritone's fragile high notes as he sings the despair inherent in mortality are, however, unbearably beautiful. As the requiem comes to its stirring close, the soprano floats brilliant top notes like silver kites above all the other musicians, and you are dazzled. Depending on your hunger for transcendence, you might even weep.

In the midst of the ovation, a young soldier comes toward the stage carrying a bouquet. His broad shoulders remind the Soprano of some officer in a romantic opera. She takes the proffered flowers into her arms and plays the role of coquette. A few loyal fans recognize the shift in bearing and cheer louder. Though curious about the card in his bouquet, she remains onstage with the other soloists and the conductor.

Backstage, before a curtain call, she quickly reads the card. The handwriting is as stiff as the soldier's uniform, but the note is not from him. It is an invitation from a Party official to join him for a late supper. "I want no part of *their* world," she tells her assistant as she hands off the card and bouquet. "I am not a political woman. Besides, he probably looks like a toad." Back on stage, the young man still standing below, the Soprano purses her lips and with an almost imperceptible shake of her head lets her answer be known. Flowers will not sweeten their recruitment efforts.

The Soprano sits by an open window and reads a review of the requiem. Her assistant stands by, anxious for word. A once friendly critic writes with hostility of the Soprano's mannerisms, her diction, even her gown. "Another one cowed," she pronounces. "Integrity fails and the papers are filled." A sudden gust of wind takes the curtain and blows it into her face. Her assistant rushes to her side and strokes the Soprano's cheek as the singer laughs.

A scarf wrapped around her throat to protect her voice, the Soprano continues her daily morning constitutionals, even as the city changes all around her. Like polluted air she has no choice but to breathe, patriotic anthems and speeches blare through the ubiquitous speakers the government has hung from streetlamps and buildings along the city's main avenues. Common citizens, as eager for the Party's approval as children courting favor from indifferent parents, sing along with nationalistic songs as they walk by her. They could at least sing in tune, she thinks.

One morning, a footbridge she has traversed a thousand times is nothing more than rubble, having collapsed from neglect during the night. She turns away and retraces her steps back home.

The Soprano's assistant answers the telephone and after a brief conversation reports another cancellation of another engagement. An opera production in which she was to star mere weeks from now. Her recording of the opera is considered one of the best by international critics. Perhaps you own it but don't play it anymore.

The Soprano turns to her practice pianist and asks him what recourse is there for her. "None in these times," he replies and tucks his hands under his legs. She looks around her apartment, rooms usually filled with flowers. Now one lone bouquet sags, dropping petals on the table in the foyer. "Why not sign their papers, become a member of their Party, and be done with it?" the pianist offers.

"I am not used to being bullied and will not accept it. Ask any conductor who has tried. What do these petty politicians know of art, my art? Have I asked to intrude in governance? No, for I am an artist, separated as it were from society so that my art may serve and enlighten it. Art will always outlast politics. Read your history and you will see this."

"But *artists* may not outlast politics," the pianist mutters. He has heard her little speech before. His hands return to the keys, but what are they to play now? The Soprano's opera role has vanished, a false pregnancy revealed.

And while the Soprano stares dumbstruck at the pianist's bowed head, across the city in a government office, a young singer in aquamarine shoes bows to an Assistant Deputy of the Arts Council. She has just signed her Party membership forms. She has told her friends in the chorus that signing pieces of paper means nothing. It's like joining a trade union, no more, she reasons. She just needs to sing, to pursue her art and this is the way for now.

Nonetheless, you are curious to know if her hand trembled when she signed, as if this would be enough to appease your moral concerns.

Piles of sheet music in her rooms. Alone, night after night, the Soprano walks about, patting them like the heads of orphans.

The Soprano reads that there is to be a loosening of restrictions on criticism. Officials are inviting critics to come into the open, for now the country is strong enough to benefit from their voices. "The soil is rich again, so let a thousand flowers of dissent bloom in the sun of the nation's glory." The Soprano thinks liberty has become a shell game but hopes for a change in her fortunes, critic by abstention that she is in the eyes of others. To illuminate the opera stage again. To tour, to record. Perhaps even to gain permission to leave the country. Dare she hope that her dreams may flower among the thousand blooms?

If you lived by M Square, you would see the dissenters who came forward, now dressed in prison garb, toiling in dirt, the occasional broken limb slowing their work. They are planting flowers in the design of the country's flag throughout the city. The perfume in the air is as strong as a narcotic. The Soprano nearly chokes on it whenever her windows are open and finally orders her assistant to keep them shut, no matter the weather.

Bees descend on the city, swarming the squares. They will sting you if try to pick a flower.

The Soprano is early for her final rehearsal with the orchestra. She sits on stage facing the empty hall. Behind her the musicians fill the chairs. There is little joking or laughter as in the old days. The conductor takes his place at the podium. He is an old friend of hers, a man who has supported her voice over the years with sympathetic accompaniment, as if he breathed with her. Perhaps there was an affair long ago: she is too discreet to say. Despite his rise with the Party's benediction, he has fought to keep her engaged for this concert. He looks up from his music and addresses the orchestra. "I have a brief announcement. The concert master has been detained. The nature of his activities is not for me to say. You, please take his place."

The Soprano turns around and watches the first row of violinists shift from their chairs over one. Some look at the conductor, imploring; others keep their eyes down. And no one says anything. The Soprano hopes that the new first violinist is up to the job. She liked the tone the other one produced during his important solo.

The Soprano's car slowly makes its way to the concert hall for the performance. Her assistant sits beside her in the back of the car, bottom lip quivering.

Some boys in uniform are standing by the stage door, looking in all directions. "Perhaps they have lost the parade they were marching in," the Soprano jokes upon exiting the car. "The government so big on parades of late. The thudding beat and bluster of marching songs, like great slabs of stone laid across the country, crushing the melodies of the past."

The Soprano's assistant noses around. The Chairman of the Arts Council is seated in the front row. "He scratches himself frequently, all about the arms and legs," she reports back to the Soprano.

"It is the prickly yearning for power that has him scratching like a dog. They say we will be at war by year's end, and he needs artists for the effort, like generals need artillery. Perhaps he has come to hear if my voice can help win a battle, if I am really worth all this effort to convert me to the cause."

As she finishes dressing, the musicians shuffle past her door and take their places on stage. The concert will feature four songs with orchestra most associated with the Soprano. She has sung them throughout career, even recorded them twice. She has sung them before many world leaders, never thinking about their policies, only the grandeur they added to the evenings.

After two orchestral pieces the Soprano takes the stage, repeating the aquamarine gown, a bow to her fading income. The applause is measured. She sings the first song in an imitation of her younger self: this made possible by her assured technique. But something happens in the second song. It feels to her as though her voice is a revving engine vainly trying to accelerate the orchestra, yet not really moving them forward at all. She stops watching the conductor's hands and looks into his eyes, the eyes of her old friend. *Is he about to cry?* An unfamiliar vibrato steals into her voice and then there is a faltering, a deflating of the voice, as she sings of disillusionment, of summers lost. She dare not reveal too much emotion for the conductor, the man, nor soften him further. She cannot undermine his purpose, for the Party requires steel of their stars.

She struggles to regain her composure during the instrumental introduction to the third song. Several bars of sweeping strings, her thumb tracing circles in her right palm, heat rising in her spine, and she is calmed. As she sings anew, you might well think it is dignity that colors her cheeks.

The new first violinist plays the solo with the simplicity and yearning of a folksong and she responds with an unadorned clarity of voice. She cherishes this: the collaboration and the fullness of the soul that comes of creating a performance with others. How will she live without this?

The assistant thinks back to a time when people waited for the Soprano in front of her home. Students, music lovers, people. Waited for her to appear, in a window, on the street. And if the Soprano did, they would cheer and her assistant would be nourished by their love even in the shadows where she dwelt.

Now the people avert their faces when they see the Soprano, if they recognize her at all. Ungrateful flowers disavowing the sun with a turn of their heads, the assistant thinks.

She tries to maintain the Soprano's way of life despite dwindling funds and the empty shops. She picks over wilted vegetables at the best of the markets, and then carefully counts out the money as the despondent grocer wraps her lot in newspapers that cheer on a war sure to come.

The Soprano walks down Avenue W, hungry, yet bloated from a diet of starchy food and cheap fats. Someone calls her name. It is odd to hear it, now that no one speaks to her any longer. *That used to be me*, is her only reaction.

A young woman touches her arm. Her hair is freshly set and her clothes are like petals around her. Something vaguely familiar about her eyes troubles the Soprano, nevertheless she follows the young woman up to her apartment, a cloud of excited babble around her.

Though small, everything about the rooms feels abundant. Flowers, cushions, drapes. "Let me get us something to eat and we'll continue our chat."

While the young woman fusses in the kitchen, the Soprano walks around, stopping at a glass case in the corner. Enshrined inside is a pair of blue-green satin shoes, dirty at the toes and heals, like precious stones dug from the earth. Now the old Soprano remembers the young woman. She has even heard her name mentioned as a rising star. A few minor roles sung in translation now that foreign languages productions are discouraged: soubrettes, feathers blown across the stage.

"I owe you so much," she declares, a tray in her hands. "The shoes were always so lucky for me. They gave me courage."

The singers sit on the sofa and sample the food on the tray. The Soprano is careful to maintain her poise despite her eagerness for the fresh fruit and lean meat. "The Party has been good to me," the young woman says as she puts down her plate.

"Don't you ever worry that it is your politics and not your talent that has won you success?" Her hunger sated, the Soprano's former boldness awakens.

The young singer dabs her mouth with her napkin, then looks over at the shoes as if to remind herself of her gratitude despite the Soprano's cutting words. "What use would it have been to not sign? Should I still sing in the chorus? Would I not still be sanctioned by them? Is a lowly fourth violinist any more pure when he takes his seat for not having signed? I sustain the people. There must be a soprano in the lead to serve the music."

The old Soprano reclines on the soft down cushions. Is the quality of youth rabid ambition instead of pride, she wonders briefly. And then she places a hand on her stomach and lets her body enjoy the sensation of having been well-fed.

The Soprano closes her eyes and listens to the radio in the young woman's apartment on Avenue W. She spends most of her days here now, coaching the young woman, feasting on food and music. And after a mere two weeks, already an important broadcast.

The Government is instituting a series of Saturday afternoon radio recitals. The programs will highlight singers that the Party wishes to promote as its new stars but will be devoid of political trappings. The old music, music without propaganda or jingoism will be performed. Even a few songs by foreign composers. Who wouldn't be tempted to listen?

Her protégé begins the first song tentatively, the voice clean but not fully open yet. That is natural, the Soprano knows. Nerves and the effort to find the sound with the piano, no matter how much the voice has been warmed.

But perhaps you would find the sheer purity of the young singer's voice enough, notes flying around your head as effortless as birds soaring, circling. And you would sigh, *oh comfort and joy.*

The second song is far better to the Soprano's ear. Notes well bound, legato much improved. But the phrasing, the color around the words, is still weak even after a thousand coached repetitions. Then in the third song, a moment of beauty, a line well sung and the heart of the poet expressed. "I gave that to her. That is my influence there." She toasts herself with raised glass and takes another sip of the young woman's liquor. "By this time next year, hers will be a voice and talent worthy of my coaching."

The Soprano's assistant walks home from the laundry where she has worked since her mistress had to let her go. She hides her hands in her coat pockets. They are so rough from the water and detergents, that they would snag the Soprano's gowns if ever comes a time when she is needed to handle them again.

On H Street, she stops in front of a book shop. The street is nearly deserted and the public loudspeakers are quiet today, so the pretty music coming from the shopkeeper's radio can be heard. Something about the singer's phrasing reminds the assistant of her mistress.

An announcer gently reminds the radio listeners that the program is made possible by the National Council on the Arts and the generous support of the Party. "A worthy voice," the Soprano repeats. How is it that she has given the Party what she withheld for so long? Her cooperation, indirect and tacit though it may be, is now clear to her. She puts down her drink and paces the room as the recital continues, her complicity like a shadow at her heels. She comes to a halt by the shrine to her shoes. She tilts the glass case back from the stand and takes the aquamarine treasures in hand, then drops them to the floor. Her worn cloth slippers pushed off, she slides into her former shoes. They are stretched out but wearable.

The young singer continues to sing on the radio, oblivious and jubilant, as if she didn't know or even suspect the truth about her benefactors. And to think, perhaps you would listen and enjoy her program, as if you didn't know the truth, couldn't see their guns at the ready, couldn't read their maps marked where the first bombs will fall, the invented enemy chosen.

But the Soprano is on the stairs and heading for the street. The reclaimed shoes undermine the steadiness of her steps but she hurries away just the same. The air outside smells excessively sweet. Prophetic promises she has sung come back to her. *For here we have no continuing city, but seek one to come.* She places a hand over her face, covering her mouth and nose. Perhaps to keep out the odor, perhaps to mute herself.

Bags

William Kamowski

Selby O'Faolain, "Sel" to his friends, family, and other listeners, was pretty much convinced that the common plastic grocery bag could be compressed in almost infinite numbers into an infinitesimal pocket of space. The physics of the matter was rather like the collapse of a universe into singularity, he would say. Only, he omitted in his simile the sequel to singularity — the expansion, the explosion, the Big Bang.

The storage bins in the basement were cramped with plastic grocery sacks stuffed into shoe boxes, corrugated cartons, coffee tins, and larger shopping bags from Kmart, Costco, Penney's. When his wife complained that she hadn't enough storage space for wine bottles and the wine she fermented, he would oblige: "I'll just compress the bags down to *four* shelves. No sense throwing them out; they'll be of use."

Scoutmaster for Troop 19, he knew the value of plastic sacks on camping trips. "They keep everything dry, clean, and organized."

As if to prove his theory of physics and demonstrate the principles of compactness in packing for a hike, he had just last weekend compressed 120 clear thin produce sacks into a Twinning's tea tin strapped shut with a muscular inch-wide rubber band.

"One hundred twenty into six cubic inches of space."

Twelve for each unimpressed Boy Scout.

His family was equally unimpressed by his physics, which seemed more fiction than science, and in any case, his physics didn't explain the rest of the collection in the basement: the Styrofoam, the jiffy bags, gift wrap tissue in the cardboard drum, bubble wrap, bottle caps, egg cartons, spice jars, milk jugs, and plastic six-pack loops. Everything except the aluminum cans from the six-pack loops — the scouts got real money for those.

In politics and in theory at least, Sel's older daughter, Reese, agreed with her dad about keeping the landfills empty. Even so, she was growing a bit unsettled by her father's "storage," especially after watching a few of those recent TV shows about hoarders.

Her father's principal excuse for warehousing the unwanted universe wore ever thinner as he reused it: "I once followed one of those freelance recyclers in his truck to the landfill where he just spilled all his sorted materials into one big pit. They charge you to take away hazardous stuff and it just ends up in your bathwater two years later."

"Really, Dad, there are other ways to recycle..." and usually Reese gave up at that point.

Kara Lee's tolerance of her father's squirreling had grown disaffected; her relationship with the basement was now over. She no longer went "down there," not since the power failure on the eve of her twelfth birthday. Candle in hand (because Dad's entire milk carton of flashlight batteries had gone dead), she was headed for the food storage and a jar of home-canned dills when her painfully creative imagination construed the headless horseman — and his head — out of the artist's easel and a twelve-inch ball of used Reynolds Wrap on the tile floor. Then, too, there were those occasional wrinkling little voices from the bags as if they resented the pressure of their confinement. Her public excuse for avoiding the cellar covered her real fears: "It's too dangerous to walk down there. There's always some stupid bag about your feet to slip or trip on. These bags have taken over the country and now they're taking over our house."

Her mother had stopped asking her to retrieve anything from the basement, and when her father made the request, she simply chilled her glare at him in a way that made a spoken "no" redundant. She had leverage over him. She knew — and told him she knew — about all the other plastic bags downstairs, densely pressed and boxed, an entire wall of Safeways, hidden by the old dust-colored dining room drapes behind the leaning wall of magazines in the spare bedroom. It was enough leverage to keep him quiet about catching her trying to drive the Cooper Mini underage and without a permit. If her mom discovered those bags, Kara Lee figured, she might just purge the cellar next time Dad went backpacking with the scouts.

Which would not have been a bad thing, actually, but Kara Lee didn't care because the basement was ignorable and, being as hazardous as she said it was, it saved her the trouble of fetching things. In *her* theory of domestic physics, a basement was an inorganic latrine; once you dumped something there, it was not to be reconsidered or retrieved. And really, when you had plumbing and garbage trucks, you didn't need latrines or cellars. The furnace would fit nicely upstairs in the hall closet, where the paper bags were currently being sheltered from excessive moisture. As for the wine, you could buy it at the grocery store like normal parents did, and as for the environment, the real world would take care of itself if it truly was an ecosystem as its friends claimed it was. Anyhow, she thought, the environment outlasts all the people who die in it—and that's everyone. You can't die outside of the environment. It always wins. Totally wins.

Between debates over green living styles and wine drinking, dinner was often a strained affair. Merla's dishes rivaled the recipes of elite French chefs, but the family palate was usually too scraped by argument to notice the riches of a *boeuf bourguignon*, let alone the subtleties of asparagus *á la normande*. Periodically, Reese raised the prospect of a vegan menu, though she never declined the *coq au vin* or *canard rôti*. Kara Lee ate everything indiscriminately until she discovered that *canard* was a duck.

Sel broke ranks with the hardcore "greenies" when it came to eating meat. "I was reading about a very revered community of monks — in Tibet, I think, or maybe Nepal, last week, was it? Tuesday, yes Tuesday — who maintain a vegetarian diet unless one of them gets sick. Then they feed their ill brother meat until he's well again. Obviously meat is held in special value even by these thoughtful vegetarians."

Whenever Dad turned pedantic at the dinner table, Kara Lee played the stubborn student. "Aren't they the same monks who take only warm water for a drink? No milk, no juice, no coffee, no tea, and NO WINE?"

Kara Lee seemed just a bit envious that Reese, not quite twenty-one, was allowed a glass of Mom's vintage at dinner.

Merla swirled her last splash of Sémillon. "Benjamin Franklin said that wine was sure proof that God loved humanity."

"And so is a good pull of beef jerky on a mountain trail," Sel chimed in with more relish than relevance.

A couple facts from last fall's science class came back imperfectly to Kara Lee. "You know, we use up more energy raising beef and other flesh than we do driving our cars—and even more reducing umpteen pounds of brisket to twelve ounces of jerky." This last tidbit from Kara's own ready-made data.

"I believe," Reese stung, "it's the plastic bag that takes the most energy to make per gram. Oh, and we use three trillion of those things a year in this country."

The wound was open. A moment of impromptu silence to let it bleed.

A siren and the rumble of an engine from the firehouse on the next block burst the moment.

Merla pushed back her chair, stepped lightly to the island countertop for the main dish, and returned to the table with a casserole of miniature ravioli in a white sauce blessed with nuances no one but she would likely notice.

Kara Lee was too busy noticing, once again, that Mom was wearing another dressy apron to dinner—like those prim-looking ladies who smiled the risqué remarks on the retro-fifties postcards. And wasn't it some point of etiquette to remove the apron before sitting down to dinner? Who, besides Mom, had a wardrobe of aprons anyhow?

Sel tested the consistency of the pasta sauce and skipped the transition to his harping point—his mantra, Reese called it: "I just think if everyone kept all their packing and packaging for reuse and sent as little to the landfill as we do, we'd all be enjoying a truly green environment."

"The bottom of our house *is* a landfill," Kara Lee said, a little too late to cut him off as she liked to do.

A slight but distinct clap escaped from the basement through the door to the stairwell.

"Sounds like something fell over down there again. Maybe we need more shelves?" Kara Lee's sarcasm was saccharine.

Saturday, the day after the dinner of ravioli and chocolate mousse, the entire wall of magazines collapsed into a slippery chaos. Sel was out, grilling hamburgers at a scout fundraiser in the Wal-Mart parking lot. Merla was the first to see the mess. Apparently the stacks had dominoed in reverse. The leaning pillar of *Sierra* magazines had gone down first, leaving the *Outdoorsmans* nothing to lean on. After that, the Rachelle Rays and Martha Stewarts slid together like two halves of a shuffled playing card deck, clearing the way for the *Rolling Stones*, *Newsweeks*, and unread hundreds of *Paris Match*. Beneath a melee of *Cosmopolitans*, the last to fall on the left, a few of many *Maxims* peeped out, leaving all the cover-girl cleavage at cross purposes with itself. Highest on the heap, the *Cosmos* seemed to Merla like a serendipitous feminist statement about "woman on top," but she shuffled aside that thought when she noticed that the weighty *National Geographics* had spilled backwards to tear down the shabby old dining room drapes.

And there they were, forming another wall: a simple row of uniform cartons, as neatly, evenly stacked as a wall of cinder blocks. Too neat, too orderly, too OCD. She reached to lift one from the top of the wall but slid to her knees on a slope of *Oprahs*. Again she tried to lift one down, but it was surprisingly heavy. Its dusty cardboard sides slipped through her palms and the box landed sharply on her instep, split open, and pushed out a glimpse of its contents. After a minute of subsiding pain in her foot, she tugged from what must have been a thousand in that carton, a single Safeway sack, wrinkled like crape paper from the pressure of packing.

It would take fifty years of grocery shopping to . . . . The thought was too frightening to finish.

The magazines were the first to go — into the nearest four dumpsters in the alley — and just as she dropped the lid on the fourth dumpster, Sel drove the Cooper into the drive.

She'd never had a shouting match with him, let alone an orchestrated one, but that was the plan and the fury. After her opening rhetorical question about what was in the boxes, delivered in that low tremolo that prefaces so many parental tirades against small sinners, and after her crescendo into the shriller ranges, mostly she just screamed, while Sel blurted his total of a dozen words in five answers he never got to finish.

"Bags . . . so many uses . . . not much space considering . . . compressed . . . almost to singularity . . . ." This last remark from him weakened by a loser's chuckle.

He said nothing after her finale: "And stuff them so far down some black hole that they come out in somebody else's universe."

Another cube of infinitely dense Safeway poly bags fell from the wall and split, the white plastic crackling, puffing outward from the wound in the carton like a mound of popping corn.

Sel spent his Saturday night removing half of an infinite number of plastic bags from the basement—half because, true to form, he did not set a pace that would have allowed him to finish that night. He was especially slow for having eaten four hamburgers in the afternoon, as had all of the growing scouts of Troop 19, to keep the surplus patties from going to waste.

Merla went out for the evening with Belle Jacobs and Melanie Smelt to the summer's first blockbuster about avatars replacing administrative assistants, food servers, and customer service staff in post-industrial America. It was a little goodbye outing since Belle's and Melanie's families, neighbors on either side of the O'Faolains, would be off in a few days for a month's vacation at their shared mountain cabin. Merla wondered skeptically how that would work out.

There are any number of reasons why one should not install ceiling fans in a basement—even a finished basement. The most obvious is that basement ceilings are low, and the taller, less attentive members of the household may find their eyebrows occasionally accented by a fan blade. According to Sel's physics, however, the fans "cultivated" a fresher, less humid atmosphere and were less complicated than dehumidifiers. "Cellars don't have to be dank to age wine," he had said to Merla's frown. A less compelling but equally good reason not to install ceiling fans in a basement is that, being so low, they swirl up very light, loose material — like Styrofoam peanuts, gift wrap tissue, and, well, plastic bags.

Opinions varied as to how exactly Sel met his death in the downstairs bedroom while clearing out the poly sacks. Drawn by a "bad feeling," Kara Lee said, she went to the basement for the first time in a year and found her dad face down in a swamp of grocery sacks, one of them encircling his face tautly like blister packing. The indisputable and immediate cause of death was suffocation. But precisely how that had come about was subject to heart-sickening debate.

The redheaded police officer concluded that Sel had been hit by a fan blade while trying to free the fan of plastic bags, for the fresh bruise on his forehead matched the blades, which were left spinning at high speed on updraft. The hit on the head could have stunned him, perhaps even made him lose his balance, though it seemed unlikely that it would have knocked him out entirely. True, the officer admitted to his colleague, there might be a flaw in this theory since it would have been better to turn off the fan before freeing it from the bags, but, "Hey, a guy who's got these fans in his basement to begin with — well?"

The bald police officer and the ambulance driver attributed the tragedy to the implications of four ale bottles — three newly emptied and the fourth almost so — in the one unlittered corner of the room.

The post mortem yielded some evidence of a mild "cardiac event" probably very shortly before death, which would explain how a seemingly healthy man would be unable to extricate himself from a smothering plastic bag.

Merla, in a dull, aching way, believed that she had bullied Sel to his death.

Reese, part cynic, but failed Stoic, could not get past the perversity of the accident and in her tears blamed the general perversity of . . . but she wasn't sure what.

Kara Lee *was* sure. The bags had killed her father and, by way of proof, she fixated on an odd detail: a plastic sack wound around the switchbox for the timer that governed the fans. "It's the bags . . . They killed him . . . I've heard them . . . Talking . . . Through the vents, I've heard them . . . They killed him."

In the week following the cremation and a scout-led memorial, the Prozac helped but did not cure Kara Lee's anxiety or her occasional, apparent delirium. For her, the sound of the bags rustling around her father's body persisted, joined by new sounds, some mere crinkles and cracklings, others thuds and snaps, plastic popping apart, more voices — all from "down there." The most troublesome noises, Reese thought, were not the ones that her sister believed she heard but those that Reese and Merla noticed.

A little over a week after the memorial came a run of windy days when the house, filled with sounds, seemed somehow vulnerable, especially with Sel gone. Still distracted by her grief, Merla became especially unsettled when the wall phone went out, presumably because of the winds, until Reese reminded her of the obvious — that they both had cell phones.

Merla was about to take down the wind chime — it had been tinkling steadily for two days — when, outside the kitchen window, she saw it fall from its hook, the suspension string snapping in an exceptionally strong gust.

Half an hour later, it was Reese who said, "There goes that wind chime again." Merla heard it too, twice, and knew it was not the wind chime, but a tinkling from the basement. Now she wondered if she'd been hearing that sound before the chime fell . . . yet no, couldn't be, must have been the chime, wasn't it, till now at least?

Reese was helping her in the kitchen with the dough for baguettes and a dozen hard rolls. Merla mimed a sign for Reese to go with her to the basement, not wanting to alarm Kara Lee who was redecorating her toenails in the breakfast nook.

"It's probably just the glass jars settling out in the crates," Merla figured aloud but doubtfully, as she led Reese down the steps.

The tinkle again—wine bottles, not jars. Disengaged by Sel's death, Merla had left her last batch of Cabernet, newly bottled, upright and randomly set across the shelves in the storage bin.

Here and there on the way to the bin, she swept aside a stray bag with the edge of her sandal. In the bin, the bags were everywhere, ankle-deep on the floor, and perhaps a dozen caught, or slung, by their handle loops over the wine bottles. One bottle of Cabernet lay on its side, cork end precariously far off the edge of the shelf, with a Rite Aid sack hanging from its neck like a gymnast from a pole.

As Merla righted the bottle, a draft called her attention to an open window. She offered the explanation that both she and Reese needed to hear: "The wind must have blown the sash open and trapped all the loose bags in here. I just can't bring myself to clear them out...It would be like pushing your father out of... Your dad said the latches needed replacing—oh, and the screens need to be put in."

"And the fans were on in the other rooms," Reese added, as if to bolster her mother's rational explanation.

Merla closed the window, turning the latch which didn't seem especially weak or loose. Reese went to switch off the timer for the fans, then returned. The bags, left as they were, everywhere, settled quietly at the bottom of the creaking house.

"Let's finish the bread."

The baguettes were cooling on a wire rack on the butcher block, the rolls had browned, and Merla had just opened the oven door to remove them when the vibration in the kitchen floor signaled that the fans had turned on again below. From the doorway to the cellar stairwell, the whoosh became audible as the bags stirred. And then... the tinkle at first, and seconds later a burst of glass, then another, and another.

Once down the steps, Reese lost the scent of baking bread and caught instead the fruity fumes of wine. In the bin, bottles of Cabernet had fallen to the floor, most of them broken; a couple intact, having landed on a veritable cushion of plastic sacks.

Reese re-latched the window that had opened again, shook her foot to escape a bag that wrapped itself about her ankle, and called in a near shout, "Mom. The wine, the bags... "

Merla left the oven door open and was on the stairs in a moment, but in another moment it was over. Her left foot slipped on a Walgreen's bag, and her right foot, working to catch her balance, caught in a handle loop of the sack. She pitched forward down the stairwell to the tile floor, her neck twisted absurdly, her forehead fractured over her open grey eyes.

Reese stumbled through the bags out of the storage bin toward her mother. She knelt, then bent to touch her mother's brow when a sack fluttered down over Merla's face. Reese's usually measured response to all that was tense, even terrible, gave way to a nauseated horror and scream that brought her sister to the top of the stairs, then, tentatively, halfway down to see the catastrophe at the bottom.

"She's dead."

"No no no."

Reese and Kara Lee were almost keening together in that futile passion of family members weakened by the shock of sudden death, until Kara Lee began to scream in pulses. "It's them, it's the bags, I've heard them, I told you I've heard them, it's them."

Reese spotted what her sister had already seen from the stairs — the bag tangled about her mother's sandals. It seemed to her, suddenly, that Kara Lee, crazy Kara Lee, was right. The bags had somehow killed their father and now their mother. She flailed at them in lame, pathetic swipes of her hands, and more of them swirled up toward the nearest fan, along with gift wrap tissue from the open cardboard drum. She tore at the sacks wrapped about the fan blades. One blade broke loose and fell to the floor. The fan spun roughly, unbalanced, as if it would rock its way out of its base in the ceiling. She ran to the windows at both ends of the rec room, yanked them open and began tossing sacks in a sob-choked rage through the windows. But the stream of sacks never stopped, so many of them had burst from their cartons and scattered since Sel had died.

The fan, now a spastic, three-armed scarecrow, tangled up the poly sacks and tissue; the motor grunted and the sparks from its housing told of a shorting circuit. The tangle of tissues and bags flamed up and shriveled into a sour smoke.

From midpoint in the stairwell, Kara heard her sister choking. She started down the last of the steps to help Reese, pushing against her fear of confronting her mother's body, when she sensed smoke above her as well. A single bag crinkled at her, curled over her fresh blue toenails. She turned round and pumped her legs up the steps as if she were escaping a snake pit.

With its door still open, the electric oven glowed at full heat, burning the rolls into an acrid smoke. Kara tried to clear her thoughts in the gray air. Close it. Close the oven. She slammed its door shut and punched the "cancel" tab on the top of the range. Good. Safe. Now. . . But at that moment, from the basement, through bitter haze came a faint, muffled gurgle, and then a stifled moan, and finally what seemed to Kara like a great whoosh of wrinkling plastic.

She thought of the wall phone, then remembered that the land line was out from the wind. Her own cell had dropped somewhere in the basement on the night Dad had died. Reese and Merla kept theirs on their hips, but another trip to the basement for a phone seemed an impossible option. She thought hopefully of the Jacobs and the Smelts who lived on either side but, as she started out the patio door, remembered that they had left for the mountains after the memorial. With the patio door open, drawing out air, a few of the sacks drifted up and out of the stairwell into the kitchen. A breath of smoke hit her throat first. No sooner did she catch enough air to scream than she found her fingers tearing away a sack that had sucked onto her face like paper to a vacuum cleaner hose. Once free of the sack, eyes burning, blurring, nearly closed, she slapped her hands along the kitchen wall until she felt the corkboard where the keychain for the Mini was looped over a push pin. In the car she would be safe, could hit the horn for help, for someone, anything, or, better, yes, drive up the block to a neighbor. Safe from THEM. Get help for Reese.

Kara Lee didn't know that it was already too late to help Reese. The smoke in the basement had not been enough to overwhelm, but in her rage Reese had inhaled a choking cloud of it and, momentarily disabled, had dropped to the floor for clear air that she sucked in convulsively — along with a clear thin produce sack that stoppered her gasp far down her throat.

Perversely, Reese would have said, the circuit breaker for the fan kicked out seconds too late to save her. The sparks and flames from the fan sputtered out, and the gusting wind shot through the basement, clearing the smoke and most of the swirling bags out the east windows in clusters, like broken cumuli sailing across the front yard.

In the driveway, Kara Lee pushed the remote, opened the door to the Mini, and dove into the driver's seat. She didn't know whether she or the wind slammed the door behind her. Brake, clutch, neutral, turn the key. Yes. Across to reverse. Clutch up. The Cooper lurched into a stall. A swirl of sacks tumbled like weeds up the windshield and over the roof.

Clutch down, key, lots of gas, screw the clutch, pop it.

The Mini banged into reverse so hard that she had to clutch and brake to avoid bolting into the street.

"Just up the block to the Reynolds—always home," she told herself. Away from THEM. Calm, calm, drive," she shivered aloud. "Calm. No mistakes. Save Reese. Drive." The wind was now roaring through the poplars so that she could not hear the engine or even sense the clutch engaging, but the smoother motion in reverse told her that she'd got it right this time.

Before she reached the street, she glanced to the right. No one coming. The wind slapped a cluster of plastic bags across the windows on the driver's side. When she looked left, she saw, pressed flat against the pane, only white plastic and the words "Safeway Ingredients for life." She took that for a good omen, listened for a short second, heard nothing but the wind, and accelerated into the street.

She did not see, and perhaps hardly felt, the recycler's truck pushing the speed limit from the left.

Racing from just a block away, the fire engine team was the first at the scene, but it was instantly clear to them that the ambulance coming for the girl in the Cooper would be only a formality.

"I'll check the house, see if anyone's home."

"I'm guessing no one is, unless they're deaf, and it looks like the neighbors from down the block are already at the doorbell."

"Was she even old enough to drive?"

"Hard to tell. Doubt it—the way he's saying she pulled straight out in front of him. 'Least he called right away. 'Course, we heard the crash from the station, but the 911 told us where exactly."

"Something smells like an old fire. That from his truck?"

"Must be."

"And what's with all the bags? They're swarming like mad hornets roused from their nest, and look at them all wrapped about that phone line by the roof."

"Must have blown out of the truck. Worst things ever born of modern technology—harder to get rid of than an oil spill. Like to pull one over the head of the guy who invented these flimsy things and tell him to breathe in the consequences."

"Too late, don't you think? More of *them* nowadays than people."

Corner Sofa

Sarena Ulibarri

I was at the coffee house again. Watered by mocha lattes and black coffee with nutmeg, I was there so often I had almost taken root in the corner sofa. I planted myself there the day after my boyfriend left me, convinced that sitting near other people and drinking coffee was different from sitting at home and drinking alcohol.

A girl bumped into the table, sloshing my coffee over the rim in a tiny wave, and a book slipped out of her bag, thumping to the carpeted floor. I leaned over to pick it up, expecting to hand it straight over to her with a small "thanks" and quick nod. But she was gone, vanished, by the time I lifted the book off the floor. I placed it beside me on the sofa, used some napkins to mop up my coffee, and waited for her to come back. I recognized her by the bulky backpack covered in political stickers. She was a regular at the coffee house, just part of the usual background, along with the big chalkboard menu and the photographs of old movie stars that lined the walls.

Half an hour later she still hadn't returned to claim the book. Curious, I picked it up and turned it over. The hard cover was black, smooth and unmarked. I flipped open to a random page just long enough to recognize it was a journal, then snapped it shut, feeling scandalized for even that glimpse. How mortified would I be if some stranger read my journal! God, all that whining about not being loved, about losing my friends during the breakup, all those detailed analyses of Cosmo quizzes. Resolutely I set the book back on the sofa, and it sat quietly in its black binding.

When I was ready to leave, I walked up to the counter with the book. The barista looked at me with superficial recognition.

"Another mocha latte?" he asked.

"No, I'm about to go to work," I said, then wished I hadn't. I didn't come here to make friends. "Hey, do you know the girl with the bumper stickers on her backpack?"

"Do I know her? No, I assume she's a student here."

Everyone who came here, besides me, was probably a student, and it was one of the reasons I chose it: no one would have any reason to know me.

"Sometimes I get you two confused, though," he continued, "You look a lot alike."

I frowned. If she looked like me, I'd never noticed. I tried to bring her face to mind, but couldn't conjure any specifics, just that ratty old backpack with the bumper stickers safety-pinned to it.

"She left something here," I said, tapping the book nervously against my palm, then changed my mind about leaving it with the barista. "I'll just give it back next time I see her. Thanks."

"Sure," he said as I turned away, "See you tomorrow!"

I worked the closing shift at a customer service hotline, and my co-workers, who I didn't get along with anyway, were always gone by ten. We stayed open late for the benefit of customers in far-away time zones, but my shift was usually quiet, and that night the phone didn't ring at all. As midnight approached, even the Internet bored me. I looked around the desk, at the plastic mail trays and oversized calendar covered in food stains, searching for something else to do.

The black book peeked out of my purse. Maybe I could find a name or a phone number, I thought. So I plucked the book from the snug matrix of my purse and held it. The black cover was smooth and solid, and felt surprisingly warm to the touch. It smelled faintly of coffee and nail polish. I opened the cover.

No name, no phone number. Of course there wasn't. It's not like I ever signed my name to my journal passages or listed demographic information in a notebook that was never meant to be seen by other eyes.

I didn't mean to read, but my eyes could not resist the words. More than anything, it was her handwriting that drew me in. Each

210

page, margin to margin, was a work of art. The lush curve of her "C," the unique connection of her "th," the way her "g" swept so wide it circled the word beneath it. So different from my tight, messy scratches. My handwriting always looked rushed, and hers looked luxurious and slow, as if she'd taken a whole minute to navigate the dramatic curves and loops of a cursive S.

"It rained all day today," the journal said, "and it was glorious. Clouds wisped over the hilltops and lay there like white sheets. The silver storm sat heavy over the city all day, its humid mass billowing like a giant quilt. I got soaked on my way to class, and as I sat through the lecture I could feel the raindrops drip off my hair and tickle down my back."

I laughed out loud at the passage, and the sound seemed to echo through the empty office. It had never occurred to me to look at rain as anything other than an inconvenience, and I smiled at her romantic description. She must be in love, I thought enviously.

But I found nothing about a lover. A few lines about the Anthropology professor she found attractive, but those were spare and whimsical. Her journal switched between poetic descriptions of everyday events and impassioned rants about political candidates or social issues, things I rarely gave a thought to. Her stories refreshed me; they were so different from mine. I read on, replacing my own blank life with her words.

The phone rang, like an alarm, and I sheepishly dropped the book. I broke company policy and let the phone ring three times so I could collect myself. Into the mouthpiece I spoke the standard greeting, the one I'd repeated so often I occasionally answered my cell phone that way.

"Could I please have your account number?" I ended.

"My parents weren't affectionate," said a female voice through the phone, "and I guess that's why I always felt like I had to be touching him. Just an arm, a hand, at least, preferably more. I wanted people to know we were together, to know we were in love wherever we went. He always thought it was inappropriate, and he'd pry my fingers off his arm and tell me not to act like such a clingy little kid."

I listened to the words — my words, from my journal — with silent horror, and then slammed the phone down and pushed my chair away from the desk. I looked at the black book, hovering on the edge of the desk, and the smooth black binding gazed back at me like Nietzsche's abyss.

My cell phone rang. I inched toward my purse and tentatively pulled it out. The screen said "Restricted Number," and I flipped it open without a word.

"I found one of his socks in the laundry today, and I'm going to keep it in my bedside drawer — "

I flipped the phone shut and jammed my thumb against the power button to turn it off. Goosebumps crept across my skin. I suspiciously surveyed the vacant office. The clock ticked noisily, marching toward one a.m. I picked up the book, careful not to let it fall open again, and tucked it back into my purse. I shut down the computer, clocked out early and locked up with shaking hands.

I rushed into my spartan apartment and tossed my purse, the book still tucked inside, on the kitchen counter. I ruffled through my bedside table drawer, tossing around sleeping pills, tattered Cosmo magazines, that damn sock. My journal, a flimsy white thing with yellow flowers on the front, was gone.

I ripped the sheets off the bed, opened drawers, crawled on the floor, looked in the refrigerator. When I'd exhausted all my options, I slumped down on the kitchen floor. No one else had keys to my apartment, and nothing else was gone. I pressed my palms into my eyes and wrapped my fingers around my hair.

Nothing was missing other than what was always missing. When my boyfriend left, he took things that weren't his, and now I had nothing on my walls, nothing on my bookshelf, nothing on my kitchen counter. Rather than reassemble my apartment, I let the lack be a reminder of all the things I didn't deserve, all the things I'd driven away by being too needy, too opinionated, too emotional.

I looked up and saw the black book had fallen out of my purse on the kitchen counter, exposing that luxurious handwriting once again. I shut my eyes and decided I had to put an end to this weirdness. The only way I could think to do it was to take the book back to the coffee house.

I drove the dark city streets, and the book sat on the passenger seat. I eyed it peripherally, as if it were a shady hitchhiker.

The coffee house was dark, as I knew it would be, the chairs on the patio chained together around their tables. Light slid down from the streetlight and I gripped the book tightly in both hands, walking toward the door with ceremonial slowness.

I turned around when I saw her in the reflection of the coffee house windows. She stood on the sidewalk, a white book clutched in her hand, her eyes wide. She did look like me, I thought, like I might look if I dressed in baggy clothes and vintage rock t-shirts, if I wore a darker shade of makeup and covered my head in a knit hat.

I held the black book to my chest. She looked at it and looked sheepishly away.

"You called me," she said, not looking at me.

"What?" I said, "No, you called me."

We didn't say anything else. We each took a couple steps forward and wordlessly exchanged the books. She gave an awkward wave and hurried away.

I looked down at my own journal, the white notebook with yellow flowers. I opened it and saw the tight scratchy handwriting inside. I read a passage, then flipped to another, then flipped again. The word drained me; they were all the same. They were meaningless. I grabbed the fragile paper with angry fingertips, tore the pages out and crumpled them. Then I threw the whole mess, white flower-decorated cover and all, into the trashcan by the coffee house door.

Through the coffee house windows, I could see the corner sofa, sitting empty in the dark room. The fabric seemed faded, the cushions more sunken than I realized, and I felt my roots beginning to lose their hold. I breathed on the window so the corner sofa was framed in fog. With one finger I slowly, luxuriantly, wrote the word "Goodbye" across its cushions, with sweeping cursive letters that decorated the window like poetry.

Meteorology For Beginners

Simon Kewin

"What makes the wind blow, daddy?"

I sit with Jade in a clearing, eating the crisps and red apples I've packed for the walk. Tree-trunks pillar around us, dark green and grey. Higher up, where the slanting sunlight catches them, their leaves glow bright orange. The forest roars in the breeze that blows up there. Jade looks up at me, crunching her apple.

"Well, see, it's caused by all the trees flapping their branches together at the same time."

"Really?"

"Oh yes. Watch them and see. Sometimes just one shakes its branches and you get a little breeze. But sometimes it sets the rest off. When they all start lashing their branches together, you get the really strong winds."

"Oh."

She peers upwards at the canopy with six-year old's eyes, smiling in delight at the sight, at the way every single leaf has its own shade of green or the way they make shapes like eyes. She looks thoughtful as she returns her attention to her apple.

"Is it just the trees that do that?"

"Oh no, it's every plant. It's just we only notice the trees because they're so big. But sometimes a whole field of grass starts to ripple and you can just about feel it."

I finish my apple and hurl the core into a nearby bramble thicket. Jade looks shocked, knowing the rules about litter.

"It's OK. It will just become a new tree."

SIMON KEWIN

She grins and overarms her own core away. It lands a few feet distant.

"But when we went to London last year it was *very* windy," she says. "And there are hardly any trees there."

I stand and offer her a hand to pull her to her feet.

"Well, you see, in the big cities they've had to build these giant wind machines because they've cut down all the trees."

"Machines?"

"Huge big fans like windmills. And somewhere there's a button they can press to start them all blowing at the same time. Depending on which machines they switch on they can have wind from any direction. There are dials too for the strength. Breath, Zephyr, Breeze right round to Storm, Gale, Hurricane."

"I think I prefer the trees."

"Me too. Those machines are forever breaking down."

We set off back through the woods, retracing our steps. The sun is starting to slip out of the sky now, down behind the swaying trees, golden light flickering through the branches. Away from the woods the wind settles down, of course, and we walk home in silence, hand in hand.

That night, when I come to tuck her into bed, I find she's been busy. All around her room are leafy twigs scavenged from the garden and set in pots, bottles, jars. Fronds of fir and fern wedged into cracks between the stones of the walls. Flowers sprouting from the pages of books.

"It's beautiful, Jade," I say.

"Watch."

I sit beside her on the bed. Hanging over her is the mobile we've assembled over the years: scraps of tin, seashells, triangles of blue plastic, glass buttons, bottle-tops, discarded computer chips, twists of wire and egg-shell shards, all hanging from a mesh of fine twines. A pine-cone from today's expedition is the latest addition.

We sit as the gloom gathers in the room, my arm around her. She is tense with expectancy, almost holding her breath. Nothing happens. She glances up at me, doubting herself now, afraid it won't work, it isn't true. This is often how she is since her mother left, her spirits easily sapped.

Then a beech twig in the corner of the room quivers and begins to wave. We don't move, afraid we'll alarm it, break the spell. One by one, the other plants respond, twitching, lurching backwards and forwards in time to the movements of the twig. I feel the breath of moving air on my face.

"Look," Jade whispers. The mobile starts to twirl and twist. The scraps of metal and glass tinkle together in the breeze, catching the moonlight shining through her window.

"It's wonderful," I say.

Smiling, she lies under her blankets and closes her eyes, the delicate jingling going with her as she drifts away to sleep.

Protected Contact

Julie Stielstra

For a long time it was warm and dark, though there were no words for it. There was motion, a gentle rock and sway, sometimes a heave and a lurch. There was noise, a pattering or braying current of sound from somewhere else, and rumbles and thumps that could be felt. That was all. Until there began a pressure, a forcing, a shoving that could not be resisted, and a sudden expulsion into cold and brilliance. He did not know how to breathe.

The calf hit the concrete floor in a crashing cataract of blood and slime. Anya recoiled from the computer screen. She had not been allowed in the pen for the birth. Only Roy, the head keeper, and Joyce, the vet, were there, waiting in a dimly lit corner. They wanted nothing unfamiliar to disturb the laboring cow elephant. Anya stared at the inert, gelatinous mass on the floor behind the cow, willing it to move. No one moved. The cow stepped gingerly aside, her ears fanning tentatively. She touched the calf, sealed in its oozing envelope, with her trunk. She nudged it with one foot, then kicked it. It stirred and the cow backed away. Her ears were fully unfurled. The calf shifted feebly on the floor. The cow raised her trunk. Even Anya could see she looked alarmed. A barred partition began to move, swinging above the calf on the floor, and the agitated cow was penned. Then Roy and Joyce and another keeper Anya didn't know were on their knees with the calf, ripping apart the sticky membranes, raising its head, moving its limbs.

"Wake up!" Anya cried to the screen. "You are born now, wake up!"

The calf twitched and strained, stretching its legs, then gave a convulsive gasp, its mouth agape below the tiny trunk. Its eyes were blank. It gasped again and again. Roy wiped and toweled, scooping out the mouth, rubbing the ribs. The other keeper was sweeping the river of blood away, down the drains. Joyce propped the calf up against her knees as Roy worked. It tried to hold up its heavy domed head. The other keeper was talking to the cow, who stared over the barrier at what had emerged from her. Anya found the zoom function and closed in on the calf. Roy wiped a thatch of dark hair from its eyes. The keeper switched on an overhead heater. As the calf began to dry, Anya could see it was furred like a collie puppy, with tiny bearlike ears barely unbuttoned from its skull. Roy suddenly looked straight up into the camera at Anya, ran his fingers through the ruff down the calf's chest and grinned. Anya began to cry. She had never seen anything born before.

Twenty two months ago, a Japanese scientist had given them an egg. An endocrinologist in Washington DC had monitored blood levels and the cow began to turn angrily away from anyone who reached for her ears. A woman flown in from Berlin had climbed up on a stepstool and inserted the egg into the uterine lining of the elephant now fidgeting behind her fence. Tonight, in southern California, an Asian elephant had been delivered of this creature. Anya picked up her cell phone and thumbed up the list of people in Japan, in Germany, in Washington, in St Petersburg, in France, in Michigan, in the Netherlands, and spelled out: "Mammoth baby born." Send.

They coaxed the cow with apples and carrots. With distraction, discipline, restraints and reassurance, she allowed the calf to nurse for three days and then no more. When he shuffled toward her, like a child clumsy in leg-braces, she stamped and fanned her ears, crashed her hips into the sides of the chute. It was not safe for anyone. The calf was removed to the quarantine room, and they upended gallon jugs of formula round the clock, concocted with the help of an elephant orphanage in Kenya. Anya called someone she knew who had worked on the milk proteins in the stomach of a frozen baby mammoth carcass unearthed in Siberia. This was why she was here, a sort of liaison among the multinational group who had engineered this animal's birth. Born and schooled in Russia, she spoke French well, English better and could get by in German a little. She had cataloged fossils at the St. Petersburg Zoological Museum while at the university, written copy for display labels, learned some conservation techniques. Her mother liked to tease her about their first visit to the museum, when Anya was five. The towering mammoth skeleton in the prehistoric animals hall had terrified her: she buried her face in her father's chest until he had carried her quickly past and set her down where she couldn't see it. She made herself look at the reflection of it in the glass of other display cases, then sneaked swift peeks when it wasn't looking. By the end of the afternoon, she stood gripping her father's hand in front of the mammoth, staring fiercely at the arching yellow tusks. She mastered the mammoth, and the giant sloths and dire wolves and woolly rhinos and lithe little proto-horses. A recommendation from the museum's head of mammals for a fellowship took her to California, to work on specimens from the tar pits of LaBrea. So she was on the spot when the zoo's female elephant was chosen, with the enthusiastic cheerleading of the zoo's director, to bear the egg stuffed with the DNA of a mammoth. She knew mammoths, she had the languages, and over the years she had met at least briefly some of the participants in this experiment. She rounded up the scientific papers on the milk proteins and sent copies to the vet, to the zoo nutritionist, and to Roy.

The mammoth calf guzzled up the formula, and a few days later broke into a foul diarrhea. More phone calls and emails; they tweaked and jiggered the recipe. Anya arrived in the elephant house to find the calf chuted and Roy carefully shaving his throat through the bars. Joyce was unwrapping an intravenous catheter to place in the jugular vein. The calf stood meekly. His hindquarters were thick with shit-coated wool. He stank. Roy carefully swept up the shorn fur and sealed it in an envelope. "Good to save everything," he said to Anya. He glanced over to see that Joyce wasn't listening and murmured, "Not to mention what I could get for it on eBay." Anya was shocked.

The catheter in place, Joyce announced they needed to set up a schedule for the calf's fluids, vital signs and meds, round the clock. Roy groaned.

"Sheila's on maternity leave," he said. "I'm short-staffed."

"Can I help?" said Anya.

"You're not trained on elephants."

"He's not an elephant. And he's just a little one."

"Have you handled livestock? Cows? Even horses?"

"My friend had a pony. I rode him sometimes."

Roy shook his head.

"That's no good."

"He's not much bigger than that pony. I have insomnia and don't sleep much anyway. I could watch him during the night. Show me what to do. You've let me feed him. I can put medicine in the fluids." She reached through the bars and stroked the calf's forehead. He raised his trunk and touched her wrist, eyes half-closed. "I can do the night shift. No one else wants to. I will call you if anything happens."

He let her.

"But remember the contact rules. You are outside the enclosure all the time, period. Okay?"

Okay.

It was warm and quiet at night. The other elephants rustled and dozed. The calf mostly slept. When she fed him, he wrapped his trunk around her shoulder and held her there as she held the jug for him. He caught his breath when it was empty, braced himself and blew another current of sludge down his back legs.

"Poor mamontyonok," she murmured. Anya walked around and closed the chute barrier. She filled buckets of warm water and began to clean him. He stood motionless as the filthy water drained and pooled at his feet.

Near midnight the phone in Roy's office deedled. It must be Roy, checking up on her.

"Elephant house, Anya speaking."

"Um, this is Tom at the east security gate. There's a gentleman here, says he's here to see the mammoth."

No one had seen the mammoth yet. There had been a triumphant press conference, of course, with the zoo's director beaming and promising that as soon as they were sure all was well with their new "little miracle of science," he would be introduced to the public in due course. Marketing was already ginning up the usual schoolchild contest for a name. But then he'd gotten sick, and the director was fretting, and daily asking when they could "get this show moving." He'd issued invitations to experts around the world and needed to let them know when they could come; they were very busy people, you know, and this was just huge for the zoo.

"Who is this man?" Anya asked. She heard Tom say something, a rapid accented voice replying.

"He says he's been invited by the director, says his name is… just a sec… Sir? Tell me your name again? Dwanyay?"

Douanier. Bertrand Douanier. They called him Monsieur Mammoth. A biology teacher at a lycée in southwestern France, he had spent all his summers for decades in a Siberian shack, looking for — and finding — mammoth bones. It was said every room in his house was filled with them, that the furniture was made out of them, that his wife had left him because of them and he was glad to see her go so he could use the kitchen cupboards to keep his collection of molars in. It was said he could smell mammoth bones as he strode across the tundra. He loved them. And there wasn't an academic scholar of *Mammuthus* who didn't have his phone number in their contacts list.

"It's all right," Anya said. "I will come meet him. He must have just arrived early." She had been introduced to him once, at a conference.

He was bouncing up and down on the balls of his feet at the gate.

"There you are! Thank you so much for coming!" he cried. "Please, I am Bertrand Douanier and I came as soon as I could. I am here to see him."

"Bonsoir, Monsieur Douanier, I am happy to meet you, but aren't you to see the director first?"

"Yes, of course, and I am meeting him tomorrow. But I could not wait. I flew and took a taxi straight here. You can let me have one look, can't you? I will tell no one, I promise. How is he? I heard he might be ill. I know you, don't I? Haven't we met?" He was shaking her hand, and then held it as he peered at her.

"Anya Kostina," she said. "Yes, we met at a conference…"

"Yes, of course, in Cleveland! You gave a nice little paper on growth plates in woolly rhinos."

She fell in love with him instantly.

In the elephant house, she gave him a clean coverall, and showed him the rubber boots soaked in a tray of disinfectant outside the quarantine room. He pulled on the smallest pair. He was a tautly feline man who had been given the large brown eyes of a spaniel. His hands were shaking as he pulled the zipper of the coverall.

"He is in here? He is ill, then? He cannot be with his mother?"

"The mother refused him," Anya said. "She was afraid of him. And yes, he seems to be ill from the formula. He has diarrhea. I tried to clean him, but…"

She closed the door behind them, and he walked slowly, slowly, toward the somnolent calf in the pen. It smelled awful; she had not had time to hose down the floor. He stood just outside the bars, gazing at the calf as though he must fill his eyes and his mind for now and forever with the sight.

"May I…" he said softly, but before she could respond, he reached through the bars and gently laid both hands on the calf's shoulders. He ran his hands along his back, stroked his head, felt his elbows and ribs. He caressed the little ears. The calf offered his trunk and Douanier cupped the tip in both his hands and kissed it.

"Pauvre petit," he murmured. "How do you feel? What do you need, little one? Are they taking good care of you?"

"I have to give him some medicine now," Anya said. She injected the medication into the intravenous line. "Antibiotics," she explained, "and something for the gut, to soothe it."

As she capped the syringe and dropped it in the waste box, Douanier opened the barrier. He slid in beside the calf, embraced him and rested his forehead against the calf's neck. He whispered something Anya could not catch. Then he briskly stepped out and left the room.

He dropped the boots in the tray, shrugged out of the coverall. He gazed at the floor for a moment, then raised his face to Anya and said,

224

"I think... I think maybe we should not have done this." He shook her hand, kissed her on both cheeks and left her.

Antibiotics, probiotics, antidiarrheals, antispasmodics — or maybe, finally, it was the slurry of saline and dung from one of the other elephants, tubed deep into his colon by enema. A few nights later, Anya woke Roy at one AM to joyfully describe the firm, glistening loaf of manure the calf had dropped on the floor. She shoveled it into a bucket, and Roy sealed a scoopful in a dated, labeled Tupperware and put it in the freezer. She wondered if he saved a scoop of it for himself.

The calf — they began to simply call him The Woolly — felt better. He gained weight again. He made little huffing noises when the keepers came into his room and eagerly caressed them with his trunk. He was afraid of the big red rubber ball someone found for him, but he seemed to like picking up an orange traffic cone and throwing it. Anya, off the night shift now, spent hours watching and documenting his activity. He cried when left alone sometimes, trunk reaching hopefully through the barrier, breathing audibly. Then she would go to him and talk to him, murmuring in Russian. He spent a lot of time lying down, sighing and wheezing as he dozed. She discovered he loved to be combed. He leaned into the steel bars with closed eyes as she tugged a wire brush through his long wool and sometimes she felt a small throb in the air, like a noiseless purr.

The paleontologists and mammalogists were summoned, the zoo director and curator of mammals paraded them through the elephant house, and sometimes Anya interpreted. Then there was another press conference, and a gala day planned for when he would be allowed to go outside for the first time, in a yard off public view. The yard was carefully swept and cleaned, the water tank scrubbed and disinfected, bushes and trees all cut back or removed.

They coaxed him down the aisle, to the open door. He stopped dead, huffing nervously. He peered out the door, looping his trunk in the air. Then he saw the other elephants in another paddock. He called out with a voice like a toy horn, and shuffled across the yard to the fence. His surrogate mother pivoted and hurried away, out of sight. The other cow stared at him, ears wide, then she followed.

He stood at the fence and cried and cried. The cameras whirred and snicked. He rambled around in the dust and sneezed. Someone brought out his traffic cone and he ignored it. Then he just stood there. The journalists went away. They brought him back inside, and when Roy fed him, he clutched at Roy so fiercely that Anya had to help him loosen the grip.

He went outside by himself every morning. They began to put out flakes of hay – alfalfa, timothy, clover. He dabbled his trunk in the hay, picking up wisps and dropping them. Sometimes he got on his knees and lipped up a mouthful, then spat it out again and lurched to his feet with an effort. He burbled around in the water tank, sticking his whole face into the water. He didn't seem to like being hosed off, shaking furiously till the water flew in sparkling arcs. Every time he cried after the other elephants, they hid from him. After an hour or so, he would pace at the gate, wanting to come in again.

Then he had trouble getting up. He levered his legs under him and grunted. Once up, he stood with bowed head, almost panting. There was snot running from his trunk and his eyes were gunked and teary. Joyce announced a fever. He coughed.

Another IV line, more antibiotics. Anya went back on the night watch. A few nights later she met Joyce swinging her stethoscope in one hand, huddled with Roy and the curator of mammals.

"I don't like the heart sounds either," she was saying. "I think we better get an ultrasound." A cardiologist flew down from UC Davis. Definitely pneumonia, it seemed, but the heart wasn't right, a valve or a chamber or something Anya didn't understand wasn't formed properly. Her notes confirmed how often he had seemed short of breath, especially when he was upset. He stood in his pen, ribs pumping, his long-lashed eye rolling and roving. More meds in the IV line, more than Anya could manage; Joyce rustled up two other vets who dropped in and out to listen and tweak and confer. Anya wrote the daily updates that the director's office approved for sending to the paleontologists.

He stopped eating, mouthing the nipple tiredly and turning away. They tried applesauce, baby food jars of strained pears, syringefuls of honey, anything to get him to nibble on something. More additives in the IV solution.

Roy called her late one morning and woke her.

"I think you better come," he said. "He's down."

He lay on his side, gasping. The director, the curator, Roy, vets and other keepers were clustered outside the pen. Joyce knelt beside him, tapping the corner of his eye, which did not blink. She shook her head.

"He's agonal," she said.

Help him, Anya said inside her head. Help him, don't let him be this way.

"I don't think there's anything more we can do for him," said Joyce. "He hasn't responded to anything. He's in tamponade. We could tap him, I guess, but..."

"Let him go," said Roy.

"Are you sure?" said the director to Joyce. She looked from him to the other vets and back to the director. She shrugged.

The calf gasped. He was not breathing, only heaving.

"Please," said Anya. No one heard her. Joyce stood up and picked up a syringe.

"Okay?" she said. The director nodded, his face dark and angry, his hands jammed deep in the pockets of his coveralls.

Joyce inserted the needle into the hub of the IV line and pushed. And pushed. It takes a lot. The gasping stopped.

No! wailed Anya suddenly inside her head. No, wait, don't!

The director marched out of the room. Everyone else stood still for a long time.

"Do you want to say goodbye to him?" Roy touched Anya's shoulder. Joyce left the room.

Anya sat on the floor. She leaned down and pressed her face against his temple, fingers wound deep into the wool. He smelled fetid and musty, of infection and dirt and misery. She hugged him and hugged him. She kissed the tip of the soft, loose trunk, she tried to twine it around her neck but it slipped off.

She had never seen anyone die before.

The director called everyone personally.

Anya called Bertrand Douanier. She managed to say to his voice-mail: "You were right. Forgive me." His message back to her said: "Pray God is willing to forgive us all."

She did not accept his suggestion that she come to his Siberian in the summer.

The necropsy confirmed several abnormalities of heart development. The museum of natural history in Los Angeles would mount his stripped skin; the director was driving negotiations with two other museums for the skeleton. An American rep from the Japanese lab flew to Tokyo with the calf's carefully dissected testicles in a small cooler in his lap. The necropsy had also found a dystrophy of the bones of his forelegs, the growth plates malformed and cartilage tattered. He had probably been in pain.

Anya heard the lab had more ova in development, and the search was under way for other elephant surrogates. Before she left the zoo, Roy called her aside and handed her a small jeweler's box. She opened it uncomfortably. It contained a russet-colored double circlet of tightly braided hair that fitted around her wrist. "I know a woman in Oklahoma who does these with horsehair. I didn't tell her what it was," Roy said.

Anya looked up from her worktable, stretching her neck and shoulders. The dry Nebraska sandhills rippled away outside the window. She dipped her brush into distilled water and painted the little mandible in her hand. The stony crust went dark with water, and she took her dental pick to it, carefully scuffing it off the tawny bone. It was a beautiful little jaw, set with a row of grinding teeth like lobed pearls. They weren't sure what it was yet—maybe a new species of early camel, or perhaps a juvenile horse. Twelve million years ago, a volcano had blanketed the plain with an ash of ground glass and the animals had all inhaled it and died. There was a lot of work to be done here at this site. She would be busy here for a long time.

Shell Fire

Nick Jackson

When Vernon held the crimped lip of the shell to his ear, he could hear the faint rush of the sea. It was a miracle to hear the waves distantly crashing, especially when he knew the sea was hundreds of miles away. He wondered which waves on which sea, as he turned the shell. He looked into the curling antechamber that led into the smooth interior, inserted a finger and waggled it around, wishing he were small enough to crawl inside and see what was within. He wanted to penetrate the innermost chambers of the shell, to sit in the ultimate and smallest recess. He was sure he'd be happy there. Then he pressed the shell once more to his ear to hear the sea.

In the weedy plot behind the house were snails. When he touched them gingerly, they pulled in the stalks of their eyes and sucked themselves into their homes. In winter they clung together in brittle bunches like desiccated grapes. But Vernon's shell was different: it had a flush of pinkish bronze and sometimes a trickle of coarse white sand emerged.

He still had the shell forty-five years later and sometimes, when he was in a good mood, he'd take it down from its shelf above the fireplace, running his fingers over the grooves and ridges.

Vernon Bradley threw his mop into the cleaning cupboard and tried to slam the door. But instead of the satisfying slam, the handle of the mop slipped forward and jammed in the door; then the mop and bucket fell out into the corridor, leaving suds on the parquet. When he had cleared up, Vernon took his broom and prepared himself for the job of sweeping leaves.

As he worked, he was transfixed by the way the wind whirled the leaves, drawing them into a tight cone and then flinging them up in an eddying vortex of russet fragments which were caught by the light as they turned. He leaned on the handle of his broom and watched this game of leaves and wind, the way he sometimes watched a breeze ruffling a puddle or the shapes of clouds over the playing fields. At these times it seemed that the world was made for him alone, and that these effects of nature were unobserved except by him.

He bent down and picked up one of the leaves, turning it in his fingers. He let it fall back into the pile of leaves and slowly straightened up. He began to sweep again, feeling contentment in the comfortable sound of the broom, the rhythmic motion of his arms, the contraction of his muscles.

The headmaster, Mr Kelly, looked out of his office window. The school playground was empty, just the acres of tarmac and the dilapidated toilet block. The caretaker was fussing in the corner with a pile of leaves. What was that man doing?

Mr Kelly tasted bile: "How long has Bradley been with the school, Miss Glacer?"

"As long as I can remember."

"He must be..." Mr Kelly examined the husk of a fly that had died on his window ledge, "... sixty, would you say?"

"Not quite that, I don't think."

Mr Kelly shuffled a pile of papers, straightening the edges. He lined up a ruler with the edge of the pages. But he couldn't prevent his eyes flicking back to the caretaker's slow movements.

"What is that man doing?"

Miss Glacer glanced out of the window. She was thinking of succulent flakes of cold chicken, with thinly sliced gherkins. "Sweeping?" she suggested.

"Could you ask him to come in here?" Mr Kelly used a thumbnail to clean between two of his front teeth. Then he brought up the budget spreadsheet on his laptop.

Vernon was sweeping the leaves into a pile. Every time he got the pile small enough to pick up with a shovel, a puff of wind grabbed them and threw them about.

He was surprised to see the school secretary walking towards him across the playground. She was hugging her mint-green cardigan tightly around her. She walked with tight little steps as though she had to keep to a line, buttocks clenched.

"Mr Kelly wants to see you in his office, Mr Bradley, if you've a moment."

Vernon looked at her sideways, leaning on his broom. The yellowed whites of his eyes slid round.

"I'll be there directly, Miss Glacer. Directly I've finished sweeping up these leaves."

"Oh," said Miss Glacer, pulling the sleeves of her cardigan tighter against the stiff breeze, "I wouldn't worry about leaves."

"I'll come now, then." Vernon put down his broom and the leaves that he'd got together began to fly off.

But Miss Glacer's buttocks were in retreat. Her heels clicked. She'd decided that after the chicken, she'd have an individual ginger cheesecake with a square of chocolate.

Vernon turned the letter in his hands, eventually he set it down on the table amongst the breakfast things. While he was eating his toast he glanced at it. He didn't like the look of the letter.

After breakfast he took it round to Mrs Crabbe who always read his letters for him.

"It's a letter," said Mrs Crabbe, adjusting the frames of her reading glasses on her nose, "from Hawksmoor Roman Catholic Middle School." She coughed and held the letter further off. "Dear Mr Bradley," she read, "due to the current round of budgetary restrictions, the school is not able to offer a renewal of all the on-going contracts for hygiene employees and given the demands of the new hygiene delivery strategy for this institution, your qualifications..." Mrs Crabbe, gave a small gasp and ran her tongue over the tips of her dentures. There was something of the lizard about Mrs Crabbe. Her narrowed eyes shuttled sideways as if she'd spotted something edible on the kitchen surface and the wattles of skin at her neck quivered.

"Oh dear, Mr Bradley," Mrs Crabbe could only give a sympathetic wince. "It looks as if you've lost your job."

"Lost?"

She licked her lips; they were so cracked and dry. "That's it, Mr Bradley, in a nutshell."

"In a nutshell?" Mr Bradley's soft brown eyes travelled down Mrs Crabbe's house-coat, its hard buttons winked like the shards of beetles.

Mrs Crabbe grasped her door handle under this scrutiny. She handed the letter back. "That's what it says." She peered out of her scaled eyes and blinked away the dust. She would go off to the mini-market presently for some water biscuits and a packet of seed for the canary. "It's these Catholic schools, if you want my opinion." She was holding the door open a crack still. "Now if it was the Evangelicals..." But he failed to catch the end of her sentence.

Back home, Vernon sat meekly in his usual chair by the window; the shadows lengthened and still he sat and a skin formed on his cup of tea. It was only now that he began to relive his humiliation: standing with his big hands dangling beyond his cuffs in the headmaster's study, looking at the trophies and framed diplomas while the man behind the desk shuffled papers. He'd begun to sweat and Mr Kelly had twitched his nostrils.

The headmaster had shown him a scrupulous politeness that, now he thought of it, stuck in his craw: "Thank you so much, Mr Bradley, for sparing the time to come and see me." Mr Kelly had said he was "a valued member of staff; one of our greatest assets." But he'd gone on about a certificate. And as he was leaving: "Oh, there's some graffiti, Mr Bradley, by the front gate. Would you be able to deal with it tonight? It's late, I know and I don't want to keep you behind but it's in a very visible area and makes such a bad impression on visitors. Would you be able to? That's excellent. Thank you so much."

Vernon realised now that he'd been fucked over, well and truly. "Yes Mr Kelly, no Mr Kelly. I'll clean your fucking graffiti off your fucking wall even though I'm working overtime for no pay!"

For thirty years, Vernon Bradley had been the caretaker at Hawksmoor Middle School. For thirty years he'd scrubbed, swept, polished and fixed; unblocked drains, gutters and downpipes; moved furniture, set out chairs, stacked chairs and cleared up after the Christmas party, kept vigil, endured... No one knew what he'd done.

Two large, unexpected tears formed; he dashed them from his eyes and began to curse everyone he could think of. When he was tired of cursing he thought he would have a drink to calm his nerves and found a bottle of rum in a cupboard that he'd been saving. He poured himself a large glass: "Congratulations on your retirement," he said to his reflection in the mirror and tossed back the rum, which burned his throat.

After the third glass he sat down on the settee and let out a resounding fart. Then he began to giggle. Old Mr Bradley, his father, was looking down from the alcove. He wore a crisp white shirt and a straw boater. He'd just arrived in England. In the photograph his black skin shone and his plump cheeks expanded to fill the frame.

"What you grinning at?" Bradley junior made a rude gesture at Bradley senior. "This fucking country you're so proud of... Never done nothing for me."

He raised his glass. "You stupid old bugger!" He knocked the bottle of rum and it emptied onto the hearthrug. Never mind, he thought, there was a case of beer in the fridge and always the off-licence.

Tap, tap, tap...

Vernon Bradley was bent over the low brick wall of a garden; it was the leaves of privet that he noticed, tinged orange in the streetlights. It was night. The dull yellow light made him want to howl. Someone was touching his arm. It was a slight, irritating touch.

"Bugger off!" he said in a thick voice.

Tap, tap, tap…

"Leave me alone!" He would have lashed out but had no strength. He was dimly recalling his journey back from the off-licence with the bottle of bacardi. He remembered sitting down to crack the metal seal on the bottle and taking a few large gulps. He was sweating now as he slumped over the wall feeling a powerful urge to vomit.

There it was again: that feather-light touch on the elbow.

"Don't!" He raised his arm. "Leave me alone." Because he was remembering, from long ago, the three white men.

He tried to focus on the face that wavered in front of him. It was a young face—one of the boys from the school. The blond kid who smelt of wee. What was he doing, wandering around at this time of night? The boy might have spoken but if he did the words were too thin and papery for Vernon to hear. Anyway he soon went and Vernon, using the tops of walls and the splintered rails of fences, clawed his way home.

She was odd, the girl in the mini-market. Vernon found her stare unsettling as he banged down the cartons of juice and milk, the loaf of sliced bread and the three slabs of cheese in their plastic wrappers.

"That all?" And she raised her eyebrows and looked so hard that he felt as though she was trying to peel back the skin of his thoughts.

"What else?"

"I don't know, do I? You don't want no fruit or nothing?"

"No."

"This all you eat?"

"Mainly."

Vernon remembered that she'd been one of the pupils at Hawksmoor School, ten or fifteen years ago. She'd had a mouth on her then and still had, by the looks of it. With her hair pulled back and the sliver of chewing gum that poked out between her lips as she spoke, the girl was making him want to rush out of the shop and back to his house. He was relieved when she began scanning his items with sulky movements, her breasts moving inside her sparkly top.

"I don't know what you want to eat this stuff for." She prodded the loaf of bread. "It's got no vitamins you know."

"It's what I eat."

"I can cook a nice meal for you." She gave a sly sideways glance as she totalled up, "I'm a good cook."

"No," he piled the stuff into a blue carrier, "I can do for myself."

"Suit yourself."

As he unlatched his front door, Vernon caught sight of himself in the hall mirror: his shabby coat, the patchy beard, the yellowing eyes. He wondered why young girls flirted like that. He imagined her sitting on his sofa, peeling off the sparkly top, her heavy breasts. He looked down at himself, at the grey flannels and baggy pullover.

"No," he said, "No, no, no." and shambled through to the kitchen. Through the back window he could see in his garden the piles of sand and cement, a trench he was labouring at, digging down through the layers of rubble into the heavy London clay. Already it was a deep trench.

When he was six or seven, his mother took Vernon to see the family back home in the West Indies. He remembered how the heat crept into his clothes, glued them to his limbs and suffocated every breath; the fierce glittering sea; the sky filled with purple clouds like the bruised flesh of a prize-fighter.

He was frightened by everything: by the huge moths that battered themselves to pieces against the lamps, by the unexpected scuffling of a small grey lizard and most of all by the swarms of cockroaches that his mother tried to ward off with a slipper. He clung to the shell that Uncle George had given him, pressing its cool hard spine against his chest. It was the one thing of beauty.

And then the storm: rain falling in torrents, hammering on the tin roofs; the wind crashing into the sides of the house and things flying past: other people's fences and roofs, clothing ripped from washing lines, a cascade of orange flowers torn from a vine, a blue plastic paddling pool... and all the while the wind roaring so that you couldn't hear yourself think.

Afterwards people said it was just a small storm, nothing like what they'd had just a few years back when whole houses were seized and flung into the air and even a cow, according to his grandmother, thrown, alive, into the top of a palm tree. No, this was nothing like a bad storm.

Vernon was breaking up some pieces of tile in his back garden when a small voice, as frail as a reed, said: "What are you doing?" He couldn't see, at first, who was speaking and began to suspect a mental aberration when the voice came again: "What are you breaking those tiles for?" A pointed face was staring at him between the broken fence slats in one corner.

His house backed onto the school playing fields. Since Vernon had previously been on the other side of the fence he didn't realise how much of his life was visible from the school. He made a mental note to have the fence repaired and made higher.

"What are you doing there? Hey?" Vernon felt exposed. "This is private property, private, hear? You're trespassing."

"Looking isn't trespassing."

"Breaking fences," said Vernon, "is a criminal offence."

"It was already broken."

"You're too lippy, by far." Vernon began to feel more and more like his father who'd lecture boys who came round to retrieve footballs. He'd always resented his father's meanness, the way he kept people at bay, and now here he was, turning into his father. As if it wasn't enough to have got his bulbous nose, his swarthy skin, he had now to endure his father's very words crawling out of his mouth.

The small face was already withdrawing when Vernon said: "But since the fence is broken you may as well come on through."

It was the same boy he'd met that drunken night—his face still tinged, it seemed, with the glow of the street lamps. He looked at the piles of hard-core, the heaps of sand, the trench that Vernon was excavating.

"What is it?"

"A building." Vernon could say nothing more. He was afraid to reveal, even to this boy, what it was he was creating. The broken tiles, the rubble, the pieces of scrap iron. Suddenly it all looked disorganised, childish, a muddle. He felt angry with the boy for intruding in his private world. "You shouldn't be here. Don't you have lessons?"

Then he looked more closely: "What's wrong with your face? How did you get those bruises? Who did that to you?"

"I'll go now," whispered the boy.

"Wait!"

The boy looked so sullen and lost that Vernon felt compelled, in spite of his revulsion, to comfort him. His shoulders were hunched as though he'd a great weight on them. Yet, the boy's moon face left Vernon in the dark, because he could never tell what a white boy was thinking.

"What's your name?"

"Carl."

"Why don't you go back to school? You'll be late for your class."

"I want to stay here with you."

"You can't do that."

First were the foundations of hard-core, then the armature of steel pipes wrapped with chicken wire and coated with mortar. It was a slow process to mould the wire and press in the mortar.

The boy came to watch, hunched in a grubby t-shirt, which he pulled over his knees and down to his ankles. The bruises were more intense, a shiny purple-black against his bilious flesh. At first Vernon felt self-conscious, with those black eyes watching his every movement but, moving around, mixing the concrete and pounding pieces of hard-core he forgot about the boy. As he worked he grunted with effort—he enjoyed the blending of the sand and cement, turning the mixture with his spade and the slopping sound of the wet malleable stuff that would soon be hard and impenetrable, soon to be shaped according to his plans.

And all the time the boy followed his movements, sitting silent and still as though he'd sprouted there like a mushroom.

As the months passed, he began to assist in small ways: handing a cold-chisel or a lump hammer; the tools hung heavy from his wrists. Then he'd wander off into a corner of the garden to play some solitary game while Vernon worked on. Seeing him, Vernon was reminded of himself at a similar age…

…crouching in the tall weeds. He'd taken his shell with him; its hardness comforted. The sun was hot on the back of his neck so that he felt their shadows rather than heard or saw the approach of the men.

"It's our little nigger friend," said the tall one because he was the leader. They were smartly dressed men who wore ties. But the leader had taken his tie off. His neck was tanned above his collar. They gave him their sunny smiles, all three of them.

Then, taking him by the arms, they led him to a corner of the field, under a hawthorn that had long since shed its white blossoms. And, smiling still, they made him kneel.

"What's this?" said one, and took the shell from Vernon and tried to smash it by hurling it against a rock but the shell was strong and bounced away into the nettles.

"Get down," they said. Face down they forced him into the nettles.

Some shells, according to his uncle, possess an operculum, Vernon remembered the scientific precision of the word, with which they stop up the entrance to their refuge when danger threatens. The creature could be inside, safe and enclosed. Nothing could enter in to disturb its inner peace.

When Vernon came to, he saw his own face: his forehead caved in, the eyes and lips swollen, out of proportion to the narrow jaw. It was his reflection, he realised, distorted by the curve of the empty bottle that lay by his head; the bottle they had used to beat him with. Stiffly, he got to his feet and stumbled over something lying in the weeds—his shell. At home his mother, busy with the washing, said: "Are you OK, Vernon?" And Vernon said that he was, that he'd fallen in the nettles but was alright. "Those nettles," said his mother, "you're always in the nettles."

One day the boy called him over. "Look." Two snails were locked together, their shells jammed close as they fought to press their glistening bodies against each other. Between them was a pulsating thread of white, binding them. There was a tiny grinding sound as the shells moved.

"What are they doing?" The boy squatted close to Vernon, his blond head almost touching.

"Mating." The snails were still. A white froth issued from between the sliding mantles. Man and boy peered close, fascinated.

Vernon started; the boy had placed a hand on his thigh close to the crotch, a subtle pressure but cold. Vernon felt the sudden chill through his jeans. As he jerked his leg away, the boy's hand drew back — a pale flash. Vernon raised his hand to strike then stopped: "You'd best go," he said. "Go on, get lost."

Vernon was having a peanut butter sandwich and taking thoughtful sips from a glass of milk that was slightly tainted when there was a soft knock at the door. He put down his sandwich; it was so unusual for there to be a knock at the door at this time of day that he felt a sense of unease in his stomach. He tasted the peanut butter that had glued itself to the roof of his mouth.

"Who is it?" he bellowed, loud enough to be heard in the street.

"It's me, Shazia."

"What you want then?"

"Speak with you." Her voice was faint but determined.

"I don't want visitors." Cold fingers of sweat were tickling Vernon's armpits.

"I got something for you."

"For God's sake!" Vernon heaved himself out of his chair. As he yanked the door open, the girl from the minimarket stepped back a few feet. She looked ready to bolt.

"What is it?"

"I made this for you." She pushed a package into his hands. He shuffled to one side to let her pass. Shazia dropped her gaze and stepped through Mr Bradley's dilapidated front door, smoothing the sleeves of her shiny jacket.

She looked round the room: "People say you're building something."

"Who that?" Vernon put the package on the table frowning. "Who says I'm building anything?"

Shazia ignored the question: "It's a flat bread," she said, as if it was her duty to bring the conversation back to the important issue in hand. "I made it myself. Aren't you going to open it?" Shazia sat on one of the dining chairs and crossed her legs. Vernon's eyes followed the line of the stockings.

He peeled back the layers of paper to reveal the pale lumpy crust, dusted with flour. The room was filled with its slightly sweet fragrance.

"You like flat bread?"

"Uh huh." He touched the soft, rounded dome of the loaf and it gave under his fingers.

"What is it you're building?" Shazia's eyes were hard and shiny in the dimness.

"That's nothing for you to know." Vernon began to gouge lumps from the bread, his fingers dug into the crust.

"Why not? Why can't I see?" She licked her lips and leaned back in the chair so that her jacket fell open. If you like, she seemed to be saying, you can kiss me.

"Because it's my private business." Vernon was stuffing the lumps of sweet oily dough into his mouth. He realised that he was hungry, ravenously hungry, he couldn't get the bread down fast enough.

Shazia turned to him. Her bottom lip was thrust out.

"I want to see," she insisted. Her eyes flicked around the room, as if searching for a bargain.

In his mind, Vernon saw it, rising in a perfect spiral, the sunlight glinting on its ridges - a great shining horn against the sky.

"It's not finished," he said.

"How, not finished?" She was growing irritable now. The painted nails curled and uncurled in her palms. "What's so special about this stupid thing?" She moved towards the door that led into the back room but Vernon caught her by the arm as she reached for the door handle.

"No."

Her hand was on the handle when he grabbed her. Her face had a startled look, as she found herself pinned to the wall, slightly winded by his abrupt force and the shock of his limbs that had the power to bend and crush her under the weight of his desire. She had no time even to close her mouth before he'd pressed his mouth into hers. He took his kiss with an angry gulping, feeling her lipstick greasy on his tongue. As he pressed back he felt the bones inside her face, behind the yielding flesh. Vernon finally stepped away and they stood panting and looking at each other.

"Come on then," she said. She shrugged off her jacket and began pulling Vernon towards the settee. She hung over him, her hair falling while he fumbled with his belt. He felt infuriated by this girl who'd forced her way in. She was unzipping him, reaching in, when he gasped as a dull pain struck him at the apex of his thighs.

Shazia stopped kneading him: "What is it?"

"Nothing," but he was limp now and pulled away.

"What's wrong with you?"

"Nothing."

"Nothing?" She stood up and began to arrange herself. "I have to go to work," she said winding her thick mass of hair into a coil and pinning it. "They don't like it if I'm late."

Soon the front door slammed, the knocker rattled and silence settled in Vernon's house.

Some molluscs feed by scraping at the clinging plants with their jaws, others rasp at the rock itself, even burrowing in, tunnelling into the solid rock. His uncle had shown him where they'd eaten away at the stone piers of the house, soon they would start on the foundations. Other shells are parasitic, piercing the soft tissues of their host to drain out the life-blood in tiny sips. The cone shell is a predator, shooting a poisoned dart, a tiny sliver of calcium, so venomous it could kill a man. It then sucks the victim, a small fish or shrimp, into its stomach.

Shells grow by small accretions, by the layering of calcite and aragonite. It is the work of decades. As he pressed each fragment into place and smoothed the grout with his fingers, Vernon felt intensely happy. In the moulding of these ribs of glass and concrete he felt he was nudging something into place. He could have been touching flesh as he pressed and poked. The foil wrappers glinted with a sudden numinous energy in the dim light as he prodded them into position. Time was unmeasured in this coiled space — his physical needs seemed to fade. Finally, a raging hunger or thirst would come over him and he would stagger into the kitchen in search of a loaf of bread or a carton of milk to fill the space. Or chop an onion and stuff it, raw, into his mouth.

A staircase spiralled up inside and there were windows at intervals in the curving walls. These windows were filled with tinted glass: amber and rose and green so that walking up the stairs you were bathed in bands of colour. The spaces between the windows were formed of fragments of glass and tile embedded in concrete. The glass was from milk-of-magnesia and Seven-Up bottles and marmite jars saved over three decades by Vernon's mother under the stairs in boxes.

In the layering of his glass and coloured foil, Vernon was unaware of the passage of time. The seasons came and went. He laboured in rain and snow, buffeted by winds and baked by sun.

Carl was back, helping now to heave the sacks of cement and grout and wielding a hammer to break up the tiles.

One day, Vernon stumbled among the glass fragments and the boy stepped forward with startling speed and stopped him from falling. His arms had grown solid. Vernon realised that he was no longer that anxious child; his face was pale and bony but no longer pinched and narrow; it had filled out and coarsened with bristles.

"How old are you?"

"Seventeen."

Vernon was shocked; he looked down at his own wrinkled hands, the splintered yellow nails and swollen veins. "Still at school?"

"No."

"You left school?" Vernon felt he should have been consulted.

Carl shrugged and hefted a bag of tiles. "Where do you want these?"

There was a sense of urgency now about finishing the structure, now that Vernon thought he could see it complete. He imagined going up the stairs, the light growing with each step, until he was at the summit. No one, not even the ghosts of the long dead, would disturb the geometry of his thoughts. Only the coloured shafts of light would enter in to soothe his meditation.

One evening as they cleared up, Vernon was compelled to make an announcement: "It's finished," he told the boy, who was at the awkward age of never looking directly, so that Vernon had no idea whether he'd heard or gone further than even Vernon himself, down some pathway of the mind.

"What then," said the boy, "do I do now?" He was full of something, though he didn't know what it was yet; he was on the verge. He stirred pieces of brick and old rusty nails with the toe of his boot.

"It's your decision, what you do with your life," Vernon said.

No one had ever spoken to the boy about deciding. He felt as though he was standing on the edge and must jump, before he was pushed.

"Maybe a building course," suggested Vernon, "if you like the idea of being a builder."

The boy looked—a quick frightened look; their eyes, for a moment colliding.

"You OK?"

The boy didn't answer immediately. "You're getting rid of me," he said finally with something like his old whisper.

"No."

"That's what it seems like."

Vernon shrugged: "What do you want?" He drove his shovel into the earth.

"Nothing." Carl walked away, kicking at the weeds and muttering.

Vernon wondered what it was people wanted from him. As the gate clicked and the boy's footsteps died away, he heard the sound echo from the entrance to the tower and a sense of emptiness reached out to him.

This time Carl wouldn't go back. He'd had enough of this old man and his crazy plans. At home he lay on his bed, naked, and began to touch himself thinking of a man he'd seen in the changing rooms at the swimming pool. His penis became stiff in his hand and soon he spilled himself, except that at the last moment his mind flicked back to the great white tower he had helped to erect; the nacreous walls thrusting up in the deserted weed-grown garden.

Late the next morning, standing in the street outside Vernon's house, Carl watched for a while but there was no sign of Vernon. He went into the garden and found some boxes and a stack of old wooden scaffolding, piling them up at the foot of the tower. Then he pulled a can of lighter fuel out of his pocket. The fire was slow to catch; Carl almost stamped it out but, once the cardboard was ablaze, he stood back and warmed himself, enjoying the sense of relief and excitement as the flames took hold. Then he ran, not looking back. He'd go to a place he knew where men hunted each other for sex among the thick foliage. It was time to do this. He would find no redemption in the walls of towers, no matter how extravagantly carved.

Mrs Crabbe's canary fluttered in its cage and scrabbled with its claws.

"What is it?" asked Mrs Crabbe. "What's wrong with you?" She stared at the bird which stretched its wings and opened its beak in a silent gape, as though in pain. Then, abruptly, it fell from its perch.

Mrs Crabbe took up the sleek yellow body. Its eyes were half-closed, then it stiffened and hopped upright on her hand. She posted it back into its cage.

"What's that smell? It's like something burning." She wondered if she'd left the grill on and went through to the kitchenette. From there she could see Vernon's garden and the peculiar thing he was working on. A stream of smoke was pouring out of the entrance. Someone had heaped cardboard boxes against the walls. The young greedy flames flickered, reaching out for support and finding the wooden struts. From there they leapt eagerly, drawn up inside the tower by the spiralling up-draughts. The windows of coloured glass glowed before exploding in a shower of sparks.

Mr Kelly put down his coffee cup. It was lunch time and the playground was filling up: some children stood in knots while others careered about; as usual, there was a cluster of bodies outside the toilet block. He went back to his spreadsheet with a frown; the figures weren't adding up. Glancing up a few minutes later he thought there seemed to be fewer children; the group outside the toilet block had broken up. The spreadsheet scrolled down.

It was only after he'd finished his lunch that he noticed how silent and empty the playground was. Leaning forward and peering round to his left, he could just make out part of the playing field. The press of bodies looked like a rugby scrum. Mr Kelly reached for his scarf and headed down the corridor.

It was a windy day; the gusts caught Mr Kelly's coat tails as he hurried across the football pitch. There were now no more than a dozen or so children at the fence. They seemed to be trying to peer through the palings at what was beyond. He wondered what was on the other side of the fence. They were mostly gardens with scraps of lawn. Behind this particular bit of fence was a large pale object. Mr Kelly was surprised that he'd never noticed it before, since it was quite visible above the top of the fence.

Three girls, holding tight to each other's hands, slipped through a large hole in the fence. Mr Kelly opened his mouth to call after them, to issue orders, but the wind, strengthening still, flew into his face and he felt his cheeks pressed in with the force of the gale. He finally reached the fence and peered through the splintered panels.

The children shouted and laughed as the flames flew into the sky. It was a twisting pillar of flames that made the young faces glow and throb to a dusky red. Some of them looked round, as Mr Kelly squeezed through the fence, but most just continued to gaze at the spectacle of the white cone that was beginning to crack. The frame was showing between the empty shapes of the windows that had fallen. The flames crackled and a burst of fire shot up the centre of the frame, sucked up by the whirling gusts of wind, and the last panes of glass shattered. Thin shards of glass arced out from the exploding window. The children covered their heads and ran. Mr Kelly clapped his hand to his eye.

There was no blood, no fragment of glass; they could not find anything wrong with Mr Kelly's eyes at the hospital. They sent him home. Yet, in the days that followed, he could only sit bewildered in his office. He stared at his laptop but the lines of figures on the white screen no longer made any sense. Instead, bursts of colour bloomed behind his eyes. Each time this happened, Mr Kelly flinched. It disturbed his ordered approach to life: to be assailed by the stuff of dreams, to have things unravelling in his mind and claiming his attention when work was to be done.

"Mr Kelly?" Miss Glacer was faintly concerned, as she nibbled a Ryvita, to see that Mr Kelly was tearing small strips from a printed spreadsheet and arranging them in concentric circles on his desk.

"Yes, Miss Glacer?" Mr Kelly was smiling as he hauled himself back from the rim of something. There was a rushing sound in his ears and a taste of salt in his mouth. He could see Miss Glacer's lips moving but her words were drowned out by what he now knew to be the sound of the sea.

Vernon watched the tower, his refuge, disappearing in smoke and thought how nearly complete it had been. He told himself that it would be possible to rebuild. Then he thought of the back-breaking work, the wasted effort. He was afraid of the hole that was left now that there was nothing and wished that he'd never tried to mould the sand and cement. It was better gone, though the impression of it stayed with him, pressing on his eyes.

He took his shell, the pink and brown one given by his uncle, from its place on the shelf. He caressed its familiar symmetry. He wondered how long a shell might last—hundreds of years, perhaps millions, like the skeletons of the dinosaurs. When he was a boy they'd told him to listen for the sound of the sea and he'd listened, entranced. He'd since learned that it was not the sound of the sea inside the shell, but the hollow echo of more mundane sounds.

"There's nothing now," he said to himself, looking at the grey flecks of a drizzle that was just beginning.

The shell seemed to throb before his eyes as if it was getting bigger in the fading light and himself becoming smaller.

If he closed his eyes the colours were more intense and other images came into his mind unbidden: twisting spirals that soared up into the cracked blue glaze of a winter sky, the curves and contours of a young woman's breast and the pale nipple at its summit. He found

246

himself walking across a shiny plateau, so vast that he couldn't see the limits of it, like an ant crossing a tabletop. Then, he found himself beginning to slide as the surface of the plateau began to undulate, to draw him in.

The ugly papered walls and the dusty carpet began to fade as if these materials were just a dull layer to be peeled away. The room was getting darker still but the shell by contrast was glowing, gathering the light, and Vernon, though less in bulk, felt himself becoming a part of the continuing thread of brightness that travelled up into the pale nothingness.

Issue 28

October 2011

Kotar's Daughter

Stuart Freyer

Gottmacher sat in the rocker six hours a day for two weeks. The new piece had fermented in his pores for months. As usual in this phase, nights passed fitfully, and every afternoon he rocked in the massive chair. Finally when he recognized the end of the cycle of contemplation he rose. At the waist high table he combined copper paints for the base and first levels. His eyes were on the massive blank studio wall but he knew the placement of the colors. Decades of expertise with pigments let him choose and blend without looking, like a smoker fishing out his pack, his matches, and lighting up. He had a habit also of drawing with his eyes closed. Several of his "warehouse erection" series were all done eyeless, examples of which hung in the Tate and MOMA.

"Ready," he said as if to something in the room, activating the intercom.

Perez, a burly man with a Moses beard and a large purple birthmark on his cheek, muttered, "about frigging time," loud enough to be heard through the door. In the anteroom he put down his paper cup half-filled with Jack Daniel's and began to motivate the 12 by 18-foot resin-surfaced cardboard-thin steel plate. A laddered easel on ball-bearing wheels glided it over polished cement into the studio's great space. Thirty feet above, motor-driven skylights allowed in the green morning of the Berkshires.

This was Gottmacher's process as long as Perez had known him. Years of experimentation, scratching off, destroying, painting over, working canvas, barn doors, then plastic, now thin metal, had evolved into a unique method. The technique was so internalized that recently every new project spewed Zeus-like, fully formed, within days. He still mingled pigments to his own specs, added the oils and solvents himself, let them evaporate just so much. Then he remixed, covered them with various cloths a gummy or mushy or semihard or drippy consistency to his desire, leaving the work fresh for later. Lately he was applying metal powders for their reflection of spectral elements. He had consulted with Chillouly the glassmaker about making metal and acrylic bubbles large enough to place their edge tangent to a surface, achieving, where desired, a laminate of color thin as a layer of cells. The present price for one of his recent works had paid for the small custom foundry waiting in the Northwest corner of the compound. The apparatus could be rolled in on tracks via its own hatchway.

Gottmacher, who could afford an army of helpers, preferred working with Perez.

"Should I remove any of the Mowers?" the entering Gargantua asked. Near the wall behind the artist stood several completed steel paintings the same size as the shiny fresh one, all on their own easels. Any resemblance to men or mowers or grass or sky came by intuition. Like a dancer, they motioned the observer to feel the surrounding air, the hauling muscles, the supporting and teeming earth straining within by texture and nuance. His reviewers came upon the term "Conceptual Poetism" to describe the oeuvre. Gottmacher's response had been, "you can call it cowshit or Mazerati for all I care." Painting was beyond description. The stuff must be seen to live.

"Yeah, take out those two," he said tilting his head to the finished Mowers, "and call me in the morning."

"You call me. I may be gone," Perez said, as he began to push the closer of the two from the great space.

"Where to? You have no life."

Gottmacher was already staring at the new metal sheet as if there was something there. He looked at the corners, the middle. His eyes drove across the plate hundreds of ways, curving, swooping, his body moving with the lines and colors in his head.

"Screw you," said Perez returning for the second giant rectangle. "Lunch will be quiche at three. You eat it or I'll nail you to the wall."

Perez went out and bolted the door of the great room. He adored the man.

Gottmacher began with a curved line of dark peach to the right of the exact middle of the quadrate. The center of the stroke, like a bobsled run, was thinner than the laterals. The topes and bone-like placements countering above and below right and left maintained the imbalance. He understood that the matchless picture is off kilter. It is disturbing to the eye, falls out of itself, a glimpse while moving. In youth he had rejected so many perfect pictures, especially the "open silo" group, because they were just that; perfect. The most arresting images break the rules.

He ate lunch standing. Six hours later, the seeds were in place and he hooded the piece with a nonporous nylon fabric. The immediate covering after each session helped to preserve and bring forth what he called "the living stain."

"Ready," he yelled into the automatic intercom.

Perez, who was preparing a supper of duck a l'orange with a salade nicoise and looking for a proper white in the temperature controlled wine cabinet, barely heard the voice crackling overhead. "Your mother," he grumbled back.

"Maybe Hattie's will help your miserable mood," smiled Gottmacher as he came out of the studio.

They both knew it was a good time. It was always good in the middle of a project.

"Maybe," said Perez.

Gottmacher's hair, still a blonde thatch, fell forward over his face almost hiding the Wicked Witch of the West nose, and he looked out through it as through a waterfall. Most women thought his square chin Superman sexy. The short solid frame still suggested the pre-art-school labor of a furniture hauler (in his case high-end furniture). In fact, the gorgeous moldings, architectural details, old masters, and luscious colors of the couches and armoires had fed his decision to cash it all in, enter art school, and become a painter. He was still practical, even frugal, about some things, an echo of bleak days in unheated flats dining on anchovy paste, flour and water tortillas cooked on a hot plate, and washed down with cheap wine. Considering the astronomical figures he currently commanded, his frequent use of house paint for certain colors (when it qualified) seemed an unnecessary quirk.

Evenings after a home-cooked gourmet dinner with Perez were commonly toots at Hattie's Bar and the grumpy giant was happy to oblige. They took their place among the crowd at the far end of the gleaming oak slab. Gottmacher's series of lovers, ex-wives, as well as his daughter, had long since given up trying to stop the nightlife. And as the merrymaking did nothing to interfere with his concentration or the part of his brain that was engrossed in the labor at hand, his agents, lawyers and galleries had not assembled much of an argument either. His artist friends, of course, loved his idiosyncrasies. "Remember Poe, Van Gogh, De Kooning," they said. "Crazy or addicts or both. Geniuses all."

How's the foundry working. Still holding at 2200 degrees? The locals treated him like another laborer who used his hands but with the respect due a master of his trade. How much of that linseed oil you use in a year? They maintained his equilibrium. Stories of life in the shops and farms fed him, added ideas to the hues and movement of the mothering woods, the hard city faces, and lush torsos already in his mental data base. A carpenter rambled about the change of cedar with time from a cool brown yellow to steel grey and everything in between; a barfly recounted how the bronze of scotch improves with each succeeding shot; a hunter described sunrise through pines. They were the back-story to everything. His horn of plenty.

Of course there were the weekenders and summer people who, like himself, fueled the local economy with their big house projects and expensively catered parties. But Gottmacher preferred to get drunk with the hoi poloi. This evening he and Perez were helped into his truck at one A.M. The three-mile drive home was automatic, though slow and unpredictable.

In the morning he rocked for a half-hour. Gottmacher first saw the chair in a Lexington Avenue antique shop. The bent oak was burnished by wear, the maker anonymous. Knowing something of its value and that it would be hard to unload, he had convinced the dealer to hold the article. He left behind everything in his pockets — which at the time was everything — returned to clean out the seller's basement and carried the oak curiosity to his tiny studio. The seat and back were now covered in silk cushions sewn by a long gone model-lover. Its size gave one the impression of a perch for a basketball star rather than a squat painter, and Gottmacher looked almost childlike hunkered in it. But it was his muse, the witness and the birthplace of his imaginings.

He stood where he had left off. In his brain only a moment had passed since yesterday. And yesterday was a page in a book, a recorded moment in a DVD, a separate world that breathed with its unique time frame ready to take up at the instant of reclamation. Composing in layered creams of oil and metal, he faithfully filled in the tempestuous spaces, dunes and arroyos lifting and scalloping the surface. The color of the reflected unsubstantial air scattered so that at different hours of the day the recurring motif would seem to evolve. It was a new story, the beginning of a cycle that was born out of the mowers, the yearning of the crops, the maternal earth below.

It would be called "woman aloft."

Perez, attempting to stay dry for the morning, called on the intercom.

"Want some coffee?"

Gottmacher was erect and inside the painting now, between the masks of oil and benzene and safflower oil, and hydrolyzed gold, cadmium yellows, coppers, transmuting together. He saw the unchartered inevitable metal islands complete. That afternoon they had worked up molten zinc for deposit to two areas. "No. Take out the foundry. And check the intercom later, there's static. I can barely hear you."

The studio-house stood by a nestled clearing in a five-acre park of ancient maple and oak. The architect had been given carte blanche with the exception of orientation to light (North), external color (Salmon), and exquisite detail about the studio itself (height of built-in tables, easel roller mechanisms, movable shelving, and the foundry niche). Perez returned the specialized beast to its lair on the far side of the yard and made for the main house. In the kitchen, while waiting for the baguette dough to rise, he pored through several chapters of a Norman Mailer novel.

And being close to the man had not been a bad thing for him. His own abilities didn't even come to the knees of such a titan. So the surrender of his own career as expert welder and dedicated amateur chef seemed less a loss than a gift. Perez had traveled with his boss, met people, seen things that few others could match. Knowing Gott- macher so well, he could picture him on the other side of the great door; the stance, the hand in perpetual motion.

On the other side of that door however the hand had stopped mid stroke. Gottmacher stood motionless. Was there a shimmer above the painting? The air shook slightly, reminiscent of a mild earthquake he lived through while sketching in Peru. He moved closer and touched the edge of the looming rectangle. His fingers reflexed away from the heat. There were convection waves coming off the picture.

"Perez, is the furnace on?"

Perez loafed in, munching on a whiskey soaked croissant. "You're right about the intercom. No, the heat isn't on. What's up?"

"Feel this."

"Maybe the sun on it?"

"Never happened before."

"You're using more metal than ever."

"Well, when I'm done, be sure to double check that the cover stays tight. If there's any dehydation overnight..."

"I know, I know."

A teenager with a crew cut and her mother's kewpie doll lips stood like a doe in the kitchen entrance.

"Dad working?"

It seemed to Perez Lisa had been shuttling the half mile between Gottmacher's compound and her mother's house since she had been able to walk.

"Probably he'll be free later," Perez replied with a sheepish grin.

"Is this a good day?" Although Tuesday was their day Lisa al- ways asked Perez if her father was free. It was a question about both his work and the drinking.

256

At least it was supposed to be a good day. They had agreed to alternate dry with debauch. Perez moved to obstruct her view of the half-filled wine glass.

"Good," she said. "*24 hours* replay is on tonight."

"He wouldn't want to miss it with you. Do your homework and come back for supper."

She took a carrot from the stainless steel refrigerator and left, showing a ballet gait that few beside Gottmacher had been able to capture in a form of expression that was—ultimately—inert. Degas showed you the dancer but Gottmacher, a reviewer said, put her in your gut. Yet who better to know that mysterious race of spitfires and sylphs than Perez's boss. Genius, wealth and fame were a powerful aphrodisiac.

That evening, in front of the TV, Gottmacher and Lisa finished Perez's paella.

"Sometimes I wish you were a forest ranger or something."

"Art still not glamorous in spite of those trips to my galleries? Too many of them?"

Since he was a child, his eye had picked up subtle gradients of color that he still had trouble articulating. Her skin, under the full spectrum lamps, was altered.

"Noo, it's just that kids tend to stay away because you're famous."

"Aha, the Princess phenomenon. How many kings have seen all forty-eight episodes of 24 since it started?"

"Not too many, I guess." She giggled and threw a shrimp tail at him.

He looked at her skin tone, then turned off the TV and looked at her again.

"What?"

"Have you noticed a color change tonight?"

"Is this a test?"

"No."

"What then?"

"Nothing, my beauty."

The light of her skin, the wall behind her, everything was altered ever so slightly, all shifted toward blue.

On the third day, muted oranges were in, blended corrosion greens added in staccato motion. The picture did not ask for anything different than what his mind had seen. Each afternoon, Gottmacher tentatively touched the steel.

Perez came in to deliver some pigments. "I turned down the thermostat. Feel the difference?"

"No. I don't think so."

He thought about phoning California but Mardus would still be in Geneva until tomorrow.

Next morning in the white studio, removing the wrap, he felt like he had sunk into a hole. What was changed about the perspective?

Perez answered his call, chewing on a biscuit laden with foie gras.

"Did you move it?" Gottmacher asked, his eyes on the picture.

"No, why? Holy shit. Look at the bottom!"

Gottmacher had seen the Issenheim Altar in a little town in the Alsace. Colmar, a bourgeois place, seemed to have no other reason to exist than its two prizes: beer and Grunewald's moving triptych of the Crucifixion. He and Lisa's mother arrived in the evening and had enjoyed the first. By morning in the tiny museum he was unprepared for the second. The broken and agonized hanging Christ made his legs soft and he had to sit on the floor. The spikes through the martyred hands had pierced his brain, spoken to him physically.

The sight before him now in the studio was more powerful. The metal sheet was elevated one inch. It floated above the easel, skimming Perez's paunch.

Gottmacher reeled back to his rocker. They looked at each other.

Perez bent to put his fist between the support shelf and the lower edge. Gottmacher leapt to clamp his hand over it and held.

"You want an amputation? What if whatever is going on changes? What if it drops? That's two hundred pounds."

"This is related to the warmth," Perez said.

"I think so too. Call Mardus."

Perez had Caltech on the line in minutes.

"He'll be on a plane out in the morning."

Jake of "Jake's Downtown Chic" was stacking boxes and he was puzzling the problem.

"Anything religious? A miracle, maybe?"

Perez was collecting the sweetbreads, lobster, arugula, and other necessities. As a rule, when alone in town, he didn't chat about Gottmacher's work although he was not under any restrictions.

"Doubt it," Perez answered. "If anything it would more likely be from the vibes of one of his spread-eagle women." He remembered that cycle with fondness and spoke with total seriousness and respect, cutting Jake off from further exploration in that direction. Joe Markel set down the organic asparagus he was delivering. He advised listening for a buzz, searching for hidden wires. A fox faced man with sleepy eyes chimed in.

"He working in metal on metal now?" asked the fox face.

"Yeah."

"And layers of plastic?"

"Yep."

"Radio condensers and thermisters generate energy from stacked metal plates. How many layers?"

"Not sure. Do I know you?"

"Just passing through, I know his work. Nice around here," the small fellow slipped out.

There were other questions Perez couldn't answer. Were there any magnetic fields in the room? Could it be a practical joke? What about very thin wires suspended from the roof? Who would do that? Who could even get in to do it unnoticed? And what about the heat? One or two at the counter looked as if they didn't believe the story at all.

That night at Hattie's, Gottmacher and Perez took a separate table after hailing the crowd at the bar.

"What do you think?" said Perez.

"How is the intercom?" Gottmacher asked.

"Still crapping out a lot."

"Do you notice anything different about the quality of light in the evenings?"

"No."

"Well look again tonight. Make yourself useful."

"You'd starve without me. You'd be eating oil and crayons," said Perez.

"I cooked before I met you," said his boss.

"Right, I heard about it. Nouveau Buchenwald."

After a half-hour scrutiny of the room and then the painting, Craig Mardus, Feynmann Professor of Physics at Caltech, and Gott-macher's second and favorite ex brother-in-law, said, "Amazing. A million monkeys."

"What?"

"I think you may have constructed a machine. You came upon the exact combination of metal and oil-based paints and plastic insulated within the structure of the picture. Like the old story about chance. If a million monkeys sit at a million typewriters for enough years, one will produce the works of Shakespeare."

"I am not a monkey and this is not Macbeth."

"I really think that in this case you are and it is. Could you write out a detailed description of how you got to this step, the ingredients of the layers, approximate thicknesses?"

"Why should I? The notes are in my head — where they belong."

"You have to record your notes. Science demands it."

"I don't think so."

"And the government might take it. It will compensate twice what the galleries pay." Mardus knew he was talking millions. "Name your price."

"And if I refuse?" Gottmacher's hands unclenched on the arm-rests of the rocker and he stood.

Mardus had heard of situations like this before among his colleagues.

"They can do things."

"Like..."

"In the case of something that might have an application as a weapon or defense there is an Invention Secrecy Act. The only way you can avoid it is to give up the copyright on your painting. There may even be other obscure preemption rulings where the Feds can obstruct the law of patent and copyright. They pyramided after 9-11."

"First, I don't want to," said the artist. He looked across into the clear eyes of the somewhat untidy man standing with him in the yellowing afternoon, then at the giant slab. "Furthermore. It's not complete. There're a few hours of work left."

Mardus returned his gaze, dumfounded. He broke into laughter and had to retreat to Gottmacher's rocker until he could regain his composure.

Gottmacher looked down at him, his face clinical and cold. His hand held a filbert absentmindedly but firmly as if it were not a brush but an arrow.

Instantly he knew Gottmacher was dead serious. Of course he was. Here was a major physics breakthrough and the man was going to…! Mardus jumped up from the chair as if shocked out of it.

"You don't mean…"

"Precisely," Gottmacher said. "I'm going to finish it."

"Change it?"

"Finish it."

The meek knock at the door that cleared the weird air in the room was welcome. Perez poked his head in.

"It's that intercom again. Comatose. And there's someone here. I told him you don't…"

A bald man with a mustache pushed through behind him. In his black suit the dark square with legs showed his credentials: Jeffrey Roucher, National Security. As Perez moved to grab his collar he backed up and raised a revolver.

"Look up," he said.

Two bull-like men were peering down through the skylights. Their shouldered rifles pointed at Perez's forehead.

Gottmacher turned fiercely to Mardus. "I'm very disappointed in you."

Mardus looked shocked but resigned. "This is none of my doing. But I'm not surprised. Only that they're here so fast."

Roucher walked slowly around the steel structure.

"This was bound to happen," Mardus said. "Gott, you know how much I respect you. This is a quadrillion to one. Like the first random collection of Nitrogen, Hydrogen and Carbon. Or the first primitive DNA. All chance. How many universes have to exist for those coincidences to arise?"

Gottmacher looked unconvinced.

"We're in just such a situation. It supersedes Art. You know I love Art not like you perhaps and we don't doubt its necessity. But someone has to examine this."

"Yes. On the wall of a gallery or a museum," glared Gottmacher.

"I mean really examine. Even the shroud of Turin or King Tut's Mummy donates microscopic fragments to provide clues to their history."

"What's next for destruction? The Sistine Chapel, the works of Picasso?" Gottmacher shouted.

Roucher looked back at them from the side of the painting. "It's the right of the government to seize intellectual property in the case of national security. In this case we understand you have invented an anti-gravity apparatus possibly valuable as part of a weapon."

Perez clasped Roucher from behind, pinned the revolver, and held his own head behind the agent's before the snipers above could adjust.

"Should I throw him out?"

"Yes," Said Gottmacher.

The angels in the skylight were gone.

"Don't," Mardus said. "Call your lawyer. Think of Lisa."

"Why should I listen to you, Judas?"

"Please, I didn't even know what you had till an hour ago. I still don't know how or why."

"This is a work of Art, for god's sake."

"This," said Roucher through gritted teeth, "is an antigravity machine and possibly an energy source that could tip trade balances, start wars. If so, the government must control it."

"Art is not controlled, it's enjoyed."

"Will you let him make a call?" Mardus said, turning to the pinioned Roucher.

Perez squeezed.

"Yes."

The snipers were through the door, their rifles stroking Perez's broad back as he loosened his hold.

Roucher waved them down.

A long discussion. Gottmacher on the phone to his lawyer who punted to a patent lawyer who immediately slapped a copyright and patent application on the painting. Let them try to copy it, the lawyer said; only the original is of value as art. An agreement was reached: the painting would be examined by portable ultrasound, CT scan, electromagnetics only. Nothing would be touched. Gottmacher was not to attempt to change the "device," add or subtract from its surface or environs. If the phenomenon was found explainable by known sources, the government would walk away. If, however it contained a scientific breakthrough, it would be confiscated for a fair market consideration. Until then Gottmacher was free to start another work. He was not to leave the grounds without permission.

"I'm under arrest?"

"Consider it federal protection. This is Mr. Bone and Mr. Carson. They'll be your companions for the next few days." Roucher rubbed his arms.

Within hours Roucher, and several new arrivals in lab coats, had set up equipment. A laptop began to pour a torrent of graphs, numbers, and scans; colored serial sections that suggested, to Perez, thin slices of a fine grade of salami.

In the kitchen Gottmacher wanted some explanations. How did they know? What would they do with it? Roucher, who had no answers or would provide none, returned to the studio. They sent out for enough scotch and beer to make up for a missed evening downtown. Mardus continued to assert his innocence. Perez was sullen.

When the three of them were drunk enough to relax, Perez blurted, "It's my fault. I should quit."

Gottmacher had recovered a little balance. "No. I fire you first. Then you quit. But why?"

"There was a funny guy at Jake's store, I thought he was a sight-seer, and I was blabbing about the thing. He must have called it in. I should have strangled him..."

Gottmacher looked over at Perez, smiled and raised his glass. "I believe you would have."

"It was just a matter of time," Mardus said. "It's not your fault."

"Here's to Kotar," Gottmacher said, raising his glass.

"Who?"

"The Canaanite God of Art and Science," Perez said.

Then they spoke about nanoparticles, women, Lisa, archeology, the chemistry of beer and the physics of color. Perez showed Mardus a card trick that Gottmacher and Lisa had seen dozens of times, still mysterious to them. The pack is thrown at the ceiling and the chosen one sticks. Never once during the evening did Gottmacher's other eye fail to see before him the finished Woman Aloft.

They were walking in the woods behind the studio playing their game about the shape and intensity of colors. When Lisa was small they had said "this is greener" and this is "bluer." This looks like a heart, like a circle, like a dog. Nowadays they used "creamier," "chromier," "restful," "happy." As she grew, Lisa knew this was a way to her father's heart. It was a language he spoke. So she conversed in color, texture and balance. The future, a time of pride and pain for both, was still years ahead.

"What will you do Dad?"

"Uncle Craig says I should give it to them."

"I know, but what will you do?"

He looked off toward a distant rise. "I guess you do know your old king."

For the next few days, Gottmacher worked in another medium. He sketched. He drew the lab workers, the way the shadows slanted in the kitchen, the guards cleaning their rifles. He took some paints, alloys and mixed tubes for later use. Mardus emailed Roucher for any late information. Nothing.

On the third afternoon Roucher called from D.C. "Here's what we know so far. The machine has been drawing minimal energy from solar and house wiring. That explains the intercom problems and what you noticed about the lighting. But not enough force to hoist a heavy object."

"What's going on?"

"Something else, something new is generating more power than we can account for — the dynes to continuously lift a 200 pound mass. Also the painting, or mechanism as we prefer to call it, follows the easel when we roll it. The two will be sent by special transport to a lab at Langley in the morning. You receive twice the figure your most valuable painting sold for. That's two point two million."

Gottmacher's lawyers had told him that in the end the only thing they could do was stall for time. Ultimately they would lose to the juggernaut, so why not sell the painting and go on? After all they had agreed not to alter it. Only remove miniscule specimens when necessary and replicate it when feasible. Even then the replication would be only that: a copy. Like a brilliant fake of the Mona Lisa. An unfinished Mona Lisa at that.

Governments. Lawyers. Brute power.

The lab people packed and left.

That evening the guards attacked the food and drink from Perez. They had come to look forward to the man's concoctions, particularly the strong coffee, which Perez said was an African blend. Neither man was able to get to the alert on his cell phone before he realized he was dozing. The added seconal worked quickly enough. Perez had plenty left from his visits to detox.

In the studio, Gottmacher quickly removed the cover, the surface still soft. The night air outside seemed expectant. The layered steel composition might be saying Where have you been?

"No matter, I'm back," Gottmacher replied to the woman within. Was she inside his mind or inside the steel? He no longer knew.

Perez stood behind him as he mixed the last batch. He added to the upper right angle, the near perfect circle of sienna in the almost center, here a line, there an impeccable smudge. He sprayed the epoxy sealer evenly like a caress and stood back.

"Now they can do what they want," Gottmacher said. He could hear a sniff behind him.

He turned around beaming and looked up at the weeping Perez.

"Thank you," Gottmacher said.

They looked at it for an hour before closing the door behind them. Gottmacher left a phone message for Roucher. It was almost morning.

The new creature absorbed the ambient light. It transmuted completely, and lifted from its mooring. There was an urge inside the woven viscera of this first child. It did not have the intelligence of its innocent creator but knew its simple purpose—to journey to more luminescence. It focused on the source.

Like a magnet drawn to some unseen pole, she crashed through the skylights and launched herself toward the morning sun.

Autopsy

Betsy Cornwell

"It's the biggest damn wolf I've ever seen."

Trudy's voice crackled over the line. Lars rolled over and stared into the clock on his bedside table. Two thirty-one. The small red light in the corner glowed AM.

Phlegm rattled in his throat as he sat up. His eyes ached with bleariness, and his lips stuck to each other when he tried to yawn.

"Yeah, don't get so worked up about it." *First time in a month I get to bed before midnight and there's a fucking wolf,* he thought.

Trudy clucked at him. "You don't understand. If there are others this size... I don't like to think of my grandchildren walking around with beasts like this loose!" Trudy sounded even older over the phone, as if the roots of an ancient tree had grown down inside her throat and lungs. Those roots wrapped particularly tight when she was worried. "It looks pregnant, so the farmer said he didn't like to kill it. You need to come down here and examine it right away."

"Don't tell me my job," Lars growled, wishing for the blank black comfort of sleep from which Trudy had pulled him.

She sniffed, and he immediately felt guilty. Like everybody else at the office, he liked Trudy, with her talent for making people feel at home—and, he'd readily admit, for making them feel guilty when it suited her.

"I'll be down in half an hour," he assured her. He stood up and stretched. The phone cord pulled tight.

"Please hurry, Dr. Ericssen," Trudy whispered. "He only used enough tranquilizer for a normal-sized coyote. I'm sure it won't last very long."

"Right," said Lars, stretching again, leaning away from his bed-side table. He heard a snap and the phone crashed down to the floor between his bed and nightstand. A frayed and broken cord hung from the receiver in his hand.

He'd fix it at a less ungodly hour. Right now he needed to get down to the office, apologize to Trudy, and take a look at this wolf.

He pulled on a flannel shirt. He found jeans in the bathroom, where he'd tossed them earlier before collapsing into bed. Instead of reaching for them, he found himself staring into the mirror. His eye-lids sagged, his mind hummed with encroaching dreams.

He came so close to sleep that his legs gave way beneath him and his head slumped over his chest. The collapse startled him awake. Exasperated, he splashed cold water over his face. After toweling off his hair and beard, he yanked on his jeans and rushed for the door.

The chains around his tires were crusted over with ice, and Lars had to chip it away for a solid five minutes before he could drive out. His truck moaned and grumbled over the frozen road. He promised himself a new heater out of next week's paycheck.

He staggered through the door, praying that Trudy had started the coffee. The acrid scent of store-brand beans greeted him under the dander and flea-powder smell that always dominated the lobby.

Trudy waited behind the front desk, a hand-knit shawl draped around her narrow, sloping shoulders. A cup of dark coffee lurked at her side.

"So, where is the old beast?" Lars asked. He'd made up his mind that as long as he had to be here, he might as well act cheerful about it.

"Operating Room B." Trudy shuddered under her shawl. "Be quick, Dr. Ericssen. The sight of that thing makes my bones ache."

"Don't worry," Lars said. "Just need some coffee first." He walked around to the back of the room. When he picked up the coffee pot he knocked over a stack of *Dover Veterinary Center* cards, and they scat-tered across the carpet like fallen leaves.

Instead of energizing him, the coffee woke up a deep headache in the back of Lars' skull. *Serves me right*, he thought to himself on the way back to the operating room. *Serves me right for opening the only large-animal veterinary hospital for miles around, and never putting anyone*

268

else on call at that. Still, this wasn't the cattle country Lars had come from. There were hardly any calls after midnight here. In Montana, he'd been raised to shoot a wolf on sight, pregnant or not—none of this tranquilizer bullshit. New England farmers were soft.

He scrubbed up quickly, humming to himself as he pulled on rubber gloves from the box by the sink. The latex grabbed at the thick hairs on Lars' hands.

The lights in the operating room were off. He could see nothing but a metallic glint on the operating table and the great, slowly undulating hulk that was the wolf breathing. Lars ignored the trickle of fear that ran through his belly.

He clicked up the ancient light switch. A hanging lamp above the table stammered awake.

His first impression was less animal than monumental. A sloping gray mountain of fur rose up from the steel table, each hair thick as a pine needle. A primal scent emanated from its matted hide, stirring all Lars' latent Cro-Magnon instincts. He snapped on a surgical mask and approached.

The wolf growled and Lars retreated to the door. He waited, still as a stone, to see if the beast had woken.

It let its gusting breath out in the slow, unmistakable sigh of a dreamer. Lars exhaled too, sweat cooling on his forehead. He circled the table to look at the wolf's face.

Its muzzle was long and angular, and three red welts slashed across its nose. Lars leaned in, breathing through his mouth to avoid the smell. Its lower jaw was completely dislocated and hung at a limp angle from its skull. He could see old scars, dozens of them, crossing over its jowls and neck. Its left eye was missing, and a string of greenish pus oozed from the swollen socket. A faint claw mark bisected the other, closed eyelid.

"How old are you, anyway?" Lars murmured. He ran his hand lightly over the wolf's matted hide. He could feel every muscle and sinew; this thing didn't carry an ounce of fat.

Still, its stomach swelled hugely. Silver stretch marks lined its underbelly.

He rolled the creature onto its back — or tried to. Lars could bench-press 200 pounds, but he couldn't make this thing move. He walked over to the door. "Trudy?" he called.

"Ye-es?" He could hear the plea behind her voice, asking him not to make her come back there. But he'd seen enough of Trudy carrying sick dogs from their owners' cars and handling unbroken stallions to know she was stronger than she let on.

"Can you bring me that big sling from the other room? I think I'm gonna need your help in here."

Reproachful silence. A sigh just quiet enough to make Lars think he wasn't supposed to hear it. "All right."

She appeared at the door, holding a canvas square and a thick length of rope. Her eyes kept flitting to the shape of the wolf behind Lars, and clear liquid thickened behind her glasses.

"Well, really, Trudy, it's just another canine…" Lars trailed off, unable to admonish her without admitting that the beast disturbed him just as much. "Here now," he said gruffly, "I'll give it another tranq first." He filled a syringe and stuck it in the flesh under the wolf's jawbone. Its head jerked a little. One lip flopped back, exposing damaged yellow teeth at least two inches long. A viscous sheen of saliva and blood slipped over its incisors.

"Okay." Lars beckoned Trudy closer to the wolf. She rolled up her sleeves — the shawl stayed safe outside — and tucked one end of the canvas under its back. The wolf huffed to itself softly, like a sleeping lapdog. Lars' and Trudy's eyes met over its great mass. Just another canine.

Lars squeezed his arms under the wolf's weight, searching for the canvas. He found it and pulled. He had to lean back on his heels, putting all his weight behind his arms, to coax it over to his side.

His hands emerged covered in clumps of matted fur and dark, clotting blood. Lars' thick brows slumped toward his nose. He looked at Trudy and saw how big her eyes had gotten.

He flexed his fingers. With this much blood, it must be injured pretty badly. "Let's get 'er on her back," he sighed. He never liked to see a beast suffer.

Trudy handed him the rope, and he linked it through the grommets on the edge of the canvas. She did the same on her side, and with the smoother fabric under it they were able, together, to hoist the wolf onto its back.

A long jagged gash trembled under its ribcage. Blood pulsed out in a slowing rhythm. Below its vast stomach Lars saw the distended bulk of its testicles—there was no way this thing was pregnant. It must have eaten just before the farmer took it down.

A nasal whine escaped the sleeping wolf's jaws. Lars pressed his left hand over the wound, knowing he couldn't staunch the blood. If the creature was dying, though, he could at least make it quick. Comfortable. He looked up at Trudy.

"It's for the best, I think," she said.

Lars nodded. He walked to the cabinet at the side of the room and selected a glass vial from the top shelf. He filled a second syringe and pressed it to the wolf's neck. A long hot gust whistled out of its nostrils. When all the air had collapsed from its lungs, the whole room seemed to sigh, too.

Lars stepped back, the better to see the dead beast. The pity he'd felt escaped him. Every angle of its bony haunches, every battle scar and bristling hair, told him this was a predator. A wolf this big could take down a full-grown man and leave hungry for more.

He heard Trudy stifle a yawn.

"You can go home if you like." He tried to smile at her, but it was hard to take his eyes off the wolf. He couldn't shake the feeling that it still might wake up and attack him. Staring at its one slit eye, he murmured, "I just want to see what's inside 'im. I'll close up after." He looked at the clock: four thirty. God knew how long this would take. "Or, you know, open for business." He tried to laugh.

Trudy walked around the table and laid her hand on his shoulder. "Thank you," she said. "I'll bring some breakfast when I come back in." She cast a last, doubting glance at the wolf and shuffled away.

A moth fluttered through the door closing behind her. It wove in curls and zigzags toward the lamplight, straying again and again from its own path. Lars watched it, glad for a momentary excuse to delay touching the wolf.

It met the lamp in a sudden graceless spark of fire. Burned wings swished down, nestling into the pale fur on the wolf's belly. The moth's exoskeleton, now brown and cracked, stuck to the bulb and smoked. He looked away.

Lars pressed his scalpel to the wolf's stomach, but the skin refused to part. Grumbling to himself, he turned to the counter and selected a longer, sharper knife, one he used for amputations and Caesarian sections. He'd delivered colts and calves with this one. He knew it would work.

As he bore down again, something jerked under the wolf's hide. A fierce kick knocked against his right arm. His hand slipped and the knife stabbed deep, releasing more blood than Lars had thought possible. Whatever was inside shuddered once more and was still.

This new blood was still bright red, though the wolf had stopped breathing some minutes before. It joined the congealing pool that already brimmed on the table. Lars opened a valve and let it all drain, thick and swirling, into a lined plastic bucket.

He cut a straight line from the wolf's abdomen to its heavy, dark genitals. Lars had neutered hundreds of dogs. He didn't know why that sight should make him stare, make him wish even more that he were anywhere else.

He retreated to the head of the table and cut twice more, carving a Y into the wolf's chest. He stuck his hands under the dermis and pulled, revealing a stringy pattern of capillaries and cream-white lines of bone.

Lars took hold of his biggest steel scissors and wedged one blade under the wolf's wide sternum. He felt his biceps start to burn as he squeezed. The sudden snap when the bone gave way made him stumble against the bulging corpse.

The wolf's ribs fanned open like parting curtains. Its lungs were twice the size Lars had anticipated, deep pink and spongy, and they let off curls of steam into the chilly room. Intestines coiled in a cramped ball above its pelvis. The spotted black liver huddled under the ribs. Every organ made way for the wolf's engorged, protruding stomach.

Lars paced around the table. The stomach lining stretched taut and shiny, thin as the skin of a bubble. Digestive tissue strained to hold in whatever lump of half-digested prey waited inside. It was stretched so tight Lars feared it would pop.

Instead it smiled under the release of his knife, easing back from the pressure within. A stench of acid and flesh streamed up to Lars' face, and he felt the jolt in his throat and tongue as he tried not to gag. After he made himself adjust to the smell, he cut further, until the tissue parted entirely from the wolf's last meal.

His incision revealed a bulk of red wool, damp with bile, wrinkled into the shape of the wolf's belly. Lars prodded it with his scalpel. There was something firm and solid underneath—as if the wolf hadn't chewed up his meal before swallowing it.

He put the scalpel down and lifted the cloth. Thick gobs of stomach acid dripped down, stinking and steaming. Tears started in Lars' eyes.

The girl's limbs were rounded and soft. Acid had burned away long strips of her skin. Her hands were round child's hands, the bitten nails pink and clear. She couldn't have been older than five or six.

Lars ripped the cloth away—or tried to. It was tied around her neck in a limp bow, and a hood clung to her head. Tooth marks punctured her blouse and skirt. The hood was still tucked tight around her face, so that her eyes and cheeks were mostly intact. Drops of acid clung to her lashes. Bile had worn away the flesh around her lips, so he could see where she'd lost baby teeth, and the nascent pink of her gums. A deep slash rent the fabric over her shoulders. Blood gathered in a still pool around her wound.

Lars' hands shook. He lifted the girl out of the wolf and wrapped the red cloak tight around her body. Her head lolled back against his shoulder. Her mouth gaped, and her acid-seared eyes seemed to stare.

Lars sank down beside the table clutching the shrouded girl. His right arm twitched, his hand remembering its grip on the knife. He jerked it back and knocked over the bucket beside him, sending the blood running in map-lines over the floor.

He was supposed to rescue her—he knew that much. She should have sprung from the belly bright and whole, laughing with him as they tore the beast apart. She should have shared Trudy's breakfast.

Lars stared down at his lab coat. It was covered in spreading stains, yellow, reddish, brown. The vomit and blood smell poured into him again, liquid-thick and sour. He choked, and a drop of spittle shot from his mouth onto the girl's cheek. He recoiled.

Unable to trust his own body, he stood, careful, still shaking. He laid the girl back inside the wolf. He curled her legs into her chest the way he'd found her, remembering crime scenes on television. Lars covered the girl's face with her hood, stroking back a few sticky brown curls.

He looked at the clock again; it was verging on morning now. Perhaps daylight lurked outside.

He moved out into the hallway, through the lobby where business cards still littered the floor, where the air still smelled like coffee. He leaned against the doorframe. A stranger called out to him from the other side of the road, but he couldn't hear. Slowly, as if still sleeping, Lars staggered into the waiting dawn.

Rules to Win the Game

Matthew Burnside

"It's a hard world for little things."
— *The Night of the Hunter*

The Game began around the time we discovered monsters were real. Theo, our eldest brother, started it the day he came into the center of the living room and declared he was no longer Theo but *The Noir*. Of course, none of us had any idea what it meant but we would learn in the coming weeks that it involved him wearing a long musty trench coat two sizes too big (it smelled like a bingo parlor), and a crushed hat with a feather gliding out of the top that would catch the kitchen light and shiver silvery, like a fish leaping out of water tickled by the sun.

Then he would hang around in corners all afternoon, smoking rolled paper while talking in a strange grown-up language none of us could translate. "You're barkin' up the wrong tree, toots," or, "Sorry dollface, but I don't know who that is," he would say, shrugging, puffing imaginary fumes whenever little Emilia would address him by the name of his old identity. The more I think about it, the more I suspect Theo might have known about the existence of monsters long before any of us.

The rules were never formally discussed but in time we all had an implicit understanding of The Game.

RULE: Everything is The Game. Everyone is a player, whether they know it or not.

Emilia got her first fifty points when she died and was reborn *The Zombie*. She began shambling, lagging one foot and slurring her speech. She would sit on the sofa eating a bowl of brains in the morning, her shredded pink bunny Pogo Rex tucked tight between her kneecaps hemorrhaging clumps of cotton, his head dangling by a string.

Not long after that, Big Little Ray got his first points by donning a green hoodie with half-cut paper plates duct taped to the back and colored to look like scaly bumps. He announced he was *The Crocodile*, warned us to avoid the floor or risk having our feet snacked on or— god forbid—our bodies devoured entirely. He would slither around, dragging his enormous belly across the carpet, snapping at toes that weren't high enough off the ground, a makeshift snout wrapped around his jaw with jagteeth and two gaping cardboard cutout nostrils. Theo would ring a bell and that would be our cue to seek higher ground. Sure, we all hated having to elevate ourselves, pinned on tiny islands of furniture, but that was his rule and there was no way around it. Later, we would learn the trick of tossing down potato chips, which allowed us to shuffle by while Ray was busy chomping on the bait. We would all use that one to get around the house.

Ben eventually caved in, too—he was the oldest next to Theo. He knotted up his greasy hair with chopsticks, strapped a broken broom on his back and began bowing to everyone and meditating on the linoleum counter top all day. He called himself *The Samurai*. Emilia didn't know what that meant, but it made her laugh to see him battling the Crocodile through the swampish corridors of the house, yapping gibberish and waving his splintered sword like a kung fu cartoon. I think he was secretly Emilia's favorite. When he would give her a paper lotus she would blush three shades of pink, slur "Fankkk yee*wwww*."

Everyone had their points except for me until the Sunday Theo slid up beside me and ignited a conversation. "Gotta light?" he asked, a toothpick stabbed between his teeth. After handing him some invisible matches, he rattled the box that wasn't there and shot me a suspicious look. "Say, what's your name lil fella?" Of course I couldn't think of anything flashy. I'm not so creative. "What you have is the look of a gunfighter—The Wild West." He was trying his best to help me out, you see, to get me into The Game. "Tough guy eh? Thanks for the tinder, kid. Twenty points for your troubles!" he said, and then winking, "I got my eye on you, mack." Then he leapt over The Crocodile, who was napping on a mattress in the middle of the floor, drizzling croc-slobber on The Zombie's leg. (She could get away with sleeping so close because she was already dead and her rotting skin was unsavory to The Crocodile's reptilian palate.)

The Noir was still sharply eyeing me from a corner when we both heard the front door creak and the sinister jangling of keys, and we knew the Emperor of Black Rainbows was home for the day.

RULE: The Game is secret. The Emperor is never to know of its existence.

Part-dragon, part-vampire, part-troll, The Emperor was the most evil monster in our tiny kingdom, and wore the face of a man as a clever disguise. He was always choosing a subject and taking them back to the Lair—what we called the peeling tin shed in our backyard with the hissing black light bulb—doing all kinds of mad scientist stuff in there. He'd come in and gather us up and choose one, just one, for the night. Then we'd watch him lead away our unlucky sibling with his mustard yellow finger-nailed hand.

It was a sinister kind of lottery. We all knew what would happen next, because we had all "won" at some time or another. He'd give you the Black Rainbow Punch—a syrupy medicine in an amber jar that always stayed full—and you'd be out cold, and when you woke up the next morning you'd be missing something: chunk of heart, lump of lung, half a stomach, quarter brain lobe. You never really knew *what* and that's what made it so scary. You might feel your heart ticking and never suspect it was gone forever, swimming in some coffee can on a wobbly shelf in the Lair. You could feel something, though. It hurt in the strangest places—embarrassing places—and you knew it was pain but only the slightest trace of it. The Punch would convince you it was all in your head. You'd believe it, because it was better that way.

The Noir would tell us to go ahead and drink the Punch because it was only when you woke up during one of The Emperor's organ-fests that you might see your lung in his hands and die on the spot. *What you don't know will keep you alive*, The Noir said.

277

These days though, he hardly ever took The Samurai or The Noir anymore; I figured it was because The Samurai had his broom-sword and The Noir, well, he was The Noir. Me, The Zombie, and The Crocodile were his favorite test subjects now, The Zombie especially, who, aside from munching on human flesh all the livelong day, was a kind and trusting soul, clueless and completely oblivious to The Emperor's evil ways.

On this day, we could tell The Emperor was feeling not-too-hot because he immediately reached for his Deathproof Tonic from the cabinet: a careful concoction of crushed bone, the ground up bits of our collective missing organs (minus the hearts — these he liked to keep as souvenirs), 12% lava, 20% dog pee, and all of it spiked with the tears of our deceased Empress, who had been a much kinder ruler to us all before dying of a Voodoo curse.

Some say after The Empress passed, that's when The Emperor went mad and began the slow transformation to diabolical super fiend, but myths abound. Hard to tell what the truth is or isn't sometimes. *The way it happened is never the same thing as the true story*, The Noir tried to explain to me once. When I asked him about the Empress he told me she had been known for her red hair, but that her spirit was locked away in the Lair now and that was that. He flicked his paper cigarette, told me never to ask about her again.

RULE: The Empress is history. Don't ask.

I suspect if it hadn't been for the Tonic, The Emperor might have been slain long ago, but with the unholy stuff swimming in his blood, he was invincible. "There has to be a way to defeat him," The Samurai often thought aloud. "No," Theo would silence him. "There is no way."

The first thing The Emperor did after getting the Tonic in his system that night was stumble into the living room and lure The Zombie over to his lap. He was quick to coax her with the Punch. "Take your medicine, creepy," he told her, pouring a capful. As she downed it he poured another. We watched him bob her on one knee, his teeth all pearly and fake. Sitting on the carpet, we could make out the rows of cavities that he hid so well from everyone else, those big black rotting stumps invisible from every other angle.

After a moment he dug around in his pocket and came out with a red rubber ball. He handed it off to The Zombie, laughing his grating laugh, and she took the bait. Just like that. Easy as pie. They were heading out the door, and the skies were growing a bruised purplish. We watched her skip all the way into the Lair, where Black Rainbows grew and twisted out of the walls like razorblade roses.

"Wonder what he'll take tonight?" The Crocodile said, twirling his tail made out of a bunch of cut up and tied-together water hoses.

"Maybe a chunk of brain. Maybe a kneecap. Who the hell knows?" The Samurai said, sharpening his sword with a coat hanger. The Noir perched on the counter, folding an Ace of Spades in half, a dark glint in his eye.

"Whatever he wants. He won't ever stop. Unless—"

We watched the Noir form the shape of a pistol with his right hand and pull the trigger. We imagined it bursting through the glass, splintering tin and burrowing itself a cozy home deep in The Emperor's skull.

That night in the fuzzy lime twilight of the living room, as we lay sprawled like mutts on the floor, I could hear The Emperor creeping back inside. The glass door opened and shut with barely a sliding hush, and his black boots grazed by my head as he deposited the sleeping Zombie on the corner of our yellowing mattress. You'd think a man as big as him would hammer the ground but his walk was a clean gutter cat prowl. No, it was the breathing that gave him away, always the breathing: the way he would suck in air like a too-narrow chimney choking on smoke before shooting it out with a crippled cough.

I heard the lock on his door. Then, somewhere in the room I heard The Crocodile fart, The Samurai shifting in his sleep to parry the phantom blast.

The eerie green light from the VCR fell upon The Noir, whose wide-awake eyes were locked on to the sputtering ceiling fan with its one blade missing. I watched him spread a ragged sheet over The Zombie's feet. He noticed me, too, and I pretended to sleep. He raised up a bit, back to the wall, put his hand inside his trench coat. (We all slept in our clothes because it was safer that way.) He came back out with that imaginary revolver. This time he polished it with a rag that wasn't there. Flicked it to one side. Dug in his front pocket and brought out nothing, but it was like he was rolling that nothing around in his hand like loose bullets. Pushed six in the chamber. *Click.* Spun it once. *Whoosh.* Clapped it shut. *Snap.* Then, he put it away, tucked it back inside that strange, oversized coat of his. Finally he curved his hat over his face and turned over to sleep.

That's when I knew The Noir was doing cartwheels on the edge of crazy.

That night I dreamed of The Empress. In it, her bones kept bending back in impossible positions. She was bald and ugly, her lips an unnatural shade of blue, all chapped and peeling and terrible. Her eyes were gone, hollowed like olives with the pimentos sucked out, and she kept calling to me from inside this giant birdcage. "Out. Out," she kept muttering. I couldn't stand how bad she looked. She had been so beautiful in pictures I had seen. Now, reduced to this. "Out. Out."

The next morning when I yanked my head from my pillow, I shook off the sweat but I couldn't shake the dream. *Out.* I kept hearing it ping around in my brain. *Out.*

Somewhere in that shed, The Empress was being held against her will, I knew it. The Noir said it himself. I couldn't stand it. Don't you know it's a horrible thing to feel trapped and powerless. It's a horrible thing to feel small. I began to hatch a plan to get her out of there.

I knew the only way I would survive inside the Lair was with Deathproof Tonic to keep the Black Rainbows at bay, so the next morning I strategically positioned myself below the cabinet where the Tonic was stored after The Emperor had already left for the day. I waited until the Crocodile lurked for his breakfast. Soon enough, that bell rattled, and we all took to higher ground.

The Crocodile slithered by, and as everyone watched him sniff The Zombie's toes through her shredded socks, I opened the cabinet and tucked the Tonic in my waistband.

Now, I knew what I was doing was punishable by torture. If The Emperor ever suspected someone of messing with his magical artifacts, we'd all pay the consequence. So as I took the bottle, I noted how it was positioned: label facing out, just left of the cracked mug with "World's Greatest Daddy." I'd have to put it back *exactly*. No room for error, not with The Emperor.

When it was safe, everyone hopped down and went about their usual routine. That is to say: The Zombie hobbled over to the television, bumping along with poor Pogo Rex by his frayed ears. The Crocodile yawned and scuttled beneath a table, going belly up and blowing snot bubbles through his leathery green snout. The Samurai folded paper flowers in the center of the living room. As for the Noir, he sat facing the window looking out over the wild tangle that surrounded the Lair, where dead trees posed like petrified bouquets of snakes, and the long brown grass and tall haunted weeds buzzed with bad omens. We all imagined freakish things in there, giant half-cricket half-dogs mutated and spliced together by The Emperor just for fun.

I knew I couldn't think too long about those kinds of things if I wanted to rescue The Empress. I locked myself in the bathroom and turned the faucet on full blast. Sat on the commode twisting the cap off of the funny square-shaped bottle, the stuff inside sloshing and glinting in the sickly-yellow light. I poured some in a Dixie cup and tried to pretend it was medicine. I clamped my nose and swallowed quick. All I could taste was the 20% dog pee, enough to make my eyes sting and water. Over and over I refilled it. I nearly threw it back up into the bathtub, but I counted back from thirteen until it passed.

Stumbling out into the hall I felt dizzy. The Noir was the only one I was really worried about getting past, and I might have scrapped the whole plan if he hadn't been so busy with his eyes glued to the television screen, watching movies The Empress would've never let us watch in a hundred years.

They all had titles like *The Big Shot* or *The Big Sleep* or *The Big Kill*—he was a sucker for anything with 'Big' in the title I guess. I didn't understand the movies but The Noir, he spoke their language. He memorized all the lines. His hero was some guy named Humphrey with a face rough enough to sharpen pencils.

As I inched by, The Noir perked up, his head turned but only slightly. I was busted, I was sure of it. But he didn't say anything then. Even when I could see myself in the TV, and I could see that he was watching my reflection in the screen crossing the room. It wasn't until I was tugging on the sliding glass handle that he spoke up. Without turning to face me, without even giving any clear indication that he was addressing me at all, he said, "Don't be late." That's what he said. For what? I couldn't tell you, but I wasn't about to hang around to find out.

Outside, I watched the shed looking mean with its zigzag rows of stripped paint like rusty, rain-rotted teeth. The high weeds waved, hiding a hundred ugly somethings I hoped would stay hidden long enough for me to get by them. When rain started to slant down upon me, I could feel my shoes turning into cast iron frying pans.

I could just make out the top of The Noir's head in the window, that feather of his shining through the dirt-caked window pane. It seemed like some magical charm to me, reminding me there were still places in the world where Black Rainbows didn't grow. Where wild colors were still able to breathe brightly, untouchable and true. With that in mind, I counted backwards from thirteen and found myself at doom's doorstep with the black bulb hissing just over me, an army of vines ready to tangle me up, but they sensed the Tonic, shrank back. One thing I was figuring out about the Tonic: it seemed to make you alert and sleepy all at the same time.

The first thing I saw inside was the long table that The Emperor splayed his subjects out on, deep fingernail trails in the wood. Row after row of dark stained cabinets. On the wall there was a board with rows of hooks that held various torture devices, surgical tools for cutting flesh and pounding bone, all brand new-looking. Shiny. You could tell he took pride in them. All around the room, there were high shelves with assorted shoe boxes, paint buckets, empty jars, potato sacks, plant pots, half-cut milk cartons, and hollowed out sleepy-eye dolls with egg-shaped heads, some with nails sticking through their faces, jutting through their noses or twisting out of their cheekbones. I knew our hearts were up there somewhere. First, I would concentrate on finding The Empress though.

I crawled up on the table to get a better look, but I was still feeling the effects of the Tonic and it was becoming tougher to focus. It dawned on me that I could have been tricked, because what I was now feeling felt a lot like the Black Rainbow Punch, and if that was the case I knew I would soon slip away and be out all afternoon, maybe forever. The Emperor would find me there on the table passed out, and he wouldn't take just a piece then, he'd take the whole thing. He'd be greedy.

So, naturally, when I went wobbly and fell from the table, landing hard on my knee cap. I was sick with shame. I had tried to use The Emperor's own medicine against him, but I should have known he was too clever for that. Real monsters always are.

RULE: You can't cheat the Game, even when it cheats you.

I might have been bleeding but I couldn't tell. The only thing I could do was drag myself to the nearest cabinet, feel my way inside before blacking out. If I was going to be found there, I hoped I would stay asleep through it all.

When I came to after what felt like only a couple of seconds, I found I was still holed up inside that cabinet. My bottom was numb, and I had a pretty bad headache pinching the right side of my brain. I poked my head out to take a look and saw that it was growing dark through a window, saw clouds like black balls of fur scuttling, oozing scab-like across the sky, dusk spreading slow over the thorny trees like a star-stained blanket. Then I could hear the mutant mutt-crickets chirping through the walls, grating their entrails like violin strings, declaring the Black Rainbow Hour begun. It was too late.

My first instinct was to spill out and head for the house on two tingly beanpole legs, and I was about ready to elbow the flap and make a break for it when I heard the shed door break first. Then the hacking cough. I pulled the cabinet door closed.

In walked two bodies, I think. The obvious presence, and another, softer one. I heard something like the thump of dead weight. Zippers zipping, buttons snapping. Hands rubbing together like sandpaper hard at work.

I tried to spy through the crack, trying so hard not to breathe. I had to wrap my arms around my mouth. All I could see was The Emperor towering over the table through a thin slit, caressing hair or — something. Sharpening blades or cleaning his surgical torture apparatus.

It was then that I saw it, high on a shelf above The Emperor's silver head of hair: a Voodoo doll with two 'X's for eyes, perfect stitch-mouth, red mangy mane of hair like a waterfall on fire. The moment I saw it I knew it had to be her. In my mind, I imagined being able to reach her and tuck her away in my pocket along with my brothers and sister, stealing us off to a bright city so deep with alleys, so crowded with people the Black Rainbows would never find us. We could be safe in a place like that, happily lost and never alone among a sea of strangers.

I guess I imagined too hard though, because in my dreamreaching, I lost my balance and spilled out of the cabinet in full view of The Emperor.

RULE: Stay safe inside your head.

He stopped what he was doing, waiting for me to stand up. I shouldn't have, but I did.

As if I had emerged through a long dark tunnel, braved the warm comfort of that darkness for so long only to smash into a blue wall of even more terrifying daylight, I saw everything upon the table. I had to fall right back down.

In the pit of my stomach I could feel it wasn't natural. The tiny body splayed on the table like that, like a living doll. The living doll spread out and open on the table like a clockwork plaything, and The Emperor with his hands upon it all, making use of it, turning those cogs, moving and contorting the mechanical parts for his own perverse amusement. My baby sister, fast asleep.

Fast asleep: the one thing I found peace in.

RULE: The way it happened is never the same thing as the true story.

Black Rainbows flitted about the room now, and I felt myself losing it, the tears came in a continuous rush. My stomach collapsed and a great wave of shame and fright flowed through me, like burning and cold all at once.

"Dear boy," The Emperor addressed me, standing over me as I lay crumpled and sobbing at his ankles. He ran his forked tongue twice over his gums. "Dear, dear boy." Whistling, he meandered over to the corner, picked out a dull-looking hacksaw. He slung it aside, gripping a hammer before finally deciding on a simple screwdriver instead. "This'll work, doncha think?" He stood over me again, smiling, his cavities fully exposed. "C'mere boy. Let's see what makes you tick."

And I don't know where he came from, but suddenly The Noir was there with us, standing at the door, his hands in the front of his coat pocket, cursive wisps crawling up from the tip of his cigarette. "Say, buster, we've got some business to settle," he said, calling out The Emperor. "I'm here to collect."

The Emperor turned to face him. Through his knees I could see The Noir, who flung me a wink before spitting out his cigarette.

"One thousand points for helping me slay The Emperor, kid," The Noir said, and then he aimed his index finger point blank at The Emperor, who began to laugh. The room flashed white, and then all that was left was a miniature fog of smoke hanging in the air, The Emperor laid out beside me on the concrete, a hole the size of a grape in his forehead gushing black blood.

The next thing I remember is being back inside the house where The Crocodile was cheering, jubilantly proclaiming to all the kingdom, "The Emperor is dead! The Emperor is dead!"

Whatever power he had held over us had fallen away, I knew it, but still something was terribly wrong. The Noir stood at the sink, frantically emptying out the Deathproof Tonic that I had left in the bathtub, the Deathproof Tonic that The Emperor had not been able to find that afternoon, which had left him temporarily vulnerable. The Noir peeked through the chipped blinds, then spoke: "You did good, kid, but they'll come for you now. They'll come for you to try to get to her, but they'll never get her will they?" He slapped me on the back and tousled The Zombie's ketchup-locks, and something about the way he did let me know it would be the last time I would ever see him —let me know that even though my sister and I were free, that freedom didn't extend to my brothers. Then, when he plucked the feather from his hat and put it in my hand, wrapped my fingers around it for me, I knew it was true.

"Here's looking at you, kid," he said, holding the front door open for me and The Zombie to escape. The Samurai and The Crocodile watched on, with their eyes exchanging the terms of a silent pact that I knew would never be broken between us. I could hear the dreamy murmur of sirens in the distance, long red and blue shrieks wailing, howling the night into a shredded song of youth. I counted back from thirteen, grabbed The Zombie, and for the first time in our lives we were free.

"Hold my hand," I said as she began to bawl. "Don't look back." Then we were off, winding through birdbath lawns, navigating by panic. Only once did I stop to tie her shoe and stab the feather behind her ear, which seemed to calm her some.

I could feel my big frying pan feet begging me to turn around. To find a good place to hide. To sprout wings and sail the marbled sky. I was afraid because I understood *every*thing now. I knew all the things we weren't supposed to know. I could feel the hollow space inside where my heart had once been, ripping itself wider and wider. Then I could see where downtown started and the old neighborhood ended, where the gravelly pavement became slick and oily, and the swaying magnolias turned into stark, soulless streetlights, where the crowns of the trees became the wide rims of soot-belching smokestacks. There was a sick, empty feeling crawling up my throat, scabs everywhere, in the bushes the trees the sidewalks the skin of my hand trembling in my pocket. In short, Black Rainbows lurked around every corner, but then I remembered something my brother once said, the day before he died and became someone else.

If you can just make life into a game, you can make it up as you go, and they can't touch you. It won't matter whether you win or lose then, because even if you lose, you win.

I hesitated, just long enough to make out a bird—or was it a bat? —diving upward into a shimmerwhite pool of sky. On a rooftop, a storm-beaten weathervane slung itself around, its brass finger pointing west, toward the city steeped in neon blur, buzzing like an electric orchard.

Finally, I understood what The Game was for, and who. I watched moonlight chase its way along the razor's edge of the feather behind Emilia's ear: our very own Black Rainbow ward, keeping the colors true.

RULE: The only way to win The Game is to never stop playing it.

"One hundred points for not crying," I heard myself say to Emilia. As we zagged through an alley, leaving our old lives behind and making up new ones along the way, I knew I was a terrible liar. I hoped I would be as good at fighting monsters as the Noir had been. "And call me *The Cowboy*." The Enchanted City lay before us in the distance, floating in a mist of melancholy dream.

My New Do

Jackie Craven

My name is Luanna Appa, but you probably know me by my maiden name, Kornacki. Some thirty years back I made headlines over that hullabaloo in Flantline, Kansas. Newspapers said I coulda been kilt.

I headed out early that morning, pointing my bike toward the 7-Eleven. Blue tassels fluttered from my handlebars, and locusts out in the yellow fields screeched loud enough to break glass. I kept on pumping, reciting the shopping list Mama gave me: milk, Dr. Pepper, two cans of tuna fish, the *Sunday Star*. I didn't hear the black Buick creep up behind me, didn't notice it till it swooped past in a poof of dust.

Then, up ahead, the Buick pulled onto the shoulder and lurched to a stop beside a shimmery mirage. A lazy crow swirled overhead. The driver's door creaked open, and a man climbed out. He slouched against his car and watched me approach.

He was a young fellow, fresh from church I guessed by the way he dressed. White shirt, red tie. Dark blue pants with a tidy crease up the legs.

I stopped beside him. "Car broke?"

His glance scuttled over me, then away. "Lost my dog?" His answer came out like a question. He touched his hair, delicately, like a woman primping. It was black as his car, all shiny and slicked back to show off a widow's peak. "You seen it?" he asked.

Now, you might think I'da been smart enough to smell trouble. But remember these were innocent times, especially in Kansas. I threw down my bike and looked around, eager to know more about the missing dog.

"A poodle," the man said in a smooth, almost girlish voice. "So small, other dogs think it's just a cat."

"I never seen a poodle, except on TV," I said.

The man cupped his hands over his mouth and shouted, "Tuffy! Here, Tuffy!"

I squinted out at the field and said a little inside prayer. Any moment and the wheat would part, and a tiny white dog—smaller than a kitten—would bound out with happy, high-pitched yips.

"Tuffy's lost. I'll never find him." Now the man's voice trembled. Well, he wasn't a man, not really. I guessed him not much older than my brother in high school. And he seemed about to cry.

Minutes later, I sat inside the Buick, trying to reassure Malcolm, because that was his name, and telling him stories about the time my own dog ran off but came home eventually, fat and happy and covered with brambles.

Malcolm pushed his foot on the gas pedal. A drop of sweat sparkled like a diamond chip on his right cheek. In the hot car, he gave off the scent of English Leather and nervousness, like my brother getting dressed for a date. It's scary, thinking you might lose something you love. I turned to watch my bicycle turn into a blue speck in the rearview mirror.

"You're going too fast," I told Malcolm. "I won't be able to see Tuffy."

Malcolm's thin, elegant hands turned white on the steering wheel. "We need to move fast so we can find him fast."

Now, this made no sense. A great big "but" formed at the back of my throat. "But," I wanted to say, "a small dog like Tuffy wouldn't have gone this far."

"But," I wanted to say, "Tuffy won't be able to catch up with us if we're speeding."

My mama always said everything after "but" is bullshit, so I kept my doubts to myself. Leaning my face out the window, I felt the sting of dry wind. We zoomed past O'Leary's old barn and the redbrick high school, and, at the junction of Flatline and Holy Mount, the 7-Eleven, where I should have been shopping.

"Mama will worry if I'm not home soon," I told Malcolm.

"We'll head home soon's we find Tuffy." He forced a smile. Sweat made his face glisten like a plastic mask. "She'll be so proud of you," he said.

By now a small voice murmured inside, warning me. But Malcolm clearly needed my help. I turned and called, "Tuffy! Tuffy!" My shouts flew back at me in a whistle of wind.

The junction, with its cluster of shops, dwindled behind us. The road became a long, straight line that seemed to drop from the edge of the world. Malcolm humped over his steering wheel. Why didn't he watch the fields? Why didn't he hang his head out his window and shout for Tuffy? I raised my voice and hollered, "Tuffy, Tuffy," as though my life depended on finding the little dog. I began to think maybe it did.

After an hour or so, Malcolm pulled the Buick into a Texaco station. A woman in striped overalls trotted over. She wiped her hands on an oily rag. "Regular?"

For an instant, I forgot about the puppy. "You're gonna pump the gas YOURSELF?" I'd never seen a lady gas pumper before.

"Shush, now," Malcolm whispered. "You shouldn't oughta talk to strangers."

"But—"

"Ain't safe," he said.

The lady crossed over to lean in my window. Her long, curly hair brushed my shoulder. Beauty parlor smells mixed with a whiff of gasoline. "You wanna help pump?" she asked.

I glanced over at Malcolm. "We're on a tight schedule," he said.

"Sorry," I told the Texaco lady. "We've got to look for Tuffy."

The Texaco lady opened my door. "You don't have to do anything you don't wanna, Luanna."

"You know my name?" Then, before Malcolm could stop me, I exclaimed, "She knows my name!" and climbed from the car.

Malcolm's face blurred behind the windshield. Suddenly the engine revved, and the Buick jolted from the gas hose. Malcolm roared off without even paying his bill.

The article that ran in the *Kansas City Star* made all this sound so dramatic, as though I'd been tied up, gagged, and stolen away at knifepoint. But, as you now know, nothing bad happened. Only afterwards, when the police fed me chocolate mint ice cream and asked all sorts of questions, did I grasp how much danger I'd been in.

In all the commotion stirred up by the police and the newspaper reporters, Mama and I never got to thank the lady at the Texaco station. A few days later we went back.

"A lady pumping gas?" asked the old man at the cash register. "What kind of place do you think this is?"

None of the fellows working in the garage had heard of the lady in overalls, so she became something of a mystery to me. What was she doing at the Texaco station that day? How did she know me?

Eventually I forgot about the Texaco lady, and then remembered her again, and forgot and remembered.

Her words always came back when I needed them. Like, when I was in tenth grade and my boyfriend wanted to go too far, I remembered that lady saying, "You don't have to do anything you don't wanna." And, when I was first married and Mama pushed for a grandbaby, I remembered. And when I got the job at the Golden Chicken and Mr. Hawkins wanted me to serve a drumstick that had fallen on the floor, I remembered. "I don't have to do anything I don't wanna," I told him, then and there. Got me a better job, working for, don't you know, Texaco.

But I never in my wildest dreams imagined who that lady really was until today at Kwick Kurls, where Francis gave me a perm. The chemical smell made my head spin. When Francis twirled me around in the chair to show me my new do in the mirror, the light shifted and my soul flipped over. There! There were those same curls that dangled through Malcolm's car window and brushed against my shoulder.

"Now aren't you the smart one?" Francis exclaimed, and I had to agree.

"Why, so I am!"

Francis, who knows about such things, says I have Rapunzel hair, and that's what saved me all those years ago. But I think all women do, if only they knew it. Don't you?

The Mnemoth and Its Uses in Dream Recall

Jeffrey Greene

The Mnemoth and Its Uses in Dream Recall

by Ivan C. Birdlaw, M.D., Ph.D.

(Reprinted from the December 1998 issue of Oneirocritique, the Journal of Dream Research, with the author's kind permission — J.G.)

Introduction:

The mnemoth (Actias memoria), an extremely rare moth indigenous to a three-square-mile area of the Peruvian rain forest, was discovered and named by Dr. Raymond Showalter in 1994. In its larval stage the mnemoth feeds exclusively on a poisonous, night-blooming vine known as the Yetziquex (a Cuiápo Indian word meaning 'Widowmaker'), and although immune to the plant's toxin, the caterpillar is itself deadly if eaten by animals or other insects. The adult moth, or imago, is not toxic, but after handling a live specimen Dr. Showalter made the surprising discovery that the wing scales of the mnemoth are coated with a psychoactive alkaloid that was absorbed through his fingertips, producing intense hallucinations of several hours' duration, the content of which he recognized as specific childhood memories. He presented his findings – the first hallucinogenic insect ever described – in a 1995 paper titled "The Mnemoth and the Yetziquex: Symbiosis and Serendipity."

After reading his paper, I contacted Dr. Showalter at Wilson College in Miami about the possibility of using the mnemoth in my ongoing research, specifically in the area of dream recall. As most people are aware from personal experience, ninety-five to ninety-nine percent of all dreams are forgotten, a phenomenon poorly understood as due to the low concentration of amine transmitters in the dreaming brain, which are needed to convert short-term memories to longer ones. To my delight, Dr. Showalter agreed to provide the mnemoths and instruct me in their use. The psychoactive effect is obtained only with living specimens, since the active chemical is very unstable and breaks down within minutes after the moth dies. Although Dr. Showalter has successfully cultivated the vine and the moths in a controlled environment, he told me that he is lucky to harvest more than ten specimens a year, and was able to provide only three imagos for our experiment. Given these limited parameters, I decided to use a single volunteer subject: Michael S., aged thirty-six, whose normal dream recall exceeds that of any of the more than three hundred volunteers I have worked with. It should be mentioned here that Mr. S. lost both his legs after being run over by a drunken boater while diving for lobsters in the Florida Keys in 1991. He sued for damages and won a considerable cash settlement, but for months after the accident he was plagued by recurrent traumatic nightmares that, along with his deep depression, resulted in a serious drinking problem. While he was under treatment for alcoholism, Mr. S.'s wife Terri read about my dream research project at the University of North Central Florida and persuaded him to contact me and volunteer his services. Thus began a fruitful six-year collaboration. After discussing the risks of the experiment with him, we agreed that the mnemoths would be administered for three trials on successive Friday nights, with a measured increase in the exposure time each week.

As in all dream research using human subjects, we had to rely on subjective, anecdotal evidence, which we present here with no claims of its unimpeachability.

First Trial, 8/18/98, 11:15 p.m.

Producing one of Dr. Showalter's specially-designed jars containing a single adult mnemoth inside a smaller holding chamber, I showed Michael how to use it. Michael's wife, Terri, who was present for all three trials, commented on the striking glossy-black color of the moth's wings and the red triangle on its back, reminding her (as it does me) of the coloration of the black widow spider. Fortunately, Michael is not phobic in regard to insects and willingly inserted his hand through a slit in the cardboard top. He then pushed the button that released the mnemoth into a cheesecloth tunnel leading to his hand.

He held the fluttering moth in his closed hand for a period of exactly twenty seconds, which Mr. Esteban Ruiz, my research assistant, marked with a stopwatch, then released the moth, gently guiding it back into the holding chamber, and withdrew his hand. The silky black coloration was noticeably thinned and depleted on the insect's wings, and the subject's palm and fingers were dusted with the iridescent black scales. Having been informed that the drug would begin to take effect in about forty-five minutes, Michael then retired to his bed in the sleep lab. EEG and EKG monitors were attached, and Terri, Esteban and myself went to the observation room to check the vital sign monitors, catch up on our paperwork and await developments.

He was asleep by 11:45 p.m. By my reckoning, the drug would take effect around midnight; however, the time came and all vital signs remained normal. At 12:30 a.m. Esteban noted the familiar loss of muscle tone and eye-rolling characteristic of REM sleep. Again, nothing unusual was noted. REM sleep occurred normally, that is, at approximately ninety-minute intervals throughout the night. The subject turned frequently in his sleep, and if anything, seemed to sleep more soundly than usual. His observers took turns sleeping as well, with at least two of us watching the monitors at all times, but nothing worth noting occurred for the rest of the night.

The subject awoke at 7:40 a.m. At first he seemed equally confused by his surroundings and the idea of eating breakfast; however, he was soon eating and talking excitely with Terri. After breakfast he wheeled himself to his computer and began recording his dreams, which in the past seldom took more than twenty minutes. When Michael was still at his desk after two hours, we realized that the drug had worked even better than anticipated. He continued recording well into the afternoon. We interviewed him, then sent him home and began perusing his dream records. Based on his verbal and written statements, we were able to make the following observations:

1. The waking mnemonic hallucinations described by Dr. Showalter appeared to carry over into the subject's dreams. He reported dreams of an intensity and emotional power never before experienced, although on reflection he did not think that the drug had affected either the content or the "current" of normal dreaming. Rather, it was

the memory of a typical night's dreams that had been improved to an astounding degree, creating a sense of absolute faith in the reality of the dreams experienced. Each dream was imprinted on his long-term memories and easily recalled — more or less in sequence — when he awoke. Any vagueness in the transcriptions was not due, he said, to an inability to remember the dreams; rather, the dreamed incidents were simply too strange or confusing to put into words. An example of this dramatic increase in dream recall was a sequence of three recorded dreams that were, as Michael put it, "dreams I had while I dreamed I was asleep and dreaming."

2. Although the number of dreams recorded was far greater than expected, their content appeared to run the gamut of normal dream experience: anxiety dreams, wish fulfillment dreams, flying dreams and many others, including trivial, erotic, infantile, traumatic, gustatory, criminal, and dreams too bizarre to classify. The subject recorded sixty-three separate and distinct dreams, but in spite of this staggering total he felt certain that he had forgotten several more. The forgotten dreams seemed to belong to a type that the subject had not previously suspected even existed, much less remembered, dreams containing symbols and events that defied translation into waking experience. Michael called this category "non-mammalian" or "cosmic" dreams, those furthest from his conscious understanding and employing the least number of earthly or familiar symbols, and felt that his inability to remember more than a scrap or two was no accident, that in fact dreams at this level were "forbidden," their content closed to conscious recall, even under the influence of the mnemoth, as if some overwhelming secret about himself or the world were being jealously guarded. That he even knew they existed, he said, was "dangerous," but was unable to elaborate on the nature of this danger. He also stated that he felt as if he had "lived for a hundred years in a single night."

3. Upon waking, the subject reported a brief sense of *jamais-vu*, or the feeling that the familiar had become strange, accompanied by an inversion of his normal frame of reference; in other words, that the world of dreams was real and the waking world illusory. After what he called his "nocturnity" of dreaming, Michael stated that he could

no longer perceive dreams as a respite from the iron-bound laws of reality, a form of play or relaxation for the sleeping brain, in which thoughts and emotions are transmuted into events without the irrevocable consequences of waking life. He now felt that the waking world was a sort of rest stop for weary dreamers, a stable but all-too-temporary refuge from the strenuous magic of dreams. He likened it to having just completed a round-the-world trip, which would normally be followed by a surfeit of travel and the need to stay home for a while. This odd feeling passed in a few minutes, and Michael agreed with Dr. Showalter's suggestion that the inversion was probably due to the subjective time dilation produced by the drug.

4. The long-term memory effect completely dissipated within twenty-four hours, and dream recall returned to normal levels by the following night. However, the subject could still recall his dreams without referring to his journal and with approximately the same degree of accuracy and detail that real events at the same remove would be remembered. Also, the subject's impression of having been on a long journey remained, with a sense of what he jokingly called "dream-world-weariness." No adverse physical side effects were reported by the subject, and he was eager to participate the the next trial.

Second Trial, 8/25/98, 11:00 p.m.

An interesting phenomenon was reported by the subject when he arrived at the sleep lab: a marked increase in the normally rare feeling of *déjà vu*, on the order of two to three times a day since the First Trial. As is usually the case with *déjà vu*, the subject could not connect these sensations of familiarity with any *specific* memories or dreams, but felt that his dream experiences of the First Trial had somehow "included" those moments that seemed strangely familiar to him. This concerned me, since Dr. Showalter had reported no increase in *déjà vu* in his waking experiments with the mnemoth, and I wondered aloud to Michael if the drug might be having some residual effect on his temporal lobes, a site where *déjà vu* sensations have been induced with mild electrical stimulation (Tortelli and Goldman, 1976). However, he stated that he felt fine, reporting no headaches, dizziness, or problems sleeping, and reiterated his desire to continue the experiment. The second mne-moth was administered as before, but we doubled the exposure time from twenty to forty seconds. The subject was asleep by 11:47 p.m.

It was my turn to sleep the first shift that night. At 1:33 a.m I was awakened by Terri, who told me that something unusual was occur-ring in the sleep lab. Esteban had noticed an irregularity in Michael's heartbeat, gone immediately to his bedside and become alarmed by the sleeper's ashen complexion and continuous, involuntary moans. I was reluctant to disturb him while he was under the influence of the drug, but after taking his blood pressure and finding it dangerously low, I sat him up and called his name several times. He opened his eyes and looked around, but all three of us had the impression that he was still asleep. Slowly he came to consciousness, and although clear-ly under the influence of the drug, he coherently related an unusu-ally intense nightmare. His lawyers had filed a damage suit against the boater who had run over him, and he had "won back my legs in court." Then, in an abrupt transition typical of nightmares, he "lost them again on appeal." His opponent's legal action was represented by a giant steel shark fin that cut his house in two and sheared off his legs at the upper thigh as he lay helplessly in bed. As I mentioned before, accident-related nightmares are nothing new for this unfor-tunate young man. What made him go into shock, he thought, was the "hyper-reality" of the dream, which had drawn on his indelible memories of the accident and produced a facsimile hardly less dread-ful than the original trauma. I offered to administer a sedative but he refused, insisting that the dream was an isolated event in a "galaxy of beauty," and stated unequivocally that he wanted to continue the experiment. By this time his vital signs had returned to normal, so I reluctantly consented, and he soon fell asleep.

As with all our sleep experiments, there was a tape recorder next to the subject's bed. Tapes of an average night's sleep will always re-veal some combination of snores, sighs, moans, lip-smacking sounds, laughter, and everything from mumbled words and disconnected phrases to clearly-spoken sentences. The tapes from the First Trial re-vealed nothing out of the ordinary. During the Second Trial, however, the tape recorder picked up sounds that none of us had ever heard before. They occurred at different times during the early morning hours, and lasted from about twenty seconds up to a minute. They might be imperfectly described as a kind of non-verbal speech — pitched almost to a whistle and containing an unmistakable element of urgency or distress, but also employing a complex and seemingly ordered series of tongue-rolls, clicks, and guttural emphases, all of which were accomplished without moving the lips, a feat I doubt the subject could have reproduced while awake, even with practice. Terri was vaguely reminded of the vocal threats male cats make when fighting over territory. Esteban, more fancifully, thought that Michael sounded "possessed by intelligent birds." I would certainly ascribe an organized, if not melodic, element to the sound, if language and music were somehow merged into a hybrid form of communication expressing emotions and ideas outside the scope of ordinary speech. What was being imparted, either to some character in a dream or to the dreamer himself, is of course impossible to say.

The next morning Michael indicated that he felt fine, but again reported the *jamais-vu* sensation of unfamiliarity with the world around him. He also reported a feeling of uncertainty as to whether he was entirely awake yet or in some transitional state between dreaming and wakefulness. The *jamais-vu* persisted much longer than the previous trial, finally dissipating about noon. He expressed the half-facetious concern that the drug might be "thinning the boundary between dreams and reality," and wondered if a third exposure to the mnemoth might cause "the bio-chemical dike to collapse and flood my days with dreams." I told him that Dr. Showalter had been using the mnemoth for four years and had not observed any changes in his brain function.

At around 3:00 p.m., after Michael had finished the lengthy process of recording his dreams, I asked him into the observation room and then played back the aforementioned sounds he had made in his sleep between 3:30 and 4:17 a.m., which Esteban had edited together into a continuous loop about two-and-a-half minutes long. My intention with this experiment was, first, to gauge his reaction, both to the strangeness and complexity of the sounds; and second, whether hearing the sound while awake might trigger a memory either of some specific dream or state of sleep accessible only at the forty-second exposure to the mnemoth. For what happened next, however, we were completely unprepared. Michael, who had been in relaxed good spirits before I turned on the tape, suddenly went rigid in his wheel chair, listening intently and with a dawning expression of what struck me at least as a kind of horrified understanding. The color visibly drained from his face, then, before we could catch him, he tumbled out of his chair in a dead faint. Fortunately he suffered only a minor bump on the head, and we were able to revive him fairly quickly. He seemed more bewildered than frightened by what had happened.

I closely questioned Michael about what he had heard on the tape and why it had affected him so profoundly, but he couldn't give me a definitive answer. He suspected that the sound was a kind of "universal dream language" spoken in one of the so-called non-mammalian or cosmic dreams described in his journal. He then leafed through the hard copy of his journal and read aloud a dream that he thought might have been the source of at least one of his vocalizations, although he couldn't be certain. The following is the text of Michael's dream:

> Straddling the city was an enormous living statue, its head lost in the clouds. I was among thousands of other people looking up at it, admiring the exotic lines and curves of its clothes or metallic covering, which was the color of dawn and sunsets, constantly shifting and changing like a humanoid piece of the sky. Its power and beauty was a coalescing of all human aspirations into a single sublime expression that might effortlessly leap into outer space or become part of the sky. I remember sobbing, overcome by its beauty and what it symbolized: a tragic joy that was unrelated to sorrow or happiness. It began a kind of oration, *though it was neither speech nor song* (italics mine—I.B.) but none of us at its feet (spiritually as well as physically) were able to understand it.

Michael repeated his belief that certain states of consciousness are forbidden or closed to the waking self, and that knowledge in the "dreamiverse" emanates at different frequencies specific to the dreamer's brainwave function, acting as a natural filter to areas of experience or insight we may not be ready to absorb or accept. When asked why he had fainted after hearing it, and why the four of us had not, he said he didn't know, but suspected that the forty-second exposure to the mnemoth had given him access to dream memories he was meant to forget, and certainly would have, had the tape not triggered a memory of something that, as he put it, "my ape couldn't handle." We three observers were unaffected, he thought, because our normal defense mechanisms were in place; in other words, our "boundaries" had not been "thinned" by the drug. I was extremely curious about the sounds on the tape, and wanted to explore them further, but a repeat of the experiment was of course out the question. At this point I was having misgivings about taking the experiment to its third and final stage, but in spite of his alarming fainting spell, Michael was emphatic in his desire to continue. With some reservations I agreed, and he and Terri went home for a well-deserved break.

To my surprise, the dream totals for the Second Trial did not differ dramatically from those of the First Trial— sixty-eight as opposed to sixty-three, suggesting that seventy to seventy-five may well be the maximum of the human dream capacity for an eight-hour period, with most people remembering between one and three percent of that figure. However, doubling the exposure time to the mnemoth resulted in a significant increase in *internal* dream recall; that is, the moment-to-moment experience of each dream was noted with far greater nuance and detail than in the previous trial. The range of subject matter was more or less the same, with one important difference: recall of the so-called "cosmic" dreams, which, for want of a better term might be called the Dark Matter of dreams, and composing approximately one percent of the subject's dream totals, was markedly improved. A comparison of the difference in quality and depth of recall of this rarest type of dream between the twenty and forty-second exposure could be illustrated by Michael's dream of the living statue, quoted above. With normal recall he probably would have forgotten it completely. At the Level One dosage he might have remembered it as a single, silent image of a giant statue, but with limited to zero context. At the Level Two dosage the dream had deep emotional and spiritual significance for him, and he could at least partly comprehend the symbolism of the living statue, but could not understand its language, which at Level Three he might not only be fluent in, but recall its meaning upon awakening.

In the week following the Second Trial the subject reported two symptoms of a psychological nature. The first was a progressive, almost hourly, increase in *déjà vu* moments, so that by Thursday he had begun to feel "as if the remaining hours of the day stretched before me like the hundredth performance of a play in which I knew every word and gesture by heart." He also reported the unnerving experience of "recognizing every face I see. I can't say where or when I've seen them before, and I know they weren't characters in my dreams. I couldn't tell you their names or anything important about them; I just know that we've all been together before in some place and time." This progressive increase in *déjà vu* would seem to favor the hypothesis that the mnemoth hallucinogen causes after-effects on the dreaming but not the waking brain, and that these symptoms are both cumulative and apparently associated with the temporal lobes.

The second symptom was far less frequent, but perhaps even more disturbing. This he termed "doubling," and seemed to occur mostly at night or when he was fatigued. Without warning, he would experience a brief, uncanny sense that he was observing himself from a second perspective. As Michael put it, "I was seeing myself out of other eyes, but they were my eyes, too." He felt as if he were looking at himself through the wrong end of a telescope, "as if the person seated in this chair weren't me at all, but a stick figure being projected or beamed onto the scene like a shadow puppet on a wall. 'I' was the projector."

It was clearly evident during the interview preceding the Third Trial that the pervasive *déjà vu* symptoms and the "doubling" effect had caused the subject a great deal of stress and anxiety, but oddly enough, he expressed no desire to withdraw from the experiment. Considering the progressive nature of these symptoms, I found his attitude troubling and expressed as much in a long-distance phone call to Dr. Showalter. He assured me that the drug was neither physically nor pyschologically addictive, and suggested that the explanation lay in Michael himself, a man infinitely less restricted in his dreams than in his waking life. He believes that Michael sees himself as a kind of "oneironaut," (to borrow a term from Stephen LaBerge, the lucid dream researcher), an intrepid explorer of his own depths, and that he would no more decline an opportunity to go further than an ocean-ographer would pass up the chance to descend into the 35,700-foot Challenger Deep. After discussing the risks with Michael, we decided to proceed with the third and final trial.

Third Trial, 9/1/98, 11:10 p.m.

The subject received a sixty-second exposure to the third mne-moth. The vital sign monitors were attached as before, and the tape recorder turned on. He was asleep by 11:30 p.m. As an added precau-tion we had decided not to take sleep breaks during this last phase of the experiment, and were drinking vast quantities of coffee in prepa-ration for a long night of watching and waiting.

The earliest indication that tripling the exposure time would pro-duce its own distinct symptoms came during the first REM phase. We observed a more dramatic loss of muscle tone than would be considered normal, causing the sleeper's body to appear noticeably smaller, as if he were shrinking in upon himself. This was followed by exaggerated eye rolling and a strange, rippling tremor of the facial muscles, like rapid waves under the skin. It occurred to me that the wave-like tremors might be facial expressions, one following the other with a rapidity impossible for the voluntary muscular system, as if the sleeper were experiencing the full spectrum of human emotion in a matter of seconds, and indeed his heart rate fluctuated wildly, although within acceptable limits. There were none of the curious vocalizations heard in the Second Trial, but several other anomalies occurred: rapid, fever-like changes in body temperature, spontane-ous orgasms, and periods of weeping and laughter, the latter of which had a sneering, breathless, malign quality altogether unlike Michael's waking personality. The periods between REM sleep were characterized by unusually slow heart and respiration rates, and virtually no turning, which often occurs forty to fifty times a night in normal sleep. He assumed a fetal position, which was maintained throughout this phase. The nadir of this hibernation-like sleep occurred around 3:30 a.m., when his heart rate fell to as low as twenty-two beats per minute. The EEG patterns at this stage were not that of deep sleep, however, but more like the alpha rhythms of relaxed waking consciousness. His extremities were cold to the touch, and respiration fell to a rate I wouldn't have thought possible for a human being. I almost terminated the experiment at this point, but as soon as the next REM phase commenced, his vital signs returned to normal.

At this point an unexpected event occurred, the implications of which will doubtless provoke controversy, if not outright disbelief, in the neuroscientific establishment. It happened around 4:40 a.m., at a moment when, by sheer chance, no one was watching the sleep lab. Terri had fallen asleep in her chair; Esteban, feeling himself fading, had gone into the break room to smoke a cigarette, and I had left the room in search of an antacid to counter the effects of too much coffee. I wasn't gone for more than two minutes; when I came back I saw that Michael's bed was empty. I called for Esteban and woke Terri, then entered the sleep lab. His wheel chair was in its usual place, so I first assumed he had fallen out of bed; however, a search quickly revealed that he was not in the sleep lab. It was possible he could have dragged himself out the door and through the anteroom connecting the sleep lab both to the office and the long outer hallway, though it seemed unlikely that in the short time I was out of the observation room he could have crawled more than a few feet down the hall. But he wasn't in the hallway either, so we immediately began a search of the rooms along the corridor, most of which were locked. At one end of the hallway was a stairwell, and on the opposite end, a good fifty feet from the sleep lab, a pair of bathrooms. Terri tried the stairwell, and Esteban and I checked the bathrooms. I found Michael curled up on the floor of the men's bathroom, sound asleep, his breathing deep and regular. Esteban joined me a moment later, and I asked him to go find Terri and bring her back here.

While he was gone, I examined Michael's face and hands for signs of injury or abrasions, and found none. I then shook him awake. He seemed to recognize me, but his eyes had that glazed aspect common to sleepwalkers, and for a few moments I was uncertain whether or not he was fully conscious. He appeared confused but not frightened at finding himself away from his bed. After helping him sit up I asked him what had happened.

"I had to go," he replied in a voice that sounded sluggish and lower-pitched than usual, like a lagging tape.

"But how did you get here?" I asked.

"I walked," he said irritably, as if it were perfectly obvious. "I'm always whole in my dreams, doctor. You know that."

"Yes, I do," I said, confused. "But are you saying you needed to go to the bathroom so badly that you dreamed you got out of bed and walked down the hall? Or did you wake up out of that same dream and drag yourself down here?"

He shook his head decisively. "No. If I'd been awake I would have wheeled myself down the hall." He looked around in sudden alarm. "Where's my chair?"

"It's back in the sleep lab," I said.

This fact seemed to jolt him into full wakefulness. He had lost his sleepwalker's aplomb and was now quite agitated. "Did somebody carry me down here?"

"No. I was out of the room for a couple minutes at most. I returned, saw that you were gone, started a search and found you here in the bathroom at the end of the hall. It's only been a few minutes."

At this point Terri and Esteban entered, pushing Michael's wheel chair. As Esteban and I lifted him off the floor, he met his reflection in the bathroom mirror and his eyes widened, as if something frightened him, but he said nothing more until we were back in the lab. There was no question of his going back to sleep now, and in fact he asked us not to leave him alone until sunrise. A fresh pot of coffee was brewed, and after Esteban had set up a portable tape deck beside Michael, we sat in a circle around him while he attempted to explain what had happened. The effects of the mnemoth had largely worn off by this time.

He began by dismissing the two previous trials as inconsequential, comparing his dreaming mind at the Level One exposure to a pebble being skipped over the surface of a pond, never penetrating deeper than a millimeter or two below the surface, and at Level Two as a man in a diving bell who reaches crushing depths but is always separated—as well as protected—from direct experience of those realities by the metal skin of the bell itself. Carrying the diving metaphor further, he stated that only at the Third Level exposure had he achieved sufficient "momentum" to thrust past the "strong surface currents of idle dreams and reveries" and descend into a dimension or "dreamiverse" where, as he put it, "everything is symbolic." He said that at this level of sleep the totality of one's dream experiences are preserved "like a Dream Library of Congress," and can be experienced as if one were at the center of a sphere and all the dreams one has ever had from birth to the present are like the innumerable points on its surface. He admitted that the subjective experience of this state is difficult if not impossible for the waking mind to grasp directly, and felt that his memories of the "four-dimensional dreams" he had could only be described by "deforming" them to fit the three-dimensional capabilities of the human imagination. He stated that just as our bodies are formed out of billions of cells not unlike those one-celled organisms from which we originally evolved, the human psyche is merely a single building block of the "mental bodies" of non-physical entities of unimaginable complexity, who exist on many levels of dream. Though "we" are in some primitive sense "them," we are no more capable of understanding the thoughts of these entities than the cells of our bodies are capable of understanding our own thoughts, although without those cells no thoughts could exist. The waking world and the dream world are part of the same continuum, separated only by barriers of perception, which, as the mnemoth proves, can be crossed, if only temporarily and with limited understanding.

At this point, feeling rather exhausted by Michael's speculations, I said: "I'd still like to know how you ended up in the bathroom."

"I'm not sure," he said with a troubled frown. "But I think something impossible happened." He then related the following dream: "I found myself in a place where every word and gesture was freighted with layers upon layers of meaning. The events that took place don't sound like much to tell, but everything had a kind of timeless shimmer about it. I was in a small room, seated at a wooden table with two chairs. There were two windows. Out of one window I could see what looked a storm of paint globules of every conceivable color, all moving in a diagonal direction across the window. The other window gave onto a vast, burn-scarred plain. Somehow I knew — with a visceral certainty — that I'd been in that room forever. Outside the room was Everything, literally everything that existed or could exist. Inside the room, where I was, was not Nothing, but the *possibility* of Nothing. Mine was a kind of eternal vigil, and there was a strangely charged atmosphere to that simple, undecorated room and my own role as its sole occupant. I knew, just as I knew what lay outside, that maintaining this vigil was of immense importance. Someone always had to be in that room, alone and separate from everything else, for without the possibility of Nothing, there was no hope for non-existence, and the nightmare of time without end would go on forever. The thing was, and it was the most amazing and troubling thing of all, was that I could leave the room at any time. I could just get up and walk out, but once I crossed the threshold and entered the world, there was no going back. My choice was horribly simple: either remain alone forever and keep the hope of this precious "nothing" alive, or selfishly leave, and doom all beings everywhere to the hell of eternity. And I should add that those familiar words so denatured and powerless here: "eternity," "infinity," "forever," carried an intolerable weight in the dream and were surrounded by the most profound taboos, as if the reality behind those syllables were too frightful to be spoken aloud, especially in a dream, where every thought and emotion has the potential of becoming real.

"At that moment (although it wasn't really a moment because there wasn't any time in the ordinary sense), something that had been building inside of me for God knows how many billions of years reached my awareness and I felt a disturbing urgency, the need to do something primal, individual, and totally absurd, considering the cosmic importance of my position: I needed to urinate. You know how a physical need can invade a dream and change the storyline.

You're thirsty, so you dream of drinking water, though dream water can't quench your thirst. You dream of urinating, but the urgency is still there. There was no toilet in the room, but my need was great, so I simply opened the door and walked out.

"I found myself in the hallway outside the sleep lab. It looked the same as it always does, though maybe it was just a construct from memory, who knows? I accepted the naturalness of it all, as one does in dreams. I walked—that's right, doctor—I walked on my dream legs to the bathroom where you found me. I felt wide awake, and the feeling was bolstered by the intense relief that followed urination. Everything was fine now; somehow the enormity of my 'crime' or 'sin'—there really isn't a word for it—had faded away as soon as I left the Room. I turned to walk out, still entirely unaware that I had no flesh-and-bone legs, and caught my own reflection in the bathroom mirror. What I saw there..." Michael paused to sip his coffee and wipe the sweat off his face. "What I saw in the mirror was *myself*, my whole self, not the legless, alcoholic, ex-surfer talking to you now. Try to imagine what your face would look like if the mind behind it were a thousand times stronger, more intelligent, more *awake* than you've ever been at the best moment of your life. The face staring back at me in the mirror looked twice as large as my own face, and seemed to reflect more light than the bathroom's dim fluorescence. I couldn't begin to describe its expression, which seemed somehow to contain all the emotions, yet was inhumanly calm and still. Its eyes were neither kind nor cruel; they looked into and through me, but during the instant in which I was able to endure its gaze, I saw all the combined moments of my life and every thought and emotion I'd ever experienced, reflected in a kind of dispassionate intimacy. It knew me infinitely better than I know myself, but there was also a dizzying sense of displacement—that 'doubled' feeling again. For the smallest fraction of a moment I realized that the face in the mirror was the dreamer and I was its dream, and because of the mnemoth this 'illegal' event had occurred and the dreamer had—purposely or by accident—shown himself to one of his dream characters. I must have passed out then, or at least passed from wherever I was into ordinary sleep. The next thing I knew you were waking me up."

Michael stated that he now understood something: the *jamais-vu* symptom that occurred after each trial is not an after-effect of the mnemoth hallucinogen, but a kind of premonitory insight into the secondary nature of the physical world. "I don't think the feeling will pass this time," he said, looking pale and shaken. "Because I know that these bodies and the atoms that form them are *literally* the stuff of dreams. Of course, I don't expect you to believe that, at least not until you've held a mnemoth in your hand for one full minute and dreamed yourself down to where I was. *Then* you'll know."

At this point, Terri, clearly concerned about her husband's mental health, suggested we adjourn. We thanked Michael for his participation, promised to keep in touch and walked him to the elevator. That same evening, while going over the data from the three trials, it occurred to Esteban to play back the tape recording of the Third Trial, in hopes of finding some aural evidence of Michael's inexplicable disappearance from his bed. Obviously we weren't surprised to hear no sounds of footsteps. What deepened the mystery for us was the fact that, past a certain moment when Michael's breathing is clearly audible, there is a gap in the tape exactly one minute and forty-seven seconds long, during which no sounds at all were recorded. This is followed by the sound of the door opening as I entered the lab and began to search for him. We at least expected to hear rustling bedclothes, or the sound of his body hitting the floor, followed by the sounds of crawling and his struggles to open the door. Instead, the tape recorded a silence that I am at a loss to explain.

I have since called Michael several times at his home in St. Augustine, but he refuses to talk to me. Terri tells me that he is physically well, but wishes to put the experiment behind him, and that even now, four months later, he is still prey to pervasive feelings of "ghostliness." In the light of our findings, and the apparently long-term nature of Michael's *jamais-vu* and *déjà vu* symptoms, I have decided not to repeat the mnemoth experiment. However, Dr. Showalter has recently informed me that he plans to use his next harvest of mnemoths for another series of dream recall experiments, using himself as a subject, and tells me that he will set aside three imagos for my own use if I wish to participate. I have yet to give him an answer.

Oceans of Darkness

Corinna Sara Bechko

Luanne sat in the window seat, surrounded by seashells. That's what she'd been calling them anyway, even though they hadn't done any testing yet to determine if there had ever been a sea out there. But seashells were certainly what they looked like. Organic, convoluted spirals. The largest, broken along its center, was almost as wide as her hand. The smallest was the size of the diamond in her wedding ring, which was to say, very small indeed.

Spreading them out in her residence was not strictly protocol. In fact, it wasn't protocol at all. But there were *so* many of them out there. Surely picking up a few for personal contemplation wasn't a crime. The career she had chosen was difficult and had scant rewards, few of them monetary. Who would possibly begrudge her a few personal tokens?

Everyone would, and she knew it. Everyone who wasn't willing to come this far out of their home system. Everyone who stayed behind and passed judgment on the things one does to stay sane in the dark, where the only light is manufactured, where the idea that it could go out and never come back on stays in the back of one's mind all the time.

She carefully repacked the shell-things into their little rubbery cases, the material shifting and realigning to accommodate their contours. She snapped the lids closed, sealing them into their cocoons. She was being selfish, she decided. The faster they got on with mapping the geomorphology here the sooner they could leave. Within certain parameters. Which of course changed all the time, depending on the whims of the company. Fuck it, she thought. Selfish or not, I'm keeping these seashells.

She heard the outer airlock hiss open and shut. Then the low rumble as the fans clicked on to compensate for the pressure differential. The world outside had an atmosphere but it was both thin and poisonous. She never liked coming inside before Jim, taking off her suit and getting comfortable while he was still out there, but sometimes the work shifts demanded it. She was glad he was back a little early.

"Anything?" she called when she heard the inner door hiss open.

"Not really. You?"

She rose from her seat as he appeared around the corner, his hair mussed from the tight-fitting helmet and his clothing stuck to his skin. His suit had been running a little hot lately, a fact that she found horribly frightening. Death by overheating on a frozen world seemed just stupid and ironic enough to actually happen.

"No, nothing. Surely we've done all we can here?"

"I don't know," he sighed, kissing her on the forehead. "All I know is that I'm tired, I smell like plastic, and alien ruins have become prosaic to me. That's got to be a certain kind of insanity, right?"

She tilted her head, a habit that reminded him of some sort of bird. A crow, maybe? A finch? He let his mind wander, imagined the place as it might have been when it was bathed in light. Were there ever things like birds here? Things with claws and beaks and feathers? That's immaterial now, he reasoned. If anyone ever figures that out he would read about it on the newsfeeds.

"Well, go grab a shower. The spray should be warm again, it's been long enough since I finished." She turned and looked out the window to the circle of ground illuminated by the floodlights hanging from the side of their habitat ring. Nothing moved outside, of course, although it wasn't as if nothing could. Shortly after their arrival she had been shocked to see some of the little shell-things rolling along the ground. Turned out that there were minor windstorms on this moon, a mystery they still hadn't quite solved. The moon rotated, of course, and that probably did create some sort of Coriolis effect. And then there was the gravity of the big, dark gas giant they circled, which might tug on the atmosphere enough to stir up the air. The truth was, they didn't know, and lacked the expertise to know. They were there for one thing only: mineral mapping. Ruins, fossils, windstorms, all these were beside the point as far as their employers were concerned.

Luanne opened her eyes to a primordial darkness. She felt she was suffocating, the weight of all that cold, all those eons of blackness, bearing down on her, pushing her further into her sleeping capsule. She took a deep, ragged breath. I control the dark, she said under her breath. I control it. If I want light, I make it. She reached up and clicked on a tiny reading bulb, fought to drag herself away from the dream she'd been having.

In the dream, she walked the ruins without a suit. The air was cold, but no more so than on a late fall day back home. The structures were black against the darkness of the rocks and the sand beneath her bare feet. When she looked up, she saw the rind of the Milky Way bisected by the disk of the huge nameless planet above them. She heard a faint mewling coming from behind one of the contoured walls and followed it. There, on the ground at the base of a tumble of oval stones, was a creature. It was organically spiraled, full of convoluted details. It had been broken in half. She reached down to touch it. It was as wide as her hand.

She shook her head and reached for the screen set into the wall, clicked on the novel she had started before bed, gradually relaxed. And then sat up, almost calling for Jim. She knew what the dream reminded her of.

It had become difficult to keep track of the days. Up until a couple of weeks before, the Corporation had updated them on Mondays, Wednesdays, and Fridays. Now they were being more sporadic. Jim had gone into the communication hutch to see if there was a new message after their last outing, and had come out swearing.

"What now?" she asked.

"What do you think? They want more tests run on the North Side. So that pushes back our departure window. Again."

313

"How long?" she didn't want to hear how long, not really. She had been having the dreams every night for at least a week now. She wanted to believe they were really leaving within the month.

"Brace yourself," he said, not joking. "A full year."

"What?" Luanne's tongue felt thick behind her teeth. Her ears were full of buzzing. An Earth year? That couldn't be right.

"That's what they said. We'll be fine as far as provisions go, especially since we started the garden. Even if they said two years we wouldn't starve. And there's plenty of water as long as the pumps work. But they've pushed the date back so many times that we're about to pass behind the planet. And then there's everything else to coordinate... Fuck."

Luanne could feel the panic rising behind her breastbone. She fought against it. It was no use. I control the panic, she thought. I control it. It was no use.

That night, after their shifts were done, Luanne leaned towards Jim over their shared workstation. She didn't want to say it.

"Jim," she stopped, frowned. "Jim."

"Hm?"

"We have to go back home. We can't stay here,"

He glanced at her, annoyed.

"No, really. I'm going to tell them that we can't stay here."

"It's too late, I already told you. They miscalculated last time. Lord knows it's hard to tell where these orphan planets might be heading, but I still think they screwed us deliberately. Anyway, either they're lying or they really miscalculated. Doesn't matter which, we're stuck."

He turned back to the work he was collating. She tried again.

"No, it's an emergency. We really can't be here."

This time he stopped, stared at her.

"What do you mean, emergency? We signed off on all contingencies. No exceptions. What's wrong?"

"I told you about the dreams? What does that remind you of?"

He shook his head, and she tried hard to remember that he hadn't experienced the dreams last time, only heard her tell about them. She cocked her head.

"They remind me of the fact that we're living in a very unnatural state. It's gotta take a toll on you, knowing there's no host star out there. It certainly takes a toll on me. Sometimes I forget we're so far from a system, start thinking that we're really far under water instead. The mind's a funny thing."

"It is, at that," she said, resigned. "I think I'm pregnant."

Teams like theirs were expensive to outfit and launch, but nothing compared to how much it cost to have a whole mining operation sent out of system. That's why they sent just two people at a time to scout a location. Robots were good for picking out likely targets, but only people on the ground could give a full overview of what conditions would be like for other *people*, who were still needed for this sort of operation.

Jim and Luanne had done quite a few turns in the past, most of them in system, on asteroids. This was their first turn on one of the so-called orphan bodies, usually big moons orbiting gas giants not attached to any system. It was incredibly odd to find ruins here, but not unheard of. At some point the planet above them had circled a star, and the moon they were living on had been full of life, or at least had been an outpost for life.

The company they worked for liked to know that the people it sent out were compatible, that they worked well together. Often this meant married couples, but not always. Married or not, a track record of not going crazy and killing each other during the long months of seclusion was helpful in their line of work. A record of not springing any surprises on the company was helpful too. The company wasn't allowed to force it's employees to prove sterility, but suggesting it often meant getting the job.

Luanne had good reason to think they wouldn't surprise the company. It was part of why they did this kind of work. Early on in their relationship, long before they had started shipping out, she had been pregnant. It hadn't lasted though, despite their plans and hopes. They had thought that it would happen again, but the doctor, when they finally went to one, had told them something entirely different. There would be no more pregnancies for them.

So they went back to school, taking courses in chemistry and physics, geology and mineralogy. They became a team. And whenever they applied for jobs Luanne was careful to put on the application, under *known health issues*, "unable to have children." She felt hollow inside for a while, knowing that their family began and ended with the two of them. Gradually they began to get more and more interesting assignments, and the feeling became easier to put aside. But she never forgot the dreams she had while she was pregnant: rich, textured, alive and strange. It was the work of hormones, she knew. But it *felt* as if the alien being growing inside her, the her/not her/Jim/not Jim, was feeding her dreams in exchange for the oxygen and nutrients she was feeding to it.

"Are you sure?" asked Jim. "How can you be sure?"
"Of course I'm not sure. But I told you: the dreams."
"Okay," he said. "Okay. So there's no way to be sure right now. And, it might not… Last anyway. Right?"
She hated him, then. She was sorry she had told him. Told him what, anyway? About a vague feeling, about some dreams? It was enough for her. She was sure.

It was a strange thing, knowing that the moon was circling, that time was passing, without any external signposts. God, I miss seasons, she thought. She wished that the people who had designed the habitat ring had thought to put a window in the roof, to show the stars. At least those should change. It was hard to tell, outside. The ruins were so disorientating. She wanted to start making sky charts but didn't know how.

She counted backwards, over and over, trying to remember when her personal season had last shifted. It was impossible. Without the regular updates from the corporation she had no markers at all. She stayed mad at Jim for a long time too, how long she wasn't sure. They still worked together, and spoke about work, but she ignored him otherwise. He tried to apologize, became frustrated, yelled at her, tried again to apologize. She let it all slide past her. All she wanted was to sleep, to figure out how to walk through the ruins without a suit, to pick up more of the shells and have them whisper to her.

At last, after a few days or perhaps a week, Jim tried again to talk to her. Her rage had subsided, but she still felt untethered. He approached her cautiously, as if she were a wild thing that might flit off at any sudden movement.

"Alright," he said. His voice was calm but his fingers were jumpy. They toyed with the frayed edge of his shirt, tried to scratch holes in the metal tabletop.

"Alright. Here's what we know: we can't leave here for almost 12 standard months. There's not another team of any sort scheduled for at least 24 months after that. The ship for our return trip will only hold the two of us, and only if we weigh about the same as we did when it brought us. Interstellar travel is not safe for children or, especially, embryos. Hell, it's not good for us either…"

She looked strait at him, unsmiling. Tilted her head, tilted it back. She knew all these things, had considered them. But her mind slipped off of them. The puzzle was inside a black box, the answer hidden from view.

"So… Options?" He looked at her, hoping for an answer, a flat statement. She didn't speak.

"You still do think… ?" He looked at his hands, at the tiny ball of string that he had pulled off the bottom of his shirt. Jesus Christ, he thought. What were they supposed to wear for another whole year? Living involved more than just eating and breathing. For the thousandth time he cursed the corporation.

Luanne watched him roll and unroll the little bit of fabric between his fingertips. She did know the options, if not the answer: leave now, despite what the corporation wanted. Hope that it wasn't too late to formulate a strait shot. Hope that they could figure out a way to keep the tiny mass of cells inside her from growing on the way home, from trying to be born. Take the dead baby out of her on Earth.

Or: figure out a way to take it out here, now.

Or: stay here, have the baby, hope to live through it, and send only one of them home next year. Not "one of them", Luanne knew. Send

Jim home. It was obvious which one of them was equipped to produce food for a baby. She would stay, with an infant, in the dark. For at least two years. The thought made her dizzy.

She remained silent. She knew what would probably happen. The baby would stop being. Soon, it would feel very silly to have worried about these things at all.

"Luanne," said Jim," are you sure that you don't know when this happened? It would help, if you could remember."

She shook her head. Of course she couldn't remember. She'd stopped paying attention to such things a long time ago. "You could try to remember too, you know." She didn't mean to be harsh. But honestly, how could you count weeks in a place like this? Five weeks, six, ten? She hadn't felt nauseous, hadn't really felt anything. Except for the dreams.

Luanne sat at the workbench, collating data that didn't really need to be collated. It was getting harder for her to work outside. The suit didn't fit very well anymore, and that could be dangerous. So Jim did most of the work in the ruins, and on the North Side. They had even determined the parameters of where a shore had been. Luanne now thought they were camped next to an ancient lakebed instead of a sea. They had found hematite, which suggested that the lake had held plain water instead of something more exotic. Jim thought that the ruins had been a harbor once, and that there was a good chance that the company would want to drill in the lakebed. Maybe they would push up the relay team's window, send another team within a year. It was possible.

They had talked, and talked, and talked, about trying to go home despite what the company wanted. In the end they hadn't done it, not so much because they felt they couldn't, or shouldn't, but simply because they had talked for too long. The window of opportunity had passed, and with it their line of communication to the corporation. They were cut off now, for at least six months, until the moon reemerged from behind the planet.

Luanne heard the airlock hiss, and presently Jim came into the room. His suit was still running hot, so now he often used hers. It was good that they were so closely matched in size, another benefit to hiring them as a team.

"Guess what?" said Luanne, looking up at him. "It moved."

Jim exhaled. "Are you sure?"

"Yes! It's alive!"

"Let me feel." He knelt next to her. Nothing for a moment. For a full minute. But finally, he felt it too.

"Okay," he said. "Okay."

"What do we do now?" she asked. "What the fuck do we do? How do we get home?"

"Home," he said. "I guess the answer is: we are home."

The Vinyl Episode

Robert A. Love

Nigel sat in the comfortable "listening chair" placed strategically in his living room at one vertex of a triangle formed by the chair and two large stereo speakers about nine feet away. As the final moments of Debussy's *La Mer* washed over him, he savored the wealth of emotions that the piece always summoned. He reflected that this performance could easily be attributed to the Berlin Philharmonic under Karajan from the mid-1960s, given the style of playing and acoustics of the hall. As he slowly exhaled and began to lift the phonograph needle off the record, his faint smile vanished as he faced the familiar bleak aftermath: It would be the last time he would ever hear this particular performance of *La Mer*.

Nigel's stereo system was elaborate, allowing him to discern fine aspects of any recording, and consisted of a sophisticated turntable and vacuum tube based electronics. Although the year was 1999, and he had begun investing in CDs, he strongly believed that vinyl albums still provided the most realistic and musical format. Simple listening tests had confirmed that, coupled with his extensive training as a musician. While his thoughts were still vivid, he walked over to a small table nearby displaying an open notebook, and struggled to write down his impressions of the performance he had just experienced. Running through his mind was the quote from Saint-Saens, "There is nothing more difficult than talking about music." Since this volume was nearly full, he carefully carried it over to a large bookshelf in the next room. There he tucked it alongside similar notebooks that were already complete. Gazing upward at several packed shelves, it struck him, "My God, almost 10 years since I began taking these notes. I need to prepare a synopsis of all my observations… "

Have I really chosen this strange journey over the last decade, or has it been forced upon me by powers that I cannot imagine? I live alone in London's Chelsea district, in a moderate-sized apartment with a partial view of the Thames River (partial enough to bring about a much higher rent). I work part-time in a music publishing firm, which provides basic sustenance. Prior to this I studied music at Juilliard (focusing on cello and later composition), and once held a position in the London Symphony Orchestra as first cellist.

In May of 1989 I traveled to Leningrad with the LSO as part of a rare tour of Eastern Europe and the Soviet Union. It was a time of remarkable thaw, both politically and weather-wise, and I often had the liberty of roaming the streets without escort. There were even rumors of the city being renamed to the original Saint Petersburg. One chilly evening I left Shostakovich Hall and strolled past Arts Square with its statue of Pushkin, and eventually came upon an old narrow street with a lone small record/book store tucked under the first level of a crumbling apartment building. After entering and browsing through stacks of Soviet era recordings, the owner appeared, a small thin fellow with scrambled gray hair and long slender fingers, which suggested the hands of a musician. To my surprise, he began a conversation in broken English.

"Ah, I saw you play last night; I enjoyed your interpretation of the controversial Shostakovich Fourth Symphony. It was presented as nicely as our own orchestras did in the 1960s."

"Well, thank you very much," I muttered humbly, truly impressed at his historical perspective, then continued, "I'm very fond of 20th century Russian composers, and I'd like to purchase this collection of Prokofiev piano sonatas." The owner nodded, but then seemed distracted in a flash of intense thought. He tugged slightly on my sleeve and motioned toward a back exit. As I followed him along a dimly lit, tunnel-like hallway, which looked disproportionally long for the building, he shouted back "I have a very special item that may interest you." We emerged into a small storage room cluttered with a variety of dusty containers and books. I wondered if I was the first foreigner to stand here.

With trembling hands (age, anxiety?) the old man handed over a thin cardboard box labeled in Russian simply *Western Classical Music*. I carefully pulled out the standard size LP phonograph record and scrutinized it for obvious defects, as I always did before purchasing. It appeared perfectly round, yet the thickness of the disc was difficult to assess by touch, which I blamed on the stiffness in my hands after the cold walk outside. The black surface had an odd featureless character, but I dismissed this perception as a consequence of poor lighting in the room. At least the album had no scratches, nicks, or breaks. Out of sheer curiosity and the low price he was offering (perhaps too enthusiastically), I bundled this item with several others of interest and paid the owner. As I exited into the crisp night air, he stood in the doorway and added, "Would you believe that I played violin with the Moscow Philharmonic in 1961 at the world premier of the Fourth Symphony under Kondrashin? Perhaps one day you will hear that performance." I made a mental note to check on any documentation of the 1961 event.

I didn't examine these purchases again until I had returned to my flat in London the next week. As I mounted the generic record on my turntable for the first time, I immediately noticed that the typical sheen arising from multiple grooves was absent, as were the gaps which normally indicate silence between tracks. Therefore I simply placed the tonearm down somewhere near the middle of the album. For a few seconds there was total silence, which was unexpected given the improbability of randomly finding a break between movements. In addition, there was a lack of background noise typical of vinyl records (hiss, pops). Soon however orchestral music emerged, and after several minutes it was clear that this was a symphony, starting from the beginning, which I quickly recognized as a work by Haydn. The performance and recording quality were so impressive that I sat transfixed in my chair, listening to the entire piece. The lack of any text to accompany the LP made it impossible to identify the orchestra, location, or conductor with any certainty.

Immediately afterward, I tried to reseat the needle in the same position, but a different selection emerged, a Mozart violin concerto from the same classical time period, again starting from the beginning. Driven on by sudden exhilaration, I next moved the needle close to the "end" of the record (near the center), and heard a performance of Messiaen's last major organ work *Livre du Saint Sacrement* (composed in 1984). Moving the needle to the "start" (outer edge) led to a string of Gregorian chants. These last two experiments were challenging because the more I attempted to focus on the geometrical beginning or end of the record, the more blurred the boundary became, which induced a nauseating dizziness. Thereafter, I abandoned any effort at precise tonearm placement in these regions of the disc. To this day, the "earliest" and "latest" musical events on the album remain undetermined. An equally disturbing observation was that the tonearm, once in play, never advanced noticeably in a radial direction across the record, even with very long pieces such as an opera. Nor could I see the small needle itself "riding" on the disc; instead it seemed to become enveloped in the ill-defined black surface, as if dipping slightly into a pool of smooth black tar.

After many weeks of trials, it became clear that the record contained an unknowingly large number of performances of "western" classical music, in roughly chronological order that they were composed. The selection to arise was unpredictable, except for approximately the time period it was written, and ranged from solo instruments to quartets to concertos and choral works and operas. Perhaps most startling: To the best of my memory I never heard the same performance of the same piece twice, no matter how accurately I tried to return the tonearm to its original position. Thus each listening event became a unique moment in time, not to be interrupted unless its permanent "loss" was acceptable.

Occasionally I had an acquaintance drop by for dinner and played some "background music" from the record, to exclude the possibility of auditory hallucinations. On these visits I didn't reveal the extraordinary nature of the disc. With more audiophile-inclined friends, who might intuitively recognize and question the continuous playback of a long piece from the single side of an album, I allowed only short works to reach completion.

In the beginning I naturally assumed that each selection corresponded to a performance occurring within the past 50-60 years, during which high quality recording equipment was available. After several months I was less convinced of this, and began to ponder the unthinkable: that with this record I might (eventually) be able to hear all performances ever given of any composition, including even a centuries-old event. It was difficult to draw definitive conclusions about time based solely on listening, given the trend of orchestras returning to vintage instruments.

Each day brought new questions. Would this album include even rehearsals, or small venues in someone's home (e.g., Chopin playing in the salons of Paris)? After several years of intense scrutiny, such diversity seemed unlikely, since I always detected some audience noise, and the acoustic character (ambience, echoes) always suggested a sizeable room. Thus I concluded that I was consistently hearing live, formal performances in large halls (even during solo instrument recitals).

Nevertheless, it was obvious that the number of events available for playback must be exceedingly large. I was comforted only by the reassuring logic that the total number of performances must be finite. Another consolation was the faint hope that I might someday hear my own LSO, assuming that I could remember sufficient details of a past concert. My optimism here was bolstered by a few instances in which a noticeable mistake had been made on a particular instrument during the performance; perhaps I would be able to recognize this sonic signature. Already, during some instances of playback, I had picked up such imperfections, which (with great relief) allowed me to conclude that I was hearing the labor of human beings and not an artificially created soundscape. (Or, had such flaws been intentionally introduced to deceive me?)

I often found myself asking: Is the disc an advanced storage device, or some kind of time portal linked to specific musical events? Why (thus far) only performances involving larger venues with audiences? Was this related to some necessary critical mass of listeners forming a "collective consciousness", if such a thing exists?

In any case, the seeming impossibility of a vinyl record physically encoding so much information was soon forgotten as the wonder of the presentations filled my modest living room. I eventually adjusted my daily schedule to revolve around playback, and didn't initiate any session without adequate preparation for listening to its entirety. Each event was like viewing a magnificent sunset that would never be repeated. In short, I became obsessed with the disc,

The uniqueness of each experience led to a number of frustrating moments, for example once during an electrical storm when power was interrupted and the stereo system shut down during an exciting interpretation of Brahms First piano concerto. I was also particularly anxious five years ago when the complete Wagner *Ring* cycle was underway, and one vacuum tube in my amplifier appeared on the verge of failing; during this lengthy marathon I found myself necessarily half-sleeping on occasion, even with the coffee pot kept on full.

I also vividly recall one instance during the second year, when an enchanting rendition of Mahler's *Das Lied von der Erde* was in progress, featuring a soprano's voice more beautiful than any I had heard before, and yet I chose to walk away and sleep, since I was unusually tired and had concerns over business matters the following day. Of course I was never able to locate this piece again, and deeply regretted the decision for months, as if I had passed up a perfect opportunity to make love with someone I desired greatly and who was in my presence for only one night.

Several incidents besides the Record (as I have come to call it) have influenced my routine over the last decade, yet these have always seemed trivial compared to the impact of the disc. Not long after after my return from Russia, I ended an engagement with a woman (a fellow musician) whom I had known for several years. A car accident in 1993 ended my professional career with the orchestra due to nerve damage in my left arm, although the limb remained functional for everyday activities. An unforeseen family inheritance in the mid-90's permitted me to stop working full-time at my firm and devote more attention to the Record, and thus better document each listening session. All of this only fueled my growing social isolation.

Eventually I began to yearn for a sign that my "duty" (if this word is relevant) toward maintenance and study of the Record had expired. One intriguing prospect emerged this week. I heard a performance of the Shostakovich 4th Symphony, almost certainly under Kondrashin and perhaps the 1961 live world premier, but not exactly the first known recording from 1962 (which I own for comparison). If correct, then I have witnessed what the Leningrad shop owner referred to years ago. Unfortunately, no further advice from that source is possible. In 1997 I traveled back to St. Petersburg and conducted a futile search for the store. Not surprisingly, that entire block had been converted into modern housing units, and the shop was gone. The old man's whereabouts were unknown to local retailers and residents that I contacted.

At this point it seems inappropriate, perhaps even perilous, to hand over the disc for objective scrutiny, such as scientific analysis at a university or museum. I fear that I have become a confidential guardian of something sacred, like a successor in a long chain of ancient priests assigned to oversee and pass along a holy relic. Perhaps I was indeed "chosen" by the Leningrad musician, who was the previous "keeper" (and may have studied the disc for a longer period than myself). Should I now seek the most promising apprentice for scholarship of the Record? There is also the matter of where my own listening notes should ultimately reside. Do they matter at all? Are there scripts from previous Record owners that should be located and merged with my own? Could other copies of the Record exist, perhaps a version with an alternate set of performances, or even a different category of music?

In the last couple of years, my thoughts have evolved toward an even higher level of speculation—that the Record's music is a manifestation of some greater, profound message. Thoreau wrote that "Music is the sound of universal laws promulgated." Perhaps the selections available are a code, waiting to be deciphered for the delivery of some incredible revelation to humankind (or at least to musicians!). This hypothesis leads to even greater anxiety regarding the fate of the disc: I may have a unique opportunity in the history of civilization to unlock a momentous secret, if only I have the patience… but to continue listening for how long? And for what, exactly? I'm not a religious person, so I cannot envisage ways in which the Record might provide spiritual enlightenment. I know it merely as a magical gift of music.

The uniqueness of each event on the Record, the regret of lost listening opportunities, and the sacrifices required to listen patiently, have all mirrored aspects of everyday life, but they lack one simple and critical component: sharing the experience with others. There exists an aching loneliness that I have ignored almost completely over the past decade. For me, this is the revelation delivered by the Record: the need for human interaction. I feel that I must now part with the disc and return to the world I knew before, even at the risk of abandoning some great insight hidden within.

As I finish the last page of this synopsis, I have packaged the Record with great care. My plan has been made, and I have contacted the appropriate people to help accomplish the final steps. I'll soon be free of this miracle and curse, and will begin the slow, painful, but necessary process of building back my life.

Epilogue:

It is now summer of 2000, and in London the great "Eye" has become a reality on the horizon, towering 450 feet above the Thames. Construction of this magnificent observation wheel has taken almost two years to complete. In the process, over 1700 tons of steel were used for the structure and more than 3000 tons of concrete were used for the foundation. This wheel, designed as a landmark for the new millennium, with its endless circular route, is to me a symbol of the Record and of the great potential it holds.

But I also believe that the Record embodies something far beyond our ability to comprehend at this time. Further, the task of finding the proper inheritor is daunting, and the responsibility on my part overwhelming, given the burden that ownership may place on a friend or colleague. It was thus my decision last year to bury the Record beneath this great symbol, until at a later stage in our history it can be uncovered and relished as an archeological treasure. I recruited a friend who was an engineer on the project, and who had access to the great pit dug for the foundation. I obtained a strong steel box to enclose and protect the Record (along with my written synopsis). On the night before the first of many layers of concrete were poured to create a massive bed of support for the wheel's superstructure, I instructed my friend to place the container at the bottom of the pit. I am confident that some future technology will allow detection of an odd metal object embedded deep beneath the Eye, just as the great pyramids of Egypt are scanned today for inner chambers. Finally, I arranged for all of my listening notes to be buried with me, in a far less interesting tomb, for future explorers to contemplate.

Meanwhile I return to my intended role here in the present, namely efforts at musical composition. As Mahler noted, "To write a symphony is to construct a world." Through my scores I hope to create emotional worlds for all, and if I am fortunate, a few performances of my work will be immortalized on the Record, for the ears of a distant generation.

I occasionally ride on the great Eye, during off-hours when the crowds have thinned. The gentle, almost imperceptible motion, combined with the wondrous views of the city, invoke fond memories of the many hours I have devoted listening to music. Today, I am also gifted with a beautiful sunset and clear skies over London. That is enough.

Contributing Authors

CORINNA SARA BECHKO is a writer who can't shake her zoology background. Her work has appeared in *All Hallows, The Absent Willow Review, The Journal of Eschatology,* and been short-listed for the Aeon Award. Her horror graphic novel, *Heathentown*, was published by Image/Shadowline in 2009. More of her comics work can be seen in anthologies from Marvel, Image, and Double Feature. She shares her home with a black cat and a brilliant illustrator. You can follow her adventures at **http://thefrogbag.blogspot.com**

MATTHEW BURNSIDE is a disciple of Yes. He is an editor for *Mixed Fruit*, an online literary magazine — **http://mixedfruitmag.com/**.

ANN CLAYCOMB is a writer living in Morgantown, West Virginia. Her work has previously been published in such places as *The Fourth River, Fiction Weekly, Brevity, The Evansville Review,* and *Hot Metal Bridge*. She finds inspiration in many places, including Meatloaf songs and — as this story surely confesses — the work of Angela Carter. She is currently at work on a novel about mermaids and opera.

BETSY CORNWELL is a second-year MFA student in creative writing at the University of Notre Dame. She grew up in the wilds of rural New Hampshire and received her BA from Smith College in 2010. She is represented by Sara Crowe at Harvey Klinger, Inc., and her first novel, a young adult fantasy, is trying to find its way toward publication. She is currently working on a second book for young people and a graphic novel for adults. You can read her blog at **www.betsycorn-well.com.**

JACKIE CRAVEN is the architecture writer for About.com and has also written articles and columns for *House & Garden, Old-House Journal, Realtor Magazine,* and many newspapers. She is the author of *The Healthy Home* and *The Stress-Free Home* (Rockport Publishers). Her short fiction has appeared in *Verdad, Fourth River,* and other literary journals. Visit her online at **JackieCraven.com.**

WILLIAM DOONAN is a writer and professor of anthropology and archaeology in Sacramento, CA, where he lives with his wife Carmen, and his sons Will and Huey. Doonan is the author of two mystery novels: *Grave Passage* and *Mediterranean Grave,* which recount the exploits of octogenarian cruise ship detective Henry Grave. For more information about Doonan and his writing, please visit **www.williamdoonan.com.**

FRANCESCA FORREST has published a handful of short stories, including "The Yew's Embrace" and "Cory's Father" (*Strange Horizons,* 2011 and 2010), "The Gallows Maiden" (in *StereoOpticon: Fairy Tales in Split Vision,* Drollerie Press, 2009), and "The Biwa and the Water Koto" (in *Lace and Blade 2,* Norilana Press, 2009). Her poems have been found hiding out in *Mythic Delirium, The Linnet's Wings, Scheherezade's Bequest, Not One of Us,* and *Goblin Fruit.* She lives by a swamp in western Massachusetts with her husband and varying numbers of her four children, plus a dog and guinea pigs.

After a career in medicine and acupuncture, **STUART FREYER** began to write down the tales he has been thinking about for years. His stories have appeared in *The Berkshire Review, Colere,* and *Timber Creek Review* among others. "Kotar's Daughter" is an early chapter in a novel he is completing. Freyer lives in Williamstown Massachusetts where he sometimes morphs into a standup comic.

JEFFREY GREENE was born in Michigan, grew up in Florida, and now lives in Bethesda, Maryland. He has published short stories in *The North American Review, Oasis, Potomac Review, Reactor Magazine, Tomorrow Speculative Fiction*, and *decomP Magazine*.

CLAUDINE GRIGGS is the Writing Center Director at Rhode Island College, and her publications include three nonfiction books and twenty articles. "Firestorm" is her first published science fiction story. Griggs earned her BA and MA in English from California State Polytechnic University, Pomona, and now lives in Warwick, Rhode Island.

Somewhere in the corner of a Norfolk field, half-buried in a hedge, **NICK JACKSON** stitches up stories out of worn out shoe leather, dried thorn twigs and maybe the odd bit of broken glass. If life is a dream within a dream, he'd like to think that in writing he gets closest to the most wakeful part of the dream. A new collection of his stories, *The Secret Life of the Panda* is due out from Chômu Press this autumn.

WILLIAM KAMOWSKI is Professor of English at Montana State University-Billings where he teaches British Literature and Mythology. His essays on Chaucer and medieval literature have appeared in *Chaucer Review* and other literary journals. "Bags" is his first venture into science fiction.

MARGARET KARMAZIN's credits include over one hundred stories published in literary and national magazines, including *Rosebud, Chrysalis Reader, North Atlantic Review, Potomac Review, Confrontation, Virginia Adversaria, Mobius, Allegory* and *Wild Violet*. Her stories in *The MacGuffin, Eureka Literary Magazine, Licking River Review* and *Words of Wisdom* were nominated for Pushcart awards and Piper's Ash, Ltd. published a chapbook of her sci-fi, *Cosmic Women*. Her story, "The Manly Thing," was nominated for the 2010 Million Writers Award. She helped write the introduction for and has a story included in *Still Going Strong*, a story in *Ten Twisted Tales* and *Mota 9*, and a novel, *Replacing Fiona*, published by etreasurespublishing.com.

DAVID EVANS KATZ is the author of the novel, *Sin of Omission* (Koenisha Publications) and numerous short stories. He was educated at Columbia University in New York and at Northeastern University in Boston. Mr. Katz was born and raised in Malden, Massachusetts and currently resides in Granby Connecticut.

ALLEN KESTEN is a writer, early care and education specialist, and former children's librarian. His stories have appeared in *The Sun, Bitter Oleander, Red Cedar Review,* and other literary journals. He lives in Cambridge, Massachusetts.

SIMON KEWIN writes fiction, poetry and computer software, although usually not at the same time. His work has appeared in numerous magazines and anthologies. He lives in the UK with Alison and their two daughters, Eleanor and Rose. He blogs about writing at **http://spellmaking.blogspot.com** and can also be found on Twitter as **@SimonKewin**. In those brief moments he likes to refer to as his spare time, he is currently learning to play the electric guitar.

KAREN LENAR is a recent graduate of the MFA program at Fairleigh Dickinson University. Her stories have appeared in *Bartleby Snopes, FictionDaily,* and *Grey Sparrow Press.* A 2011 Pushcart Prize nominee, she lives with her husband in Boston, where she is currently working on her first novel.

ROBERT LOVE has worked as a research scientist at pharmaceutical companies in the field of structural biology, unraveling the three-dimensional architecture of proteins. He received his PhD in Biophysics from UC Berkeley. His publications are primarily technical in nature, but here he ventures into fiction, incorporating his longtime passions for music and philosophy. He lives in San Diego along with his wife and two daughters.

CHRISTOPHER LOWE's fiction has appeared or is forthcoming in *Bellevue Literary Review, Third Coast, Fiction Weekly, New Plains Review, Swamp Lily Review,* and *War, Literature, and the Arts.* His writing has also been anthologized in Sundress Publication's *Best of the Net* series. He teaches English at McNeese State University in Lake Charles, Louisiana, where he lives with his wife and daughter.

MICHELLE NICHOLS grew up on a cotton farm outside of Lubbock, Texas. Her fiction has appeared or is forthcoming in *Babel Fruit, Bitter Oleander, The Distillery, et cetera, Harbinger, Juked, Pank, Product, Squid Quarterly, Texas Review,* and *Twenty-First Bird Review.* She has been nominated for an AWP Intro to Journals Prize, a Pushcart Prize, and in 2009, she was recognized for teaching excellence. Michelle holds a Ph.D. in Literature and Creative Writing from the Center for Writers at The University of Southern Mississippi, and currently she works as an English Lecturer at Southern Polytechnic State University in Marietta, Georgia.

Retired professor **TOM SMITH** lives in Vermont with his wife Virginia enjoying visits from sons and grandchildren. Meanwhile, he writes poems and fiction and grows flowers. He has published nine volumes of poems, most recently *Jack's Beans: A Five-Year Diary* (Birch Brook Press 2006). His long story "The Christmas Shopper" won the A.E Coppard award for 2009 and was published by White Eagle Coffee Store Press.

JULIE STIELSTRA resides (for now) in the Chicago area, but lives part of every year in rural Kansas. Her writing has appeared in the *Chicago Tribune, Potomac Review, New Plains Review* and *Copperfield Review.*

R. I. SUTTON writes stories in an attempt to transmute lead into gold. Her short fiction occasionally surfaces in journals in Australia and the U.S and in 2010 was nominated for the Pushcart Prize. She is currently studying to become a teacher of creative writing. You can visit her website at **www.risutton.com.**

SARENA ULIBARRI has published fiction and poetry in *Scribendi, Conceptions Southwest* and *With Painted Words.* She won the 2005 Western Regional Honors Council Award for Poetry and received Honorable Mention in the *Alibi's* 2007 Appallingly Short Fiction Contest. She graduated from the University of New Mexico in 2007 and is on her way to the MFA program at University of Colorado Boulder this fall.

LAURA VALERI's debut collection of short stories titled *The Kind of Things Saints Do* (U of Iowa Press) was an Iowa/John Simmons Award winner, and winner of the Binghamton University sponsored John Gardner Award. Her work appears in *Glimmer Train, Big Bridge, Gulfstream, Literary Potpourri, Night Train, Waccamaw, SN Review, Fiction Writers Review, Soundzine, Clapboard House,* and *Adirondack Review.* Her short memoir "These Innocent Lambs" was featured in Lee Gutkind's anthology of Creative Nonfiction essays by Italian American writers titled *Our Roots Are Deep With Passion,* published by Other Press in collaboration with Creative Nonfiction. Laura Valeri has an MFA from Florida International University and an MFA from the Iowa Writers' Workshop. She was a Walter E Dakins Fellow at the Sewanee Writers Conference in 2008 and a Hambidge Fellow in 2010. She is Assistant Professor of Creative Writing specializing in fiction at Georgia Southern University.

Contributing Artists

MICHAEL FILIMOWICZ is an American Midwest transplant and interdisciplinary artist working in the areas of digital photography, experimental video, sound design, public art, interactive art and creative writing. He teaches in the School of Interactive Arts and Technology at Simon Fraser University in beautiful British Columbia. Visit his website: **www.filimowicz.com**

TERESA FRAZEE, born in Brooklyn, New York, has been a visual artist for over 30 years. Having exhibited in well over 100 solo and group exhibitions world wide both juried and invitational, including The Biannual International Contemporary Art, Florence, Italy, The Boca Raton Museum of Art, Boca Raton, Florida, The Cornell Museum of Art, Delray Beach, Florida and The Palm Beach International Airport, West Palm Beach, Florida, as well as having received numerous awards and honors.

At the same time Teresa has been pursuing her other love, writing, and has been published in many venues. Inside her world of make believe, she paints and writes what she knows to be true. Bound by the creative force, she leaves reality entirely up to you. Visit her website at **www.frazeefinearts.com**.

JOHN PAPPAS has been an abstract expressionist painter for 30 years. Born in Oakland, California, he has lived in Los Angeles since 1974. Today he resides in Long Beach with his wife Caren and their Golden Retriever Niko. He has exhibited paintings at several solo venues in Hollywood, Silver Lake and Long Beach and his works are on display in private homes in Europe and in the U.S.A. Pappas is also an award winning actor and a writer. He received 2 Dramalogue awards for: Greg Suddeth's *Very Cherry and Extra Clean,* and Gilbert Girion's *Word Crimes.* In 1990 he received a Los Angeles Weekly best actor award for Girion's *Bad Country.* Visit him online at **http://www. adivingduckpicture.com**.

JEFF FOSTER has been doing photography since 2000. Self-taught, he has been influenced by Bosch, Darger, and Saudek. He runs a cleaning business to make ends meet. His photographs are on display in galleries in Missouri and Kansas. Visit his website at **http://www.seclu-sionimagery.com**.

www.ingramcontent.com/pod-product-compliance
Lightning Source LLC
Chambersburg PA
CBHW031105030726
47496CB00002BA/386